DADDY DEFENDER

BY
JANIE CROUCH

First Published in Great Britain 2017
By Mills & Boon, an imprint of HarperCollins*Publishers*
1 London Bridge Street, London, SE1 9GF

© 2017 Janie Crouch

ISBN: 978-0-263-92931-7

46-1117

Janie Crouch has loved to read romance her whole life. The award-winning author cut her teeth on Mills & Boon Cherish novels as a preteen, then moved on to a passion for romantic suspense as an adult. Janie lives with her husband and four children overseas. She enjoys traveling, long-distance running, movie watching, knitting and adventure/obstacle racing. You can find out more about her at www.janiecrouch.com.

This book is dedicated to my aunt Terri and uncle Mike. Thank you for being a wonderful example of God's love and goodness to so many. And for being two of my favorite people on the planet.

Chapter One

"Ashton, it means the world to me that you would come here to fix this first thing in the morning."

Ashton Fitzgerald, top sharpshooter for Omega Sector Critical Response Division's SWAT team, had his head and half his large torso under the kitchen sink of a condo unit in Masking Ridge, a community just south of Colorado Springs.

He knew Summer Worrall, owner of said sink, didn't expect much of a response from him, so he just grunted as he put a little more elbow grease into tightening a stripped nut on her piping.

"I don't know when it started leaking, but it was definitely bad when Chloe got me up this morning."

As if in agreement, nineteen-month-old Chloe began gurgling in her mother's arms and clapping loudly. She obviously wanted to be let down onto the floor to play with Ashton, but Summer was keeping her out of the way.

"It's no problem," Ashton muttered.

Actually, it was a problem. He was going to be late into Omega Sector's SWAT training facility. Not that there would be any true harm in that; the team was just running exercises today unless something real came in. But as soon as they realized *why* Ashton was late—because Summer Worrall thought he was the maintenance man again—they were going to tease him mercilessly.

Again.

They all knew, or at least knew of, Summer and Chloe. Her husband had been killed in a hostage situation gone wrong nearly two years ago. Then she'd been kidnapped by a psychopath eight months ago in another incident involving the Omega Sector's Critical Response Division, an elite interagency task force with some of the country's best agents.

So no one on the team actually begrudged Ashton helping out the young widow. What they found so hilarious was the fact that Summer thought he was the handyman for the entire condo complex.

And Ashton could admit he was a pretty mechanically minded guy. Growing up on his parents' farm in Wyoming had given him a lot of skills with his hands. He could fix most household problems, given the time and tools.

"I think I've got this under control," he said. "It's nothing big, just some piping that needed to be realigned and tightened."

"Oh good. I didn't want to turn a big, formal request in to Joe."

Joe Matarazzo, the main hostage negotiator at Omega Sector, who also happened to be a billionaire, owned the condos in which Summer and Chloe lived. That's how this crazy misunderstanding had started in the first place. Summer had needed a handyman and called Joe. Joe had said he'd send someone trustworthy right over.

But then Joe had an emergency with Omega and asked Ashton if he could take care of Summer's problem. Instead of calling someone, Ashton had just gone over to

Summer's home himself. He'd had no intention of misleading Summer, and had even introduced himself as Joe's friend.

Evidently she'd taken that to mean Joe's *handyman* friend.

When he'd given her his number, telling her to call him if anything else came up, Summer had taken him up on that offer. Eight times in the last few months.

Now Ashton had no idea how to tell her the truth.

And that wasn't even the worst secret he was keeping from her. He grimaced and worked his way out from under the sink.

"Okay, I think I've got it all fixed under here. I just need to turn your water back on in the basement."

Ashton pulled himself the rest of the way out from under the sink and stood. He smiled at Summer, trying not to let himself be taken aback again by her beauty. Petite, with rich auburn hair, pale skin with freckles dusting her cheeks and nose. It was colder weather now, but Ashton knew from the tank tops she wore in warmer temps that her shoulders were dusted with freckles, also.

But he definitely did not want to be thinking about her bare shoulders or how he'd love to play connect the dots on them with his fingers or—even better—his lips. Summer wouldn't be interested in any law-enforcement lips after what she'd been through. Especially his.

"Ah-ta!" Little Chloe squealed and threw herself forward from her mother's arms, reaching for Ashton. He caught her, taking her from Summer and pulling her to his chest.

"Sorry," Summer murmured.

"Don't worry about it." It happened every time he came by. Little Chloe loved to see him. Not able to say the word Ashton, she'd taken to calling him *Ah-ta* last month.

"Hey, gorgeous." He smiled at the baby. "You shouldn't be so quick to jump out of your mama's arms."

He knew he wouldn't be.

Chloe put both her tiny hands on his cheeks. "Ah-ta."

"Yeah, but I might not always be there to catch you." He adjusted his tool belt so her little feet didn't get snagged on anything. The belt didn't bother him at all. It was quite similar to the SWAT utility belt he wore in other circumstances.

"Ashton, thanks again for making this your first stop. I'm sure you have other places to be. Other units higher on the priority list than mine."

He shook his head. "Don't worry about it. It was no trouble coming by here."

Summer's green eyes filled with distress. "You mean you only came here for me? You're working out of another complex today? I'm *so* sorry."

Ashton never knew what to say, so he said as little as possible. "Yeah, I'm working at another complex today." That wasn't technically untrue; the SWAT training facility was definitely another complex. "Don't worry. I never mind coming by here."

Ugh. Now he sounded like he was about to ask her out for a date. He was sure she'd shut that down real quick.

"I-I just mean…" He trailed off. Was he actually stuttering now? She must think he was a complete moron.

She touched him on the arm. "I understand and I truly appreciate it." She reached over and tickled Chloe. "This little wiggle worm does too. She always loves to see you."

"I'll just take her downstairs with me to turn the water back on. Is that okay?" Chloe was currently playing with his ears. Pulling on them with her surprisingly strong little fingers.

"Sure," Summer smiled. "Give my arms a break for a few minutes. I'll put this stuff back under the sink."

Ashton turned with the baby and began walking down to the basement. He knew where it was from a hot-water-heater problem a few months before. As a matter of fact, for a newer condo, this place tended to have a lot of issues. But he definitely wouldn't complain.

It gave him a chance to see Summer. Even if it was as the handyman.

Little Chloe began jabbering to him in her baby language, laughing as he bounced her as he went down the stairs. He didn't know why the little girl liked him so much, but he would take it while he could.

Someday she would find out Ashton was the reason her dad had died. Then neither she nor her mom would want anything to do with him.

SUMMER LOVED HEARING her daughter squeal with delight as Ashton took her down the stairs. She felt safe leaving Chloe with Ashton. Not only had he proven over and over again that he was patient and gentle with her, Joe Matarazzo—one of Summer's closest friends—had vouched personally for Ashton.

Joe had first sent Ashton over when she'd had a garbage disposal problem a few months ago. She'd somehow found multiple reasons for him to come back since. He must think she was completely useless around the house. But he never seemed to mind coming over to help with whatever she needed.

So Summer kept calling. And Ashton kept showing up.

With his tall, gorgeous body and thick brown hair. Muscular arms that stretched the sleeves of his T-shirts.

She had to admit, she didn't mind the view whenever he was here.

She hadn't gone so far as to actually break anything herself to get him to come over, but she'd never tried to fix even the smallest problem when it occurred. Since the unit was really bigger than she and Chloe needed— three bedrooms, two different levels, plus a basement— there did seem to be a lot of different things she could call him for.

Summer began putting back the cleaning supplies she'd moved out of the way before Ashton had arrived. Ashton barely ever talked while he was there. At least, not to Summer. She could hear him keeping up a steady stream of conversation with Chloe, but the most Summer got were short, direct sentences. He was shy and a little bit awkward. Unbelievable in a man with his looks.

Not that Summer would know what to do if the man could get a full sentence out and began to really talk to her. Then she'd be the one stuttering.

So she kept her one-sided attraction to herself. She was sure she wasn't really his type. She didn't know what that type may be, but it was probably someone more into things he was into…

Like being quiet.

She knocked her head softly against the sink cabinet door. She didn't really know anything about Ashton. She knew some basics—that he'd been raised on his parents' farm, that he still went out to Wyoming to see them as often as he could. She knew he was kind and gentle with her daughter and always polite to her. But she had no idea what he was into, what he liked. Only knew he tended to be reserved. A man of few words.

And that he had a face, hair and biceps to die for.

She would've totally given up on any possibility of anything ever happening between them if she didn't catch him looking at her with heat in his eyes every once in a while. Like he felt the same attraction she did but couldn't seem to move on it. He *never* moved on it.

Maybe because he was too shy.

Or maybe she'd just imagined those looks.

She put a stack of sponges where they belonged before closing the cabinet and resting her head against the wood. It had been too long since Tyler died. Too long since she'd had a man's attention focused on her. And as much as she'd like that focus to be from Ashton, she didn't see that happening any time soon.

"Okay, got your water turned back on and everything should be great."

As she stood back up, Summer couldn't help but notice his shirt had gotten a little damp, probably while he'd been under the sink, and clung to his midsection, showing off the perfectly defined abs underneath.

Weren't plumbers and maintenance guys supposed to have beer bellies and ill-fitting pants? She may not know what Ashton did on his time off, but it definitely wasn't sitting around watching TV and drinking beer, that was for sure.

And then she noticed how he kept Chloe up high in his arms so her little legs wouldn't get damp from his shirt.

And darn it if that wasn't almost as sexy.

"Ashton, thank you again for coming by. Especially since you weren't planning to work in our complex this morning."

He looked a little sheepish, she had no idea why. Chloe reached for her. "Ma-ma."

Summer took her daughter, nuzzling her soft hair. "Hey, sweetheart. You have fun with Ashton?"

Chloe began jabbering an entire story only she could understand.

"Are you sure you don't want me to pay you extra for your time? Coming out here—out of your way? I feel bad."

Ashton's eyes widened. "No. No. That's *really* not necessary. You definitely cannot pay me. Summer, I should—"

He stopped, rubbing a hand over his forehead.

"You should what?" she finally asked when it became apparent he wasn't going to say anything more.

As usual.

He gave a tiny sigh, then a smile. "Nothing. Really, it was no problem helping you. Just call me if there's anything else you need."

What if she needed to ask him to dinner? What would he say to that? No doubt he would stutter and get embarrassed.

But would he stutter yes or stutter no?

Summer had been out of the dating game for a long time. She and Tyler had been married three years when he'd died nearly two years ago. So it had been over five years since she'd asked anyone—or been asked by anyone—for a date. She wasn't sure she even knew how to start now.

All she knew was that it was nice to be around a man who didn't know that her husband had died suddenly and tragically. Didn't look at her with barely veiled pity in his eyes.

She turned toward the kitchen counter and grabbed a plate. "Well, I made you some muffins. Blueberry."

She thrust the plate holding the half dozen oversize muffins toward him.

"You didn't have to do that."

Now she felt like an idiot. "Oh. Yeah, well, I just felt like baking." At four o'clock this morning when she'd realized he might be coming over in a few hours to fix the leak. "And thought you might like some. I can't eat them all."

She wished she'd never brought it up.

"Oh, well, they look delicious. Thank you very much."

He took the plate. She ignored the tiny bit of guilt she felt over the knowledge that he'd probably return the plate in the next couple of days and she'd get to see him again.

That was *not* why she'd baked him muffins.

He was a single guy. He probably didn't get a lot of home-cooked items. That's why she'd baked him muffins.

He glanced at his watch and winced. "Okay, I've got to get going. Just call me if there are any other problems, okay? And thank you." He held up the plate.

He reached over quickly and tickled Chloe's cheek, causing her to laugh. "Bye, you little heartbreaker. Be good for your mama."

He was out the door before she could say anything else.

What would she say anyway?

Bring me back my muffin plate tomorrow and when you do, ask me to dinner!

She wished she had the guts.

Summer put Chloe in her high chair and set some Cheerios in a small plastic bowl on the tray. Within seconds, they were spread out all over the tray and she was trying to feed herself with both fists at once.

Chloe wasn't much of a conversationalist either.

Summer had lost her husband to useless violence so long ago now. She missed Tyler every day, wished he was here to see his daughter and what a beautiful, smart, delightful baby she was. But Summer had long since accepted Tyler wasn't coming back. He wouldn't want her to waste her life pining over what couldn't be changed. He would always live in her heart.

So maybe someday soon she would ask Ashton out. He seemed like a good man, if a little shy, but solid, steady, dependable.

And hot as all get-out.

Summer could use a little solid-and-steady, even if the words sounded boring to her. She'd had enough excitement in her twenty-six years. First Tyler's death, then eight months ago when a crazy stalker linked to Tyler's case had taken her and Chloe and trapped them in a burning building.

Some Omega Sector agents who worked with Joe Matarazzo had gotten her and Chloe out. Joe had been able to stop the stalker and save his wife, Laura—whom the psycho had also taken—although only barely.

Summer didn't remember a lot of what had happened in that building. She'd been drugged so everything had been hazy. She just remembered a man in full combat gear, breaking through the door of the small room where she and Chloe had been placed and carrying them both out to safety—as if carrying them had been no difficulty for him at all. The whole scene had been so chaotic, Summer hadn't even been able to thank him.

So yeah, she'd had enough of excitement. Was ready

for a little bit of boring, like maybe a quiet handyman. Although she doubted Ashton was boring once someone got to know him. At least she hoped not.

Summer almost absently gave Chloe more Cheerios before reaching down to grab the ones that had been knocked to the floor and throwing them in the trash.

Summer dreamed a lot—almost every night. Vivid, lifelike dreams. For a while they had been terrifying ones of Tyler's death. Thankfully those had gone away.

Now she often dreamed about her kidnapping and the fire. She dreamed about the man who'd gotten her out. Who'd carried her safely in his arms.

Capable. Strong. Calm and steady under pressure.

But in every dream, no matter how it started or what she did differently, there was only one face she ever assigned to her hero: Ashton's.

Ashton Fitzgerald may be strong. And even capable in a lot of situations. But he was no rush-into-a-burning-building sort of hero. Which was fine. There were all types of heroes. Ashton was just the type who came by early and fixed sinks, rather than leaping tall buildings in a single bound. Summer had no problem with that.

She just wished she could convince her subconscious.

Chapter Two

About an hour north, in a building the polar opposite of any of the lovely condos in Colorado Springs, Damien Freihof was bored.

And generally when he became bored, people started dying.

He took a deep breath and feigned interest in what the other two men were saying inside the abandoned warehouse just outside of Denver, where they all had agreed to meet since none of them knew each other.

One waxed poetic about the need for change. He wore an ill-fitting, charcoal-gray suit with a red tie and paced back and forth. He kept a baseball cap pulled low on his head to make his features, if not exactly indistinguishable, at least more difficult to describe.

"We will rewire the entire American law enforcement system," he argued from the shadows. The man obviously wanted to keep his face—as he had wanted to keep his name—out of the equation.

Which was fine for now.

Damien raised his fist in the air. "Yes! Fight the power." He barely restrained from rolling his eyes.

Red Tie stopped his pacing. "We *will* fight the power. We will change everything by destroying the law enforcement status quo. Once Omega Sector crumbles, other law enforcement agencies will follow. We will stop the corruption."

It was obviously a rehearsed line. Damien had no idea how deep Red Tie's following went, whether the man had only practiced his speech in front of the mirror or if he had dozens of soldiers lined up for his cause of restructuring the law enforcement system.

But Damien knew he worked relatively high within the elite law enforcement group of Omega Sector and wanted to destroy it.

That made Red Tie Damien's new best friend. Inconsequential things like names and faces could come later.

If Damien guessed, he would say the man was some sort of active agent or SWAT member, based on his general discomfiture with his suit. He obviously didn't like the restriction and was probably used to wearing the superhero uniforms the SWAT team wore. Plus, he was definitely fit. Maybe not quite right in the head, but definitely physically capable of doing harm.

The other man, Curtis Harper, the man Damien had contacted and brought to this meeting, had no qualms about standing in the open, his face and identity known to everyone.

Harper tended to be much more whiny and annoying in general. He finally spoke up.

"Dude…"

Damien had found in his years of experience that nothing intelligent ever followed the word *dude*.

"Dude," Harper said again, "I'm not interested in no revolution. I just want to get revenge on the man who killed my father."

Red Tie stared at Harper, his arms crossing over his chest. Everyone stood in silence for a long time.

"Damien." Red Tie turned to him. "I'm not sure we're all on the same page he—"

Damien held out a hand to stop the man's words. He didn't want Red Tie to scare Harper away. Harper served an important purpose.

An important, *disposable* purpose.

Damien walked over to Harper, putting a friendly arm around his shoulders. He led him away from Red Tie, toward the door of the warehouse. "Mr. Harper, you want revenge. Rightfully so."

"Damn straight." Harper nodded and moved his jaw strangely. Damien realized he had chewing tobacco in his mouth.

The urge to snap the man's neck right now rushed through Damien's body. He could feel the tingling need zip through his arms and fingertips. He'd be doing everyone a service by killing this uneducated, woe-is-me bigot right now. But Damien resisted the urge.

Barely.

"I understand," he said instead, keeping his hand around the man's shoulder. "And I want to help you get that revenge against Ashton Fitzgerald."

Harper's eyes narrowed. "That bastard killed my daddy. Murdered him in cold blood."

Damien doubted very seriously that the Omega SWAT team sharpshooter had murdered anyone in cold blood, but he knew not to say as much. "Indeed. And he deserves to pay."

"I should just grab my .45 and blow his brains out."

If Harper had the backbone to do that, he would've done it in the four years since his father had died. Damien just squeezed the man's shoulder. "You could, of course. I know you've got the guts. But why don't you make Fitzgerald suffer a little beforehand? The way you've had to suffer."

Curtis Harper lived every day of his life—before and after his father's death—with a victim's mentality. That's how Damien had found him. How he'd been able to draw him into his scheme.

It was how he would use Harper to chip away at a little piece of Omega Sector. To kill off just one member, that, when it was said and done, would seem like an isolated event from a lone redneck bent on revenge.

Damien wondered how many isolated events Omega Sector would endure before they realized the events weren't isolated at all, but carefully orchestrated by a great puppet master.

And now who was waxing poetic?

"Curtis, you go on home now and get ready." Damien put just a bit of a Southern accent—totally fake—into his words. He wanted Harper to think they were cut from the same cloth. "I'll be in touch soon with a plan I've got in place that will make Ashton Fitzgerald pay. It involves hurting Ashton Fitzgerald not only physically, but through the people he cares about as well. The worst kind of pain."

Harper wasn't worthy of knowing Damien's entire design, his blueprint. Harper wouldn't comprehend its enormity even if Damien told him. But Harper didn't need to grasp or appreciate it in order to be useful.

Curtis Harper wouldn't understand the plan, but he would help make the members of Omega Sector understand it.

Harper nodded. "Okay, Damien. Thanks."

The man turned and spit to the side. By the time he looked back at Damien, Damien had managed to wipe the sneer from his face.

Curtis Harper was a means to an end, nothing more. Omega Sector agent Ashton Fitzgerald wouldn't survive the next week, but then again, neither would Harper.

They shook hands and Harper left. Damien turned and walked back into the building.

"Curtis Harper is not the type of person we're looking for to further the revolution," Red Tie said. "He's filthy and sloppy."

Damien shrugged. "Not everybody can be a general in the war. You need foot soldiers also. *Expendable* foot soldiers."

That seemed to appease the other man.

"Attacking one person isn't going to bring Omega down." Red Tie began his pacing again. "It's not going to change the status quo within law enforcement. I've got no beef with Fitzgerald in particular."

"No." Damien held himself perfectly still in direct opposition to the other man's pacing. "But attacking one person will split Omega's focus. Then the next hit will split their focus more. And the one after that, et cetera, et cetera."

Red Tie stopped his pacing. "But eventually we have to hit them hard. Not little hits. One giant strike with great force. I've already got something in the beginning stages."

Damien smiled, showing just the right amount of teeth to make it look authentic. "To begin the revolution."

"Exactly."

"Be patient. We'll make our most deadly strike once everything is in place. Until then, we just continue to wound them—both people inside Omega and those connected to them—without them realizing how much they're bleeding out. Omega will limp along until it's time for you to make your move. Bring the whole organization down for good."

A huge grin spread over Red Tie's face. "They've always underestimated me. They'll never see it coming."

So Red Tie wasn't truly about the revolution after all. He'd been slighted and wanted personal revenge. Of course, he probably couldn't see that in himself, had convinced himself of his visionary status.

Damien didn't care either way. He would use whatever tools became available to him in his fight to take apart Omega Sector. Whether they thought of themselves as visionaries or just wanted payback, Damien didn't care.

He would use them all. And when they were no longer useful to him, he would discard them all.

"Are you going to tell me your name?" Damien finally asked the man.

He tilted his head in suspicion. "I don't think so. I'm not sure I can trust you."

The first intelligent thing that had been said all day.

"Shall I just address you as 'hey you'?" Damien crossed his arms over his chest. He didn't really need the man's name. Honestly, at this point he didn't care.

"You can call me Fawkes."

Damien gave a short bark of laughter. "As in, Guy Fawkes, the man who tried to blow up the British Parliament? Okay, Mr. Fawkes, let me know when you want to meet again." Damien turned to leave.

"Wait, that's it? What about planning the attack? The big one."

Damien turned back around. "It's not time yet. If we

strike now, we'll fail. We weaken Omega Sector one little piece at a time. And when they're hollowed out? That's when we strike."

Damien was nothing if not a master planner. He'd always excelled at chess because he played four moves ahead of where the pieces currently sat on the table.

Fawkes didn't looked pleased. "Maybe you're afraid. Maybe I've come to the wrong person."

Damien didn't rise to the bait. Wasn't even tempted. He walked closer to Fawkes and touched his tie, waiting to see if the action would spur Fawkes to violence. Fawkes tensed but didn't do anything.

Good. More self-control than Damien had given him credit for. Fawkes would need it in the weeks ahead.

"You'll have your revolution when the time is right, Mr. Fawkes. Be patient. Continue gathering your intel, both on those inside the organization and those connected to it. Finding vulnerable spots we can stab quickly, retreating before they know they're wounded. Never knowing the largest wound is yet to come."

The younger man still didn't like it. But he nodded. Damien smiled and slapped him on his shoulder. "Good. Then, until we meet again, Mr. Fawkes."

He turned to leave but then stopped at Fawkes' final words.

"You know, you're awfully trusting with who you give your name to. I know who you are. Even Harper knows who you are. Aren't you afraid Omega Sector is going to find out about you?"

Damien didn't turn back around. "Not worried at all. Omega Sector already knows about me. They're the ones who created me in the first place."

"When they stopped you from blowing up yourself and all those people in that bank nearly five years ago?"

Now Damien turned around, eyebrow raised. "You've done your homework, Mr. Fawkes."

"I always check every possible angle."

Damien doubted this man could even see every possible angle, much less check them. "If Omega hadn't interfered, I would've been long dead by now. But they did. Thankfully, I must say."

And what Fawkes didn't know—what Damien himself hadn't even known until recently—was that Omega Sector had created him long before they stopped him from blowing up that bank. Long before they'd thrown him in that prison.

They'd created him when they'd killed his precious Natalie seven years ago.

And now they would pay. Would know the agony he'd known at her death.

Damien took a few steps toward Fawkes. "I have no doubt Omega Sector will eventually figure out it's me behind the little attacks. Honestly, I hope it's sooner rather than later. *You* are the one we've got to keep hidden."

"Don't worry, they'll never suspect me."

"Make sure, Fawkes. Because your revolution will never get off the ground at all if they do."

"You worry about your part, I'll worry about mine. I've already got something in the works that will start shaking them up."

Damien raised an eyebrow. "Anything I should know about?"

The other man smiled. "No. Just an extra little something to splinter their focus. Like you said."

Damien fought a grimace. The problem with working with someone like Fawkes was that the man was just smart enough, just ambitious enough, to have plans of his own. Plans Damien hadn't created and therefore didn't control. But Damien knew when to back off. This was one of those times.

"Okay, then. Just be careful. Don't lose the war just to win one battle."

Fawkes shrugged. "I won't. I know the endgame."

Fawkes *thought* he knew the endgame. He didn't. But Damien just nodded at him. "I'll look forward to our next meeting."

He turned again and walked out the door of the warehouse, putting on sunglasses as he stepped into the bright sun shining over the Rockies framing Denver. He'd be in his car in two minutes. Five minutes after that, he would change his appearance enough that he'd be able to walk right by Fawkes or Curtis Harper and neither of them would ever recognize Damien.

It was just one of Damien's skills and one of the reasons he'd been able to avoid capture by Omega Sector for the last ten months since he broke out of prison. They were looking for someone who didn't match Damien's description at all.

Damien Freihof was the greatest criminal mastermind Omega Sector had ever battled. He didn't care if he was waxing poetic now. Truth was truth. Omega was at war, they just didn't know it yet.

They'd targeted him for years. Now it was their turn to become the target.

Chapter Three

"All I'm saying is that she thinks you're the janitor," Roman Weber said as he ran at Ashton.

Ashton grimaced as Roman's boot hit his linked fingers. He used his leg and arm strength to boost his teammate up onto the fifteen foot wooden wall, part of the obstacle course the SWAT team regularly completed.

It was supposed to not only build fitness, but promote teamwork. Right now, Ashton just wanted to push his teammates over the wall, then run the other way.

"That's about as firmly parked in the friend zone as you can get. Janitor." Lillian Muir, Omega's only female SWAT agent, snickered. Being the lightest, she would be the last up the wall, since any of the other team members could pretty much hoist her up one-handed.

Derek Waterman, SWAT team leader, stood beside Ashton to boost other members up the wall and shook his head. "Let's focus, people. Plus, we have a guest."

Tyrone Marcus, not yet a full-fledged member of the SWAT team, had joined them for this morning's training and was next over the wall. The younger man smiled at the banter as he flew toward Derek and Ashton, jumped into their waiting hands and pulled himself the rest of the way up. But he didn't say anything.

Ashton knew he liked that kid for a reason.

Derek nodded his head up, indicating it was Ashton's turn. Ashton jogged back about ten feet from the wall, then burst forward in a sprint. As he jumped onto Derek's waiting hands, Derek's push upward helped propel Ashton to the top. From there, the other team members helped him climb over.

Ashton immediately turned and reached his arm down, along with Roman. Derek was already running toward the wall, using his huge size to propel himself up and catch their arms. Ashton and Roman pulled Derek, then reached back down so they could do the same with Lillian.

She was much lighter and faster and soon the whole team was over the wall, the final obstacle on the course. Everyone sat, catching their breath.

"I don't know that he's in the friend zone," Liam Goetz, hostage rescue specialist, said. "She did make him muffins."

Ashton shook his head. "You guys give it a rest, will you?"

"Uh, she made muffins for the *janitor* who came over to fix her sink," Roman argued, blatantly ignoring Ashton.

Lillian reached over and high-fived him. "That just means Fitzy is parked in the VIP section of the friend zone. Still the friend zone."

Ashton closed his eyes, wishing that would make them all go away. Even the new kid was grinning, although he still hadn't said anything about it.

Not that anything anyone had said was untrue. How he'd let this situation with Summer, the only woman he'd had real feelings for in years, get so out of hand he didn't know.

"She doesn't think I'm the janitor. She thinks I'm the building's maintenance man. There's a difference," he muttered.

Mistake.

Everyone burst out laughing, now arguing the difference between maintenance man and janitor. They all jumped down from the wall and walked back toward the building, except for Ashton and Derek.

"Hey, we're hitting the new gas and airborne substances simulator in an hour," Derek yelled out after them. "But not you this time, Tyrone. Sorry. Everyone else, be ready."

They all nodded and responded, slapping Tyrone on the back. He'd make a good team member after another few months of training.

Ashton just leaned back against the wall, enjoying the quiet.

"You need to tell Summer who you really are," Derek finally said. "Not telling her is going to bite you in the ass eventually."

Derek wasn't one to run his mouth like the rest of the team. He didn't share his opinion for no reason or generally participate in the teasing. So when Derek spoke, people listened.

Ashton opened his eyes. "I know." He grimaced. "Although I'm so concerned about saying the wrong thing around her, I can barely get a sentence out. She must think I'm a moron."

Derek chuckled. "I doubt it. Maybe a little shy or something."

Ashton rolled his eyes. "If my mother could hear

someone calling me shy. The one of her three kids who never shut up. She would have a field day."

"Everybody likes Summer. And you have too many mutual friends for her not to find out who you are eventually. It'll be better coming from you."

Ashton hit the back of his head against the wooden wall. "If it was just about her thinking I was the maintenance guy, I would tell her."

"But you're worried about the situation on the day her husband died."

As always, the bile pooled in his stomach at the thought. "I had the shot, Derek. I could've taken that hostage-taker out. Tyler Worrall and those others would still be alive. Summer would still have a husband and Chloe would still have a father."

"We've all been over the footage, Ash. Us as a team. Steve Drackett and the review board. Taking the shot that early would've been a mistake. Joe thought he could talk the guy down. We all thought he could talk the guy down."

But there had been a second, right before the man pulled out the hand grenade that killed nearly everyone in the room, that Ashton could've done something. He'd been on the building across the street with his sniper rifle.

He should've taken the shot. His gut had told him to take the shot. But he'd ignored it.

And people had died.

Ashton shrugged. "Well, I don't think Summer is going to be interested in dating the guy who could've saved her husband's life."

"You know, Joe Matarazzo already tried to claim blame for Tyler Worrall's death. Summer wouldn't let him. What makes you think she's going to hold you at fault?"

Because she didn't know—*nobody* knew—about that second shot Ashton could've taken as the man was pulling out the hand grenade from his pocket. Ashton's hesitation had lost the shot, then cost everyone in the room their lives.

Ashton shrugged. "Gut feeling."

Derek slapped him on his shoulder. "Well, sometimes our gut feelings about women leave a little to be desired."

Ashton stood up. "Let's go battle with tear gas. That should be more fun."

A GOOD MAJORITY of the SWAT team's time was spent in training. Running different scenarios so they would be more prepared once they were out in the field.

A lot of exercises—like the obstacle course they did this morning—were for physical fitness and general team building. They knew each other's strengths and weaknesses. The team often had to go into situations with multiple unknown or rapidly changing variables. Their training exercises ensured team cohesiveness.

Most of the training was routine: do it once, do it again, until there were no mistakes. They spent hours at the firing range together. In simulators together. Rappelling down walls. Studying hostage rescue, shields, vehicle assaults, even tactical medicine.

Despite the jokes this morning, most of the SWAT team's training was taken seriously by everyone. It required focus, tenacity and teamwork. Often pushing themselves to the brink of mental and physical exhaustion.

It was hard. But that's why not everyone did it. Only the ones who made the cut.

You could damn near see the excitement in the room now as everyone on the team gathered around the training techs to hear about the new challenge they were about to undergo.

Facing something new as a team had them all itching with enthusiasm. You never got a second first chance.

"Alright, boys and girls." Steve Drackett, director of the entire Critical Response Division, was present for this inaugural training session. "Sadly, responding to tear gas and airborne elements is almost becoming routine in this day and age. We need a place where all SWAT teams can train. It won't be just us using this facility, but departments from around the country."

Drackett turned to the half dozen people standing around—some in lab coats, some in suits, a few from other SWAT teams besides Omega Sector's.

"The designers—made up of analysts, computer experts, airborne terrorism experts, chemists and some of the best video game developers in the country—have pulled exactly zero punches with this new training facility. This is about as real as it gets outside of an actual combat zone, including actual tear gas."

Steve smiled, but nothing about the facial movement felt comforting. "Participants might wish it wasn't quite so real by the time they're through, including the physical stimuli that will occur when someone gets shot. But I can guarantee you will be more prepared for your next critical response call involving gas or a possible airborne bioterrorism attack."

Ashton shifted from where he was leaning against the doorframe. "Sounds like the developers are taking a little too much joy in our pain, boss."

One of the men in a lab coat, complete with pocket

protector and glasses, shrugged. "If you don't get shot by anything, there won't be any pain."

Ashton cracked a smile. So the nerds wanted a fight. "Fair enough."

He saw Lillian's fist stretch out from where she stood next to him and he tapped it.

"The sensors are worn over your normal gear," the lab coat guy continued. "Light and flexible enough that it shouldn't impede your movement or speed in anyway. It will just…notify you when you've been hit by a subject's weapon."

Everyone noticed the slight hesitation and ghost of a smile on the tech guy's face as he said *notify*. Evidently the notification wouldn't be pleasant.

"Enough talk." Roman Weber smiled, although no one in their right mind would call the facial expression inviting. "Let's get to the action. Bring it on."

The SWAT team was dressed in full tactical gear, just as they had been when they ran the obstacle course this morning. It only took a few minutes to get from the briefing room to the warehouse-sized simulator. Knowing everyone would be watching from the briefing room kept the pressure up, but that would be the least of their worries in a few minutes.

"We've got a big audience, people, so you can expect that they're going to be throwing everything at us, up to and including the kitchen sink," Derek told them. "Look sharp and watch each other's six."

Because the scenario involved possible tear gas but didn't guarantee it, none of them had their masks on yet. The ability to get the masks situated quickly was an important part of a real-life airborne attack.

They stood inside the holding room. In just a moment,

the door would open and the clock would start. One of the revolutionary parts of this simulator was its ability to mechanically reset rooms and situations. Every time the door opened, the team entering would be facing a different scenario.

Just like real life.

The door flew open and they got into formation, entering the darkened hallway so that everyone was facing a different angle. Using abbreviated sign language, the six-person team motioned to each other about who would take the lead and who would bring up the rear.

Everyone was focused but had the slightest smiles pulling at their faces. The team lived for this sort of challenge.

The scenario was a dark alley, amazingly lifelike. Ashton reached over and touched one of the "city" walls. He couldn't feel the texture through his gloves, but it obviously had weight behind it, like a real wall.

An announcement from what would be the equivalent of dispatch came in through the earpieces they all were wearing.

"SWAT team, we have intel that a group of five men is attempting to exit a bank two blocks to your north. Be advised suspects have hostages and have released tear gas into the vicinity."

"Masks on, people," Derek said as they began jogging toward the north, staying close to the wall. Soon they were around the corner from the bank.

The bad guys the team was combatting resembled life-like robots. They had sensors on their frames that could pick up on any movement or sound within human parameters. If a person could see or hear the SWAT team, the robots would be able to also.

And shoot accordingly.

Not real bullets of course, but the entire team's gear was covered in a netting that held sensors. The same ones the lab guy had explained would *notify* them when they'd been hit. Shots the bad guys took and the team received would be marked and counted against them. A direct shot to the head or enough shots to the chest—even with vests—would "kill" the SWAT member and they would be unable to help the team any longer.

Basically it was a game of laser tag but much more intense.

"Ashton, Liam, I want you to find some way to get to higher ground so we can take shots if needed. Lillian, Roman, keep lower."

The sound of gunfire—scarily realistic—could be heard throughout the building.

Everybody scattered, each going to their assigned place.

It really was an amazing facility. Ashton jumped up and grabbed a fire escape ladder and pulled it down. It easily supported his weight as he climbed up. If he didn't know he was in a simulator, he would swear he was on a city street at night. The creators had captured the chaos of a hostage situation with eerie accuracy.

Ashton spotted the window he wanted to get to. It would give him excellent vision into the bank.

He looked at Liam. "I'm heading up to that window."

"Roger that. I'll stay here."

Ashton had to make a pretty big leap over to the next "building," but grabbed the balcony and pulled himself up with no problem. He eased along the ledge to get to the window he wanted. Carefully.

Simulator or not, a fall from twenty feet would do some serious damage.

Once he made it through the window, he pulled out his mock sniper rifle.

Ashton spoke into his mic. "All set, Derek. I have visibility on the targets."

"Roger that."

"I'm in position, too, Derek," Liam said. "Ashton and I can take out at least three of the perps."

"Hold. We're working our way around behind them."

From his riflescope, Ashton watched as Roman made his way down the edge of the wall, using the smoke for cover. Ashton couldn't see where Lillian moved, but that wasn't unusual. Her smaller size gave her a distinct advantage in situations like this.

"Whoa, Roman, bogey on your six."

Ashton saw the human-looking robot step out from around the corner and aim at Roman. Ashton took the shot, even though he knew it would be too late.

The robot immediately powered down as Ashton's electronic bullet hit him, but the damage had already been done. Roman's suit lit up in the shoulder.

Roman's obscenities flew over the comm units. Ashton watched through his sniperscope as Roman grabbed the shoulder that had been "hit."

"Damn it, that hurts." Roman's voice was tight with pain.

"What?" Everyone asked it at the same time.

"Those sensors," Roman said, teeth clearly gritted. "Shocked the hell out of me when I got hit and it's still sending a pretty damn painful pulse every few seconds."

Not unlike what you would feel if you got shot in real

life while on a mission. Although probably not nearly as painful.

"So I guess you're not dead," Liam said.

Roman cursed again under his breath. "No. Just wounded. No wonder that lab coat bastard was all but laughing."

"Alright, that's it. Let's finish this. If they're going to use force, I'm not going to hesitate to order you all to do so, too," Derek said.

It was over less than two minutes later.

Ashton and Liam picked off three more of the six— five had been bad intel from the beginning, a nice little twist in the game—Lillian was able to take the other two from where she'd successfully sneaked around behind them.

The lights came up, and all mechanical bad guys stopped moving. The good guys had won that particular scenario.

"Alright, people, we're going to need to debrief. Not just our actions but how everything worked in here," Derek said. "Meet in the control room in fifteen minutes."

Ashton took off his gas mask now that overhead ventilation units were sucking all the residual tear gas and smoke out of the building.

He stood up and looked around the room he had crawled into to take his shots. It looked just like an apartment living room. Maybe the room would be part of another scenario—domestic hostage-taking or something.

He turned to walk to the window so he could crawl back out and find a way to the ground when metal shutters suddenly dropped from the ceiling, covering the window, blocking his route.

Great. There went that exit. When the scenario finished, obviously everything shut down. Literally.

Ashton turned toward the door on the other side of the room; the only other exit. He'd find his way back down using that.

But the metal shutters dropped from the ceiling there, too, covering the door.

"Um, Derek, I've got a situation here. I think Big Brother just locked me in the apartment building room I was using as cover."

Liam laughed. "I guess they don't have all the bugs worked out."

"Roger that, Ashton." Derek responded. "The control room should be able to hear this conversation and let you out soon."

"But until that time," Roman piped up, "please use your isolation to reflect on how you plan to move yourself out of the friend zone with the lovely Ms. Worrall."

Ashton rolled his eyes and gave a mock laugh. "You know what? You guys can kiss my—"

His words froze up as every sensor on his clothing and gear began to jolt him repeatedly. Ashton dropped to the ground, his muscles seizing up from pain, as almost every inch of his body was bombarded by a near constant flow of electric shock.

Chapter Four

All Ashton could do for the first few moments of the shocks burning throughout his body was survive. The pulse faded and he struggled to heave breath into his lungs, cursing through gritted teeth as the shocks amped up again.

"Fitzy, what's going on?" Ashton could hear Roman's voice but couldn't respond, unable to unclench his jaw. He could feel his vision begin to fade but knew if he lost consciousness he'd die here in this room.

Ashton slid toward the metal shutters that had covered the window he'd climbed in and slammed against it with his foot as hard as he could.

"Ashton, report." Derek was in full team leader mode, but Ashton couldn't speak. He slammed his foot against the shutter again. Vaguely he could hear orders barked over the comm unit.

The shocks eased again. Ashton reached for the light netting-like material that covered his SWAT garb. The sensors, like the ones that had shocked Roman when he'd been "shot," were giving the shocks. Although obviously malfunctioning since Ashton didn't think death by electrocution was supposed to be part of the training simulations.

"Sensors malfunctioning. Shocks." Ashton barely managed to get the words out before the voltage cranked again.

Through the agony coursing through his body, Ashton could hear Derek demanding that the control room shut off all the suits since they seemed not to be able to isolate Ashton's. Could hear Roman and Liam attempting to get under the metal shutters at his feet.

And a whole lot of cursing from just about everyone.

They weren't going to make it to him in time.

Ashton tried to pull the netting holding the sensors off of himself, but they just snapped back into place like they were supposed to, designed to keep from hindering any movement.

Too bad they could work that detail out but not halt the overloading of electrical voltage that was going to kill him right here on the floor. Ashton reached for the knife in his boot—almost from a distance, he could hear everyone screaming in his ears, the team, the control room, telling him to hold on—but he knew he was going to lose consciousness before he could cut the netting off himself. Not to mention sticking a metal object into live voltage probably would compound the about-to-die problem.

Damn it, he did not want to die in this simulator. The voltage amped up again and Ashton didn't even try to stop the deep grunt of pain that fell from his lips.

Then everything fell into complete blackness. Every light blacked out, every sound stopped.

The voltage stopped, too. Had he passed out? No, he could still think. Could still feel the pain echoing through his body even though the sensors had stopped their attack. He rolled over onto his back, too exhausted to even remove them in case they switched back on.

Lillian's voice came over the comm unit. "Main power outside completely cut."

Now that an electronic lock wasn't keeping the shutters closed, Roman and Liam were able to use their strength to open the one over the door. Liam held it open and Roman rolled under, shining his flashlight onto Ashton. He nodded his head toward the other man.

Roman knelt down next to Ashton, knife in hand and began cutting the netting material that held the sensors against their clothing. "Ashton is down, but alive. I'm getting these damned sensors off of him. I suggest everyone else do the same."

"Roger that," Derek said. "Steve has a medical team on the way."

"I'm okay," Ashton finally managed to get out. "I can move everything, at least, and don't seem any more brain-damaged than normal."

"Just sit tight," Derek continued. "It's going to take a minute to get to you since we're in complete blackness out here."

"Hey," Lillian huffed. "I didn't have time to finesse it. I just shot the hell out of the whole power box. I'm probably going to get fired for this."

"Thanks, Lil," Ashton said. Her quick thinking—shutting down all the power rather than trying to isolate the problem—had probably saved his life.

"No problem, Fitzy. How else am I going to get homemade muffins if you're not around?"

It wasn't long before people swarmed the training warehouse. Temporary lights were set up and a medical team got Ashton onto a gurney and out of the building. They took him back to the main Omega building where he could be thoroughly examined.

He had two noticeable burns—one on the back of his shoulder and one on his waist—and generally felt like he'd been hit by a truck, but he would live.

The entire SWAT team, plus Steve Drackett and the lab coat guy from the control room, was now crowded into the medical holding room with him.

"We're glad you're okay, Ashton," Steve said, leaning back against the wall.

"What the hell happened in there, Steve?" Derek asked. "That was well beyond not having the kinks worked out."

Steve gestured to the glasses lab coat guy. "This is Dr. Castillo, one of the main contracted developers of the training facility."

Dr. Castillo cleared his throat. "We're not exactly sure what happened. And it will be a little difficult to find out since Agent Muir basically decimated the power box."

Ashton just lay back in his bed as the entire team started defending Lillian's actions all at once. Loudly.

Steve finally shut them down. "Nobody is blaming Lillian. That was smart thinking and probably saved Ashton's life."

Lillian just shrugged from where she leaned against the bed. Ashton held out a fist toward her, which she immediately tapped with her knuckles.

"The truth is," Dr. Castillo continued. "I don't know what happened. All I know right now is that it wasn't just one problem. Yes, the sensors malfunctioned on Agent Fitzgerald's suit, but multiple other problems occurred. Problems that didn't happen when we tested the facility before you went in there."

"We're going to need answers, Dr. Castillo," Steve

said. "As to whether this turned ugly due to human and/or mechanical error or if there's something bigger at play."

Dr. Castillo scrubbed a hand across his face. "Yes. Absolutely. Finding out what transpired here is my team's number one priority. And not that it's worth much, but we're all terribly sorry and completely flabbergasted at the situation, Agent Fitzgerald. Please accept my sincerest apologies."

Ashton nodded. "Just figure out what happened so it doesn't happen again."

Dr. Castillo agreed, said a few more things to Steve, then left.

Grace Parker, Omega psychiatrist and in this case Ashton's physician, entered the room. "Okay, this place is not intended for the entire SWAT team. Steve, Derek, are you guys done debriefing?"

Steve straightened from where he leaned against the wall. "For the moment. Until we get a better sense of what the hell occurred in there today."

"I'll tell you this much, you're lucky it was Ashton in that suit that malfunctioned," Grace said as she lifted the edge of Ashton's shirt so she could see one of the worst electric burns on his waist.

"Lucky me," Ashton muttered.

Grace chuckled. "No, what I mean is that you have a lot of body mass, so those defective sensors were spread out further. For someone smaller—" she turned "—for instance, you, Lillian, the sensors would've been closer together and would've resulted in far greater damage. Maybe even death."

The team glanced at each other, saying nothing. They'd all just chosen random sensors as they'd entered the facility. It could've easily been someone with less body mass than Ashton.

"Well then, we're glad Ashton took one for the team." Derek slapped him lightly on his unwounded shoulder. "Does he need to stay overnight, Grace?"

The older woman checked out the other burn on Ashton's shoulder, then returned his shirt to its place. "No. No damage here that won't heal on its own. Even your burns don't look like they'll blister too badly." She smiled at Ashton. "You'll just be sore for a couple of days, so take it easy."

After showering gingerly, with cooler water than he would've liked because of his burns, he met the team at the Omega canteen to get their first meal since Summer's muffins.

Nobody knew exactly what mood to be in. Everyone was glad Ashton wasn't hurt any worse, but also hadn't expected anyone to be in any danger to begin with.

It wasn't a loss. But it wasn't a win.

"Hey, who wants to go get a drink?" It was late, already after 9:00 p.m. Their day had been long, but no one wanted to go home.

Everyone nodded and looked at Ashton.

He smiled. "Sure. I'm buying."

That certainly cheered everyone up. Derek begged off since his wife, Molly, and baby son, Sebastian, were waiting for him at home.

Ashton was just walking into the bar the Omega team often frequented when his phone rang.

Summer.

Why would she be calling him at nearly ten o'clock? He stepped back outside so he could hear more clearly.

"Summer?" he said by way of greeting.

"Hi, Ashton. I'm so sorry to call so late. You weren't asleep were you?"

"No, not at all. What's up?"

"I feel like an idiot."

"No, I promise, it's fine. What's going on?"

"The power in my condo went out. I checked the breaker like you showed me, but couldn't find anything wrong. I called the power company—they said they would eventually get here but had other priorities."

"Do you want me to come check it out? See if there's anything I can do?"

There was silence on the other end for so long Ashton worried they'd been disconnected.

"Summer?"

"No. No, that's not necessary. I'll just wait for the power company. One night won't kill me."

She laughed but it sounded brittle.

"It's not just the power, is it?"

"I thought I saw someone looking in the window. Which is ridiculous, I know. I'm being ridiculous," she repeated.

"No. It's easy to get frightened when you're alone. Everybody deals with that."

"It's just…something bad happened the last time my power went out. Somebody…" She faded out again. "Something bad happened."

She'd been kidnapped by a crazy woman. He knew. But Summer didn't know he knew. He didn't blame her for being a little spooked.

"Look, I'll be there in just a few minutes okay?"

"No. It's silly. You were already over here once this morning. My condo is not your only job."

Her condo wasn't his job at all. Ashton scrubbed his

hand across his face, wincing as it pulled on the burn on his shoulder. Like Derek had told him, he needed to tell her who he was before it bit him in the ass.

"It's no problem. Just for both of our peace of minds. I'll see you in a few minutes."

"Are you sure? Please, Ashton, you can tell me if this is inconveniencing you. Augh, who am I kidding, of course this is inconveniencing you. Just don't worry about it."

"Summer." He waited until he had her attention to continue. "I promise I don't mind. I'll be there in about fifteen minutes." He disconnected the call before she could begin to berate herself again.

"Looks like I'll be buying the rounds." Roman walked up to the entrance behind Ashton.

Ashton lifted his shoulder in a half shrug. "I've got to go. Summer needs—"

"Summer needs to know what you do for a living. Who you are."

"I'll get to it."

"Get to it soon, brother. It's going to be hard enough now. If she finds out on her own…" Roman shook his head.

"You're right. I'll tell her."

Because ultimately telling her he worked for Omega was going to be much easier than telling her he could've saved her husband's life two years ago.

How exactly did one phrase that?

He wouldn't worry about it tonight. Summer was upset, needed help. Honestly, Ashton didn't mind being the person she called. He just wished it was because she wanted to see him, not because she thought he was under contract with the building.

Because he sure as hell wanted to see her. Maintenance problem, boogie man or for whatever reason she called.

He liked hanging here with the team, drinking a couple of beers. But he'd rather be with Summer and Chloe any day of the week.

Roman was right. He had to tell her. There were too many other things he was keeping from her—planned to continue keeping from her—to let his occupation be a secret.

He'd almost died today. In his line of work, he could honestly die at any time—it was a risk they all accepted as part of the job.

He hadn't had any grand moments of his life passing before his eyes earlier when he'd been electrocuted. But he did know one thing for sure: he needed to come up with a plan when it came to Summer. Figure out what truth he could give her and what he couldn't and see where that left him.

It was time. Past time.

Chapter Five

Summer felt like she had set women's lib back a hundred years. What sort of grown female called a man over to her house just because the electricity went out?

She walked into Chloe's room to check on her again. Found her daughter sleeping peacefully in her crib just like she had been the last two dozen times Summer had checked.

And that face at the window had just been a figment of her imagination. Nobody was standing outside her condo.

Right?

Summer was willing to cut herself a little slack. The last time the power had gone out, a psychopath had drugged and kidnapped her and Chloe and trapped them in a burning building.

So she had reason to be wary of her power being out. Of course, Ashton didn't know any of this. He was just going to think she was a coward.

Or maybe he was going to think she wanted to see him. Seduce him or something.

She wasn't sure which was worse. At least if he showed up here and she was waiting in some kind of negligee, he wouldn't think she was terrified of being alone in the dark.

But would he be interested?

She pushed the thought away. That was *not* why Ashton was on his way over.

But she promised herself this was the last time she would allow herself to call. She was taking advantage of him. Of his politeness.

The knock on the door startled her out of her thoughts.

"Summer? It's Ashton."

She opened the door. "Thank you again for coming over. I'm sorry. It was totally unfair for me to ask you to come back again today. Especially so late at night."

He completely surprised her by putting a finger up to her lips. "It's okay. Don't apologize."

He dropped his hand back to his side almost immediately, but Summer still felt shocked. She didn't think Ashton had ever touched her except to shake her hand or in passing Chloe between them.

And more than that. He looked *different*.

She opened the door farther to allow him entrance, shaking her head. How could he possibly look different when she'd seen him just over twelve hours ago?

But he did. Just in how he carried himself. How he was looking her in the eyes without looking away.

How he'd just touched her.

"Are you okay?" he asked.

She tucked a lock of hair behind her ear. "I know you must think I'm a hot mess, but the last time the power went out something…" She swallowed. She really didn't want to get into the details. "Something bad happened."

Ashton cocked his head sideways, studying her for a long minute, but he didn't ask her what she meant. "It's always better to be safe than sorry. Let me double-check the fuse box, then I'll go to the main breaker near the street."

She stood at the top of the stairs as he made his way

down into the basement/laundry room of her condo. He was back up in just a few minutes.

"You were right. There weren't any fuses tripped in the box," he said softly, making her appreciate his awareness of Chloe's sleeping state.

She smiled at him. "I'm glad. If you had been able to come over here and fix the power in under ten seconds, I would've never been able to show my face in this town again."

He smiled. "It looks like you're free to show that beautiful face whenever you want to because there's nothing you could've done about the power."

Summer just stood staring at him. Not only did he just speak an entire sentence to her without stuttering, but did he just *flirt* with her?

"Oh. Oh, okay. Good." Now who was stuttering?

"Let me go check the larger fuse box out by the street."

Summer watched him walk back outside, trying to get herself under control. Maybe Ashton was just more confident and talkative at night.

If she thought she was attracted to him before, now she felt like she was smoldering inside.

Maybe she *should've* met him at the door in a negligee.

She needed some water to cool herself down. She turned away from the window—because staring at him probably looked a little desperate—and walked into the kitchen.

And found the same hooded face pressed up against her kitchen window.

This time she knew it wasn't any figment of her imagination.

She ran to the front door, then stopped. She couldn't leave Chloe alone in the house.

"Ashton!" she yelled.

He looked up from where he crouched at the fuse box by the street. He got one look at her face and began immediately running toward her.

He grabbed her arms. "What? What happened?"

"The face in the ski mask. It was back. At my kitchen window." She could hardly get the words out around her own breaths.

"Go inside and lock the door, okay? Don't open it for anyone but me. Call the police and tell them what happened."

"But—"

"Summer, just do it, okay? I'll be alright. I promise."

She nodded and did what he said, locking and deadbolting the door. She grabbed her phone and called 911.

ASHTON PUSHED AWAY all physical discomfort from his injuries as he bolted around the building and into the woods behind Summer's unit, Glock in hand. He knew how much she loved the privacy these trees provided. He hoped this incident wouldn't change her opinion.

The electrical box near the street had definitely been tampered with. The lock on the outside was broken, wires inside had been hacked. Someone wanted the power out in Summer's home, maybe the entire condo unit.

Ashton didn't know if it was some punk kid playing pranks or someone with much more sinister intent. If he was still around here, Ashton would catch him.

He wished he had his sniper rifle with him. Not because he planned to shoot the guy outright, but because looking through the scope for an enemy target was Ashton's forte. Hiding from Ashton when he was in a secure location with his riflescope to his eye was damn near impossible.

But instead, Ashton got to the cover of the trees and stopped. He held himself still, looking for any sign of movement in the darkness. One thing Ashton had learned as a sniper was patience.

But nothing moved. After long minutes of holding himself completely still, he felt sure he was alone in the trees. Whoever had peeked through Summer's window evidently had taken off as soon as he'd realized Summer had seen him. Which was good. That probably meant it was some sort of sick Peeping Tom or burglar, not someone who meant true harm.

Although who would mean true harm to Summer? Bailey Heath, the woman who had kidnapped Summer and Chloe, had died that day on scene.

Stupid punk teenagers out to cause trouble and damage buildings was a much more likely scenario than someone intending to hurt Summer or her daughter.

Ashton made it back to Summer's door and knocked, letting her know it was him.

"Oh my gosh, are you alright? I was worried about you." She threw open the door, grabbed his shirt and pulled him inside. "Did you see anything? Are you okay? The police should be here in a minute."

She ran her hand from his shirt to his arm, but didn't let him go. He didn't wince even as her fingers hit some of his sore spots.

"I'm fine. I searched the woods but didn't see anyone."

"You could've gotten hurt!" Now she had both of her hands on his arms.

This was the perfect time to tell her, he realized. It would only take ten seconds and he could get it out, at least letting her know that he was law enforcement. He didn't have to provide details.

"Summer, there's something I should tell you."

Her big gray eyes looked up at him expectantly. "What? Do you think it was someone with a gun? Someone trying to break in to the house?"

"No. I mean about—"

A knock on the door stopped him. It was too loud and it woke up Chloe. She started crying as the police identified themselves outside the door.

The moment was lost.

"You answer the door," he told her. "I'll get Chloe."

Ashton made his way into little Chloe's room. He didn't turn on the light, hoping he'd be able to soothe her into going back to sleep. But as soon as she saw it was him and not Summer in the dim glow from the night light, she scooted herself around onto her little bottom and pulled herself into a standing position on her crib.

"Ah-ta! Ah-ta. Ah-ta." Glee tainted her tone. She held her arms out to him.

He couldn't resist her, didn't even try. "Hey there, sweetheart." He swung her up in his arms. "I'm sorry all the racket woke you up."

"Ah-ta. Mama."

"Yes, your mama's right out in the living room. Let's go see her, since I'm sure you'll scream bloody murder if I put you back in that crib right now."

Summer was telling the two police officers what she saw at the window. A man in a ski mask.

"As soon as I looked over there, he disappeared. I called for Ashton who was out at the power box at the street and he went to look out back."

Ashton nodded at the two men. "Here, you take this wiggle worm," he said, handing Chloe to Summer, "and I'll take the officers outside and show them what I saw."

He didn't want to talk shop in front of Summer. It wouldn't take much of a slip before she realized he knew way more about crime scenes and pursuit tactics than a condo handyman should.

When the door closed behind him, he immediately identified himself, pulling his credentials from his pocket. "I'm Ashton Fitzgerald, with Omega Sector." The two officers introduced themselves as Jackson and McMeen.

He showed the men where the wires had been cut in the main fuse box and they went around to where the perp had been looking through Summer's window. Sure enough, a footprint was clearly evident in the soil beneath Summer's window.

The two men looked at each other. "This matches a couple other calls we've gotten the last few days. Mostly apartments and condos, but a couple of houses," McMeen said.

"Dangerous?"

Jackson shook his head. "No. Power cut, some graffiti. General building damage. Nobody has actually seen them before Ms. Worrall."

"Whoever it was took off immediately as soon I headed their way."

McMeen wrote something down in his notebook. "That would be consistent with our theory that it's some teenagers just looking for a little trouble."

That made Ashton feel better. He knew it would Summer, too.

The officers left and Ashton made a call to the power company. They assured him they'd have someone out there first thing in the morning to look at it. By the time he made it back inside Summer's house, she was laying Chloe back in her crib.

"Did they find anything?" she whispered as she came back out, closing Chloe's door behind her.

"There was definitely a footprint under your kitchen window and some of the wiring to all the units had been tampered with down at the box by the street."

"Why? Do the police have any idea who it is?"

"It looks like it's probably some high-school kids trying to make trouble. They've had other similar calls around town this week."

Some of the tension eased from Summer's shoulders. Stupid kids were just stupid kids.

Now that the immediate danger was past, Ashton could feel every bruise and burn on his body from the electrical shocks earlier today. God, he was tired.

Evidently it showed.

She touched him gently on his arm. "Thank you for coming over here tonight. I was a mess."

"No, you were fine. Anyone would be a little frightened in these circumstances. Kids didn't mean any harm, but that doesn't mean it's not scary." He remembered carrying Summer and Chloe out of that burning warehouse a few months ago. If anyone had logical reason to worry about a masked face in a window, it was her.

She turned away. "I guess so."

"The power company said they'll be out here first thing in the morning, so that's good."

"Yeah. I'm glad it's not too cold out yet. We should be able to sleep comfortably." But her eyes darting around the room said otherwise.

"Summer, are you going to be okay? Do you want me to stay? Camp out here on the couch?"

Or so much more. He wanted to do so much more.

She studied him for a minute but then swallowed whatever it was she'd considered saying. She wrapped her arms around herself. "No. You're tired, I can tell. We'll be fine. Like you said, just kids, no danger."

Disappointment hit Ashton in the gut. He hadn't realized how much he'd wanted her to ask him to stay. Even if it had just been on the couch.

In any other situation, he'd just tell her that was what he was doing regardless. He'd wink at her and offer to be her own personal SWAT security.

And tell her she was welcome to join him on the couch if she got scared at any time. Or he'd be happy to bring the security detail into her bedroom.

But he couldn't laugh and wink and make jokes and charm his way into staying.

There were too many secrets between them. Too many lies.

He walked over to the door. "I'll call you tomorrow to make sure the power got turned back on. If not, I can call the power company again."

"I'm sure it will be." She opened the door and looked at him again like she wanted to say something, but then her gaze slid to the ground. "Thanks again, Ashton."

He touched her arm, wanting to do so much more than that.

"Good night."

He heard the door shut and lock behind him and he walked down to his truck. He eased his sore body into it then, staring back at her condo, started the ignition.

Then promptly turned it back off.

He wasn't leaving her.

Yeah, it was probably just kids trying to scare people, but Ashton didn't care. On the off chance it was someone with a more sinister intent directed at Summer, he wasn't leaving her alone.

He slid his seat back in an effort to get more comfortable inside his truck.

It was going to be a long night.

Chapter Six

Summer could make a list of all the ways she'd been an idiot tonight, but it would probably take too long.

But Ashton offering to sleep here and her turning him down? That would be at the top of said list.

She'd been fascinated with the man for months, hoping he would ask her out. Finally he'd done something that could be categorized as romantically encouraging—or at least protective—and she shut him down.

Not to mention they still didn't have power and she was pretty nervous. It was past midnight already. She wondered if she'd be able to get any sleep.

Even though she'd already double-checked them all, Summer went around to make sure she'd locked the windows. When she got to the bay window, she saw Ashton's truck still parked out front.

Why was he still here?

She moved the curtain more to the side so she could get a better look. Maybe he was on the phone or something and just hadn't left yet.

It didn't take long to realize Ashton was watching out for them in his truck.

Warmth bloomed in her chest and tears actually welled in her eyes.

Ashton Fitzgerald may be too shy to ask her out, but he cared enough about her and Chloe to stay out in his vehicle and make sure they were safe.

Summer opened the front door. She'd been an idiot enough tonight. Now was her chance to rectify that.

Her eyes met his as she crossed from the side to around the front of his truck. His didn't widen, his expression didn't change. He just watched her as she came around to stand next to the driver's side door.

They stared at each other through the glass for a moment. There was more than just protectiveness in his eyes. The warmth she'd felt at his concern now grew hotter. A heat pooled inside her.

She opened the door to his truck. "Hi."

"I just wanted to make sure you and Chloe were safe."

She nodded. "It means a lot to me that you would do that. But come inside. It's silly for you to be out here."

He studied her for a moment and she thought he might refuse. But then he straightened the seat and got out, groaning a little as he did so.

Summer stepped closer. "Are you hurt? Did something happen when you were chasing that guy in the woods and you didn't tell me?

"No." Ashton closed the door behind him. "There was an accident while I was…working today."

She noticed the slight pause but didn't press it. "What sort of accident?"

They walked back to her house.

"Electrical."

She opened the door and they went inside. "Great. I'll bet the last thing you wanted to do was come here and deal with more power-company-related problems."

"I never mind coming over here to help with anything. Truly."

Now that she had him back in her house, she wasn't sure exactly what to do with him. When she gestured toward the couch, he eased himself onto it as if standing was too much of an effort.

"Let me get you a pillow and blanket."

He bobbed his head. "Thanks for coming out there to get me."

She smiled, wishing she had the guts to lead him into her bedroom.

When she came back out with the bedding items, Ashton had slipped off his shoes and was lying all the way across the sofa. He was too big for it—one leg hung off the arm of the couch and the other was bent with his foot on the ground. He'd thrown one arm up over his face which had caused his T-shirt to slide up, exposing a brief measure of sexy abs and some sort of bandage.

"Ashton, how hurt are you?"

He slid his arm down slightly so she could see his eyes.

"I have a couple of electrical burns, one on my side, one on my shoulder. And I generally feel like somebody decided to use me as a punching bag."

He sat back up as she crossed the room.

"You shouldn't have gone off sprinting after my Peeping Tom."

"Catching someone in the process of committing a crime like this is almost always easier than trying to determine the culprit from any evidence they leave at the scene."

She sat down next to him. She couldn't help it. He was conversing—even if the subject matter was a little strange—not stuttering and looking away from her like he normally did. On the contrary, he was looking at her the way a man looks at a woman he's interested in.

God, how she'd missed this feeling.

She scooted just a little closer. "Oh yeah, do a lot of crime fighting on the side, do you?"

His brows pulled together quickly. "Um. Ha. Ha. Well, actually I—"

Now he was back to looking away and stuttering. Summer reached over, hooked an arm around his neck and kissed him.

He paused for just a moment and she was afraid he would pull away. But then he groaned and scooped her up and placed her on his lap so her legs straddled his hips.

He kissed her with shattering absorption, as if he couldn't get enough of her. Whatever timidity had possessed him each time they'd spoken over the past few months was gone now.

Her hands slid up his shoulder and she felt the edge of another bandage. Not wanting to hurt him in any way, she slid her fingers up around his neck and into his thick brown hair.

His arms wrapped around her hips, pulling her more tightly against him. She barely restrained a gasp at the feel of her breasts crushed against his chest.

How long had it been? She'd forgotten how good it felt to have strong arms wrapped tightly around her.

His tongue traced her bottom lip before slipping into her mouth. Summer sank deeper into him, her fingers clutching him to her.

The kiss went on and on until she couldn't think straight for the need pulsing through her. But vaguely she became aware that Ashton was slowing the kiss down. Drawing it out.

Easing back.

She pulled away from him so she could look into his soft brown eyes.

"Want to take this into my bedroom?" She could hardly recognize the husky voice as her own.

He put his forehead against hers. "I do. More than I want to take my next breath, I want to move this into the bedroom. I want to keep you in there for about the next month."

"There's a huge but in here, and it's not mine." She began to pull away.

He grabbed her buttocks and pulled her back against him. Both of them gasped slightly at the contact. He thrust his hips gently against hers.

"You cannot doubt that I want you right now. Because I do. And yes there is another but in here that is not nearly as fine as yours."

"What is it?"

"We haven't even been on a date yet, Summer."

She began kissing along his jaw. "Will you have dinner with me, Ashton?"

He groaned as she made her way down to his ear. "Yes. I most definitely will. And we'll talk. And after that, if your bedroom is still an invitation, I will most definitely take you up on it."

She sat back so she could see his eyes. "Do you have something bad to tell me?"

He sighed. "Not bad. Just…complicated. Right now isn't the time to go into it all. It's late and it's been a long day for both of us, filled with all sorts of crazy. Let me take you out on Friday night. We'll have a nice meal, just the two of us, and talk."

She narrowed her eyes. "You say it's not bad, but I feel like it is. Like you're trying to get out of being intimate with me right now."

He sighed. "I'm not. I promise. Trust me, I'm calling myself all sorts of a fool. But if you still want me after we talk on Friday night, I promise you—" now he leaned forward and began to kiss her jaw the way she'd been kissing his, working his way down to her throat "—I will take you back to that bedroom or this couch or hell, the kitchen counter—maybe all three—and make love to you until neither of us can move."

She moaned as his lips nipped gently at her throat.

"Ashton, are you involved with someone else? Is that what you have to tell me?"

"No."

"Are you a criminal?"

"No."

"Then fine." She leaned back so she could look at him more clearly. She didn't understand why he wanted to wait, but she would respect his reasoning. Plus, it would give her a chance to be prepared with some underthings that were a little more sexy. She hadn't been expecting this—him, *them*—tonight. "Friday it is. But I fully expect to take you up on your promise to not be able to move Saturday morning."

He already had part of her heart. She was ready to give him more.

Chapter Seven

Two days later, on Friday at four o'clock in the afternoon, Ashton left Omega Sector to go home. Three quarters of the way there, he spun his truck around, nearly causing an accident behind him.

He needed to go to a florist. To get flowers.

For the date of doom tonight.

He grimaced, waving his hand in apology as horns blasted all around him at his insane driving antics.

The last two days had been hell. He'd been relegated to desk duty at work to allow him time to heal. Fortunately the SWAT team hadn't been sent out on any missions, but Ashton hated missing the training and physical exercise. He needed it. Needed some sort of outlet for the tension running through him.

Waking up with Summer cuddled against him on the couch on Wednesday had not been hell—the opposite in fact—despite the aches in his body.

All his good intentions had almost flown out the window right then, looking at her delicate form pressed up against his. It had only been Chloe waking up and starting her sweet jabbering in her crib that had stopped him.

A good thing, too. At the very least Summer needed

to know he worked for Omega Sector before they became intimate.

If they became intimate.

Ashton was hoping she would laugh it off, that he would be able to explain how he'd meant to tell her but couldn't figure out how. How he really hadn't minded helping fix anything—glad to use the skills he'd developed growing up on the farm. And that it gave him an excuse to see her.

He would've used just about any excuse to see her.

Hopefully just explaining that he worked for Omega Sector and that was how he knew Joe Matarazzo—her friend and landlord who had introduced them—would be enough. Ashton would mention SWAT if he had to. And maybe even the burning warehouse when Omega had been on the scene and gotten her out.

But he prayed she didn't bring up any questions about her husband's death.

He would just blow up that bridge—and probably himself—when he got to it. He pulled into the parking lot of the florist, resisting the urge to beat his head against the steering wheel.

Right now, flowers. Something to smooth the way. He laughed when he looked over and saw the actual name of the shop.

The Blooming Idiot.

He was definitely in the right place.

Maybe a huge beautiful bouquet would help ease the jagged path Ashton would be walking tonight. He wasn't sure what type of flowers to buy. Hell, he didn't know much about flowers at all besides the obvious. He sat for a minute trying to think of what Summer might like, then gave up. He'd have to ask the florist for help.

Since it was so big, he'd parked his truck a little farther away even though there were closer spots. Ashton glanced around as he walked. He felt like someone was watching him.

But there was no reason to think that—nobody he knew would think to find him here. Not to mention almost taking out a half dozen cars as he'd made his psychotic U-turn had definitely gotten rid of anyone tailing him.

Still, Ashton had been living with his gut feelings for long enough to know not to ignore them. He crouched to the ground with the appearance of tying his shoe. It gave him the opportunity to look around without seeming like he was studying anything.

Nothing.

Maybe he was just jumpy about tonight. About the conversation he'd be having with Summer. Maybe he just hadn't gotten the exercise over the past few days his body was accustomed to. Too much energy. Too much frustration. Ashton stood and walked the rest of the way into the florist.

He was no less jumpy in here.

Petals of all shapes and sizes assailed him. How the hell was he supposed to pick something Summer would like?

The manager, an African-American man in his late forties whose name tag said Marcel, finally took pity on him after a few minutes. He walked over and slapped Ashton gently on the shoulder, his uninjured one thankfully. "Don't worry, whatever it is you've done or you're about to do, we've got the right flowers to cover it."

Ashton tried to smile, but he was sure it didn't come across correctly on his face. "I'm going out with a woman for the first time tonight."

"So something simple." Marcel tapped a finger against

his lips. "Maybe a daisy or two. Less is usually more for a first date."

Ashton gritted his teeth and nodded, sighing audibly.

"Okay, that face tells me there's more to the story than just going on a first date."

Ashton decided to just jump right in. "I've basically been lying to her for the past seven months. She thinks I'm someone I'm not."

"More than daisies, then." Marcel chuckled and pulled him toward the roses. "How big are these lies you've been telling?"

Ashton rubbed his eyes. "Pretty big."

"Have you considered the Louis Vuitton store?"

"What?" Was that a different florist?

Marcel chuckled again. "Never mind. C'mon, I'll get you set up with something that will hopefully give your date something else to think about besides what a lying bastard you are."

Ashton grimaced. That was going to take an awful lot of flowers.

Marcel made a beautiful bouquet, Ashton had to admit. It wasn't roses—possibly the only flower he would've been able to identify. Instead, the bouquet was made of lilies, artistically arranged to look stunning but not overwhelming.

The flowers were lovely and full of life, just like Summer. Ashton told Marcel that.

"You be sure to tell your lady friend you think she's lovely and full of life. That will go a long way toward whatever news you need to tell her that's so bad."

Ashton paid and made his way out the door toward his truck. He heard the bells on the shop's door ring and Marcel's voice call out.

"Be sure to keep those out of the sun until tonight. Won't do you any good to bring her wilted flowers along with your lies."

Ashton chuckled and spun back to give the older man a smart-aleck response.

An action which saved Ashton's life.

The flowers in his hand—right where his chest had been a second before—exploded into a thousand pieces of brightly colored petal confetti. A second shot flew over his shoulder and into the window of the shop, shattering the glass.

Ashton had pulled his Glock before the glass finished breaking and scurried back to the cover the tires of his truck provided.

"Marcel, get inside," he yelled.

The man's eyes were wide in his face. He stood motionless.

"Marcel, inside now!" Ashton yelled again.

It took the older man a second to process what Ashton was saying before he ran back through the door.

"Call the police!" Ashton yelled after him.

He turned around and peeked over the bed of his truck, only to immediately duck back to the ground as another bullet came spinning for him. He let out the vilest curse he knew when the next two shots took out the back and side windows of his truck.

The shots were coming from an office building across the street. Whoever it was had a relatively high-powered rifle—probably a .308 Winchester—and was fairly skilled in its use.

Fortunately not highly skilled or Ashton would now be lying dead in The Blooming Idiot's parking lot.

And thankfully he'd parked his truck on the far side of the lot so the gunman had to shoot while he was walking rather than picking Ashton off as he stopped and unlocked the door to his vehicle.

He got his cell phone out of his pocket and called the first Omega number he came to: Roman's.

"Calling me for advice about your date, Fitzy?"

More shots rang out. Ashton could see people in a parking lot down the street trying to figure out what was going on.

Ashton didn't waste time. "Roman, I've got some asshole shooting at me from a building across the street." He gave the address. "Nobody is injured, but the guy has me pinned down behind my truck."

He could hear Roman running, yelling to the other members of the SWAT team.

"Are you out in the open?"

"I'm okay for now as long as he's working alone." If the gunman had a partner who was in the process of making his way to this side of the building, Ashton was in trouble. "But there are civilians all over the place."

"Alright, we've already got locals on their way to you. ETA four minutes. We're five minutes behind them."

Another shot rang out, creating a grinding sound as it hit the metal of Ashton's truck. "You guys hurry." He disconnected.

Other people were starting to realize what was happening. Panicked cries came from farther away. Ashton tried to move from behind his truck, but a volley of shots rang out.

There was no way he was getting out from behind this vehicle.

Damn it, he had one more call to make and all the lies he'd told over the past few months dictated he do it right now before the sirens of local law enforcement arrived.

Hunkered down behind his truck, looking at the destroyed flowers he would've been giving Summer in a few hours, he called her.

"Hey, Summer, it's Ashton." He tried to keep his voice light.

"Hi. I didn't expect to hear from you this afternoon. Everything okay?"

"Well, actually, unfortunately something has come up. Something at work. I need to see if we can reschedule."

Silence met him from the other end. *Damn it.*

"Summer—"

A set of shots rang out and another one of his truck windows blasted out, blowing glass near him. The gunman was obviously trying to get Ashton to leave the cover of the vehicle. He cringed. There was no way Summer hadn't heard the window breaking.

"What was that?" she asked.

"The work thing I was telling you about. Another window just broke." The gunman was also firing into the florist shop. Ashton needed to return fire, he couldn't take a chance on Marcel getting hit. But he didn't want to take a chance on Summer hearing the gunfire.

"Summer, can you hang on? I have to put you on hold for just a sec." Ashton didn't wait for an answer, just pressed the mute button, raised his head over the edge of the truck and fired four rounds based on where he estimated the shooter was coming from—the roof of the three-story office building across the street.

Hopefully, Ashton's return fire would pin the gunman down for a few minutes.

"Marcel?" he called out. "You okay in there? Hurt?"

"No. But that bastard shot out my window!"

"Just stay back, okay? Police are on their way."

Ashton pressed unmute. "Sorry. I'm back." Although

his voice was calm, another piece of glass from the shop fell to the ground making a loud shattering noise. He grimaced. "Things are a little chaotic here."

"I can tell. I thought you were just making the whole work situation problem up. That you had just changed your mind."

"No, no, I promise I would be there if I could." He heard the sirens begin to ease their way up the street. In another thirty seconds, they'd be unmistakably blaring. He tried to keep his voice as conversational as possible. "Can I call you tomorrow and we'll work out another time to go out?"

"Are you sure that's what you want, Ashton?"

He could hear the hurt in her voice and wished he had time to reassure her the way he wanted to. "I'm very sure."

That was all he could give her. All the secrets he'd kept from her were now racing toward him in the form of sirens. If he'd been honest from the beginning, he could've been honest now.

"I'm sorry, Summer." Ashton disconnected the call, cursing. But for now he had to push Summer out of his mind. He needed to make sure Marcel and the other civilians weren't hurt.

The guy was firing at the shop again. Ashton leaned from the back of the bed this time and fired again, hoping to pin the man down, or at least draw fire back to the truck. But he'd now used nine of his fifteen-round magazine.

A few seconds later, the bullets flew toward the truck again, which was what Ashton wanted, although he still grimaced at every hit the truck took.

He smelled it before he saw it, but he saw it close afterward. Gasoline. The shooter had punctured the truck's large gas tank and it was leaking everywhere.

A well-aimed shot would in essence make the truck a giant explosive.

The local squad cars had arrived and were now causing chaos in the street between the shop and the shooter. Ashton knew he had to take a chance and leave the cover of the truck.

"Marcel, stay inside, as far back as you can," he yelled.

"What's going on?"

"He's punctured my gas tank. It'll blow if he hits it right. I've got to get away from the truck."

Ashton didn't waste any more time talking. He pushed away from the truck and began a random weaving pattern as he ran. To anyone else it would look like he was drunk, but Ashton knew firsthand that a target weaving in and out with no discernible pattern was more difficult to hit.

Or at least kill.

Ashton would have to take his chances.

Shots didn't fire out at him but he heard them hitting the truck.

The gunman had decided to aim for the stationary target. And hit it.

Ashton dove for the minimal cover of an air-conditioning box on the side of the building. He felt heat sear over him as all the gasoline in his truck caught fire and blew up in a cloud of deadly flames.

He stayed down against the unit for a few more seconds before peeking around. His truck was burning, barreling smoke into the air. It at least provided cover.

Ashton made his way around the side of the building, where the shooter hopefully wouldn't be looking, and crossed the street. He kept his Glock low at his side so he blended in with the other people standing around staring at the brouhaha in the florist parking lot.

Ashton knew the shooter would still be on the roof of the office building and moved directly for it without running, in case the shooter was still waiting for a chance to pick him off. He knew he should make himself known to the local law enforcement, but there wasn't time.

He put his Glock back in the hidden waist holster of his jeans. If someone saw it and got hysterical that wouldn't end well for him.

Roman and Derek's vehicle came tearing into the office parking lot just as Ashton got there.

"You okay?" Roman asked.

Ashton nodded. "Shooter has to be up on the roof. It's the only place he had a clear vantage point."

"You two head up there," Derek told them. "The rest of the team and I will help the locals. Keep everyone from becoming any more panicked."

People poured out of the building, being evacuated due to the fire and shots. Roman and Ashton made eye contact. They both knew the shooter could be walking right by them and they wouldn't know it.

They fought their way up the stairs through the swarms going down. As they reached the roof access, Ashton signaled to Roman. He would take the lead.

Roman threw the door open, gun in hand and pointing toward the most visible area. Ashton took two steps around him, Glock held with both hands at shoulder height, ready for anyone who might be waiting.

It didn't take them long to realize the roof was clear. On the side closest to the florist lay a .308 Winchester, leaning against the roof's ledge. Dozens of shell casings surrounded it.

But the shooter was gone.

Chapter Eight

Monday morning the SWAT team met in one of the Critical Response Division conference rooms. They'd gone over what had happened on Friday night at the florist. Thankfully no one had been hurt, although there'd been some pretty extensive property damage.

Ashton's truck was a total loss. Marcel's Blooming Idiot would be closed for quite some time.

But right now they were studying a picture on the screen of Curtis Harper. Twenty-nine-year-old son of George Harper.

Brandon Han and Jon Hatton, two of Omega's top profilers, searched through the files. Most of the SWAT team remembered what had happened with George Harper four years ago without having to look at the file.

Derek pointed to the picture. "Harper Sr. was the genius who tried to rob a jewelry store, then took four people hostage when the plan went south. He killed one hostage before Ashton took him out via sniper rifle."

Everyone around the table murmured their agreement. They all remembered. The girl who died had been a part-time college student. Nineteen years old.

"Ashton's kill was deemed a clean shot," Lillian pointed out. "Internally and by an external review board."

Derek nodded. "That's correct. No one is calling the case into question. Except evidently George's son, Curtis Harper." He pointed to the picture again.

Jon Hatton closed the file he'd been studying. "Harper's fingerprint was found at the crime scene. He wiped down the rifle he used, but evidently he touched one of the shell casings. We also caught him on camera inside the office building."

Ashton stood up, unable to sit any longer. "So he, what, followed me to the florist and set up shop across the street?"

Brandon shrugged. "He might have been waiting for an opportunity for days or weeks and this happened to be it."

Ashton scrubbed a hand over his face. "George Harper has been dead for four years. Why would his son want to get revenge on me now? That doesn't make any sense."

Murmurs of agreement floated around the room. "We're not sure," Brandon replied. "We're going to see what we can find out about him and do a full profile."

"He'll have gone to ground now." Ashton leaned against the wall, studying the man's picture. "Every law enforcement agency in Colorado is looking for him. He won't just be wandering around."

"Agreed," Derek said. "But everyone needs to watch their back, especially you Ashton. He might be hiding right now, but we can safely assume he's not finished. If Harper decides…"

He trailed off as everyone's phones began to buzz. Within moments, everyone was standing.

The Omega SWAT team had just been called in for duty.

Derek walked over to the computer, speaking as he

read the update. "Alright, people, looks like Harper isn't the only idiot who's decided to go crazy this week. We've got a hostage situation at a grocery store at the corner of Broad and Michaels. Everybody suit up, we're out in ten minutes."

"Who takes hostages in a grocery store?" Roman muttered. "That's like the worst tactical situation on the planet."

Ashton shrugged. "Is Matarazzo going?" Joe was Omega's top hostage negotiator.

"He's already on his way," Derek said. Everyone ran out of the conference room to grab what they needed.

Curtis Harper would have to wait.

LITTLE CHLOE LOVED to be outside in her stroller. Now that she was becoming more secure at walking, she often wanted to toddle beside it rather than be in it, but that didn't bother Summer. Summer couldn't resist the huge smile that lit her daughter's face every time they went outdoors.

Right now they were walking, as they did a couple times a week if the weather permitted, to the grocery store a few blocks away. Summer used to be able to get there and back pretty quickly when she could push the stroller, but now the toddler set the pace.

Summer felt thankful once again that she had a job that allowed her to work from home and around Chloe's schedule. Joe Matarazzo had provided that job—because of his wealth and media attention, he'd needed someone as a personal social media specialist/press secretary. Joe kept his Omega Sector work as separate as possible from his personal life, but he'd needed someone he could trust that would speak for him online. Summer also searched for and helped spin any damaging stories others might try to publish about him or his business ventures.

Summer was thankful for the work that challenged her mind and offered creative avenues and had found herself quite good at it. Joe had probably only offered her the job after Tyler had died because of his guilt about his part in Tyler's death, but it had worked out for both of them.

Summer had never blamed Joe for Tyler's death. She'd only ever blamed the person fully responsible: a disgruntled ex-employee who had walked into Tyler's office building with the intent of killing everyone. Tyler had been one of the casualties before Joe and his Omega Sector team could take the killer down.

Even though she didn't blame Joe, she'd still taken his job offer since she'd been six months pregnant and totally alone. But after a few months they'd both found she had a knack as an online personal assistant and she'd taken on the social media presence for some of Joe's charitable organizations and businesses as well.

The condo she lived in was also owned by Joe and his wife, Laura. Summer's rent was probably highly reduced—again, out of some misplaced guilt on Joe's part—and soon Summer would have to confront them about that again. She'd tried to make her arguments a few months ago when they'd come over for dinner that a reduced rent rate wasn't necessary, but Laura had just touched Summer on the arm.

"Joe wants to do this. We both know you don't blame him for Tyler's death, but knowing you're not under any financial pressure helps Joe. I promise if we need the money, I will let you know."

The Matarazzos were billionaires so she doubted

Laura and Joe would be demanding more money from her any time soon.

But maybe she would check with Joe or Laura and make sure they knew how much extra time Ashton had been spending at her condo over the past few months.

Her face heated. Well, she wouldn't mention the time she and Ashton had spent making out on her couch last week, but the times he'd come over to fix things. She just wanted them to know how helpful he was. What a great employee he was.

Chloe lost her balance and plopped backward onto her diapered bottom.

"Uh-oh," she said, looking over at Summer.

"Yeah, uh-oh. You okay, sweetie?" She helped her daughter stand and wiped the dirt off her back. Chloe immediately started her not-quite-steady forward progress again, holding on to the edge of the stroller.

Right back up and on her way. Summer wished she could be a little more like her daughter sometimes.

She'd talked to Ashton briefly a couple of times since he'd broken their date on Friday. She didn't know exactly what had happened, but she knew it had involved his truck. Evidently it had been totaled. That had been part of the chaos she could hear when they were on the phone Friday. Summer didn't imagine a handyman's job was overly exciting, so she looked forward to hearing about whatever mess had happened.

Except they'd yet to exactly reschedule.

Ashton wasn't overtly avoiding her, she didn't think. And she knew he'd been busy with work; breakdowns didn't stop just because it was the weekend.

He'd told her he had something to say. Something he thought she wouldn't like.

She wished he'd just come out and say it, whatever it was. How bad could it be?

As they rounded the corner bringing the grocery store in sight, Summer knew right away something unusual was going on. Police cars were haphazardly parked all over the lot, lights blazing. A couple of news vans and pockets of people milled around recording everything with their phones.

Chloe became immediately entranced with the lights and action and began walking that way.

"Oh no, little missy. If we're going to go check it out, then you're going to have to get in the stroller."

Chloe stiffened her back, making it more difficult for Summer to get her in the seat. "Hey, if you don't go in the stroller, we'll have to go home."

She knew her daughter couldn't possibly understand the whole sentence, but she evidently comprehended the word *home* because she became much more compliant.

"Good girl." Summer kissed the top of her head as she buckled the belt around her waist to offset any escape attempts.

They walked toward the chaos. At the outer edge of spectators, Summer asked a woman she recognized from the store—a cashier in uniform—what was happening.

"I wasn't in there, but I heard some guy came in— obviously high—and demanded the manager open the big safe. But it's on a time lock, so Brad couldn't do it."

"Oh no."

"They were in the office for a long time with the guy yelling at Brad. Somebody called the police. But I think it's over now. Nobody got hurt."

Summer put her arm around the lady and hugged her. "I'm glad you weren't in there when it happened."

"Me, too. Sorry, it looks like the store won't be open for a while, if it even opens at all today." She bent down to smile at Chloe. "You'll have to get your food somewhere else, cutie."

Chloe giggled at the lady's silly voice.

Summer didn't really need any food. This was really just more for her and Chloe to get some sun—winter and all its snow would be coming soon enough. It also allowed Summer to get out of the house and talk to some adults, even if it was just for a few minutes.

But she was very thankful she hadn't been a couple hours earlier. Would not have wanted to be inside with Chloe when the man on drugs decided to break in.

Chloe babbled from her stroller, still enjoying the lights and noise, so Summer walked along the outside of the parking lot to get some exercise even if they couldn't shop.

Joe Matarazzo stepped out of a large law enforcement van a few yards away. She wasn't surprised to see him here but didn't call out to him since he was obviously here on official business.

Chloe had no such compunctions. Summer wasn't sure if it was Joe she recognized or just wanted to get closer to what was going on, but she started clapping her hands and talking her gibberish so loudly that Joe turned toward them.

He smiled and waved and jogged over.

"Hey gals." He pulled Summer in for a hug before reaching down to tap Chloe on her nose. "What are you doing here?"

"We walk here sometimes just to get out of the house, and we saw all the action. You've probably got to go." She gestured toward the store.

"Nah. This entire situation had worked itself out before Omega even got here. We set up camp, but the locals didn't need us."

Chloe began to squirm and fuss now that the stroller wasn't moving anymore. Summer unhooked her and picked her up, but she just wanted down to walk. Summer set her down, keeping a tight hold on her hand and walking her back and forth.

"I'm glad no one was hurt. I guess sometimes it's nice for you not to be needed."

Joe smiled. "For sure. I would much rather a situation resolve itself than for me to need to go in."

Chloe walked her in circles around the stroller.

"But it's hard," Joe continued, "for the entire team to get wound up, game faces on, then nothing. The SWAT team will be more cranky than that one—" he pointed at Chloe "—at her most nap-ready worst."

Summer laughed. "I can imagine. Although I doubt anyone could be as bad as this little terror at her worst."

The little terror was babbling and trying to pull Summer toward the store.

"Okay, I better get back to the paperwork. Which is less than if I'd had to go in there, but still enough to make me cry." He hugged Summer again.

"Give Laura my love. We'll get together soon. Hopefully not when you're working."

"Yeah." Joe grinned a little sheepishly. "Laura might have a little news to be sharing soon."

Summer's eyes got wide. She knew instantly what news Joe meant. "Oh my gosh, are you serious?" She let go of Chloe to clap her hands. "I'm so excited!"

"It's early, so Laura doesn't want to tell anyone. And

practice your surprised face in the mirror so she doesn't kill me when she tells you."

"I promise." Summer laughed and hugged Joe again, keeping an eye on Chloe who was still circling the stroller. "I'm so excited for you guys."

Joe grinned and jogged off toward all the action.

Summer smiled. Joe and Laura would make such good parents. And after what they'd been though, she was thrilled they were starting a family.

But now it was probably time to get her little family away from this chaos. She picked Chloe up to put her back in the stroller. But both Chloe's arms reached over her shoulder and she began to yell and strain away from Summer.

"Ah-ta! Ah-ta!"

"Honey, Ashton isn't here. It's time for us to go home. Maybe we'll see him later."

"Ah-ta! Ah-ta!" Chloe was all but climbing over Summer's shoulder.

"Chloe Marie, Ashton is not here." Summer spun around, knowing reasoning with an almost-two-year-old was pointless, but willing to try. "He—"

But Chloe was right. Ashton was here. He was walking toward the law enforcement van Joe had gotten out of a few minutes before.

He was dressed in black from neck to toe, holsters of some kind on both hips and wrapped around both thighs. His vest had multiple pockets holding gun clips and other items Summer didn't recognize. Full tactical gear. He held some scary-looking rifle in his hands.

And blazing across the middle of his chest was the word *SWAT*.

He was talking to someone else dressed almost exactly

the same, but about a foot shorter than him. A woman, Summer realized, although her hair was pulled back in such a tight braid it was hard to identify her as such at first glance.

"Ah-ta! Ah-ta!"

Summer stood holding her daughter, staring at the man she thought she'd known so much about but obviously hadn't.

SWAT.

She saw the exact moment Ashton heard Chloe. A smile brightened his face as he looked over at them.

Then faded as he obviously remembered where he was and realized what just happened.

The woman next to him clapped him on the shoulder and took his rifle, then walked away. Obviously she knew who Summer was and that Ashton had been keeping his profession a secret from her. That maybe hurt even worse.

They stared at each other from the yards that separated them. Chloe kept yelling for him and trying to get down.

At least now Summer knew what Ashton had wanted to tell her that she wouldn't like.

Her handyman was SWAT.

Chapter Nine

How could she have been such an idiot?

Ten hours later, Summer paced back and forth at her house. Ashton would be there in a few minutes so they could talk.

She'd turned and left the grocery store this morning without a word. What could she say to him there, surrounded by his colleagues, surrounded by people who obviously knew who he was and who she was?

She could tell by the looks on their faces that his SWAT colleagues had all known he was in trouble. Which meant they'd obviously known he'd been lying to her for months.

Chloe had thrown an absolute fit when she'd been unable to go to her precious Ah-ta. Summer hadn't cared. She let her daughter wail as she'd stuffed her stiff legs into the holes of the stroller and buckled her in. They'd both been crying by the time they'd made it home.

Why would Ashton have lied to her for all these months?

Just to make sure she had the facts straight, that Ashton didn't work for Joe on the side or something, she'd texted Joe.

Need to clarify: does Ashton Fitzgerald work for you?

It hadn't taken Joe long to reply.

Works with me. Not for me. At Omega.

Does he do handyman jobs on the side? Is that why you sent him to fix the garbage disposal in my unit a few months ago?

It had taken Joe much longer to respond to that one. He must have gone to talk to Ashton to find out what the hell Summer was talking about.

Evidently there was a miscommunication a few months ago. I asked Ashton to find you a handyman. He knew he could fix the problem himself so he did that.

Logical. Summer had to admit it. Joe had asked Ashton to do him a favor, and Ashton had just done the work himself rather than call in a stranger. Ashton had been able to fix everything she'd needed him to over the past few months, so it wasn't like he wasn't capable.

Why didn't he just tell her from the beginning he was a colleague of Joe's? At least then she wouldn't have kept calling him back to fix every little thing. Pulling him away from his real job.

A sick feeling pooled in her stomach. She texted Joe again.

Did Ashton know about Tyler? About how he died?

A few moments later, her phone rang. But it wasn't

Joe, it was Ashton. She let it go to voice mail. She couldn't talk to him right now.

But she pretty much had her answer, didn't she? The rest she could piece together.

He had known about Tyler all along. Had come back to help her all those times because he felt sorry for the poor widow of the man Omega Sector couldn't save. They probably all did.

Her phone pinged. Joe again.

Ashton wants to talk to you.

I don't want to talk to him right now.

Give him a chance, Summer. He's pretty torn up.

After that, she'd set the phone down and cried again.

By the time Summer had pulled herself together, Chloe had been waking up from her nap. Snuggling with her daughter—as Chloe was so prone to do when she was first waking up and sitting with her sippy cup—made everything a little better.

When Summer picked her phone back up, she had six missed calls from Ashton. And a text.

We need to talk about this. I'm coming over tonight at seven.

She texted him back.

Fine.

So here it was, almost seven. She had taken Chloe over

to Joe and Laura's to spend the night. One, because she didn't want her daughter to hear all the yelling she was sure would happen when Ashton got here. Two, because damn it, Summer's heart all but melted every time she saw Ashton and Chloe together. He was so gentle around her. Cared about her so much.

Maintenance man or SWAT, Ashton still loved her daughter. And Chloe loved her Ah-ta right back.

Summer didn't want any distractions—any chinks in her armor—when it came to giving Ashton a piece of her mind. Seeing him with Chloe was both.

He rapped on her door right at seven.

He was wearing a dark blue T-shirt tucked into his jeans. She didn't know if he picked it out because it framed his chest and abs so well, but if he hadn't, he should have.

She opened the door wider to let him in and noticed his eyes darting around everywhere that could be seen from the doorway. She'd always assumed he'd done that because he'd been too nervous to look her in the eye. But now she realized he was scanning the room, looking for any potential danger.

Ingrained training. Ashton probably wasn't aware he was even doing it.

Once his eyes rested on hers, she could see his discomfiture. His hesitancy.

He reached out with a small bouquet of lilies.

"These are for you."

She hadn't been expecting that. "Oh."

"I actually bought a similar bouquet before our date on Friday got…cancelled."

She took them. They were lovely. "Friday got canceled because of work. I'm assuming that had something to do with Omega Sector, not with having to rush over to fix someone's toilet."

He had the grace to look sheepish. "Did you see anything on the news about a shoot-out at The Blooming Idiot on Main?"

Summer could feel her eyes widen. "That was you? Your truck was the one I saw burning all over the news?"

Ashton shrugged. "Yeah. Calling you without giving away everything was difficult."

"You know what could've solved that?"

"What?"

"You telling me the very first time you met me who you were and what you did for a living."

SUMMER WAS MAD.

Not that he'd really expected any differently, but Summer mad didn't really fit into his mental image of her. Her personality had always matched her name. She'd always been lighthearted, kind and smiling.

Her smile was nowhere around now.

She'd at least taken the flowers, and was now in the process of putting them in a vase.

He could tell her the story of how he'd tracked down Marcel, the owner of The Blooming Idiot, to find out what had been in Friday's original bouquet and where he could purchase them. He could tell her how Marcel had laughed when Ashton had told him he was definitely in the doghouse with her now. But he wasn't sure if she would appreciate the story or not.

Honestly, he was just glad she'd let him through the door.

When he'd heard Chloe's sweet little voice this morning calling out to him with such joy at the grocery store, he'd been thrilled. He wanted to squeeze her little legs and hear her talk to him in her gibberish like she always did. And he'd known, without even consciously thinking it, wherever Chloe was, her breathtaking mother wasn't far behind.

When Summer turned around, face devoid of all color, he'd remembered where he was. That he was in full SWAT gear. What he was doing.

He remembered every secret he'd ever kept from her.

Lillian had patted him on the shoulder and taken his rifle. "Good luck, dude. You're going to need it."

Ashton wasn't sure what he was going to say to Summer, but he knew he had to say something.

Then she'd turned and left. Without a word. Chloe's cries breaking his heart.

He'd wanted to go after them right then and there. To explain. To at least try to get Summer to listen to him.

But he couldn't. He couldn't leave an active crime scene while he was on the clock, even if it looked like the crisis had already passed.

Plus, what exactly would he say to Summer there in front of dozens of other people?

So he'd watched her walk away, worry burning like acid in his gut. He'd been terrified that her rigid back and quick pace in the other direction might be the last time he ever saw her.

When Joe had hunted him down this afternoon, asking Ashton what the hell was going on with Summer, demanding why she wanted to know whether Ashton worked *for* Joe, the situation had gotten worse. Ashton had explained the misunderstanding about him being the handyman, since he'd fixed her garbage disposal himself a few months ago.

Nobody blamed him for that.

He'd told Joe what happened, how it had basically just accidentally grown over time. Joe wanted to know the same thing Ashton was sure Summer wanted to know: why hadn't he just told her afterward that he wasn't the normal handyman? Maybe she would've laughed.

Haha. My mistake. If I can't pay you, can I take you out to dinner?

Maybe that's how it would've gone, what she would've said. And Ashton wouldn't be standing here now afraid he was about to lose the person who had been his first thought in the morning and last thought at night for the past six months.

Now she was glaring at him where he stood awkwardly in the middle of her living room, "Where's Chloe?" he finally asked.

"She's at Joe and Laura's house. I didn't want her to be around for a bunch of yelling."

He winced. They stared at each other.

She took a step closer, then stopped. "You told me you were the condo's handyman."

"No. I never said that." He shook his head. "That first afternoon, I told you Joe asked me to deal with the broken garbage disposal, that I wanted to look at it myself first and that we could call a specialist if needed."

"But you knew what I thought."

"I didn't. Especially not that first time. You offered to pay me, but that wasn't so unusual."

Her eyes narrowed. "I've called you back like eight times in the last six months. You had to have known I thought you were the maintenance man for the condo!" Her volume rose.

He winced again. "Look, I'm not saying I handled it well. I didn't. I was wrong and I'm sorry."

That didn't seem to appease her in the slightest. "I thought you were *shy*. I bought that 'I grew up on a farm in Wyoming' stuff hook, line and stupid. Was any of it even true?"

Ashton ran a hand through his hair. "Of course it's true. It's all true." Now his voice rose slightly. "I wasn't trying to lie to you, Summer. The only thing I wasn't fully up-front about was the fact that I'm Omega Sector."

But that wasn't the complete truth, now was it? Yet he couldn't bring up her husband's death now. Not until the initial shock of his sudden career change had been dealt with. Maybe not ever.

"I feel like an idiot that I didn't figure it out." She wrapped her arms around herself.

Her hurt look was much, much worse than the angry one. "Summer, no. Don't feel that way. It wasn't like that. I wasn't trying to trick you."

"Then why? Why didn't you just crack a joke when I called you the second time to come fix stuff?" She deepened her voice to imitate him. "'Hey, Summer, let me get you the number of a real maintenance guy. I'm pretty good at fixing things, but I work with Joe at Omega, so I won't always have time to help you.'"

It sounded so simple to hear her say it.

"After I missed my early chance, there just never seemed to be the right time to say it."

"You should've *made* the right time, Ashton. Even if we both were embarrassed."

He ran a hand through his hair. "I know, okay? But I thought you wouldn't have me around anymore if you knew. That you wouldn't be interested in spending time with a member of law enforcement."

She stared at him for a long minute, seeming to battle some inner emotion. He thought maybe he was off the hook, but then her arms dropped and her eyes narrowed.

"It was *you*." She pointed her finger at his chest.

For a terrified second, Ashton was afraid she meant the situation about her husband. But she couldn't know that. No one knew that.

"It was me who what?" he asked hesitantly.

"It was you who got me out of the fire, wasn't it? A few months ago, when Bailey Heath kidnapped Chloe and me, *you* were the one who carried us out."

She seemed quite upset about that.

"Yes?" It shouldn't have been a question but it came out as one, wary of her reaction.

She stormed over to him. "I dreamed it was you. And convinced myself I was absolutely crazy, because how could the handyman be the person who had gotten us out of a burning building?"

Oh damn. "Summer—"

"That couldn't possibly be right. You were shy. Timid, even." She began to pace back and forth right in front of him, her voice getting louder and louder. "Which was fine, I had no problem with that. But you just weren't the type of guy who would be a part of Omega Sector. I've met some of them. They're all alpha male, save-the-world sorts of guys who could lead a crowd to safety at any moment. But you seemed more comfortable chatting with my *toddler* than talking to me."

She turned and poked him in the chest. "I convinced myself that I was delusional. I mean, yeah, you had the muscles, so maybe physically you could've been a part of Omega. But not in personality. In mindset. I berated myself that I was so desperate for some sort of knight in shining armor that my mind was trying to make you something you weren't. I felt *horrible*."

This was so much worse than he'd thought it would be. "Summer. Don't."

"But now, come to find out, my subconscious was right the whole time. You're not shy. You *are* one of those alpha males—a take-charge kind of guy. You're the absolute epitome of Omega Sector." She stood there and glared at him. "Everything I thought I knew about you was completely wrong."

He took a step back, surprised at how hollow he felt at her words. He'd known all along Summer wasn't interested in becoming involved with someone in law enforcement. This was it. The end.

Over before it even began.

"And that's not what you want, is it?" he asked quietly. The least he could do was give her an easy way out.

She stared up at him. "Are you kidding? I get all hot inside just thinking about it."

Chapter Ten

He didn't look like he believed her.

And she was standing here feeling like her insides might incinerate any minute. Part of it was anger, sure—she was pissed at what he'd done.

But more of it was the attraction she'd felt for him for the past seven months, since he'd first walked through the door. She'd let herself get convinced that she wasn't really the type of woman he wanted—since he was so *shy*, he would want someone more demure, less outgoing.

He wasn't shy. She wasn't demure. The urge to throw him down on the couch again and have her way with him was damn near overwhelming.

And he was looking at her as if he didn't believe she was attracted to him.

"Ashton, for months I've looked for every possible thing wrong with this condo to bring you back over here. I didn't actually break anything myself, but I have to admit, I thought about it."

He smiled a little at that. "I wouldn't have minded fixing it, if you did."

"That's just it. I thought you were a shy, tongue-tied handyman who was raised on a farm. Who was nice

enough to come over whenever I called. Just being polite."

"I'm not shy. Not really tongue-tied. I just didn't want
to lie to you so I thought saying the least I could about
anything having to do with my job was better. That's
why I stuck to stories about growing up."

Thank goodness. This all would be a nonstarter for
her if he'd been lying to her the whole time. Or probably
if he was really that shy. "I see that now."

"And that's not the kind of man you want? The shy,
kind-of-bumbling guy?"

She took a step closer. "No. I was attracted to you *despite* the shyness. Not because of it."

He tilted his head to the side. "Good. I never minded
being here, you know. I wanted to. I always hoped you
would call."

She took another step forward like a magnet pulled
her. Her fingertips itched to touch him.

"And, of course, I wanted to help. Because I knew..."
He trailed off, looking down at the ground. "I knew what
happened with Tyler."

The heat building inside her completely dissipated
with his words.

She should've known, of course. Should've guessed
that he knew about Tyler. Omega Sector wasn't that big.
Ashton obviously knew Joe and so it made sense that
he'd know about Tyler's death.

She could feel something inside her shriveling. Shy or
confident, Ashton still hadn't been here all these months
because he wanted her.

"Summer, what? What just happened? Tell me."

She took a step back, studying the ground. She
couldn't say it. It was too hard. She shook her head.

But he just stepped closer. "What, Summer? Tell me." He slid a finger under her chin, the first time he'd touched her since he'd walked into the condo.

"I thought you were here because you liked me, okay? *Me.* Everybody else in my life knows about Tyler. Knows how he died. Thinks of me—to at least some degree—as the poor young widow and single mom who lost her husband tragically." She threw up her arms, volume rising again. "I thought you were the handyman who didn't know anything about me! Who was just too shy to ask me out."

"Summer—"

She stepped back farther. "But instead, just like everyone else, you were just here because you felt sorry for me. Wanted to make my life easier. I just want someone to want me for *me.* For that desire to be completely untainted by the 'poor young widow' scenario."

He threaded a hand through his hair. "It wasn't like that at all. Was never like that."

"But you knew about Tyler's death before you started your handyman duties."

He took in a deep breath. "Well, yeah. Everyone knew."

Exactly. *Everyone* knew. She turned her face away, letting out a sigh.

"And that's always going to be the case, isn't it? You're never going to be able to see me without it being through the widow filter. You're never just going to see me as Summer, the woman."

Vaguely aware she was being unreasonable, fussing at a man who'd done nothing but help her for months but seeming unable to stop, she turned toward the kitchen.

"Summer—"

She didn't turn back to look at him. Couldn't look at that gorgeous face, those brown eyes. "I get it, Ashton. I really do. You're a decent person. You don't want me to struggle. But I don't think it's *me* you really want."

She walked into the kitchen but barely made it two steps before his large hands snaked around her waist, spinning and pushing her up against the counter.

She gasped, unaware he could move so silently or quickly, although she shouldn't be surprised. She grasped his biceps to keep her balance.

"Our history will always be complicated because of my involvement with Omega, but you damn well can put away any doubts that I don't want you," he said, leaning in so their faces were just inches apart. "Because mistakes or no mistakes, secrets or not, I have always wanted you with a ferocity that eats through me."

Then he kissed her, his hand reaching to curl around her neck, the hold possessive. His tongue traced her lips before thrusting into her mouth.

Heat coursed through her instantly.

He pulled her hard against his body in a way that could leave no doubt whatsoever that he wanted her. His mouth was hot, wet, open against hers, gentleness nowhere to be found.

Good. She didn't want gentle. Didn't want to be treated as if she was fragile, breakable. Gripping his waist, she pulled him closer, her tongue dueling with his.

He kissed her like he planned to never stop, kissed her in a way she never dreamed shy, handyman Ashton was capable of.

But this Ashton—the *real* Ashton—was capable. His breath gusted hot along her jaw as he shifted slightly, grabbed her waist and hoisted her up onto the counter.

His hands moved to her hips as he slid her forward until they rested against each other, her hips cradling his.

Summer moaned as his lips moved down to her neck, sharp little nips by his teeth immediately soothed by his tongue. One of his hands moved up, fisting a handful of her hair to keep her in place.

All Summer could do was hang on. She felt her hips thrust against his of their own accord. She wanted him. Wanted this man. Right now.

"Ashton." She groaned his name out as his lips moved back up to hers. Could feel his movements becoming as frantic as she felt.

"Don't ever doubt I want you," he said against her lips. "I've wanted you every hour of every day since the moment you showed me this garbage disposal." He hooked a thumb toward the sink right next to them.

He slid his hands under her buttocks and pulled her all the way off the counter. She hooked her legs around his waist as he carried her to the bedroom and proceeded to show her exactly how much he wanted her.

SUMMER ROLLED OVER in her sleep, scooting closer against him. Ashton smiled. If the woman got any closer, she'd be sleeping on top of him.

Which would suit him just fine.

He rubbed a hand up and down her back. By whatever means he'd managed to dodge a bullet in this situation, he'd thank his lucky star and whatever other mixed metaphor. He slid his hand down to Summer's naked hip and pulled her closer.

Pity was the absolute last emotion he felt for her. It had nothing to do with why he'd come around here. And yes, he'd been willing to settle for less, to be a sort of silent guardian. He'd wanted to help out wherever he could—not just with handyman stuff, but any part of Summer's life where she'd needed help.

He still hadn't told her about Tyler's death. That he'd been there. That he'd had a shot.

He doubted very seriously she'd be lying here so trustingly with him if she knew. He brought a hand up to his face and rubbed his eyes. He never should've let things get so far without telling her the entire truth.

And he'd wanted to, had planned to ease into it. Trying just to break one piece of bad news at a time. But then she'd looked so distraught at the thought that he'd only been hanging around her because he felt sorry for her.

Proving that wasn't true had taken priority over everything else. He'd honestly just meant to kiss her. To pull her up against him and prove there was no way he didn't want her.

Because he had. He'd wanted her from the first moment he met her. Hadn't been interested in another woman since the first time they'd spoken.

He'd known of Summer for a long time, since the day her husband was killed. Joe—feeling even more guilty than Ashton had about Tyler's death—had started a friendship with her. Ashton had sort of watched that from afar.

But then when that psycho had taken Summer and Chloe, and Ashton had carried them out of that burning warehouse…something had changed for him. It was like once he'd had actual contact with Summer, he couldn't force himself to stay away any longer. So when Joe had asked him to deal with her maintenance problem, Ashton had been happy to.

He'd never spent one minute with her because he'd felt obligated. It had always been because he wanted to be with her. In whatever capacity she would allow. The team had teased him for months about the friend zone. But the friend zone hadn't bothered him. At least he'd gotten to see Summer and Chloe regularly.

He'd hoped it would turn into more over time. But even his hopes for a romantic future with her could never have lived up to this. He'd never dreamed he'd be holding her sleeping body next to his after the hours of mind-blowing lovemaking they'd just discovered together.

First in her bed, then in her shower.

Hell, he'd almost taken her right on the kitchen counter where they'd started, when he'd realized at what perfect height that had placed her. But he hadn't wanted that to be where they first made love, so he'd hustled her to the bed with very little finesse.

Summer hadn't been overly concerned about finesse either, ripping both of their clothes off as soon as he'd had her in the bedroom. She'd had a few moments of insecurity—it had been a long time for her. She'd had a baby since she'd last been in any sort of physical relationship with a man. But proving how breathtakingly beautiful she was to him had been no hardship. Showing how perfectly they fit together had been an easy task.

And he'd be damn sure to take advantage of that kitchen counter in the near future. Maybe right after breakfast in the morning. And again in a couple of days.

The future. He never thought he'd even be thinking about a future that included Summer. But what had happened between them tonight? He knew this physical relationship wasn't something either of them took lightly.

Before it went any further, he needed to make sure she understood all of the connections between them. That she knew he'd been there the day Tyler died. About the shot he didn't take. She wouldn't forgive him if he didn't tell her, not after what he'd already kept from her.

If by some miracle she could forgive him for that, then maybe they truly could have a future together.

Tomorrow, he promised himself, everything would be clean between them tomorrow.

Ashton stretched a little, raising one arm over his head. The woman in his arms murmured something in her sleep before flipping herself over so her back was pressed into him.

Her very naked back. Ashton rolled onto his side, spooning her, and pulled her closer, forcing himself not to do anything else. Certain parts of his anatomy were having more trouble with that directive than others, but they both needed sleep. The sweet smell of her hair and curves in all the right places lulled him into closing his eyes.

The silence awoke him.

Ashton's eyes opened and his body tensed, senses immediately aware that something wasn't right.

Summer still slept against him, her back to his chest, her head resting on the crook of his elbow. She'd tucked her small feet between his calves.

Had she done something to wake him? Ashton wasn't used to sleeping with his body in a constant state of contact with someone else. Maybe she'd had a dream or sudden movement and woken him.

But soon Ashton realized the silence was too crisp. Too encompassing. There was no hum of electricity whatsoever. The power had gone out again.

Then he heard it. The soft sound of someone forcing a lock open. As best he could tell the sound was coming from her garage.

Someone was in the house.

Chapter Eleven

Curtis Harper's face immediately came to Ashton's mind after last Friday's shoot-out at the florist. And the man's total disregard for collateral damage and innocent bystanders.

If it was Harper breaking in, getting Summer out of here was imperative.

Ashton wrapped his arms tightly around her, shaking her slightly.

"Summer," he whispered in her ear. "We've got trouble. Someone has cut the power again and I'm pretty sure is breaking in your garage door."

He hated to feel her go from soft and pliant to tense and fearful, but it couldn't be helped.

"We need to get out of bed and hidden from whoever is breaking in here."

She nodded.

Damn it, Ashton wished he hadn't left his sidearm at home. It had been a conscious decision—he thought bringing a gun to Summer's house when he was there to talk about his secret SWAT life might be a little insensitive.

But given the choice between insensitive and dead, he'd take insensitive.

They got out of bed, Ashton slipping on his jeans and Summer pulling his shirt over her head. It was almost completely black outside, with no moon out to provide light through the windows and all electricity off. Ashton took her hand and led her out into the hall, closing the bedroom door behind them softly, before making their way around a corner.

All the time he'd spent in her house fixing things came to his aid now. He knew where every room was, where every potted plant and baby item lay. He was careful not to make any noise.

He heard a low creak at the bottom of the stairs. If it was Harper, the man wasn't wasting any time. Ashton pulled Summer behind his body near the linen closet door.

The man made no further noise as he came up the stairs. Fortunately, he didn't look around the hallway before moving directly into Summer's bedroom.

The perp knew where the room was. That wasn't good news. Burglars would be looking around, trying to ascertain the most valuable items, not making a beeline for a certain place.

As the man passed them, Ashton caught the faintest gleam of metal in his hand outstretched in front of him. A gun.

He'd cut the power to silence Summer's alarm and was making his way toward her bedroom with a gun in his hand. This didn't look like a robbery. It felt like an assassination.

Ashton knew he had to get Summer out of the house, couldn't take a chance tackling an armed man not knowing if the guy had any backup with him. Ashton could feel Summer's hands holding onto his waist from behind him. As soon as the man had cleared the hall enough for Ashton and Summer not to be seen, he took her hands and guided them both down the stairs.

It wouldn't take the guy long to figure out whoever he was looking for—Ashton had to believe it was him and not her—wasn't in the bedroom.

Unfortunately, Ashton's car keys and cell phone both were.

As he and Summer moved past the kitchen, Ashton stopped and spun to look at her, putting his hands on her shoulders. "Where's your cell phone?" he whispered.

"Upstairs," she answered just as quietly, bringing her hands up to grasp his wrists.

Ashton knew they were running out of time and options. They couldn't run far in what little clothes they wore—a Colorado November wouldn't allow it and opening and rustling through a closet was out of the question. They had no car keys and no way to call for backup—not that backup could get here quickly enough.

The best Ashton could do was get Summer out of the house while he tried to take the man down. Thank God Chloe wasn't here.

"You have to run, through the garage the way he came in. Go wake up a neighbor. Get them to call the police."

"Come with me," she whispered.

He pushed her toward the door. There was no way he was going to let Harper, or whoever it was, get away without at least trying to stop him.

"I'll be out in just a minute. You go now." In order for Ashton to be able to fight an armed man and win, his focus couldn't be split worrying about Summer's safety.

He felt Summer's nails sink into his wrists as they

both heard three muffled shots come from up in her bedroom.

The unmistakable sound of a handgun with a silencer.

Time had just run out.

"Go, okay? You have to trust me, Summer."

He saw her nod, then scoot through the garage door that had been left propped open. He hid himself over in the corner near the door that led to the basement. The man would be much more wary now that he hadn't been able to complete his objective of killing them in their sleep.

Ashton wished he had time to make it into the kitchen to grab a weapon, knife, scissors, hell even a rolling pin, but the bottom-stair creak let him know the man was already back down on the first floor.

He'd only have one chance for a surprise attack. And the man had already proved himself willing to kill.

He waited until the guy was almost directly in front of him, looking toward the garage, then jumped quickly out of the shadows. Ashton piled into the man, knocking him into the living room, but the gun remained in his hand.

In the dark he couldn't tell if the attacker was Harper or not, so Ashton didn't waste any time trying to figure out if it was. Whoever it was, they wanted to harm him or Summer or both.

His fist found the man's face. Ashton took a hard punch to the gut and saw the man's hand swinging up with the gun. He spun and ducked, a shot from the gun barely missing him, the bullet screaming past his head finding a place in the wall behind him. Even with the silencer on the weapon, the sound echoed through the room.

The man howled as Ashton continued his spin, his

elbow smashing into the man's nose. The guy fell backward and Ashton knew he had him.

But then Summer's entire living room window shattered and Ashton felt a burn across his upper arm, jerking his body to the side.

Damn it, someone was shooting from outside the house.

And Ashton had sent Summer right out into the line of fire when he'd sent her to get help.

Ashton ignored the pain—he'd been in SWAT long enough to know when a gunshot wound wasn't serious—but knew he was in trouble. The breaking glass and shot from outside had given the other man the time he needed to recover and bring his gun back around and pointed toward Ashton.

"So long, Fitzgerald. I hope you rot in hell. Tell my father hello."

So it was Harper. Damn it.

But the shot never came. Instead Harper tumbled over as he was hit across the back and shoulders from behind.

Summer.

She'd just saved Ashton's life.

Harper dropped his gun but wasn't unconscious. He rolled over on the ground and reached out and yanked her leg, pulling her to the ground with him, his fist flying toward her face. She raised her arms to cover her head but Ashton still heard her cry of pain as the man's fist connected.

Ashton leapt for Harper, rolling him away from Summer. He had no doubt he could take Harper, but it was the other man, the man who had just proven reckless enough to shoot through a large window, obviously not caring too much if Harper got hurt in the process, who worried Ashton. Ashton just needed to get Summer out of here.

Live to fight another day.

"Get my car keys upstairs," he said to Summer. "Stay low and away from windows. Harper has a partner out there." Ashton blocked a gut punch from the man beneath him, one that would've certainly knocked all the wind from Ashton. He reached for the gun Harper had dropped, but the other man kicked it to the opposite side of the room.

Summer ran up the stairs.

Ashton threw two punches at Harper's head, followed up by a blow to the midsection, making sure Harper's attention didn't focus on Summer.

"I've got them." Ashton saw Summer's legs before he heard the words. He took a punch to the ribs, but then cracked Harper along the jaw. While Harper was momentarily stunned, Ashton jumped up and grabbed Summer's hand, running for the garage door.

A shot splintered the doorframe as they ran through. Ashton couldn't tell if it was from Harper or his partner. Ashton clicked the automatic unlock button for his rental car as they ran outside of the garage.

"Get in," he told Summer. "And stay low."

Ashton got in and started the ignition, throwing the car in reverse and dipping low in the seat as Harper ran out of the house. He pushed Summer's head down as shots shattered the glass of two of the side windows. Other bullets slammed into the metal of the car's frame.

Damn it, this was his second shot-up vehicle in a week. And the car rental insurance probably didn't cover bullet holes.

He spun the car in the street and stepped on the gas,

keeping his head so low that he could hardly see over the steering wheel. Only after they turned the corner did Ashton sit up. But even then he didn't slow his speed. Those guys had a car, too, and he wasn't sure how far they were willing to take this.

He sped them out of Summer's neighborhood and began weaving through different side streets, turning every few blocks. Only after he was sure Harper and his partner weren't following them did he slow down and pull Summer up from where she hovered in the floor-boards.

"Are you okay?"

She nodded, climbing into the seat. "A few little cuts from the glass, I think, but overall I'm okay. You?"

"That first bullet skimmed my shoulder but didn't do real damage." He wrapped an arm around her and pulled her close, leaning over to kiss her temple. "I thought I had lost you when I realized there was a second shooter out there. Thought I'd sent you right into his line of fire."

"I never even left the garage. I thought you might need help. Which you did."

He kissed her again. "Yes, I did."

"I don't know who those guys were, Ashton, or why they would want to kill me. Do you think they were robbers? What would I have that they would want to steal?"

He kept his arm around her as he drove. "Let me call Omega, get people on the scene at your house as soon as possible. They weren't after you. They were after me."

Curtis Harper trying to take his vengeance on Ashton, and Summer had just been collateral damage.

"What if Chloe had been there?" Summer began to shudder. "What if she'd been in her crib when that guy broke in?"

Ashton stopped the car at a dark gas station, pulled far to the side where the car couldn't be seen from the road. He put it in Park, then yanked Summer across the seat and into his lap.

She only had on his T-shirt and the windows had been shot out. He rubbed his hands up and down on her arms and legs, trying to instill some warmth back into her body. But it was the thought of her daughter being hurt that had her body shivering—no amount of external warmth would heat that frozen place inside. Ashton knew, because the thought of Chloe or Summer being hurt brought on the same chill in him.

"Summer, I promise we will figure all this out and I will get you and Chloe both somewhere safe, okay?"

He held her tightly to his chest as sobs broke loose from her. No one could blame her for the breakdown. Ashton just held her close, murmuring words of comfort.

"Let me get us to Omega Sector, sweetheart," he said against her forehead as her emotional storm ran its course. "Get a team out to your place and make sure you and I are safe and warm."

"I've got to get Chloe, too," she said between shuddery breaths.

He nodded, understanding the need to have her close. "Joe and Laura will bring her. They'll meet us there."

Ashton eased her back to her seat, then stepped outside to use the payphone. The sooner Omega could have a forensic team at Summer's condo, the sooner they'd have answers.

He dialed Steve Drackett's cell phone, a number he had memorized.

"Drackett."

"Steve, it's Ashton. I've got a situation at Summer

Worrall's condo. Curtis Harper just broke in and tried to kill us, and he had a partner on the outside."

All sounds of sleep erased from Steve's voice. "Are you secure? Injured?"

"We're secure. Minor injuries. I'm bringing Summer into HQ. We need a team at her house right away, armed agents before the lab people get there. I'm assuming Harper and the other guy are gone, but send someone armed just in case."

"I'll take care of it. You just get Summer somewhere safe. The baby?"

Steve and his wife, Rosalyn, were about to have their own child, so Ashton wasn't surprised his boss asked. "Chloe is with Joe and Laura. We're going to need to get a safe house set up for Summer and Chloe. I doubt my house is secure."

"You're sure it was Curtis Harper?"

"Yes. And he's way out of control if he's breaking into Summer's house to get to me."

"Alright, I'll see you at HQ in a few. I'll let them know you're coming."

Ashton hung up with Steve and turned back to the car. Summer had her legs tucked under his shirt and her arms wrapped around herself.

He wanted to hit a wall. After everything she'd been through in her short life, Summer deserved to live free of all danger.

He would do whatever it took to make Summer and Chloe safe again.

Chapter Twelve

Summer felt like she may never be warm again. Even now, two hours after being inside Omega Sector headquarters, fully clothed, with a cup of coffee in hand, she still felt chilled. She wore a black shirt and cargo pants provided by Lillian Muir, the only female member of the SWAT team and the closest person to Summer's size. Summer remembered seeing her at the grocery store yesterday.

Yesterday? Was it truly less than twenty-four hours ago?

Summer felt as though her entire life had changed in twenty-four hours. Finding out Ashton wasn't the handyman, that he worked for Omega Sector, that he knew about Tyler's death.

That Ashton had wanted her from the first time he'd come to her condo.

Making love to him last night had changed everything, also. She could still feel the soreness in muscles that, before last night, hadn't gotten much use in the last couple of years. The thought of their lovemaking was almost enough to break the chill inside her.

It had been everything she'd dreamed lovemaking

would be with Ashton. And he very, very definitely was not shy.

But then she remembered that man breaking into her house. With a gun. Intending to kill her. That was enough to bring a chill to her bones from which she felt she'd never recover.

What if Chloe had been there? What if she had cried or giggled when Summer picked her up? Would the man have shot at her, too? Summer didn't know. Couldn't bear to think about it.

She tried to focus on the fact that she was safe. Ashton had gotten them out relatively unscathed. Chloe was safe, too. She'd already personally talked to Laura on the phone. Summer had decided to just let Chloe finish the night there rather than wake her up and disrupt her routine. They'd bring her when she woke up.

A medic had gotten the few pieces of glass out of her arm, none of them big or needing further medical attention besides a bandage. Ashton's arm had also been bandaged, the wound more of a burn than anything else. Another wound to match the electrical burns on his torso.

Summer looked across the room at Ashton speaking with Omega colleagues about…stuff. She didn't know what. She'd basically tuned everything out unless someone asked her a direct question. As if he could feel her eyes on him, Ashton looked up and over at her.

He said something she couldn't hear to the two men around him and then walked out of the room in a different direction. Summer could feel herself begin to panic with him out of her sight but tamped it down. She refused to become a driveling idiot. She could handle this. Would handle this. As soon as she got warm.

A couple minutes later, Ashton showed up next to her

chair. He took the lukewarm cup of coffee she'd been barely sipping out of her hand and helped her stand, then wrapped a blanket around her.

"You look a little cold."

She shrugged. "I know I shouldn't be. But I just can't seem to get warm."

He trailed his fingers down her cheek. "Part of it is shock. I'll have somebody bring you more coffee and some food. Getting sugar into your system will help."

She pulled the blanket more tightly around her and sat back down. "This helps, too."

"We're working on a safe house for you and Chloe. Somewhere that's suitable for her, too. Just for a few days until we get this figured out."

"Do you know who was in my condo?"

"We think so. But we're waiting to see if the forensics team can provide us anything concrete." He crouched down next to her chair. "I will say this. I think those guys were after me. Not you."

"Why were they after you?"

Ashton blew out a frustrated breath. "It's someone named Curtis Harper. He's mad at me because I shot and killed his father—someone who had taken hostages in a jewelry store and already killed one person—four years ago."

"But you don't think it's Harper?"

"I do, but it just doesn't make a lot of sense that now, four years later, Harper would suddenly decide to become all vengeance-bound. Why not a week after the incident? A month? A year? But *four years* later? That seems an excessively long wait."

"It's not the anniversary of his dad's death like it was when Bailey Heath took Chloe and me hostage, is it?"

"No. It's no special date as far as we can tell."

Summer just sat looking at him for a long time.

"Thank you," she finally said.

"For what?"

She rubbed her hands together. This probably wasn't the time to say any of this, but she wanted to anyway. "I always wanted to thank the person who had gotten Chloe and me out of that fire. I never knew it was you. I should've asked Joe, but he just wanted to put the whole situation behind him." Considering his wife, Laura, had almost died, Summer hadn't blamed him. She'd just wanted to put it behind her, too.

He smiled at her, eyes soft. "That's when I knew I couldn't leave you alone. If you hadn't mistaken me as the handyman, I would've found another way to be around you."

"You should've told me the truth and done that anyway."

He winced. "I know."

"When do you think you'll hear from the forensics team? I'd like to get some stuff. My phone especially so Laura and Joe can call if there's any problem with Chloe."

"I need mine, too. So I'll have them sent over right away. Agents had to go in first to make sure the crime lab team wouldn't be ambushed."

"Ashton, can we get your input over here?" One of the two men standing at the large conference table called him over. He kissed her forehead, then jogged to them.

Summer just sat watching him for a long time. Ashton was obviously well respected and liked by his colleagues. Here it was, the middle of the night, or early morning, she wasn't sure which, and they'd all come in to help him.

She still felt a little silly that she could ever have thought him shy. The way he so easily talked and interacted with everyone here fairly screamed the opposite.

She snuggled farther into the blanket. There were so many things she needed to do but she was so tired. It was probably good that Chloe was still with Laura and Joe. Summer didn't know if she had the energy right now to keep up with a nineteen-month-old.

"You look pretty deep in thought there." The SWAT team lady sat down beside Summer. She had a plate of food in her hand.

"You're Lillian, right?"

The other woman smiled. "Yes, Lillian Muir. I'm on SWAT with Ashton."

"Thanks for the clothes." Summer gestured to herself with her hand. "Much better than roaming around in just Ashton's T-shirt."

Lillian smiled. "No problem. I'm not used to anything I wear fitting someone else."

The woman was petite, no doubt, and would be dwarfed by Ashton and some of the other men on the Omega team with her. Small-boned with dark brown hair that fell over her shoulder in a braid. Brown eyes and a darker skin tone that spoke of some sort of Latin or perhaps Asian heritage.

Lillian Muir was lovely. Although she looked like she might punch someone in the face if they gave her any such compliment.

"I brought this for you from the Omega canteen. Ashton said you needed something in your system."

"He's probably afraid I'm going to break down again on him like I did in the car. Sob fest."

Lillian handed her the plate. "Well, I think any time

someone breaks into your house in the middle of the night and tries to kill you, you're allowed a few tears. It's in the rule book."

Summer picked up a piece of bacon and began eating it. Somehow she doubted Lillian would've cried if anyone had broken into her house.

"I have to admit, I'm a little surprised Fitzy was at your house given the look of death you gave him at the grocery store yesterday."

Summer shoveled a forkful of eggs into her mouth. "Yeah, I wasn't too happy about finding out his real profession that way. I thought he was my condo's maintenance man."

"If it helps at all, he's wanted to tell you for a long time. Once we found out what was going on—you make delicious muffins by the way—we ragged him unmercifully."

Summer shook her head. "That should make me feel better, shouldn't it? But it doesn't. You all knew about what he was doing. Laughed about it. You must have thought I was an idiot. *Ashton* must have thought I was an idiot."

Lillian just smiled, her dark eyes full of compassion. "Not at all. We thought *he* was an idiot. And made no bones about letting him know that. But he would never have let anyone say even the slightest bad thing about you. Even if any of us had thought it, which we didn't, he wouldn't have let us say it."

Lillian didn't strike her as the type who would lie just to save someone's feelings, but it was still hard to believe that was the truth.

Summer shrugged. "He's a good guy. I know that.

Maintenance man or member of SWAT, he's still a good guy."

"Definitely true," Lillian agreed. "I would want Fitzy at my back in any situation. He's a hell of a shot."

"Is that his specialty?" Summer asked glancing at the other woman. "To be honest, we didn't get that far in our conversation about his work. Just that he worked at Omega."

"He's one of the best sharpshooters I've ever seen. He's got instincts and patience that make him stellar in multiple situations. Particularly hostage ones."

Summer took a bite of the food Lillian provided as she studied Ashton again from across the room. He was still talking to other people and poring over a computer. "I believe that. He's solid. Focused."

"I'm just glad you were able to get past everything. Fitzy cares a lot about you. But with the whole situation with, you know—" Lillian glanced over at her, waving her hand "—everything, he's overthought it all to death."

"I don't understand."

Lillian shrugged. "That's a problem all SWAT members have, particularly snipers. When a situation goes wrong, we overplay it in our minds. Trying to figure out what we would've done differently to get a different result. Almost like a reverse chess game."

"If you had done such and such five moves ago, maybe the end result would've been different—that sort of thing?"

"Yeah, exactly. All of us hate it when a hostage situation goes wrong. But Ashton really tore himself up about it. Even though he's been completely cleared. There was no shot to be made."

"I don't know why he would feel that way," Summer

responded. "He got Chloe and me out. I don't know what more he could have done."

"No, I'm talking about—" Lillian abruptly ended her sentence. She shook her head. "Never mind. It's late. Let's just leave it that Fitzy overthinks everything. Like you said, he tries to be too many moves ahead."

Summer felt like she was missing a critical piece of a puzzle she hadn't even realized she was putting together.

Or maybe she was just exhausted.

"You should eat." Lillian pointed to the plate. "You don't realize how fast your body burns calories when you're in shock. You'll need the nourishment."

"Somebody tried to kill us tonight." She took another bite. Lillian and Ashton were right. The food was helping. She felt less like she might crumble at any moment.

"Yeah, everyone is pretty focused on that. We take it pretty seriously when someone tries to harm one of our own."

"Ashton."

Lillian smiled. "Not just Ashton. I know we're all pretty new to you, but you're not new to us. First because of Joe and then because of Fitzy."

"They're putting Chloe and me in a safe house."

"That's the best place for you. It's not wonderful, but it's not too bad. That way, Ashton and the team can concentrate on catching this guy and not be distracted with worry about whether you and your daughter are safe."

Summer nodded. "I'm not looking forward to that."

"You'll have a guard. You'll be safe."

She'd have a guard, but it wouldn't be Ashton. She wanted him by her side for more than one reason. But she refused to be a burden.

She just wanted to get her life back under control.

Chapter Thirteen

Ashton heard little Chloe before he saw her. Gibbering away to Joe and Laura as they walked down the hall.

Summer immediately threw off the blanket she'd had wrapped around her the last couple of hours and rushed to her daughter. Ashton heard the toddler's exuberant "Mama!"

He walked out of the conference room and turned the corner so he could see them. Summer had her arms wrapped around her daughter, her face buried in her neck. Shudders wracked her body.

The look Joe and Laura shot him spoke volumes of concern. But Ashton knew what Summer was feeling— well, not totally, because no one could love a child the way a mother did—but the knowledge that Chloe was safe rocked him, too.

He walked up and put his arms around both of them, almost sick with relief when Summer didn't pull away.

"Ah-ta!"

Chloe's bright smile clenched his heart. He smiled back at her as she dove for his arms the way she always did.

"Hey there, sweetheart."

Chloe immediately started talking her gibberish to

him. He nodded as if he understood the important story she obviously told.

Summer used the time to wipe her eyes and pull herself together. She smiled over at Ashton, nodding that she was okay.

Chloe soon wiggled to get down and walk. Ashton let her grab a finger on each hand so he could walk behind her, balancing her, even though he looked a little ridiculous hunched so far over doing so. Everyone else walked with them.

"Are you guys okay?" Joe asked.

"Yes," Summer said. "Some cuts and Ashton got shot in his arm."

Ashton shrugged. "A burn more than a shot, thankfully."

"The damage to the condo was pretty bad, Joe," Summer said.

He threw an arm across her shoulder. "Don't you worry about that at all. I'll see what we have empty and you can move in immediately while the repair work is going on."

Ashton spun Chloe around so they were headed back toward her mom. "We're going to put Summer and Chloe into protective custody. We've got a good safe house picked out for them."

Joe nodded. "Okay. But I thought Harper was after you, not Summer."

"Harper obviously doesn't care about collateral damage, so we're just going to make sure Summer is completely out of harm's way."

Joe's wife, Laura, hooked her arm through Summer's. "You know both you and Chloe are welcome to stay with us. Joe snores, but we can lock him in the attic or something."

Summer smiled. "No, I don't want to even potentially bring danger or stress your way."

Laura turned to her husband and smacked him on the arm. "Damn it, Joseph Gregory Terrance Matarazzo, you told her."

Joe took a step back. "What? Me? All she said was that she didn't want to bring any possible danger to our house."

Laura narrowed her eyes at him. "Summer would've at least considered it if she didn't know about me being pregnant. Now did you tell her or not?"

Joe gave her his most charming smile and sauntered toward his wife, arms held out in mock surrender. "Okay, counselor, busted. You're super sexy when you get all smarter-than-everyone like that." He pulled her in for a kiss.

"Get a room," Ashton and Summer both said at the same time. Ashton winked at her.

"And don't think you can dazzle me with your flattery, Matarazzo," Laura said against her husband's mouth. "You're still in big trouble."

"If it helps, he told me to practice acting surprised so I wouldn't blow it for him," Summer told her friend.

"Not at all. That's even worse." Laura laughed and they began walking again.

Summer wrapped her arm around Laura's waist. "Congratulations, Mama," she said softly.

"Thanks." Laura beamed.

They made it into the conference room where Chloe took turns charming the pants off everyone and running in circles. Ashton helped as much as he was able, knowing Summer was as exhausted as him.

They both looked relieved when Steve announced an hour later that the safe house was ready, reasonably baby-proofed and had a crib set up. It had been used by a young couple in witness protection a few months ago. They'd also had a toddler.

An Omega guard would be posted in the front hallway twenty-four hours a day. Plus no one outside of Omega Sector would know where she was. Especially not Curtis Harper.

A few minutes later, when someone showed up with some of Summer and Chloe's items from their condo, they were free to leave. Summer said her goodbyes to everyone. Chloe continued her reign of charm by blowing kisses at everyone on her way out.

Roman and Lillian walked down the hall with them. They would be following in their car to help ensure no one was tailing Ashton and Summer to the safe house. Probably an unnecessary precaution, but Ashton wasn't taking any chances.

"I hope your kid runs for president one day, Summer. I'd vote for her." Roman chuckled as Chloe began running down the hallway on wobbly legs.

"She's quite a character," Summer agreed.

Roman nudged Lillian with his arm. "Lil, do you think any kid you popped out would know how to reload a Glock from birth?"

The smaller woman smirked. "I don't plan to find out. I'm not parenting material, if you know what I mean."

"You and me both, sister." Roman held out his fist and Lillian tapped it.

"But that one is pretty cute," Lillian said, pointing at Chloe.

"Yeah, she's a riot unless she needs a nap or has a dirty diaper," Summer muttered.

Ashton laughed at the horrified looks that crossed his fellow SWAT members' faces. He'd been witness to said dirty diapers and knew they were definitely something to fear.

The car ride to the safe house proved uneventful. The trip took them an hour, although it could've been made in twenty minutes. Ashton wanted to make sure nobody could possibly be following them. He knew Roman and Lillian did the same.

When he received a text from them that they hadn't spotted anyone either, Ashton finally took Summer and Chloe to the house. Chloe had long since passed out in her car seat.

Summer gently removed the baby from the restraints and walked inside with Ashton leading the way. He showed her the room with the crib and Summer laid her daughter down. They brought in the rest of the stuff from the car.

Ashton gave her the tour of the small house, glad he was familiar enough with it to do so. It really only consisted of two bedrooms up a small flight of stairs, a kitchen with an eat-in section and a small living room on the bottom floor. Its only unique features were the number of exits: the front door, a back door and both bedrooms which led out to a small balcony that also had a staircase leading outside to a wooded area.

He showed her the safety features of the doors. Except for the front, all of them could only be opened from the inside.

"Don't walk out on the balcony and let the door close behind you because you'll be locked out."

She shook her head. "I hope I'm not going to be here long enough to want to do any sunbathing."

God, Ashton hoped so, as well.

He showed her where the guard would be posted in the outer hallway and introduced her to Patrick, the one who would be on duty for the next twelve hours.

"I'll text you with the identity of the new guard. They change every twelve hours, so hopefully we'll have Curtis Harper after only a couple of shift changes."

Summer paced a little in the living room. "Okay, good. I wish…" She faded off, staring down at her feet.

Ashton grabbed her hand, pulled her a little closer. "What? Tell me."

"I wish you could stay with me."

He pulled her all the way into his arms and kissed the top of her head. "I want to. Believe me. If I didn't think I would be one of the most useful tools in catching Curtis Harper, I would stay."

A plan was already formulating in his mind about a trap, using himself as bait. If Harper wanted him so badly, Ashton would be glad to set that up for him.

With the help of his SWAT buddies, of course.

But to do that, he had to know Summer was safe. She would be, here.

"I know," she whispered. "I'm being selfish."

He wrapped his hands around both her cheeks, threading his fingers into her beautiful auburn hair and tilting her head back. "You're not selfish. Or if you are, I am, too. Because I'd much rather be here with you and Chloe." He kissed her. Gently. Briefly. He wanted more, but this wasn't the time.

"But your team needs you."

He shrugged. "I'm sure they'd do okay without me, but yes, we're most effective as a team."

"I know you have to go, and this probably isn't the best time, but can I ask you something?"

"Sure."

"It's about something Lillian mentioned when we were talking at Omega headquarters."

"Okay." He smiled. "Unless it involved something I've done at any of the multiple bachelor parties that have been held for Omega agents in the last year. Then I have no recollection of any of those events."

She smiled, but it didn't reach her eyes. Actually, Summer had been pretty quiet most of the day. He'd chalked it up to exhaustion and stress—both definitely plausible—but maybe something more was bothering her.

"Summer, what? Just ask me okay?"

"She mentioned that you sometimes overthink things."

"Sometimes, sure. I think maybe all law enforcement officers do."

"Like things in the past. Situations that had gone wrong. Playing them over and over in your head."

Ashton could feel dread pooling in his stomach.

"Yes." He nodded slowly. "When things go wrong. You want to figure out what you could've done differently. What could've resulted in a better outcome."

"She mentioned that you tended to overthink the situation that had to do with me. About how that could've gone better. She said you did that even though you'd been completely cleared."

"Summer." He stepped back from her slightly. This was not the time or place he wanted to do this, but he wasn't going to be able to get around it. He damned himself for not telling her before now.

Her eyebrows furrowed. "I thought she meant when I was kidnapped by Bailey Heath a few months ago. But then I realized that situation ended successfully. There would be no reason for you to pore over that mentally. She meant something else. She said something about a shot."

Ashton tried to prepare himself, but he still flinched at her next question.

"Were you on the scene the day Tyler was killed?"

"Yes."

She stepped all the way back so they weren't touching. "So you knew who I was not only before I first thought you were the handyman, but before you carried me out of that burning warehouse seven months ago."

"Yes. I knew of you, but I didn't know you personally."

She nodded slowly as if she were trying to process everything, to make sure she hadn't missed important details.

"What is it you're not telling me, Ashton? I thought we had gotten all the secrets out yesterday, but evidently we haven't."

There was no avoiding it now. He took a deep breath, then pushed the words out in a rush. "I was the primary sniper on the roof across from your husband's office that day."

"Okay."

"That means I was responsible for eliminating the hostage-taker if necessary. For recognizing if Joe wasn't going to be able to talk him down and taking the shot if needed."

Summer wrapped her arms around herself. "Ashton,

Joe didn't mention your name, but he already told me all this when he came to see me right after Tyler was killed. He told me the sniper had the shot but that he didn't let you take it because Joe thought he could stop the killer without lethal force."

"Yes." Ashton said. "That's true. Joe always wants to try to talk the hostage-takers down if he can."

"And you did what Joe asked. If I don't blame Joe for what happened, I'm certainly not going to blame you. The man had a hand grenade. Nobody could've expected that."

He couldn't bear how she stood there, looking at him so expectantly, like this was something about to be cleared up. Put behind them.

He took a slight step closer, then stopped himself. She didn't understand. "I had a shot, Summer. For just a brief second, after everything escalated, I had a shot. I could've saved your husband, but I didn't.

Summer stood staring at Ashton, like she couldn't figure out how to process his words.

"I don't understand."

He wanted to walk toward her, but he didn't. "Joe— and Derek, because he's actually the team leader—originally told us to hold our fire, so we did."

She nodded.

"But then things escalated pretty quickly. I could see the perp was getting more agitated. Knew in my gut the situation would turn ugly."

He reached a hand toward her but then withdrew it. She wouldn't want him to touch her now. Instead he brought his hand up and rubbed it over his gritty eyes.

"I had the shot, Summer. If I had just trusted my instincts, I could've taken it right then and Tyler and three other people would still be alive. But I didn't. And they died."

She sat down slowly on the couch, just staring at him.

"But they told you not to take the shot," she said softly. It was like she didn't want to believe him. But who could blame her for not wanting to think about the fact that the man she'd just spent the night having sex with was responsible for her husband's death?

It tended to taint things slightly.

"They told me not to shoot when things looked like they could possibly be salvaged. Once they turned ugly—when the perp reached to pull something out of his pocket—I should've taken the shot right there."

"Because of the grenade."

Ashton nodded, his heart breaking. "Yes. That's what he had in his pocket. If I had taken the shot, he would've never had the chance to pull it out, much less use it to kill himself and four other people."

She just stared at him like she didn't even see him.

Ashton didn't blame her. "But I didn't follow my instincts, and because of that, your daughter will grow up without ever knowing her father."

Summer cupped her face in her hands. Ashton had never felt so helpless in his entire life. He crossed to her, he had to. He couldn't stay away when she was hurting like this.

"Summer. I'm so sorry." He gently touched her on the shoulder, grimacing when she flinched.

She brought her hands down from her face. She wasn't crying like he'd been afraid, but he wasn't sure if that was better or worse.

"I think you should probably just go, Ashton. I just

need to be alone right now. Everything… It's all just too much."

He stuffed his hands in his pockets. "Yeah, sure. I understand. I'll call you later, okay? Make sure you two are alright."

"Yeah, okay."

She didn't get up, didn't say anything more as he walked away.

There was so much he wanted to say. To do. He'd give anything if he could erase the stunned, devastated look on her face. But he couldn't. Nothing could change the past.

He opened the door. "I'm so sorry, Summer."

"I know," he heard her say softly as he closed the door behind him and walked away.

Chapter Fourteen

Damien Freihof sat across from Curtis Harper and the ever-secretive "Guy Fawkes" in the townhouse he'd rented here in Colorado Springs. He'd invited them over for a civil meeting of sorts.

Not that you could tell from all the screaming.

"Harper, you're an idiot." Fawkes, red-faced and eyes bulging, stood only a couple feet from Harper, looking like he might pounce on the other man any moment. "First, a shoot-out in the middle of a crowded area of town, then trying to attack Ashton Fitzgerald last night while he was at someone else's house?"

Harper, looking much worse for wear after the skirmish with Fitzgerald two nights ago, pushed himself from the wall. "We agreed that Fitzgerald deserved to be killed for what he did to my father. I almost had him, too. I know I shot him in the arm."

Damien bobbed his head up and down patiently as if Harper's story was completely true. Evidently the man wasn't intelligent enough to figure out he'd had help from outside Summer Worrall's condo.

Help from Damien.

He'd been the one who shot through the window, who'd known all about Summer's house from when he'd cut the power there and peeked through her window last week. *He'd* been the one who had told Harper where the bedroom could be found.

He'd been the one who'd injured Ashton Fitzgerald.

He'd been the one waiting for Summer to come running out of the house, but she hadn't, unfortunately. It would've been the perfect time to implement the first part of his plan.

But Harper and Fawkes didn't know any of this and Damien didn't plan to tell them.

"Killing *Fitzgerald*, sure." Fawkes still looked steamed. "He's part of the law enforcement system that needs to fall. As a matter of fact, Fitzgerald ironically happened to be the one who got caught in my special little trap a couple of days ago."

Damien's eyes narrowed. This was news. "What little trap?"

"The one I mentioned to you briefly at our last meeting. Some settings I rewired in the new SWAT training facility. I wasn't trying to catch Fitzgerald specifically, just ended up that way."

"What did you do, Fawkes?"

Fawkes smiled, showing his teeth. "Well, Fitzgerald got electrically shocked to within an inch of his life. But more important, the brand-new facility got shut down. No training can be done there until they double and triple check every single piece of programming and wiring. Definitely sets Omega back."

Damien relaxed a little. He still didn't like anyone moving outside of the stage he'd created, but in this case it sounded like Fawkes' actions were helpful for the "cause."

"But that's an example of keeping our fight set on Omega agents, not civilians," Fawkes continued, glaring at Harper. "You can't take out Ashton Fitzgerald by breaking into a civilian's house. Can't put her in danger too. And what about all the people who could've been hurt with your rifle stunt on Friday?"

Damien leaned back a little farther on his couch, stretching his long legs out in front of him. Fawkes was pretty damn self-righteous for someone whose ultimate plan involved the death of hundreds, a lot of them civilians. "Harper wants revenge for his father's death," he told Fawkes. "He's willing to go after that now even if it means innocent people are hurt."

"This isn't what we discussed last week. The plan was to dismantle Omega Sector and cripple law enforcement in general. To start a revolution."

"Revolutions take time, Fawkes. We talked about that, too."

Fawkes rolled his eyes. "Harper's actions are not part of the revolution."

"You guys quit talking about me like I'm not even here," Harper finally spoke up. "I'm not a part of no revolution. I just want revenge for what happened to my dad."

Fawkes looked like he was ready to pounce on Harper again. To kill the smaller man. That wasn't good. Damien still needed Harper to fulfill a purpose.

Damien stood and walked over to the two men. "Curtis, let Mr. Fawkes and me talk privately for a while. You get some rest. Our plan to eliminate Ashton Fitzgerald is still in play, don't you worry. I'm going to help you. I have a plan."

The plan also involved both Summer Worrall and Harper's deaths, but that was probably better left unmentioned.

Damien put his arm around Harper's shoulder and

walked him to another bedroom. He showed him "the wall"—an impressive collection of maps, pictures, newspaper clippings. Like something straight out of a super-spy movie.

Some of it was junk, but not all of it. Damien had no doubt when the brilliant profiling minds at Omega finally saw the wall, they'd be able to put together the clues. To follow the breadcrumbs Damien was leaving them about his next intended victims. And there were many.

Whether they'd figure it out in time wasn't really Damien's problem. If they did, he'd just move on to someone else.

Of course, Agent Fitzgerald wouldn't be helping them figure out the next victims. He'd be too busy mourning the current ones or hopefully be dead himself.

How well Damien remembered those early days of losing Natalie. When the grief was so fresh he couldn't breathe because of it, much less do anything functional.

Omega Sector would know that grief. The unbearable grief. And then Fawkes would take over with his revolution and tear the entire place down.

Harper walked over in awe of the wall, as Damien knew he would be.

"Wow, this looks like something from out of one of those CSI shows or something."

Damien smiled. "A good plan is the backbone of any successful mission. And we have one." Damien gestured at the wall. "You just need to trust me. You know you can trust me, right, Curtis? We want the same thing."

Harper nodded, obviously as clueless as he'd ever been. "Yeah, Damien. I know I can trust you."

Damien talked to Harper for a few more minutes,

promising him his revenge against Ashton Fitzgerald soon, before walking Harper to the door.

"I'll be in touch, don't worry."

Harper smiled. "As long as Fitzgerald's dead at the end of this, I'll give you the time you need."

You had to admire a simple-minded man's single focus. He slapped Harper on the back. "Absolutely."

He closed the door behind him as Harper left.

"Harper is an idiot, you know." Fawkes had relaxed a little with Harper's exit, although Damien doubted the man ever relaxed completely. Some people didn't.

"Harper is weakening a piece of Omega's Critical Response Division, no matter how small. That's all that matters."

"They know it's him. They already found forensic evidence of him on the roof. I'm sure they'll find more at Summer Worrall's place. They'll be hunting him."

Damien rubbed his palms together. "That's fine. Because Curtis Harper is expendable in our greater plan. Don't forget that."

Fawkes sighed. "Harper isn't smart enough to stay out of Omega Sector's clutches for long. They've been studying his patterns and known associates all day. They'll catch him soon."

"Hopefully not before he's served his ultimate purpose, but if so, we can adapt."

"Aren't you afraid Harper will implicate you? I know he only knows your first name, but I'm surprised you brought him here at all."

Damien smiled and walked into the kitchen. "Curtis leading Omega agents here is part of my ultimate plan."

"But they'll know who you are. They'll be hunting you."

"They're already hunting me. This will just make

them a little more diligent about it. So I hope Curtis Harper's limited information about me will lead them straight here and eventually directly to me. I want Omega's eyes wide open about who they're fighting. I want them to know from where their destruction comes."

"If they 'know from where their destruction comes—'" mockery tinged Fawkes' voice "—they're going to be much more likely to try to defend themselves. Don't underestimate them."

"I don't underestimate them." Damien lifted a shoulder in a half shrug. "I just don't underestimate myself, either."

Fawkes sighed. "Why is Summer Worrall even being brought into this? Our fight is not with her."

Natalie's face came to his mind. Her face right before Omega Sector had burst into their home, killing her. She hadn't even looked surprised.

Oh yes, his fight very much was with Summer Worrall. She was a loved one of Omega Sector. Just like Natalie had been a loved one of his.

Therefore she had to die.

He looked at Fawkes. "Our fight is with anyone who has aligned themselves with members of Omega Sector. If we keep their focus outward, they'll miss what's really happening until it's too late to do anything about it."

Fawkes didn't know it, but Damien had already put into motion the next strike against Omega. A more indirect hit this time, against two people in Texas who had helped them with a case last year. The super-spy wall would help point them in the right direction so they didn't miss it.

Split their focus yet again.

Damien nodded at Fawkes. "But I understand your fight is not with civilians. You've made that very clear. I'll make sure Harper focuses on Fitzgerald, not Summer."

Damien's focus would be on her, though.

Fawkes just rolled his eyes. "I don't think that Harper is competent enough to kill Fitzgerald anyway."

"Don't worry. I will help him with that. Like I told him, I have a plan. He probably won't like the end result, but it's still a plan."

"I don't want him going after Summer Worrall. They've moved her into a safe house, but Harper is idiot enough to try to find her if he thinks it's a good idea."

"Where is the safe house? I'll make sure Harper doesn't go anywhere near it."

Fawkes gave him the address. "It was hard for me to get that info, so make sure Harper doesn't go there and screw it up."

The safe house was in an area just on the outskirts of town. Damien smiled at Fawkes. "Don't worry, I'll make sure Harper goes nowhere near Ms. Worrall's location."

Damien, on the other hand, had no such compunctions.

"So we've confirmed that Curtis Harper is working with someone else," profiler Jon Hatton told the team as they sat around the conference table.

It had been a long damn day. Ashton had wished for the obstacle course or an escaped criminal they had to chase down or even some cat caught in a tree that required a SWAT rescue. Anything that would get him out of this room and provide him a physical release for the frustration coursing through his system.

Summer's face when he'd told her about his part in Tyler's death yesterday. Eyes open or closed, it seemed to be the only thing he could clearly see.

They'd talked a couple of times on the phone so he

could be certain she and Chloe were okay. He'd even dropped by there this morning to drop off one of Chloe's favorite toys. A fire truck.

Summer had been polite but distant. Ashton hadn't pressed. Like she'd said, there was too much going on right now to concentrate on what had happened in the past. He could see the weight of all the stress wearing on her. Her normally light and happy features were pinched and pale.

And the fault lay squarely at his feet.

"A security camera caught this footage of Harper and an unknown second man just after the florist shoot-out last Friday," Jon continued. He put a picture up on the screen. "We haven't gotten a hit on the second man in any of our facial recognition databases."

"We also checked the picture against all family members of anyone that the SWAT team, particularly Ashton, had any sort of official contact with in the past few years," Brandon Han said. "In case they'd started a club or something."

"Anything?" Ashton asked.

"No. You don't recognize him, do you?"

Ashton studied the second man. There didn't seem to be anything striking about him whatsoever. His hair was brown, generic. Skin pale. His cheekbones were just short of puffy. His clothes were ill-fitting. He could've been anywhere from thirty to fifty years old and probably got passed by on the street all the time without anyone noticing him at all.

"No. Hell, I'm looking at him right now and am not sure I could describe him to anyone else."

Brandon and Jon looked at each other, nodding. "We think that's what he wants. That he's wearing a pretty effective disguise."

Ashton studied the picture again. Granted, he wasn't an investigating agent like Brandon or Jon, but he was still pretty observant. "I don't disagree with you. But it's a pretty damn good disguise if it is one."

Both men nodded.

"Do we think this is the same second guy who was at Summer Worrall's house when Fitzy got shot?" Roman asked.

"We definitely know, like Ashton reported, that there was a second gunman at the scene. Interestingly, he did not use a rifle to shoot through the window. The casing forensics found was from a .357 mag revolver."

Ashton wasn't surprised by that news. "Good thing for me. If he'd been using a rifle and had any accuracy at all, I'd probably be dead."

"It was pretty risky of him to shoot through the window since his partner was inside wrestling with you. He could've just as easily hit Harper," Lillian pointed out.

"If they both only had handguns, it would've made more sense for them to go inside the house together." Ashton leaned back in his chair. "Or at least for the guy to have rushed in once he realized Harper had trouble."

But thank goodness the second guy hadn't, because if he had, both Ashton and Summer would probably be dead right now.

"We think this unknown guy is calling the shots. A puppet master of sorts," Jon continued. "That maybe he's the one who got Curtis Harper riled up enough to try to kill Ashton."

"I wondered about that," Ashton said. "Why would Harper suddenly decide to come after me four years after his father's death? It didn't make any sense to me. But someone egging him on? That makes more sense."

Steve Drackett, head of the Critical Response Division, walked in. "We're going to continue to search for the identity of this man. In the meantime, there's still an APB out for Curtis Harper. All locals are looking for him. We're also starting to use nonofficial channels."

Omega Sector had resources—both computerized and human—that most law enforcement agencies didn't have. When Curtis Harper had started shooting at Ashton in the middle of a crowded city street, he'd become someone Omega would use all their resources to find and apprehend.

"By all reports, Harper isn't a criminal mastermind. Or mastermind of any sort," Brandon said. He tapped the screen at the picture of the unknown man. "This man is key. I know it. He's manipulating Harper. Using him to do his dirty work but staying clean himself."

"If it's true, that's a pretty elaborate scheme," Lillian said. "Most people don't sit around creating henchmen to eliminate law enforcement personnel."

Brandon smiled, unoffended. "You're right, of course. Creating henchmen, as you put it, takes time. Of course, Curtis Harper was already a henchman. He just needed someone to bring it out." The profiler studied the picture more carefully. "There's something familiar about this guy. I don't know what it is. But it's something."

Brandon was the most brilliant agent any of them knew. If he said this unknown guy was important, everyone would listen.

"We also have an update on the training facility accident," Steve said. "Except I can't call it an accident. Turns out it was definitely sabotage."

Ashton cursed under his breath. "Is it possible that Harper was able to manipulate the training facility in some way? Trying to take me out?"

Steve shook his head. "No. Definitely not. This was an inside job. The problem is, we don't know inside where."

Ashton sat up straighter. "So maybe not inside Omega Sector."

Steve shook his head. "I sure as hell hope not. There were a number of different individuals, even whole firms in some cases, who were involved in the creation of the simulation vests. Not to mention the programmers and the electricians. Any one of them could've been bought off to sabotage it."

"Great," Roman murmured. "Fitzy's got enemies crawling out of the woodwork."

"Actually, it doesn't look like Ashton was the intended target. He just happened to choose the sensor suit that had been tampered with."

Ashton rubbed his temples against the headache brewing there. "Well, that seems par for the course with my luck this week." The worst of it having little to do with people trying to kill him and everything to do with one petite woman who had every reason to hate him.

"Sorry about that, Ashton." Steve's glance was sympathetic. "The training facility will remain shut down until we figure out what's going on, which may be weeks. Like Dr. Parker said, if it had been someone else who'd put on those sensors—someone with not as much body mass as you—we'd be at a funeral now. We can't take any chances."

The thought sobered everyone even further.

"Alright, people, it's late." Steve closed the file in front of him. "Time to head on home—get some rest. I'll keep everyone posted if we hear anything about Harper or our mystery man."

The team got up and began dispersing. Steve was right. The best thing they could do now was be ready when they needed to move. That meant allowing themselves some downtime while they could get it.

"You heading to the safe house?" Roman asked as they walked toward the locker room.

"No, I don't think I'm welcome there."

"Really? I thought you and Summer were a thing now. Looked that way when she was here yesterday morning."

"Yeah, that was before she found out that I had the shot that could've saved her husband two years ago."

Roman whistled through his teeth. "She blames you?"

"Wouldn't anybody?"

"Fitzy, I'm no sniper expert like you, and I wasn't up there that day. But we all know you would've taken the shot if you could've."

Ashton was tired of everyone being so quick to forgive him. Everyone except Summer, who was the only one who mattered.

But he just shrugged. "Thanks, man."

"I'm sure all of this has been pretty hard on Summer. For a civilian, that woman has seen way more than her fair share of violence. Let things blow over with Harper. She'll come around."

Ashton wished he could be so sure.

He turned back as Jon Hatton called his name from down the hallway. "Hey, Harper has been spotted in a bar across town. We're going to apprehend him, think he's less likely to run if we go in rather than uniformed locals."

Ashton ran down the hall. "I'm coming with you."

"We don't need SWAT for this one. We can handle him," Jon said. "I just wanted to let you know."

But Ashton was already jogging back toward him. "I know you can. I'm still coming."

Chapter Fifteen

Summer felt numb. Had felt that way since Ashton left yesterday.

She hadn't handled that situation well at all. She probably should've had him stay, gotten more details, heard his side of the story. Instead she'd asked him to go.

His face told her that was nothing less than he expected. Nothing less than what he thought he deserved.

She'd cried herself to sleep last night. It just all seemed overwhelming and impossible.

But now a day later, not quite so exhausted, she was seeing a little more clearly.

Learning that Ashton had been there the day Tyler died had caught her off guard. He blamed himself for Tyler's death.

But Summer knew she didn't blame Ashton. The same way she hadn't blamed Joe when he'd wanted to take responsibility. Both Ashton and Joe had done their jobs. Sure, able to replay it over and over in their minds, they wished they'd done things differently. But like Lillian had said, playing God was tricky for mere humans.

Summer should've told Ashton that. She couldn't bear to think he'd spent the last day and a half thinking she blamed him. When he'd brought Chloe's fire truck by, the air between them had been taut with awkwardness.

He'd barely looked at her. Their chats on the phone to make sure she was okay hadn't been much better.

She knew he was needed at Omega Sector, but had hoped he would come by after work. But why would he? Why would he come back somewhere he obviously wasn't welcome? She'd made him feel that way.

Now it was nearly 9:00 p.m. She'd heard from Ashton last at 6:30 p.m. when the guard switch had taken place. Patrick from yesterday was back.

She couldn't let this go on any longer. She picked up her phone and texted Ashton.

Come over. Let's talk. I don't want things to be like this between us.

It didn't take long for him to respond.

I'd like that. We're on our way to arrest Curtis Harper. I'll be over as soon as I can, but it might be a few hours. You'll probably be asleep.

A pressure inside Summer eased. She and Ashton would work this out. He still wanted to see her. Hadn't given up on them. Neither had she.

She smiled as her fingers flew over the phone. Things really would be okay.

That's still fine. Especially if you can think of an interesting way of waking me up.

When he didn't respond right away, Summer began to get worried.

Oh, I can think of quite a few. See you soon. I'll have Patrick let me in.

Summer smiled, feeling better all the way around. If Ashton was on his way to arrest Curtis Harper, then hopefully she and Chloe could go home soon. And with all the danger gone and no more secrets between them, maybe she and Ashton could just start completely over. Allow what was between them to grow into what it was supposed to be: something permanent.

She wanted that with a ferocity that surprised her.

She decided to take a shower and get some sleep until Ashton got there. She hadn't had a decent night's sleep in days, and it looked like tonight might be another semi-sleepless one.

Although for a much better reason than last night.

After getting out of the shower, she checked on Chloe, careful not to wake her, and closed her door. Summer lay down in bed, wishing she had some sort of sexy lingerie or nightgown or something to wear. All she had was the oversize T-shirt she always slept in and a pair of Snoopy pajama pants.

Nothing screamed, "Take me, you hot stud" like Snoopy pajama pants.

Oh well, he'd just have to peel her out of them.

She placed her cell phone and the baby monitor on the nightstand and rolled onto her side, pulling the other pillow close to her.

She fell asleep thinking of the ways Ashton might wake her up.

ASHTON WAS STILL smiling about Summer's text when he, Jon Hatton and Liam Goetz entered a bar named Crystal Mac's on the north side of Colorado Springs.

"Why would someone name a bar as a spin-off of a drug known to induce paranoia?" Liam asked as they entered. "Not to mention be illegal as hell?"

"Moreover, who would want to frequent it?" Jon responded.

Evidently someone as stupid as Curtis Harper.

They were all in jeans and casual shirts, not wanting to draw attention to themselves as federal agents. Harper was certain to run if he knew law enforcement was coming through the door.

An anonymous tip-off had led them here, but Ashton didn't care how they got Harper as long as they did.

He wanted this behind him. And thank God, it sounded like Summer did, too.

They opened the door and were immediately assaulted by loud rap music. All three men glanced at each other, rolling their eyes.

"I'll take the bar," Ashton told Jon and Liam.

Liam jerked his thumb towards the back area. "I'll take the pool tables."

"I'll find any side doors and be watching."

They swept the place thoroughly, but twenty minutes later it became obvious that Curtis Harper wasn't there.

Ashton felt the frustration boil through him. Damn it, he wanted this over with.

"He's not here, man," Liam said. "Let's talk to the bartender."

Less worried now about people knowing they were law enforcement, Liam and Ashton showed the bartender their IDs and a picture of Harper.

"You seen this guy around?"

Bartender nodded. "Yeah. An hour or two ago, maybe. He took off with some woman."

Ashton grimaced. "Does he come in here a lot?"

Bartender shrugged. "Not enough that I remember him. I only remember him today because his face was all beat up."

Liam pulled out a card. "If he shows back up, give us a call. We won't forget it."

The bartender studied them. "Yeah, okay. Sure."

They walked out the door. "Think he'll call if Harper does show up?" Ashton asked. Liam had DEA experience before coming to work at Omega Sector and had used informants all the time.

"Maybe. People like to think of law enforcement as owing them one."

The men walked out to the car and began the twenty-minute drive back to HQ. The only thing good about not having Harper in custody was that it would allow Ashton to get to Summer sooner.

The only thing he needed to decide about now was how to wake her up.

He showered quickly in the Omega locker room, then jogged out to his car. Patrick was on guard duty, so Ashton texted him to let him know he was on his way.

Five minutes later when Patrick hadn't responded, Ashton called the man's cell phone, frowning. Whenever Patrick had been on shift and Ashton had requested an update, the agent had been quick to respond.

But now the call went immediately to voice mail.

Ashton put his phone in hands-free mode and called Steve Drackett's office. Cynthia, one of Steve's four executive assistants, answered.

"Cynthia, it's Ashton Fitzgerald. I just tried to reach the guard assigned at Summer Worrall's safe house and it went straight to voice mail."

Cynthia didn't waste any time. "Hold while I check the system, Ashton."

Guards checked in every hour with a code only they knew.

Cynthia came back on the line. "Patrick missed his assigned check in four minutes ago. One more minute and it would've alerted everyone in the system." Guards were given a five minute grace period.

"I'm on my way there now. ETA twenty minutes."

"I'll get uniforms out there, also. But it will take them ten minutes at least."

If Harper had found out the location of the safe house and left the bar an hour or two ago like the bartender said, he definitely could've already made it to the safe house and taken Patrick out.

Ten minutes was way too long. Ashton pushed the gas pedal down further. He disconnected with Cynthia, knowing the woman would do what needed to be done on Omega's end, and called Summer's phone.

SUMMER HEARD THE door creak open downstairs and smiled. She should pretend to be asleep just so she could see how Ashton decided to wake her up.

Her phone buzzed on the nightstand and she grabbed it.

Ashton?

"Why are you calling me if you're coming into the house right now? When I said to pick an interesting—"

"Summer." He completely cut her off. "It's not me in the house and we can't get in touch with the guard. Take Chloe and get out now. Right now. Use the balcony."

Summer sat straight up. Oh God. Someone was in the house and it wasn't Ashton or one of the guards.

She flew out of bed without wasting time. She had no idea how long before the intruder would make his way upstairs. She pulled her door behind her as she exited, hoping it would buy her time, and eased Chloe's door open. She saw her tennis shoes where she'd left them in the bathroom before her shower and grabbed them, toeing them on.

The silence was terrifying. All encompassing. Summer struggled to control the sound of her breathing. To her, it sounded like a freight train.

Did the intruder have a gun? Of course he did. Otherwise how would he have gotten by Patrick outside? Summer couldn't even think what that meant.

"I'm in Chloe's room," she whispered into the phone as she closed the bedroom door behind her.

"Do you have shoes? A jacket? You're going to have to run."

"Shoes, yes. No jacket."

"Okay. Hurry."

She picked up Chloe, praying her daughter wouldn't wake and cry. She grabbed the blanket and drew it around her and the baby.

Chloe remained asleep. Summer went to the door leading to the balcony and opened it.

"I'm outside now. Chloe's still asleep."

"Help is going to be there in about eight minutes. You've just got to keep away from him until then."

Chloe hurried down the stairs and across the open area into the trees. "I'm running toward the woods."

She screamed and almost dropped the phone as a tree to her left splintered into pieces and a boom filled the air. She dove for cover behind other trees.

"Summer!" Ashton's voice roared into the phone.

"I'm okay. He shot at me but missed. I'm in the trees now." She could feel Chloe start to stiffen. "I've got to keep moving or Chloe's going to cry."

"Stick your hand out from behind the tree quickly, then bring it back in."

She didn't understand but she trusted Ashton. "I did it. Nothing happened."

"Run deeper into the woods. He didn't shoot at your hand so he's probably working his way down the stairs."

Summer began moving again and felt Chloe relax. She kept her daughter tight against her chest and forced herself to run as fast as she could. After just a few minutes, all she could hear was the sound of her own breath as it sawed in and out of her chest.

Chloe's sleeping weight became almost unbearable.

She stopped to rest for a moment. "Ashton, I don't know where he is or how long I can keep running." She said the words around her breaths.

"I'm at the house now. Keep this line open. I'm tracking your phone. Don't try to talk. Just keep moving, okay?"

"Yes." She tucked the phone inside the blanket with Chloe and began moving again. Another shot rang out. Not as close as the first one, but close enough for Summer to realize the man was almost on her.

She picked up speed again, trying to use the cover of the larger trees, struggling to keep her footing in the darkness, arms burning in agony. She felt like she had run forever and knew she had to stop and rest for a minute. If she fell and broke an ankle she and Chloe would both be dead.

"Have to stop— For a minute," she said as close as

she could to the phone that was tucked in with Chloe. She hoped Ashton could hear her.

She found a large tree she could sit behind and sank to the ground, rocking Chloe back and forth in hopes of keeping her asleep. She felt something crawl across the upper part of her foot but didn't let it faze her. Her fear of bugs and snakes definitely took a back seat to her fear of a maniac chasing her with a gun.

How much time did Ashton need? Was he already in the forest with them? Would her phone pinpoint her location or just give him a general idea?

Should she start running again?

The questions spun through her mind so quickly it made it hard to think. What was her best course of action?

And then the man stepped out from behind the tree in front of her, gun pointed right at them.

"I'm sorry," he said, shrugging. "This is nothing personal."

"Wait. I don't know who you are." She had to try to buy some time.

The man actually looked sympathetic. "I know. And like I said, I'm sorry it had to be you. I just have to take from them what they took from me. They have to understand the agony of grief."

Before Summer could say a word, even beg for her daughter's life if not her own, a shot rang out in the darkness.

Chapter Sixteen

Ashton plowed his car through the small ravine next to the safe house and drove as far as he could into the woods before the axel got caught on something. That was the third car he'd totaled this week, but he couldn't care less.

He dove out the door and immediately began running in the direction of Summer's location, Omega feeding the info directly into the map on his phone.

He could hear Summer's ragged breathing through their open phone channel as she struggled to move forward with the heavy load of a sleeping Chloe in her arms. She was keeping it together, that was all he could ask of her.

Ashton pushed himself faster, Glock already out and in his hand. They were only about a thousand yards, not quite half a mile, ahead of him.

If Harper caught her, a thousand yards might as well be a million.

Ashton wished he had his rifle and scope with him, but the Glock would have to do. He was pretty darn accurate with it, too. He knew exactly how accurate he was with his Glock 23 with 180 grain Blazer Brass .40 caliber ammo, which was what he was carrying.

Two hundred thirty yards was his best record.

He heard Summer's breath get more ragged and knew she'd have to stop soon. He wasn't surprised to hear her muffled words.

"Stop… Minute…"

He didn't take the time to reassure her, just kept running as fast as he could, no regard whatsoever for his own safety. He knew he was closing the gap.

But where was Harper?

Six hundred yards. At this pace, he would be at her in less than two minutes.

Hang in there, baby, he willed. So many things could go wrong. If Chloe woke up and started crying. If Harper just stumbled on them.

He was three hundred yards out when he heard the man's voice.

"I'm sorry. This is nothing personal."

Summer. "Wait. I don't know who you are."

Ashton's stomach dropped out. Harper had caught them. Ashton could barely make the man out in the darkness two hundred and fifty yards in front of him.

He stopped running. Running wouldn't do him any good now. He took a deep breath to steady himself and brought the Glock up in a shooting position.

This was the longest shot he'd ever taken with a Glock. And the most important.

His finger rested lightly on the trigger.

The man's voice came over the phone he'd slipped in his pocket. "I just have to take from them what they took from me. They have to understand the agony of grief."

Ashton blew out his breath in a long narrow stream. His finger gently squeezed the trigger, his arms absorbing the shock of the gun's recoil.

The sound of the gun firing echoed through the night.

He heard Harper call out and knew he'd at least wounded him in some way. Ashton didn't wait, he immediately began running toward Summer again. A few seconds later, he fired again while running. His aim wouldn't be as accurate, but hopefully it would keep Harper away from the girls. His girls.

He heard Summer's voice on the phone. "He's gone, Ashton. You hit him. He's gone."

He didn't take it out of his pocket. A few moments later, he made it to them. He wrapped Summer and Chloe to him with one arm, but didn't drop his Glock with the other. Harper was still out there, perhaps only minorly injured and biding his time. Ashton needed to get them out of here.

"Let me take her," he said to Summer, noticing her arms were shaking from holding Chloe for so long. He hefted the baby's slight weight up onto his chest, keeping the blanket over her head, and began walking.

When he found a secluded overhang where they were protected on three sides, he sat down and brought Summer down with him. They would stay here until the rest of the Omega team arrived. Ashton wasn't taking any chances that Harper might double back. At least here no one could sneak up on them from behind.

"Are you okay?" he asked Summer. She hadn't said a word since he'd arrived.

"Yes." She closed her eyes. "When I heard that gunfire, I thought for sure he was shooting Chloe and me."

Ashton's teeth ground together. "I'm so sorry."

"But it was you." She moved closer to him.

He wanted nothing more than to put his arm around her, but he had to keep his gun hand free. He leaned over and kissed the top of her head. They sat in silence for long minutes, both reveling in being alive and unharmed.

Eventually Chloe began to squirm and stretch under the blanket, unused to being held for so long. Summer reached over and pulled the blanket off her daughter's head.

"Mama." Chloe's sweet voice was beautiful to both of them. She turned to Ashton. "Ah-ta." She smiled at him like there was nothing unusual about them sitting outside in the forest in the middle of the night. Ashton squeezed her nose and she giggled.

She reached out a hand and grabbed a lock of Summer's hair and began playing with it.

"How far out were you when you took the shot?" Summer asked.

"Too far out to get a kill, evidently."

"But he's the only person who could've made that distance. Two hundred and sixty yards," a female voice said, coming in closer to them. Lillian. "I don't think even *I* could make that with a Glock 23."

"Is everything clear?" Ashton asked.

She reached down a hand to help Summer stand. "We're still combing the woods for Harper, but nothing."

"Any sign of the second man?"

"None."

"What about Patrick?" Summer asked. "Whoever broke in had to get past him to enter the house."

Lillian shook her head. "He didn't make it, you guys. I'm sorry. Harper, or the unknown man must have taken him out."

Ashton saw Summer wipe tears from her eyes.

"I'm taking Summer back to HQ," he told Lillian. "She'll stay there. We've obviously got some security problems we need to talk about with Steve. Nobody, especially Harper, should've been able to find out where Summer was located."

Lillian nodded and winked at Chloe in his arms. "Yep, no argument here. I'm going to escort you out."

Ashton agreed. He wanted Lillian's eyes with them, looking out for any further trouble. He knew one hundred percent for certain he could trust her. But an Omega guard down and Summer and Chloe almost getting shot meant there was a traitor inside Omega who clearly couldn't be trusted.

ASHTON BROUGHT THEM to some sort of studio apartment inside Omega Sector's headquarters. It had a bed in one corner and a couch and coffee table in the center. A small kitchenette with an island for dining made up the other section. Obviously the apartment wasn't meant for long-term living, but it was certainly adequate for a few nights for her and Chloe.

And Ashton would be staying with them. He hadn't left Summer's side for even a moment since he'd found them in the forest. He'd sent Lillian into the safe house to get what she and Chloe needed for the next couple of days—including Chloe's fire truck.

He was currently cutting up a banana for her to eat in the baby seat they'd attached to a chair at the island. Chloe didn't seem to care that it was three o'clock in the morning. She had her Ah-ta and food. Life was good.

"The more I think about it, the more I feel like we should get you out of here," Ashton said as he cut.

"Because you think Omega has some sort of mole or something?"

"I don't know that it's an actual person. Maybe it's a

computer security problem. Someone hacking in from the outside. Either way, I don't want you and Chloe's safety to be compromised again."

"Is Harper a computer whiz? Is that how he found us?"

Ashton cut another piece of banana. "Curtis Harper isn't a whiz at anything as far as we know. And moreover, why would he come to the safe house when he knew I wasn't there? He wants revenge on me. It shouldn't have anything to do with you."

"He certainly looked serious when I saw him. Said you guys needed to learn the agony of grief the way he had. He must have really loved his father."

"Yeah, we got a recording of everything he said while I was tracking your phone. The profilers will analyze the words, see if they can come up with anything. But I have to admit from what I heard, it didn't sound like something Harper would come up with on his own."

"Do you have a picture of Harper? I didn't actually see him when I cracked my lamp over his head a few nights ago."

He nodded and got out his phone, finding the picture and handing it to her.

"This is Harper? Like, a recent picture?"

"Yes, from last Friday. We caught him on a security camera."

Summer stared at the picture. "That's not the man who almost shot me today."

She watched as Ashton wiped Chloe's banana-smeared face with a wet washcloth, not even thinking twice about it. He tweaked her nose and she laughed.

"Are you absolutely sure?"

Summer nodded. "Yes. There is no way this is the same man I saw in the woods."

Ashton flicked his screen to another picture. "What about this one?"

That picture was much more similar. "Yes. He didn't look exactly like that, but we'd both been running through the woods for a while. But I would say that is the man I saw."

Ashton picked Chloe up out of the chair. "I need to call this in. We know Harper is working with this guy, but we don't know who he is."

"Me, neither. He doesn't look familiar to me at all."

Summer took Chloe from Ashton and changed her diaper and clothes while he made his call. Ashton paced back and forth as he spoke, upset as everyone probably was at the whole situation. Upset that anybody had found the safe house. Upset over the loss of an agent. It didn't matter if it was Harper or this mystery man.

The night was catching up to both Summer and Chloe. Now that her belly was full and all the excitement seemed to have passed, the baby's eyes were beginning to droop.

Summer went and laid her on the bed so she could stretch out, then sat down on the couch. When Ashton was done, he joined her.

"Steve Drackett, my boss, agrees that we should probably get you out of here. I don't like it, but until we figure out exactly what's going on, I think it's probably true."

"I could go to my sister's house in Atlanta."

"Yes, that would be good. Lots of flights. There's an FBI field office and we can make sure they're aware of the situation. I will personally call their office and talk to someone who can be trusted."

"Okay. When should I leave?"

"Early tomorrow would be best."

"Oh." Summer was torn. She wanted to be safe, to

get her daughter to a safe place. But she didn't want to leave Ashton.

"Believe me, I don't want you to go." He slipped an arm around her shoulder, pulling her closer. "But I do want you to be secure, so I'll let you go. I don't like it."

"There's something I need to say to you, Ashton." She sat back a little bit so she could see him better.

"Okay. It's about Tyler, isn't it?"

She nodded. "I didn't handle our last talk about him, about that situation, very well."

"It was some shocking news, Summer. You handled it the way anyone would."

"I want to tell you what I told Joe Matarazzo when he tried to take the blame for Tyler's death. I don't care if you had the shot or not: you're not the killer. The man who walked into that office building with the intent to hurt others and pulled out that hand grenade. He's the only one to blame."

His name had been James Hudson. But Summer tried to say his name out loud as little as possible. She didn't want to give him that much credit or space in her life. He'd taken enough.

"But I could've stopped the killer," Ashton said softly.

Summer stood up and took a few steps away. "Says you and your crystal ball. Somebody hitting him with their car in the parking lot that day could've stopped him, too. Or maybe if he'd learned stress-management techniques in high school."

"But I had a rifle trained on him."

She shook her head. "If there's one thing I know about Omega Sector, it's that you guys are the best. You made the call you made. A split second changes everything in SWAT stations, I'm sure."

He stood up, too. "I don't think you understand—"

"No, Ashton, I don't think *you* understand. I get it. You could've taken James Hudson out. You hesitated and the moment was gone."

Ashton looked at her like he expected her to rage across the room and kangaroo kick him. That he almost wished she would.

She walked over to him. Reached up and cupped his face. "If you could go back and change it, I know you would. You would take the shot. A thousand times over you would take the shot."

"Yes." He looked a little surprised that she understood. "I know that."

"You don't hate me? Not even a little bit deep inside?"

"You thought I would?"

He shrugged. "I thought you *should*."

"No, I don't hate you. I could never hate you, Ashton. Especially not for this. You did your best. On most days, that's enough to save everyone involved. And when it's not, it's usually because of something you can't control."

His arms folded around her. "I just wish that day I could've done it. Could've controlled the entire situation."

She shrugged one shoulder, smiling softly. "You two would've liked each other, you know. Tyler was easygoing like you. Funny. Smart."

"I know this sounds really weird because I'm about to kiss you, but I would've like to have met your husband, too."

Summer smiled more fully, leaning back so she could look up into Ashton's eyes. "I will always love Tyler. He was a good man. And because he's Chloe's father, he'll always be a part of me. But I know he wouldn't want me to be alone. To pine for him."

She raised up onto her toes so they were just inches apart. "So yes, Agent Fitzgerald, please kiss me."

He obliged, lifting her off her feet with his arms wrapped around her hips. Neither of them let the kiss get too far, aware of the baby sleeping just feet away. After a few minutes, he reached down and swept her completely up in his arms and carried her over to the bed. He laid her down on one side of Chloe, then she felt him reach down and pull off her shoes.

"Scoot over," he whispered.

She did, laying Chloe between them on the bed. Ashton got in on the other side.

"This wasn't exactly how I thought the night would go when I first texted you earlier," she said, smiling at him. She watched him lay a hand on her sleeping daughter's belly.

"Me, either. But there's no other place I'd rather be."

THAT BASTARD ASHTON FITZGERALD *shot* him.

Damien hadn't thought there was any way someone from Omega would make it to the safe house in time to stop him from killing Summer, especially since he'd sent them on a wild-goose chase looking for Harper on the opposite side of town.

Fitzgerald must have already been on his way to the safe house when Damien entered. Damn it, Damien should've taken that into consideration. That Fitzgerald would rush to Summer when they didn't find Harper at the bar.

Damien was getting a little tired of failing to kill Summer Worrall. He wasn't used to failing at anything.

He winced as the gauze wrapped around the wound on his shoulder pinched him slightly. The wound wasn't bad, just a burn, really just Fitzgerald returning the favor for what Damien had done to him earlier this week. Damien knew Fitzgerald was Omega's best sniper; he should be glad Ashton hadn't been any closer or Damien would've needed more than gauze.

Fawkes would throw another temper tantrum when he found out a second attempt had been made on Summer Worrall's life. Damien would blame Harper, of course, and agree that it was time to eliminate him.

Because it *was* time to eliminate Harper.

Damien looked down at the woman lying on the floor bound and gagged—a stranger, picked out days ago solely because of the fact that she lived alone and the location of her apartment. Her eyes begged for mercy. Damien reached down and smoothed a bit of hair out of her eyes.

"There, there. This will all be over soon, okay?"

Somehow that didn't reassure the woman. She began thrashing around on the floor. Damien stepped away from her. Let her rub the ropes more fully into her skin. That would help sell the story.

Damien needed the entire SWAT team out here at this apartment. That was the only way he could be sure Fitzgerald wasn't going to deliver Summer and her daughter to the airport and plane himself. There had to be a crisis big enough that Ashton's conscience wouldn't allow him to turn away for personal matters—even getting his girlfriend on a plane to her sister's house.

Fawkes would be so proud of Damien. Damien had been able to hack into Summer's online credit card statement and see the purchased ticket himself. No secret Omega info needed. Figuring out she had a sister in Atlanta hadn't proved difficult, either.

It was time to put the plan into action. First, he needed to call Harper. He hit Send to the man's number, tapping his foot impatiently as it rang three, four times.

"Hello?" Harper finally answered, obviously having been sleeping.

"Mr. Harper, it's Damien."

"Dude, it's like six o'clock in the morning."

"Actually, it's nearly eight."

"Whatever."

Damien shook his head. "Harper, I'm going to deliver what you need to kill Ashton Fitzgerald today."

"You are?" Now the other man sounded much more awake.

"Indeed. I need you to meet me at your father's house today at noon."

"Dude, my dad's place is all rundown. It got fore-closed on."

All things Damien already knew. "Yes. But a fitting place, don't you think, for Agent Fitzgerald to meet his end? Since he is ultimately responsible for the state of your father's house."

"Yeah, yeah, you're right. That's like poetry justice."

Damien rolled his eyes. It really was time for Curtis Harper to die. "It is definitely poetic justice. I will see you at noon and will explain the plan."

He disconnected the call before Harper could say something stupid.

Say something *else* stupid.

And now it was time to get this show on the road. Damien got out his burner phone and dialed 911.

"911. Please state your emergency."

"Oh my gosh!" Damien deliberately pitched his voice as high as he could, breathing rapidly in and out to add a sense of panic. "I think my neighbor's ex-boyfriend is holding her hostage inside her apartment. He used to come here all the time and knock her around and threaten to kill her. I saw him go in there with a gun this time, screaming. Oh my gosh, should I try to help?"

"No, sir," the respondent was quick to tell him. "Leave that to the proper authorities. Please give me the address of the apartment."

Damien rattled off the address. "Oh my gosh, I think I might have heard two men yelling. What if that sicko brought his disgusting friend? That was why Tamara broke up with him last year, you know. I told her."

Damien looked down at the woman on the floor, shrugging apologetically at all the ridiculous lies he was making up.

"Oh my God!" he yelled. "I just heard a gunshot. I've got to get out of here."

Damien ended the call and dropped the phone near poor Tamara. He went over and made sure the drapes were tightly closed. Closed drapes would buy more time.

He walked over to the door, cracking it open and fired his gun into the ground twice. That would definitely be loud enough to gain more neighbors' attention. 911 would probably soon be getting more calls.

Damien walked over to Tamara.

"I'm sorry. It's nothing personal. Just part of the plan."

He shot her twice in the chest and watched her head roll to the side, dead.

It was time to go. Damien had a plane to catch.

CHLOE WOKE UP first and saw Ashton.

"Ah-ta. Ah-ta. Ah-ta." She showed no signs of stopping as she climbed up onto his chest.

Summer pried her eyes open. She really, really, really needed to get a decent night's sleep. She hadn't been this exhausted since she'd been a single mother with a newborn.

Today looked to be another long day, involving taking an overstimulated toddler on an airplane.

She needed to be at the airport in a couple hours for her flight that left at eleven. Hopefully Chloe would sleep through part of the flight since it would be sort of her nap time.

Summer got Chloe's breakfast together and Ashton supervised feeding the baby while she took a shower. She changed into the one other set of clothes she had that Lillian had grabbed from the safe house. At this point, she was just going to take whatever she had to Atlanta and buy the rest there. Good thing Joe paid her a decent salary.

She packed their items into a small suitcase as Ashton played with Chloe, chasing her around the couch.

Summer watched the pandemonium. "Good, help her get out as much energy as possible before she has to sit still on the plane."

"Have you got everything ready?"

Summer nodded. "Yeah. I'm just not going to worry about it. I'll beg, borrow or steal whatever I need in Atlanta. At least there are supercenters on every corner."

Ashton grabbed Chloe up in his arms and walked over to Summer. "You're going to be gone a few days. A week max. And if it will help, I'll fly out there so you've got an extra set of hands with this munchkin coming back."

Summer leaned into him. She was so tired and having someone to depend on, someone she knew loved Chloe very much, was nice.

More than nice. Something she could definitely get used to on a more permanent basis.

"I might take you up on that," she said against his lips, standing on her tiptoes.

"Good, because I mean it."

Chloe tapped them both on the cheeks with her hands and they pulled apart.

Ashton smiled. "Alright, let's get you ladies to the airport."

They were almost out the main door of Omega headquarters when Ashton's phone began buzzing.

"Hold on," he said, stepping to the side of the hall. "I've got to take this."

It didn't take long to realize it was some sort of emergency. The SWAT team—and Ashton—were needed.

She could tell Ashton was going to try to argue his way out of it. She touched his arm. "I'll be fine. Chloe and I can take a cab to the airport."

"No. I'm not sending you there alone."

"Then send another agent with me. They only have to keep me safe for one thirty-minute ride. Nobody knows where I'm going." She could see how torn Ashton was. She touched his cheek. "You're needed, Fitzy. Something important. We'll be fine."

She could tell he was still hesitant but a few moments later when another agent came rushing down the hall and announced that Steve Drackett had sent him to escort Summer and Chloe, Ashton finally relented.

"Tyrone, you're not to let them out of your sight for even one moment. Okay? This isn't a drill. Isn't practice."

The large, dark-skinned young man nodded. "Yes, sir. I'll walk them all the way to the gate. Even past security."

"You won't be able to bring your gun through without

the proper clearance which we don't have time for, so leave it in the car. But they will let you through security by showing your badge."

"Yes, sir. I'll be stuck like glue."

Ashton nodded at the other man, then turned to Summer. He pulled her close. "I'll see you soon. Call me as soon as you get there."

She touched his cheek. "Be careful."

"Always."

He kissed Chloe on the nose, brushed Summer's lips with his, then was gone, sprinting down the hallway.

Summer realized this was how life would always be with Ashton. He could be called away at a moment's notice when his SWAT skills were needed.

But she was willing to live with that. What Ashton did—what all of Omega did every day—was important. Of course, she and Ashton hadn't even talked about the future yet.

But she couldn't imagine hers without him.

Summer turned and faced the big, young agent who'd been assigned to her.

"I'm Tyrone Marcus, ma'am."

"Thanks for doing this, Tyrone. I'm sure it can't be too exciting for you."

He took her bag and began walking with her and Chloe back toward the main exit.

"It's no problem. Agent Fitzgerald and the other SWAT members have really taken me under their wing. They're role models for us all."

"How long have you been an agent?"

"Three years. And I've just been accepted into the SWAT training program. Pretty excited about that."

They were almost to the door when they passed another man, who seemed to be staring at Tyrone.

Tyrone gave him a short wave. "Hey, Saul, they announced the new SWAT training acceptance group starting in the spring. You in this time, man? You were so close the last couple of times."

Saul, young and muscular like Tyrone but with sandy blond hair that made him look like a surfer, pulled tightly on his tie as if it bothered him, then shook his head. "Nah. I withdrew myself from consideration. I've decided to go another route."

Tyrone nodded. "That's cool. Everybody has to do what works for them."

"Exactly. I think I've finally found something that works for me." The two men shook hands. Tyrone's smile definitely seemed more sincere than Saul's. Probably jealousy about the SWAT acceptance. Sour grapes. Summer felt a little sorry for the guy. She tried to give him her friendliest smile as he walked away.

Tyrone led her to the car in the parking garage. "Omega SWAT competition is tough. And it's not just physical. They're looking for the whole package. Even going through this training doesn't guarantee I'll be selected for the team."

"I'm sure you'll make it."

"It's all I've ever dreamed of doing. I've been practicing some with the team for the last couple of weeks. No missions yet, but still absolutely fantastic." He flashed her a toothy smile. "Heard a little bit about you and some muffins."

Summer rolled her eyes. "Don't get Ashton back on my bad side."

Tyrone chuckled. "I wouldn't dream of it."

He'd make a good fit for the team, Summer could already tell. She hooked Chloe's car seat into the back seat of the car. Chloe was climbing all over the front seat with Tyrone next to her attempting to keep her from doing any damage to herself.

"I'm going to sit back here with her if that's okay," Summer said. "Try to stop her from falling asleep which she normally does as soon as we get in motion. I want to keep all her sleeping for the plane, if possible."

"That's fine. But it's hard to believe anyone with this much energy could fall asleep so quickly."

Summer rolled her eyes. "Believe me, it's like a light switch. And she won't be happy that I'm keeping her awake. The drive to the airport will not be pretty."

She got the car seat situated and stepped out of the car. A shriek escaped her when a man moved out from the dark shadows of the garage too close for Summer to feel comfortable.

Tyrone immediately shot out of the car, weapon in hand.

"Damn it, Carnell, what the hell are you doing?"

The man studied them both with eyes that seemed too deep for his face. "Director Drackett asked me to escort you to the airport in a second car."

Carnell glanced around like he either expected an attack at any moment or didn't like to make eye contact with other people for that long. Summer reached in and scooped Chloe off the passenger's seat. Either way, he gave Summer the creeps. She was glad Tyrone was driving them to the airport and not the other man.

"I think I can handle this." Tyrone obviously wasn't happy about Carnell's presence.

"I won't be coming inside the airport. Director Drackett is just more cautious after what happened last month."

Tyrone glanced at Summer, filling her in. "Drackett's wife, Rosalyn, was kidnapped last month."

Carnell interrupted, "While an agent was escorting her back to Omega headquarters. The attacker killed the agent and took Rosalyn."

"Oh my God." Summer had thought she would be more than safe enough with just one agent. Evidently not.

"You're talking to a civilian, Carnell. Why don't you tone it down a little?"

Carnell studied Summer and Chloe in a way that made her uncomfortable. Like they were a science project or something.

"I didn't mean to shock or offend you. I just believe everyone should have as many facts as possible."

"Well." Summer began buckling Chloe into the car seat. "Let's just get to the airport."

Carnell got into a car a few spots down and Tyrone started theirs. "Sorry about Carnell. He's a strategic genius but not particularly great with people as you can see. He doesn't really have a filter."

"I'm surprised your boss would send someone like him to help escort us."

"Phillip has a mind like a computer. He can spot traffic deviations and dangers before I could ever begin to see them. If something is going down near us while we're driving, he's a good person to have around."

"Okay." Summer felt better. Kind of.

"Unless he gets on the radio and starts talking about the need for a revolution. Dude is a fanatic about how law enforcement needs to evolve in order to stay ahead."

Thankfully the ride to the airport was uneventful except for Chloe's irritation at being kept awake. But once she was given free rein to toddle down the airport hallways, she perked up again.

Summer checked them in and true to his word, Tyrone walked them through security all the way to the gate. Summer gave the man a hug and Chloe blew him goodbye kisses as they walked down the corridor and onto the plane, one of the first ones on since they needed the extra time to get situated.

She attached Chloe's car seat to the seat next to her and put Chloe in it, immediately giving her a sippy cup and cereal to feed herself. Then she sat back and watched as the other people loaded onto the plane.

Something ached in Summer's chest. A worry about Ashton. She knew how talented the Omega SWAT team was but just couldn't shake the bad feeling she had in the pit of her stomach.

Ashton had to be okay. He had to.

She reached partway over Chloe to look out the window. She felt a tear leak from her eye before her daughter's tiny hand reached up and caught it on her cheek.

"Ah-ta," Chloe said soberly.

Summer kissed her forehead. "Yes, Ah-ta. We'll see him soon."

The rest of the people boarded and Summer prepared for the flight—and days—ahead. Days without Ashton.

Then an announcement came from the front.

"Summer Worrall, if you're onboard the plane, please press your flight attendant call button."

Chapter Seventeen

Summer pressed the call button, wondering what in the world was going on. Soon two flight attendants made their way back to her.

"Ma'am, there's a federal agent back in the terminal that has asked that you come off the plane. We can help you with the baby and your luggage."

Tyrone? "Was it a tall, African-American man? Young?"

The female shrugged, giving her a sympathetic smile. "I don't know. I'm sorry. They just called it down to us."

Something must have happened. Maybe they already caught Curtis Harper and Ashton was trying to keep her from leaving.

Her stomach clenched again. Or maybe something really bad had happened.

"Okay," she told them as she began to unhook Chloe from the car seat. One of the flight attendants got her suitcase from the overhead bin and the other carried the car seat while Summer made her way back up the aisle, feeling everyone's eyes watching her.

It wasn't often someone was escorted off a plane right before it was scheduled to take off.

When they got to the terminal, it wasn't Tyrone waiting for her or even the creepy Phillip Carnell, it was a different middle-aged man. He looked vaguely familiar. She must have seen him at Omega sometime the last couple of days.

"Where's Tyrone?"

The man shifted just slightly. "He was called away to a scene so Ashton Fitzgerald asked me to escort you." He pulled out a badge and ID that looked just like Ashton's. "I'm Agent Jennings. We need you to come back to Omega Sector immediately."

"Is Ashton okay? Did something happen?" She still couldn't shake the bad feeling she had in the pit of her stomach.

"Honestly, ma'am, I'm not sure exactly what is going on right now. If you want, I can radio once we get to the car and see if I can get any information for you."

She nodded. "That would be great."

Refusing to let herself think the worst, she walked back through the airport with the agent. Chloe was already beginning to fall asleep on her shoulder, a dead weight, but thankfully Agent Jennings carried her suitcase and the car seat.

"I'll hook the seat in for you, ma'am," Agent Jennings said at the car. "I've had two of my own go through the car-seat age."

Summer smiled, thankful. She slipped her phone out of her purse. She knew Agent Jennings said he would ask through official channels when they got in the car, but if she could just text with Ashton, know he was okay, maybe it would ease this sick feeling in her stomach.

I know you probably can't talk. I just need to know if you're okay.

She sent the text. He probably didn't even have his cell phone with him. She remembered what he looked like in his SWAT gear. Personal cell phones probably weren't part of the equipment the team took with them.

"Do you want to put her in the seat or do you want me to?" Agent Jennings asked.

She smiled at him. "I'll do it. Hopefully I can keep her asleep. I'll sit in the back with her, too, if that's okay."

"Smart." The other man smiled back, looking so familiar to her.

"Did we meet at Omega in the last couple of days? It's been so crazy. I don't mean to be rude," she asked as she slid Chloe into the car seat, careful not to wake her.

"We met but it was very briefly. I don't expect you to remember me."

Her phone buzzed in her hand.

Hasn't your plane already taken off? You shouldn't be using a cell while in flight you know. Talk to you soon.

Relief flooded Summer. Ashton was safe.

"Was that Agent Fitzgerald?"

She nodded. "Yes. He's fine. I was worried. It's been a stressful couple of days."

The agent smiled. "Did you tell him you were off the plane and I was bringing you in?"

"No." Summer shook her head. "He was actually fussing at me for…"

She trailed off. Fussing at her for using her cell phone on the plane. Where he thought she was. Summer suddenly realized what a mistake she'd made. She'd been so worried about Ashton's safety she hadn't even stopped to think that he wouldn't have sent someone she didn't know without preparing her. Especially if he had access to his phone.

She turned and looked at Agent Jennings, who was now standing right behind her.

But he wasn't really an agent at all, was he?

It came to her. "You're the man from the woods last night." He looked different. His hair was lighter, thinner. His eyebrows were bushier. But it was definitely him.

He shrugged. "Like I said, you only met me very briefly. I don't expect you to remember me."

She felt a sharp pinch in her arm and realized he'd injected her with something.

"What do you want?" The world began spinning around her. Summer grasped the car to keep from falling.

"To use you as bait."

It was the last thing she heard before everything faded to blackness.

THE FIRST THING Summer knew when she woke up was that she wasn't in a car. She was lying on some sort of couch. An old, dirty, smelly one. She sat straight up, moaning and grabbing her head as dizziness and nausea assailed her. She realized her hands were tied in front of her with a zip tie.

"Careful there, Summer. The effects of benzodiazepine can be pretty long lasting. You'll probably be dizzy for several hours."

It was the man who had called himself Agent Jennings. The one who had tried to kill her in the woods last night.

"Where's Chloe?" she croaked the words out, struggling to open her eyes to look for her daughter.

"Right next to you in her car seat. I thought it better to keep her strapped in. Not that she'll be waking up for a while."

"What did you do to her?" Summer could see her now, a few feet away. She tried to stand but found her hands tied to the couch by a longer piece of rope. "Did you drug her?"

"Your daughter has only been given diphenhydramine, Ms. Worrall. There won't be any long-lasting effects from that but should keep her sleeping for a few hours." The man narrowed his eyes at her. "I'm sure you'd prefer that anyway."

Summer struggled to push through the fog in her head. Diphenhydramine. That was an allergy medicine. Benadryl. It shouldn't have lasting ill effects on Chloe. Just cause her to have a nice long nap.

If the man was telling the truth. At this point, Summer just had to pray he was.

But he was correct about one thing: Summer would prefer Chloe be asleep as long as possible until she figured out how to get out of this. She could see Chloe's little chest moving as she breathed. That was enough for now.

"What do you want? Why are we here?"

"I'm about to give you to Curtis Harper as part of the grand plan for him to get his revenge on your boyfriend."

None of this made any sense. "But last night you were about to kill us in the woods. Why don't you have a gun pointed at me now?"

"Oh I do. It's just a different sort."

Summer wasn't sure what that meant but knew it wasn't good.

She heard loud music blaring from a car outside as it pulled up. Most of the windows in this house were knocked out and it looked like it hadn't been occupied in years. The couch she was attached to had definitely seen better days.

"Ah, here's Mr. Harper now. I'll just go ahead and apologize for him. He's a little difficult to bear."

"Alright, Damien. I'm here. What's your brilliant plan?"

The younger man came storming into the house, half tearing the door off the hinges, obviously not caring how much noise he made. This house—such as it was—definitely must be pretty isolated.

"Here's the lovely Ms. Worrall and her daughter. All that you need to get Agent Fitzgerald out here alone."

"You really think he'll fall for that?"

Freihof smiled at Summer. "Oh most definitely." He stood from the dusty armchair where he'd been sitting. "But don't worry, I'm not going to leave you alone to deal with him."

Harper walked farther into the room, leering at Summer in a way that had her flinching back from him. "You won't?"

"No, I'll be outside with a gun trained on Fitzgerald. All you have to do is lead him into this room and right next to the couch. From there, I'll be able to take him out. You'll finally have your revenge."

"What about Summer here?"

Freihof smiled. "You can do whatever you like with her."

Summer felt revulsion rip through her as Harper took a step closer. She realized this was the man who had broken into her house. "You touch me and I'll break your nose again like Ashton did. I don't need him here to do that."

Harper's eyes lit with fury, but at least he stopped moving toward her.

Summer wanted to point out all the flaws in this plan

to Harper and Freihof. Ashton wasn't going to come alone, he was part of a SWAT team, for heaven's sake. They worked together to secretly infiltrate places and rescue hostages for a living. Did Harper really think Ashton wouldn't bring the team just because Harper wanted it that way?

The Omega team might not walk through the door with Ashton, but Summer had no doubt they'd be around.

Summer studied the two men. Freihof *knew*. Harper may not be smart enough to see the holes in the plan, but Freihof did.

Freihof was creating the holes.

Creating discord between the two of them was probably her best bet.

"He's playing you, Harper." She turned to the younger man. "Think it through. You're the one in here with a member of SWAT, probably a whole team of SWAT." She stuck her thumb toward Freihof. "He'll be outside, easily able to get away."

Freihof's eyes narrowed at her. "Probably best to stop talking now, Ms. Worrall."

"Why? Because I'm smart enough to see what he can't? That you're using him to—"

Freihof walked swiftly over and backhanded her. Dizziness assaulted her again as she fell onto the filthy couch.

"You're just trying to save your lover's life. Curtis won't fall for your lies."

"But she's right," Harper said. "I'm the one left here. The one taking all the chances."

Freihof walked over and put his arm around Harper. "She's just trying to save herself and Fitzgerald. To make things more complicated than they need to be."

Summer wanted to argue further, to try to make Harper see what was really going on, but she was afraid Freihof would hurt her, or worse, threaten to hurt Chloe.

"With this plan, you'll get to be up close and personal when Fitzgerald dies," Freihof continued. "Your face will be the last thing he sees. His body will fall in your father's house like we talked about."

Harper's smile became wider. "Yes, I like the sound of that."

Freihof squeezed his shoulder. "And we're a team, you and I. We've been in this together since day one. You can trust me to take care of Fitzgerald. You can trust me to take care of everything."

"Okay. I trust you, Damien. And Fitzgerald will finally get what he deserves."

Freihof smiled. "All you need to do is lead him over to the couch. I'll have a clean shot from there and will take care of the rest. Look, I even got these so we'll be able to communicate with each other."

He pulled out two communication earpieces and handed one to Harper. "So we'll be able to talk through it and make sure everything is going according to plan."

Harper visibly relaxed. Obviously Freihof had regained the younger man's trust. "That will be pretty cool. Like a movie and stuff."

"Exactly. Like a movie and stuff. You do your part of the job and trust that I'll do mine."

"What about her?" Harper looked over at Summer.

"I suggest you gag her, first off, so she doesn't warn Fitzgerald. But once he's gone, really you can do whatever you want with her."

Summer shuddered as Harper looked her over.

"Okay. I'll call Fitzgerald. It's a good day for him to die."

Chapter Eighteen

The woman—her name was Tamara Snell—was dead long before SWAT ever arrived at her apartment building. But due to the pandemonium, they hadn't realized it for a while.

911 had received multiple calls about a gun being fired in Tamara's building. Most callers couldn't give an exact apartment number, but one person had. The same guy who had said he saw Ms. Snell's abusive ex-boyfriend holding her hostage.

Well, there was no abusive ex-boyfriend around now and Tamara was definitely dead. Shot twice in the chest.

The SWAT team had established a normal hostage situation perimeter. After a bit of reconnaissance, Ashton had determined his best angle for a sniper shot, if needed, would be across the street out on the fire escape of another set of apartments. After communicating with the team where he was going, he got into place and waited.

And waited.

He listened as Derek Waterman attempted to make contact through the victim's cell phone. No one picked up. And nothing—no movement, no light—could be seen behind the thick curtains covering Tamara's windows.

When both a visual and audio wire probe under the

door obtained no results, everyone began to fear the worst. When a second probe through the apartment upstairs had shown a shot woman on the ground, the team had immediately breached the door.

They'd been too late. Way too late to help Tamara Snell.

Local investigators would come in from here and take over. Ashton was just a little pissed that they'd come all the way out here and hadn't been able to do a damn thing to help. Especially when he could've delivered Summer and Chloe to the airport himself.

Then he'd gotten her text.

I know you probably can't talk. I just need to know if you're okay.

Ashton had shaken his head. It was nice that she was worried about him. But she should've already been in the air by then. The flight must have been delayed.

Hasn't your plane already taken off? You shouldn't be using a cell while in flight you know. Talk to you soon.

He hadn't heard back from her again, so she must've started following airline rules and put her phone away.

Lillian and Roman met him at the SWAT truck.

"Her ex-boyfriend must have run out immediately after he shot her," Roman said. "Because that scene was about as cold as any hostage situation I've ever been to."

"I'm no profiler." Lillian shrugged. "But generally, domestic violence cases are more personal in their violence. Yeah, the vic was tied up and yeah, she was shot. But there were hardly any other marks on her."

Ashton shrugged. Lillian was right, domestic cases tended to be some of the most brutal ones they worked. But he was glad the victim hadn't suffered a great deal before she died.

The locals would be taking over the investigation from here. Omega SWAT had been called because they were best at first response, but now it would be taken over by the Colorado Springs detectives.

"Let's get back to HQ." Derek shook his head as he walked toward him. "There's nothing we can do here."

Everyone helped secure the equipment and soon they were on their way back.

"Anybody heard about any action happening anywhere else?" Derek leaned back against his seat as they drove down the highway.

"Like, trouble?" Lillian asked.

"Yeah."

Everybody doubled checked their phones to be sure.

"No, nothing," Lillian said first, then looked around. "Anyone else?"

"What's up, Derek?" Roman asked from the driver's seat.

"911 dispatch said the man who called this in said Tamara Snell's violent ex-boyfriend was back. Had a gun and was holding her hostage. That's why we were called rather than just the locals. A number of other 911 calls confirmed that shots had been fired."

They all nodded.

"I overheard neighbors talking as I was coming out. Ends up that Ms. Snell did not have ex-boyfriends," Derek continued.

"What, like she was married?" Roman asked.

"Widowed. Basically a recluse."

Ashton looked more closely at Derek. "Could she have had a boyfriend before?"

"Neighbors have known her for ten years. She's never had a boyfriend in that time."

Ashton shook his head. "Why would someone call 911 and report an ex-boyfriend if there wasn't one?"

"Exactly." Derek gestured down at Ashton's phone. "Where are Summer and Chloe?"

"They're on their way to Atlanta. I didn't want them going to the airport alone so Tyrone Marcus escorted them. I got a text from him about an hour and a half ago saying she'd gotten on the plane and he was heading back to HQ."

Derek nodded. "Good. I was just checking."

Something wasn't sitting right with Ashton. "But then I got a text from Summer about twenty minutes ago. Asking if I was okay."

"Shouldn't she have already been in the air by then?" Lillian asked.

"That's basically what I said. That it was dangerous to use a cell phone in flight. She didn't respond."

Ashton took his phone out and immediately dialed Summer's number. Straight to voice mail. That could just mean she'd done what he'd asked and turned her phone off.

His second call was to the Omega switchboard, which could connect him to Tyrone Marcus.

"Ashton, hey," the other man answered.

Ashton skipped all pleasantries. "Did Summer and Chloe get on the plane?"

"Yes, sir."

"You escorted them all the way to the gate?"

"Yes. I waited until they got on the plane before I

left. Ms. Worrall was one of the first people on since she needed extra time to get Chloe settled."

Right. That all made sense. Ashton nodded at the rest of the team who were watching him.

"Thanks, Marcus. I appreciate you taking them."

"Any time."

Ashton knew he should feel better, that this tightness in his gut should go away. Summer and Chloe were on their way to somewhere safe. They hadn't used any Omega computers to book the tickets, so if there was a computerized or personnel leak at Omega, the perp wouldn't know about Summer's plan.

But something about Summer's text didn't sit right with him.

I know you probably can't talk. I just need to know if you're okay.

Why would she be worried about him? When Ashton had handed her over to Tyrone Marcus's care, he hadn't given her any information about the op he was about to go on. Had the text been just general concern?

The truck pulled up at Omega headquarters.

Something wasn't right. Ashton knew it. Last time he'd ignored his instincts, Tyler Worrall had gotten killed. Ashton wasn't going to ignore his instincts now.

"Derek, something's off, man. You felt it, and I second it. That whole situation with Tamara Snell seemed…" Ashton wasn't sure what the right word was.

"Staged," Derek finished for him.

"Yes." That was it. Staged. Ashton pinched the bridge of his nose. "Almost like how we went off looking for Harper across town last night based on an anonymous call, only to find Harper hadn't been there for hours. Then today, 911 gets an anonymous call about a violent ex-boyfriend only to find out the victim didn't have any ex-boyfriends."

Derek nodded. "I agree. Something's headed our way." He turned to the rest of the team. "We all stay prepped and ready until Ashton has official word that Summer and her daughter are safe."

Staying in full SWAT gear definitely wasn't comfortable but none of the team complained.

"I need to get in touch with someone from the Atlanta Bureau field office to escort Summer and Chloe to Summer's sister's house once they arrive. I'm not taking any chances."

"Got someone you can call?"

Ashton had been working law enforcement long enough to have made friends all over the country. "Yes. It won't be a problem."

He was in the process of dialing when another call came through. A local one.

"Ashton Fitzgerald."

"Hey there, Ashton Fitzgerald," a mocking voice said. "I've been trying to get your attention lately."

"Curtis Harper." The heads of everyone in the van whipped around to look at Ashton. "You've done more than just try to get my attention."

Ashton brought the phone down from his head and switched it on to speaker mode so everyone could hear.

"I have to admit, you've been more difficult to kill than I thought you would be," Harper said.

Ashton shook his head. Evidently Harper wasn't intelligent enough to realize that he'd just confessed to crimes they'd linked him to but didn't have hard proof. And he'd done it on a federal agent's phone which could be recorded at any time.

"Sorry to disappoint you."

Harper laughed. "Don't worry, I have a new plan now. Wanna hear it?"

"Absolutely, Harper. Nothing I would like more."

Derek was already up and on the phone. Probably with Omega Sector to see if they could trace Harper's call.

"How about you come to my father's house? Or what was my father's house before it was abandoned and repossessed. Thanks to you." Harper rattled off an address. Roman wrote it down.

Derek circled his finger in the air signaling for Ashton to keep Harper talking.

"Sure, Harper, want to give yourself up?"

"No. I thought you would come alone and give *your-self* up."

"And why would I do that?"

"Because maybe you're willing to trade your life for Summer Worrall and her daughter."

Ashton's grip tightened on the phone. He forced his voice to keep calm. If this was some sort of fishing expedition on Harper's part, Ashton didn't want to give him any info. "Ms. Worrall has already headed out to visit friends in Los Angeles. I'm sure she's already enjoying the sunshine." He didn't even hesitate to lie.

"That might have been true if we hadn't taken her off the plane heading toward Atlanta a little while ago."

Ashton's eyes flew to Derek's. This was bad. Too many details that rang true. One, that Harper knew Summer and Chloe had been heading to Atlanta, and two, that he mentioned getting her off the plane.

Out of the corner of his eye, he saw Lillian get on her phone.

"If you have Summer, let me talk to her."

"Sure thing."

"Ashton?" The dread in his stomach solidified at the sound of her voice. That was definitely her.

"Summer? Are you okay? Chloe?"

"Yes, we're fine. We're okay."

"I'm coming for you, okay? Just hang on."

"No, Ashton, it's a trap. It's—"

He heard the sound of skin connecting with skin before Summer cried out.

"I think that's enough talking to her."

"Damn it, Harper," he roared into the phone. "If you hurt her—"

"You have thirty minutes to get here, Fitzgerald. It's time for you to pay for what you did to my dad. Come alone. If I see anyone else, she dies."

The call disconnected. Roman immediately spun the truck around and they were on their way.

Ashton felt stunned. How had Harper gotten Summer?

"You can dump us half a mile out and take the truck in yourself," Derek said. "We'll get into position and radio you with what we find."

Ashton just stared at the team leader for a long moment. Derek reached over and clasped both hands onto Ashton's shoulders. "I know it's tough, but you have to focus. She and Chloe are still alive. That's the most important thing."

Derek knew from firsthand experience what it was like to have the woman you loved held by someone with plans to hurt her. His wife, Molly, had been kidnapped by a terrorist intent on torturing information out of her.

Ashton nodded. Derek was right. He had to focus. Work the problem. This was what the team trained to do.

But it was so much damn harder when it was the people you loved on the line.

They were all already in full gear. All already situated with comms. Harper had given him thirty minutes, thinking it would be a crunch, causing Ashton to panic and not be able to bring the team with him, but he'd been wrong. They were ready and Harper was going down.

"I just talked to my contact at the airport. Evidently an 'Omega agent—'" Lillian put her fingers up for quotations "—flashed a badge, stated there was an emergency and got Summer and Chloe off the plane."

Damn it. That would've been after Tyrone Marcus had left. He'd seen Summer and Chloe onto the plane. There was no reason to think someone would dare take her off it afterward.

"Here's a picture of the agent." She passed her phone around.

"That man is definitely not Curtis Harper," Ashton said.

"It could be the same guy Harper met with after the shoot-out on Friday. Different appearance but same height and build," Lillian pointed out.

"We still have no idea who this guy is, right?"

Lillian shook her head. "Jon and Brandon are working on it, but nothing as of right now."

"I've got the details on the address. It's a foreclosure property. Been empty for years," Derek said. "It's a large, dead-end lot. Shouldn't be anybody else just hanging around."

Ashton checked the clip of his sidearm as if he didn't already know it was ready to go. "Good, we don't want any friendlies in the way."

"HQ is coordinating with locals," Derek continued.

"There will be a roadblock on all roads about two miles out from the house. If Harper tries to run, they'll stop him. Bomb squad and medics are on their way just in case. They'll come in stealthy so as not to aggravate the situation."

"He's got a lot of advantages, Fitzy," Lillian said softly. "He knows the house. He has this second person. We're going in blind with little prep time."

"I know."

"He could shoot you outright and we couldn't do anything to stop it," Roman continued from the driver's seat, all signs of his usual jesting nature gone.

Ashton shrugged. They weren't saying anything he didn't already know. "But you'd be able to get Summer and Chloe out. That's the most important thing."

"Alright, people, cut the goodbyes. That's not what we do," Derek said. "Everybody stay frosty. Ashton, you get in there and don't get killed. We'll get the tactical positions we need and call it in to you."

"Okay." Ashton slipped the earpiece into his ear. "But Summer and Chloe are the most important thing. Nobody lose track of that. You see a chance to get them out, you take it. I don't care what happens to me."

Years of training were the only thing that kept the panic from swallowing Ashton. He couldn't let himself dwell on how frightened Summer had to be. And Chloe's little face—he had to push that away entirely. If he didn't, he wouldn't be able to focus the way he needed to.

Summer and Chloe *would* get out of this.

If Ashton walked away, too, that would just be a bonus.

"You keep your Kevlar and your helmet on," Derek told him. "If mystery man number two is around with a rifle, we'll find him. But it will take a little time. Let's not give him a free shot."

"Buy us time with Harper, Fitzy," Roman said. "We'll have your back."

"I wish I had some pointers from Joe Matarazzo." Joe was the best hostage negotiator any of them had ever seen.

"We'll patch Joe through from HQ," Derek said. "But you've heard him enough to know a lot of his tactics. Just keep the perp talking as much as possible. Listen to him. Give us time to do our job."

"I'm better with a gun than words," Ashton muttered. "Always have been."

The truck stopped and the team filed out. Ashton had been trusting them with his life for years. Trusting them with Summer and Chloe's was harder, but he knew he could.

"You guys," he told them as he got into the driver's seat. "These girls are everything to me."

Derek and Lillian nodded.

"We've all known that from the first muffin, man." Roman winked. "We'll get them out."

Chapter Nineteen

Ashton made no attempts at stealth as he inched the SWAT van toward George Harper's house. He had to force himself to go slowly, just like he'd had to force himself to not speed immediately to the house once the rest of the team had sprinted off for their tactical positions.

Everything in him screamed to barrel down the road, to burst into the house guns blazing, to make sure Summer and Chloe were safe again. Only the knowledge that his not-so-elaborate plan would do more harm than good stopped him.

Give the team time to get into place. Harper should be glad it wasn't Ashton positioning himself with his sniper rifle. For the first time in his career, Ashton wasn't sure he would wait for the green light to take the shot.

His watch beeped. It was now twenty-eight minutes since Harper's call. Show time.

He pulled the truck up the isolated road and into the Harper driveway. Grass grew two feet tall all around him. There'd been no upkeep at the place for years. A nondescript vehicle was parked in the cracked driveway.

"Got a gray early-model Camry at the front of the house," Ashton told the team as he checked inside. "Empty."

Most of the windows in the house had been knocked out by nature or vandals. Some were boarded up. The front door leaned off its top hinges and sat at a canted angle against the floor, barely upright.

Ashton turned off the truck and got out. "I'm about to enter." Ashton wouldn't be able to say much once he was inside if they wanted to keep up the appearance of him being alone.

"Roger that," Derek responded. "Roman is moving in toward the back to check out closer around the house. Lillian is establishing sniper positioning. So far we've had no sighting of Harper's accomplice."

There was a hell of a lot of empty ground where the other man could be hiding.

"Backup is on the way. ETA five minutes. We'll have thermal imaging soon, Ashton. Just draw it out as long as possible."

"Roger."

Of course, if Ashton walked in there and Summer or Chloe was hurt—or, oh God, he could hardly bear to think about it, *dead*—drawing it out wasn't going to be an issue.

As if he could read Ashton's mind, Roman muttered, "Fitzy, training, man. Not emotion."

"I'll try." But his promise sounded weak even to himself.

He made his way through the overgrown grass, eyes scanning everywhere for anything that might be useful or pose a threat. The porch steps made a loud sound as his booted feet landed on them. That was fine, Ashton wasn't attempting stealth.

"So you made it," he heard Harper say, although he

couldn't see the man. "I had wondered if you would make it in time."

"I'm coming in, Harper." Ashton slid the broken front door back as far as he could and stepped inside. The interior state of the house—if it could even be called that with the amount of broken windows and doors—wasn't any better than the outside.

Ashton stepped over a pile of trash and rounded the corner of what used to be a coat closet that faced the front door. This brought him into what looked like a dining room. A few more steps brought the back room into view.

Harper stood there, grinning like an idiot, gun in hand. Next to him, sitting on the couch, gagged with her arms tied in front of her, was Summer. Chloe was in her car seat on the floor a few feet away from Summer, sleeping.

Something eased slightly in Ashton. They were alive. He would damn well make sure it stayed that way.

"I see Summer and Chloe are alive. Is it really necessary to gag Summer and tie her up?" The info was for the team, apprising them of the situation.

"I'm in charge here, Fitzgerald. You do what I say." He swung the gun around at Summer. "Or she's the one who gets dead."

Ashton held his arms out in front of him. "Okay, Harper, you're the boss. Whatever you want, that's what we'll do."

"That's right, I *am* the boss. Why are you in your SWAT gear?" Harper's eyes narrowed.

"Because I was at a hostage situation across town when you called. I came straight here."

"Take out your gun and put it on the ground slowly."

"Why don't you point your gun at me? I'm the one you have to worry about."

Ashton didn't like how shaky Harper's hands were, especially with the gun pointed so close to Summer.

"I'm not stupid, Fitzgerald. I know keeping this pointed at her is the only way to keep you in line."

Harper was correct about that. If Lillian had a shot available, she might take it if Harper had his gun pointed at Ashton. She wouldn't take the chance if Summer or Chloe's lives were at stake.

"Alright, Harper. Here's my gun. I'm putting it on the floor."

"Kick it away from you."

Ashton did, but probably not as far as Harper would like.

"Take off your helmet. I want to be able to see your face clearly. I want to know that you wish you hadn't killed my father."

Ashton took off his helmet and dropped it to the ground, but tried to stick to the wall. If the second man was out there, ready to take a shot, Ashton wanted to give him as small a target as possible.

"I'm willing to talk about that with you. But you need to let Summer and the baby go first."

"Why don't I kill them both and then we'll talk?" Harper sneered.

Ashton swallowed the panic. "You do that and there's going to be nothing keeping me from diving across this room and you and me fighting one-on-one. Remember what happened last time we fought, Curtis?" Ashton tapped his nose, reminding Harper of his broken one.

Wrong thing to say. Harper brought the gun even closer to Summer. "That won't happen again, trust me."

Ashton tensed to pounce, but then Harper brought a hand up to his ear for just a second, then seemed to relax. He eased the gun away from Summer's head.

"Fine," Harper said, sulking like a child. Ashton wasn't even sure what he was talking about. "Did you come alone?"

"Yes."

"How am I supposed to believe you?"

"The only thing I care about is getting Summer and her daughter out of here unharmed. You can make that happen. Let them go right now and you can do wherever you want with me."

Harper brought his hand to his ear again. "Is everything a go?"

Ashton stared at the man. What was Harper talking about?

It dawned on Ashton. *Damn it.* The man was talking to his partner through a radio comm channel, just like Ashton was with his team.

"Who you talking to on that comm unit, Harper? Your partner?"

Harper's gloating laugh filled the air. "Just because you're here alone doesn't mean I'm stupid enough to be." Harper touched his earpiece. "You're sure he's here by himself?"

While Harper and his partner spoke, Ashton's team reported to him.

"Ashton, we've got no evidence of a partner out here." Derek's voice filled his ear. Ashton didn't want to answer and tip his hand to Harper that he wasn't, in fact, alone. "Thermal imagining report in the next two minutes. The rest of the Omega team is here. Tyrone Marcus is making his way around to help Roman."

Harper was looking at Ashton with glee in his eyes.

"I told you I was alone, Harper. Now let's stop messing around. Let Summer and the baby go."

"You killed my father, Fitzgerald. In cold blood."

"I killed your father because he'd taken people hostage. Had hurt people."

"He was forced to do that!" Harper's tone bordered on whiny.

Ashton shook his head. "We gave him every chance to surrender before using lethal force. He'd already killed one of those hostages—a young girl who'd just started college and had never hurt anyone. And he was about to kill someone else."

As he spoke, Ashton could see a myriad of emotions cross the other man's face: disbelief, guilt, acceptance, fear. Harper knew what Ashton said was the truth.

Ashton lowered his tone, tried to be more friendly, approachable like Joe Matarazzo would do if he was here handling the negotiation.

"It was an unfortunate situation, Curtis. If I could take it back, I would." It was a partial lie. Ashton would change shooting George Harper if he could, but only if it meant the other victims wouldn't have been hurt also. "The Omega team always tries to get everyone out alive if they can."

He was getting through to Harper. The gun in his hand wavered and lowered. But then his partner obviously said something to him, because Harper stopped and looked away, holding his ear. Whatever the other man said worked. At his words, Harper obviously pushed the other emotions away to hang on to what justified his actions now: righteous anger on his father's behalf.

"No," Harper said. "Omega Sector does what it wants.

Shoots first and asks questions later. *You* shot before you had all the facts."

Derek's voice came on again. "Ashton, thermal imaging confirms there is nobody out here. I don't know where Harper thinks his partner is, but no one out here has a bead on you."

No partner.

This changed things. Yes, Harper still had a gun, but if he didn't have a partner out there with a sniper rifle, the odds just became much greater in Ashton's favor. All he needed to do was get the gun pointed at him and not Summer.

But where was the partner? If their goal was to kill Ashton, this was a great opportunity. But the other man had left Harper without any backup. What was their plan?

Ashton stepped closer. Summer started shaking her head.

"I shot before I had all the facts?" Ashton ignored Summer and took another step closer to the couch. He needed to be close enough to attack Harper if things turned sour. "Is that what you really believe, Harper, or was that what someone told you to believe?"

Harper's eyes narrowed. "What are you talking about?"

"You've known I shot your father for four years. Why are you just now deciding to take revenge?"

"Because you deserve to rot in hell for what you've done."

"That may be true, but why are you just now deciding that's the case? I think you had to be talked into it. I think maybe you know your father was wrong, but when someone started talking about revenge, that sounded interesting so you went for it."

Harper's eyes darted around the room, and he rocked his weight back and forth, agitated. Ashton knew he was on the right track.

But the voice in Harper's ear refused to give the man too much time to think it through. When Harper looked at Ashton again, his face was full of resolve.

"Shut up or she dies right now."

"Ah-ta!" Little Chloe's voice drew everyone's attention. Harper's gun swung around to her and Summer stood, terror in her eyes.

"Harper, calm down," Ashton said. "Point the gun at me, not at the baby."

Tears streamed down Summer's face, but Ashton forced himself not to focus on her. He needed Harper to point the gun away from Chloe.

"Harper, you have to admit, that baby has absolutely nothing to do with this. You're not going to shoot her, are you?"

Chloe began to cry, upset that Ashton was ignoring her. "Ah-ta. Ah-ta. Mama." She stretched her arms, trying to get free of the restraints of the car seat where she was buckled. It didn't take long for her cries to turn into wails.

"Somebody shut that kid up!" Harper yelled, agitated.

"Let her mom get her out of the car seat," Ashton argued. "She's a baby, Curtis. She doesn't understand what's going on."

"I have a confirmed shot on Harper." Lillian's voice sounded in his ear.

Ashton immediately held a fist up at shoulder level. It would look odd to Harper if he noticed, but to the team it would be an indication to hold. It was too dangerous to take the shot when Harper had the gun on Chloe.

"Ashton signals to hold fire, Lil," Derek said. "Harper has the gun pointed at the baby."

"Roger," Lillian said.

"Let her mom pick her up and she'll stop crying," Ashton said.

Harper put the gun against the back of Summer's head. "If you try anything, both you and your daughter are going to die."

He saw Summer flinch, but she nodded. Harper pulled out a knife and cut through the long rope that kept her bound to the couch. She walked over to Chloe, Harper with her the entire time, knelt down and unhooked her daughter as best she could with her hands bound with zip ties, and helped her out of the car seat.

Chloe wrapped her tiny arms around her mother's neck and stopped crying as Summer scooped her up awkwardly. "Mama." She patted her mother's cheek and touched the gag wrapped around her face. Summer just snuggled up against her.

Ashton took another step toward the couch, which drew Harper's gun away from the girls and back to him, which he wanted.

Harper actually smiled that Ashton had moved closer. "Is that close enough?" he said into his communication device.

Close enough for what?

"Hey, are you there?" Harper tapped his ear. "What are you waiting for?" The man said something to him as Harper listened. "Wait. Are you *driving*?"

With Harper's shock, Ashton finally figured it out. Harper thought his partner was out there. But he wasn't. He'd left Harper here alone, and Harper obviously wasn't expecting that.

"Guys, something's not right here. Tyrone and I are trying to get under the house and it's locked up like Fort Knox," Roman's voice said through the comm unit. "Weird, considering the state of the house. What would someone want to protect under there?"

Ashton looked over at Harper who had pulled the communication device out and hurled it down in anger. What would someone be willing to go to great lengths to protect under the house?

The plan.

There was obviously some elaborate plan going on here and Harper didn't know about it, probably because he was expendable to the unknown second man who'd been pulling the puppet strings from the beginning. A plan put in place by a man willing to kill Summer last night and willing to kill her now again.

A plan that didn't require the man to be here, but required that no one interfere with whatever was under the house.

"Lillian, take the shot now!" Ashton called, not caring anymore if Harper knew he wasn't alone. Ashton was already leaping toward Summer and Chloe when the shot rang out. He didn't wait to see what happened to Harper. Lillian wouldn't miss.

"Roman, get out!" he roared into his comm piece as he scooped Summer into his arms with Chloe in hers and continued his forward motion toward the back door, bursting through it with his shoulder.

They'd barely cleared it when the house exploded behind them. As the force of it propelled them through the air, Ashton could feel heat singeing his exposed skin. He twisted his body to the side so he wouldn't crush Summer and Chloe as they landed.

His arms wrapped more tightly around them, his hands covering Summer's who was covering Chloe's head. He felt his shoulder pop out of socket as they slammed against the ground, but immediately turned so the girls were on top of him.

It took him a second to get any words out. "Are you two okay?"

He felt Chloe wiggling between him and Summer as she struggled to get up. His eyes met Summer's. She nodded.

He grimaced as he forced his shoulder to move to untie the gag from Summer's mouth. She stretched her jaw, then lay back against Ashton's uninjured arm.

Chloe just got up on Ashton's chest and started wiggling, laughing.

"Ma, Ah-ta. Ma. Ma. Ma." She kept hitting the fingers of her two tiny hands together.

"I think she wants you," Ashton said as he let the girl wiggle. "She's saying Mama."

"Oh no," Summer responded, shaking her head. "She's saying *more*. That signal she's doing with her hands is a little piece of sign language I taught her."

"More?" Ashton asked. "More what?"

Summer laughed and threw her arm around them both. "I think she wants you to blow up another building."

Ashton just pulled them both closer.

Chapter Twenty

The next couple of days went by in a blur for Summer.

It was amazing what money could do to ease the way when you wanted quick repairs done to a condo. Especially when you were talking about the type of money Joe Matarazzo had. By the time Summer got back home from the hospital the day after she and Chloe had been taken, the front window had been replaced and the entire place had been cleared out and cleaned as if the shooting had never happened.

Joe also had a new and much more advanced alarm system installed. One that still worked even if the house's power was cut. Heck, it might work even after a nuclear holocaust.

Summer, Chloe and Ashton had spent last night in the hospital. Ashton had dislocated his shoulder getting them out of the house and had some burns on his skin that had been exposed—the back of his neck and part of his arms and hands.

Nothing serious. Unbelievably.

Summer and Chloe had been kept overnight just to confirm there was nothing in their systems that would cause any long-lasting harm. Both of them were fine. There was no way Summer was going to allow Chloe out of her sight, so she'd been glad the hospital had worked with them, bringing a crib from the children's ward so Chloe could sleep next to Summer.

Summer hadn't liked being away from Ashton, but figured he could take care of himself. He probably wouldn't wake up scared and crying like Chloe might.

Although he would have good reason if he did.

That was the second time Ashton had gotten her and Chloe out of a burning building safely. Summer just prayed it would never happen again.

She'd felt so helpless there on the couch, unable to communicate with Ashton, afraid he would walk too close to the couch and Damien would shoot him.

But Damien hadn't been there at all.

Thank God Ashton had figured it out in time, because Summer sure hadn't. She'd known Damien was playing Harper, using him, but she hadn't thought Damien would actually try to kill the other man.

Although from what she understood, Damien hadn't actually succeeded in killing Harper. Harper was still alive. Barely.

But Damien had killed young Tyrone Marcus in the explosion. Summer brought a hand up to her face to wipe away the tears at that thought. He'd been so excited about the possibility of joining the SWAT team.

"Hey, you okay?" She felt Ashton's hand trail up her side, then along the arm she'd raised to her cheek.

She and Ashton had left the hospital together yesterday morning. Neither of them could stand the thought of being away from each other, so when they'd heard Joe had graciously rushed her condo's repairs, Ashton had just come home with her.

He hadn't really left since. They'd gone together to

pick up a few of his things, for Summer to see where he lived—a confirmed bachelor pad in an apartment complex about five miles away—then returned home.

Chloe couldn't be happier to have her precious Ah-ta around. Even if his arm was in a funny cast. She was now napping and they were taking advantage of the calm to do the same.

"I was just thinking about Tyrone Marcus."

Ashton sighed. "Yeah, he'll be sorely missed."

More tears leaked from her eyes. "I thought they were going to kill you. That I was going to watch you die in front of me."

"I'm amazed you even want to be here with me right now. Nobody would blame you if you didn't want to be involved with someone who works in law enforcement. You've been privy to way too much personal violence in your life."

Summer shrugged. "I wasn't there when Tyler died, so even though that was horrible, I didn't really experience it. When Bailey Heath kidnapped us a few months ago, she drugged us first. I was never fully conscious for that. Don't even remember much, unlike Laura and Joe."

She took a shuddery breath. "But *this*. I thought they would kill you and then Chloe and I would be at Harper's mercy."

He put his good arm around her and pulled her close. "Even if they had killed me, the team was out there. No way Curtis was going to get to you."

"I can't believe he thought you would actually come alone."

He kissed her forehead. "If there's one thing Curtis Harper seems to excel at, it's deluding himself."

She snuggled closer. "I might not ever be able to let you out of my sight again."

"I know the feeling." She felt his lips against her hair. "When Harper told me you'd been taken off the plane... When he had just enough details for me to know he'd somehow really managed to kidnap you and Chloe... I almost couldn't function."

So many things could've gone wrong. If Ashton had been five seconds later in figuring out that Damien had placed a bomb under the house, they would both be dead.

But they weren't.

She kissed the side of his chest and, twisting around, pushed herself up until she was sitting across Ashton's hips, straddling him. "I say, since we're both so dang grateful that the other is alive and relatively unhurt—and since the baby will be sleeping for another hour—that we should celebrate life."

"Sounds perfect to me."

She saw him wince as he moved his injured shoulder reaching for her. She put a finger in the middle of his chest and pushed him back down.

"But in this celebration, you're going to let me do all the work."

The sudden flash of his bad-boy grin stopped her heart. He tucked his good arm under his head as he looked up at her, heat smoldering in his eyes. Had she truly ever thought this man shy?

"By all means, I would never turn down the request of a lady."

She heard him suck in a breath as she pulled her T-shirt over her head, and felt him harden beneath her hips. She loved that she had this effect on him.

"That's right, you save your strength for figuring out

who this Damien guy is tomorrow. But right now—" she leaned down to kiss him "—right now is just for us."

ASHTON DIDN'T WANT to leave Summer to go back to the hospital the next day, but he knew he had to.

Curtis Harper had woken up. The man had survived the explosion. If Lillian's shot in his shoulder hadn't propelled him across the room, he'd most definitely be dead now.

The rest of the Omega Team wasn't so lucky. Not only had promising young agent Tyrone Marcus died, but a few halls down, Roman Weber lay in a coma, back and arm covered in second-degree burns. The locked door he'd found leading to the crawl space under the house—the one that had tipped Ashton off that they were all in grave danger—had blown off and hit him on the head. For all the damage it had done, it had also probably saved Roman's life, covering him and protecting him from much of the heat of the explosion.

Between Tyrone's death and Roman's severe injuries, whoever this mystery man was who'd masterminded the entire scenario had just jumped to the top of Omega Sector's wish list. Not a comfortable place for any criminal to be. The mystery man had no idea who he was messing with.

But he was about to find out.

But for right now, they had Harper. He wasn't dead, but he probably wished he was. He'd be in the hospital for a long time, recovering from the burns that covered a great deal of his body. And then once he did, he'd be going to jail.

The only advantage to Curtis Harper's injured state was that his fury no longer directed itself toward Ashton. Harper had a much bigger enemy to hate now: the "partner" who'd left him as bait and planted a bomb directly under his feet.

So Harper was willing to talk to Omega. Wanted to tell everything he knew about his *partner* to bring the other man down.

"He only told me his name was Damien. I don't know if that was his first name or last."

Jon Hatton sat at Harper's bedside, now three days after the explosion. It would be weeks, if not longer, before Harper was in any condition to be questioned anywhere but at a hospital. The man was handcuffed to the bed, although the chances of him escaping right now were almost nonexistent.

Jon was questioning the man, but Ashton watched from where he leaned against the window. He wanted to know everything there was to know about the unidentified man who had almost cost him everything. Cost him the woman he loved.

Jon pulled out a copy of the picture they'd gotten from the security camera last Friday when Harper had been caught talking with the other man.

"Is this Damien?"

"Yes. Bastard." Harper spit the word out.

"How did you meet him?"

"I was in a bar, a place called Crystal Mac's."

Jon nodded. "Yes, I know the place."

"We started drinking some beers and eventually we got around to talking about our dads. When I told him my daddy had been killed by someone in Omega Sector, Damien mentioned how much he hated Omega, too."

Ashton's eyes narrowed. So the unknown man, Damien,

wasn't a garden-variety psycho who just wanted to hurt or kill random people. He was targeting Omega, too.

"He told me he could help me get revenge on Fitzgerald—" Harper's eyes darted over to Ashton "—for killing my dad."

"So Damien had the plan from the beginning?"

Harper latched onto the idea that he wasn't at fault for everything. "Yeah, it was always Damien's idea."

"The shoot-out downtown at the florist?" Jon asked. "That was him?"

"No," Harper admitted sheepishly. "That was me. I followed Fitzgerald. And when I saw him stop at the florist, I knew the office across the street would be a good place to set up my hunting rifle. Just like hunting deer."

"But you talked to Damien afterward. Once the police got there and you left."

"Yeah, he caught me and pulled me into a building around the corner. Told me to let him help get Fitzgerald. He's the one who told me about Summer Worrall's place. That I could break in there and finish Fitzgerald off before he even knew what happened."

Ashton turned and looked outside so he could resist the urge to go over to the hospital bed and beat the hell out of an already severely injured man. Killing Ashton was one thing, but Harper had been willing to just rush into Summer's bedroom and shoot them both, even though she had nothing to do with any of it.

That was why Jon was doing the interviewing and Ashton was a member of SWAT.

"And when that didn't work…" Jon prompted.

"Then Damien showed me his planning room. Told me he had a plan to help me take Fitzgerald down. Bastard," Harper murmured again.

But Jon zoomed in on the important thing Harper said. "Planning room? Can you tell us how to get there?"

"Maybe. What will it get me?"

"For one thing, it will get you the knowledge that you helped bring to justice the man who put you in this hospital bed. For another, it gives the District Attorney someone else to throw some blame at once indictments start being handed out."

Harper didn't even try to resist; he rolled over immediately. He gave them the address of Damien's house. Harper had barely finished speaking before Jon and Ashton were heading out the door.

They rode together, calling it in to Omega on the way. This wasn't a location that could be rushed. Only after the bomb squad deemed it clear—after searching meticulously for any booby traps or explosives—could anyone enter.

Even afterward, Glock in hand, Ashton made sure every room was clear. That no one hid in any closet, bathtub or under any bed. He made extra effort to look for any traps the bomb squad might have missed, anything that might not be an explosive, but still dangerous, but found nothing.

The house was clean, at least from danger.

Ashton caught sight of what Harper called the "planning room" in the midst of his sweep, but couldn't take time to study it then. Couldn't even wrap his head around something that complicated.

Then forensics came in to see if they could find anything usable. It was an important part of crime fighting, but waiting for them to finish seemed to take an eternity.

"When Harper said *planning room*, he wasn't kidding, Jon," Ashton told the profiler as they stood at the car waiting for the go-ahead from forensics. "Elaborate is not a strong enough word."

When they were finally allowed in a couple hours later and Jon saw the room, he immediately turned to Ashton.

"Call Brandon Han. Tell him he needs to get over here right away."

Brandon was a genius. Like, certified genius. Two PhDs and a degree in law or something like that. If anyone could make sense of the wall full of newspaper clippings, photos, drawings, police reports, Google search printouts, fingerprints and whatever other unknown pieces of information were on the wall in that room—with different colored strings connecting them all in mind-boggling, crisscrossing patterns—Brandon Han could.

"This thing is giving me a nosebleed just looking at it," Ashton rubbed his forehead.

"Yeah." Jon continued to stare at the wall and its massive amount of information. "Whoever did this is..."

"A nutcase?"

Jon chuckled. "Probably. But also a genius. Harper never had a chance against this guy. He was just a small measure of this man's much larger symphony."

"I don't think I like what you're saying, Jon. A symphony implies that there's a lot more music yet to come."

Jon looked over at him and nodded, gesturing to the wall with his hand. "You're right. Whoever this is, he's just getting started."

Chapter Twenty-One

Freihof watched all afternoon and evening from his true apartment—across the street from the one they were searching—as the Omega team carried out section after section of his wall of clues.

He was glad to see Brandon Han and Jon Hatton on site. He knew the other two men would appreciate the gift he'd left them.

It almost made up for the frustration he felt at the ruination of his original plan. Neither Summer nor Ashton had been killed in the explosion he'd set. Curtis Harper had one simple job to do: get Fitzgerald over to the sofa with Summer. The idiot hadn't even been able to do that correctly.

Fawkes had warned Damien not to underestimate Omega Sector, and Damien could admit that maybe he had. Damien had known the SWAT team wouldn't be far behind Ashton, but he hadn't thought they'd figure out the plan so quickly and adjust accordingly.

The plan hadn't been a total wash. From his visit to the hospital yesterday—and he'd been there right under a dozen agents' noses—he'd discovered that one agent had died and one of the SWAT members was in a coma.

So not the win he wanted, but a win nonetheless.

SWAT weren't the only ones who could adjust accordingly as situations changed. And Damien planned to be in this for the long haul. His next play was already in motion. He'd had plans in motion long before he'd ever even spoken to Fawkes or Curtis Harper.

It involved a different state, different pawns, different victims. But it was still part of the bigger plan. What remained to be seen was if the Omega Sector agents could figure it out in time.

Damien was glad to see Omega was at least taking his clues seriously, moving sections of the wall piece by piece out to the truck with care.

Interestingly, Fawkes was on scene, too, helping load items from inside onto the truck to be taken back to Omega Sector. Damien wondered if that was the man's job or if he'd volunteered when he'd found out what location was being searched. If he worried his own prints might show up.

Damien received a call on one of his burner phones. His business associate from Texas.

"Hello, Mr. Trumpold," Damien answered.

"We're ready to put the plan into action. They need to pay for what they've done."

"I'm glad to hear that."

Convincing the Trumpolds that their brother had been wrongly accused of being a serial rapist, framed by two people in Corpus Christi, had required quite a bit more work than convincing Curtis Harper that he needed to go after Ashton Fitzgerald.

Damien had to doctor some evidence this time, make it look like it was all a setup. But ultimately the Trumpolds had been eager to believe their older brother—who they'd idolized—was innocent of all crimes. And since the man had died very early in prison, he wasn't around to say one way or the other.

A little twisting of the truth, a sympathetic ear and he'd been able to convince them to take their revenge on the people who'd so wrongfully cost their beloved brother his life.

The Trumpolds had no idea that the people they'd be targeting happened to be closest friends with two members of Omega Sector.

Damien spent the next few minutes encouraging Trumpold, reminding the man that he was doing the right thing. The *just* thing. That the mission he was undertaking was a righteous one.

That the mission would also serve Damien's purposes—picking apart yet another piece of Omega—was beside the point.

This time the plan wouldn't fail. This time Damien would ensure Omega Sector knew his pain. Knew the agony of grief.

They'd won once, but they wouldn't again. Damien would make sure they understood pain.

THE NEXT MORNING when Ashton arrived at Omega HQ, Jon and Brandon, along with some of the likable nerds from the forensics lab, had rebuilt the entire "wall of crazy" in one of the conference rooms.

They'd been at it all night and were obviously way pleased with themselves for the exact replica they'd created.

Ashton and Lillian arrived at the conference room at the same time. Ashton shook his head as he entered. "Jon, you're getting married in two weeks. Does the lovely Sherry know you're spending your nights doing such kinky stuff?"

"And with Brandon," Lillian continued, "who if I'm not mistaken has his own lovely fiancée at home waiting for him."

"Our women," Jon responded, "I'll have you know, were very understanding and supportive of our need to get this project situated absolutely perfectly."

Lillian turned to Ashton. "We're going to need to talk to them about enabling."

"Yes, sadly."

Ashton and Lillian sat down at the table to study the wall as Brandon and Jon gave their thanks to the three lab techs who were leaving.

"Can you guys really make sense of any of this?" Ashton asked.

Jon shook his head. "Not yet, but we will. We've already gotten rid of some of the string. It had obviously only been added for confusion."

Ashton and Lillian tried to help, while at the same time stay out of the way, as Brandon and Jon bounced theories off each other for the next few hours. They isolated and narrowed down concepts and patterns—connecting parts on the wall with their own string. The two men identified patterns Ashton couldn't recognize even when they were pointed out to him.

"Both Summer and Curtis Harper stated how this Damien character told them that Omega Sector needed to suffer. To know the agony he'd known. That Omega needed to be forced to know what it was like to lose a loved one," Jon said.

"So it's someone who we've 'hurt' in some way," Brandon said. He sat down in one of the conference room chairs. "You know, we've been working on the assumption that this secondary guy—since he was willing to kill both Harper and Summer—gave them a false name. What if he didn't?"

"Damien Freihof," Jon muttered, shaking his head. He sat down, also. Quiet.

This wasn't good. Ashton looked over at Lillian. She just shrugged. "Who the hell is Damien Freihof?"

"We put him in jail five years ago when he tried to blow up a bank full of people," Jon said.

Lillian scoffed. "There's no way he's doing this from jail."

"He escaped last year." Brandon rubbed his neck, studying the board again. "He's definitely smart enough for this." He threw his hand out toward the board. "And to manipulate Harper into wanting to kill Ashton."

"Has there been any contact with him since he escaped from prison?" Ashton asked.

"Freihof was the guy who took Andrea last year and nearly killed both her and Brandon," Jon explained.

Brandon's voice was icy, his eyes closed, remembering. "He hung explosives around her neck right in front of me."

Ashton flinched. The thought of finding explosives around the neck of the woman you love, as Brandon had, was enough to bring out the hardness in anyone.

"Freihof almost killed Andrea and me both," Brandon continued. "He was injured by his own explosives, but he got away."

"Looks like he might be back," Lillian muttered. "With a definite vendetta to fill."

"Damien wanted to kill Summer, not me," Ashton said. "Harper wanted me, but the second man was always after Summer. The explosives would've taken both of us out. A bonus, I guess."

"Damien Freihof is a psychopath. Completely evil.

But he's also a genius and loves games. Puzzles." Brandon stared at the wall again. "I have absolutely no doubt this wall is his way of giving us clues to keep the game interesting."

"If we can figure them out," Jon muttered.

Ashton shook his head. "That's part of the game, right? If we can't figure it out in time, then we can't stop whatever he has planned."

"Exactly." Jon nodded.

"I'm looking at this mug shot of Freihof." Lillian spun her laptop around. "Granted he was arrested five years ago, but that picture doesn't look like the man we caught on security footage talking to Harper."

All three men studied the picture. "Different facial structure," Ashton pointed out. "Fuller cheeks, hair and eyebrows different. But he meets the same basic height and build so it could be him, if he's got some expertise in disguise."

"It would certainly explain how he's eluded us for so long," Jon agreed. "If he knows how to change his appearance enough to fool facial recognition software."

After notifying Steve Drackett of their fears and taking a short break for lunch, everyone headed back to study the wall again.

By midafternoon, Ashton hated that thing more than he'd ever hated any inanimate object.

"I don't know how they do stuff like this every day," he said to Lillian. "A profiler's life is definitely not for me. Give me a building to rappel down or a window to break through any day over this."

Jon and Brandon, with the occasional help of Molly Humphries-Waterman, Derek's wife and genius in her own right, had narrowed down whatever it was they were looking for until they were studying one small area near the left bottom corner.

Jon walked over and pointed to a newspaper cutting on the opposite edge of the wall. "This clipping is about a playing card company that decided to start using a new type of ace card."

Brandon pointed out another section of the wall. "And the string was attached to these sets of dates: June 3, 2010, June 23, 2011, June 7, 2012, May 30, 2013, and June 19, 2014."

Ashton walked closer to the wall. "Do you think those are crimes? Something happened on those days connected to Omega?"

"We don't think so." Brandon turned to Lillian. "Can you look up Catholic holidays?"

Ashton stared at the wall he couldn't make any sense out of whatsoever. The dates weren't familiar to him at all. "Catholic? Is this guy some sort of religious fanatic? Takes religious beliefs and slants them for his own selfish purposes?"

"No," Jon said. "We don't think so."

"Those are all dates that the Catholic Church has celebrated the Feast of Corpus Christi over the last few years," Lillian said.

"Corpus Christi," Brandon whispered.

"I don't get it," Ashton said. "What does a Catholic holiday have to do with the deck of cards company or our guy?"

"It's not the card company," Jon said. "It's the fact that they have new aces."

"Nueces County, pronounced new-aces, is where Corpus Christi is located."

Ashton might have studied this wall for the rest of

his life and never put those two clues together. "Okay, I'll buy it. And Corpus Christi has something to do with whatever you're talking about down in that corner." He pointed to the opposite edge of the wall.

"It's a newspaper clipping about a restaurant in Chicago that burnt down a few years ago named Wales and Gill," Jon said.

"Did Omega have anything to do with that? Did we investigate or make arrests?" Ashton didn't remember anything of the sort. He wanted to beat his head against the wall.

"No." Jon shook his head, then turned and brought up something on one of the laptops sitting on the table. He spun it around so Ashton and Lillian could see it. "I worked a case eighteen months ago in Corpus Christi. A serial rapist. The local detective who worked the case with me is Zane Wales. The rapist's last victim before he was killed was one of my fiancée's best friends. Her name is Caroline Gill."

Wales and Gill.

"We need to warn them that a madman might have them in his sights. At the very least make them aware that it looks like Freihof is back in the picture and possibly targeting people with ties to Omega," Brandon agreed.

"They're both coming to the wedding in two weeks but that might be too late," Jon said. He had his phone in his hands and was walking out into the hallway.

"Zane, it's Jon Hatton," Ashton heard the man say as he walked down the hall. "Got a minute? I've got some bad news."

It sounded like Jon's friends had been through enough. Ashton hoped this could stop more potential pain for them.

He turned back to the board. "Okay, that's one. We know there has to be more. Let's find a way of beating this bastard at his own game."

MANY OF ASHTON'S days as a SWAT member were physically exhausting. Today had been mentally exhausting.

And honestly, he hadn't even been the one figuring out Freihof's pattern. Just watching Jon and Brandon weave their brains through that psycho's "planning wall" had been exhausting enough for Ashton. Besides Jon's friends, Zane Wales and Caroline Gill, they'd found another possible clue connected to Brandon. His fiancée Andrea's good friend Keira Spencer had been mentioned.

Unlike Zane Wales, Keira wasn't law enforcement. She was an exotic dancer in New Mexico like Andrea once had been. Local law enforcement would be keeping an eye on her.

One thing was for sure. Like Jon had said, Freihof was a master composer and his symphony was just beginning. Exactly how long, how loud or what the next measure would be was anybody's guess.

But Omega would battle Freihof the way they battled every terrorist who threatened the safety of the people and country they loved: together.

Right now, though, the only people Ashton was interested in being together with waited inside the door of Summer's newly renovated condo where he was pulling up. Over the last few days, more and more of his stuff kept getting moved in there. She'd even given him a key. He'd been there with his girls every moment he wasn't at Omega.

Because there was nowhere else in the world he'd rather be.

Eventually they'd have to talk about the fact that they were basically starting to live together. Because that wasn't going to work for Ashton.

Summer would have to marry him first.

She opened the door as he walked up, Chloe in her arms. "The munchkin saw you from the window."

"Ah-ta!"

He grabbed Chloe with one arm and slipped the other around Summer's waist. "I feel like I'm home."

She reached up and touched him on the cheek. Chloe immediately imitated her mother on his other one. "You are home."

"If that's the case, we're going to need a few rules."

The slightest bit of worry fell over Summer's features. "We are?"

"Well, one in particular."

"What's that?"

"You're going to have to make an honest man out of me."

All the worry vanished and a smile that stole his breath away covered her face. "Well, you know if we get married you're stuck with both me and this rug rat for life."

He pulled her closer. "I wouldn't have it any other way."

"Good, because I just hung a new honey-do list on the fridge. In case you haven't heard, my condo lost its handyman."

"Nope." He stepped inside, bringing the girls in with him. "You didn't lose one. You gained one permanently."

* * * * *

It was an argument they could have later, assuming they survived the next few minutes...

It was an argument they could have later, assuming they survived the next few minutes...

"Ready, Becca?"

"One second." She fisted her hands in his jacket panels and pulled Parker close. Her lips met his with an urgency that shot through his veins like a bolt of lightning.

He wrapped his arms around her, bringing her flush against his body. At last, he indulged the fantasy of claiming her mouth. Becca's lips parted and his tongue stroked across hers. The pleasure and heat wove a spell around him. Parker ran his hands up over her ribs, his thumbs following the soft curve of her breasts.

The soundtrack of heavy boots thundering on the stairs brought him slamming back to reality. Breaking the kiss, Becca's taste lingering on his tongue, he pushed open the door and they ran...

RELUCTANT HERO

BY
DEBRA WEBB
&
REGAN BLACK

© 2015 Debra Webb

First Published in Great Britain 2017
By Mills & Boon, an imprint of HarperCollins*Publishers*
1 London Bridge Street, London, SE1 9GF

© 2017 Debra Webb

ISBN: 978-0-263-92931-7

46-1117

Our policy is to use papers that are natural, renewable and recyclable products and made from wood grown in sustainable forests. The logging and manufacturing processes conform to the legal environmental regulations of the country of origin.

Printed and bound in Spain
by CPI, Barcelona

Debra Webb, born in Alabama, wrote her first story at age nine and her first romance at thirteen. It wasn't until after she spent three years working for the military behind the Iron Curtain—and a five-year stint with NASA—that she realized her true calling. Since then the *USA TODAY* bestselling author has penned more than one hundred novels, including her internationally bestselling Colby Agency series.

Regan Black, a *USA TODAY* bestselling author, writes award-winning, action-packed novels featuring kickbutt heroines and the sexy heroes who fall in love with them. Raised in the Midwest and California, she and her family, along with their adopted greyhound, two arrogant cats and a quirky finch, reside in the South Carolina Low Country, where the rich blend of legend, romance and history fuels her imagination.

For my dad, the first hero in my life, who nurtured my independence and taught me to believe without limits.
—Regan

Chapter One

San Francisco
Thursday, October 14, 6:20 p.m.

Rebecca Wallace had an itch between her shoulder blades, warning her it was well past time to get out of the office. She'd turned off the three monitors on the wall, all of them muted, that were tuned to the television network she worked for and their top two competitors. She scrolled her mouse over to power down her computer when a new email icon popped up on her monitor.

She should ignore it. Needed to ignore it. She had a date tonight—the first in months—and she already knew she was going to be late. Late wasn't a behavior she tolerated in others, so she did her best to be prompt as often as possible. Her career as a producer for an acclaimed investigative journalism show frequently put her at odds with her aim to be on time. While the weekly show was scheduled down to the second, when important stories broke, she felt an ob-

ligation to be available to support the stable of reporters the network had in the field.

Knowing the news cycle had wound down for the
day, she exercised self-discipline and shut down the
computer. She would read the email on her phone
during the commute home and then delegate any response if necessary. With a longing glance at her laptop, she left it behind as well. Carving out a personal
life had been one of her primary intentions for this
year. Considering this was only her tenth date for the
year and it was October, she scolded herself for letting an important goal slide.

Deciding the email would wait until the morning,
she set her phone to vibrate and dropped it into her
purse. Her team had the next big story in the works
already. Last week, she and her lead journalist, Bill
Gatlin, had started digging into an anonymous tip
that alleged an elite team of US Army soldiers serving in Iraq had stolen a fortune in gold.

She would have blown off the mysterious lead if
not for the list of six names and the date of the pur-
ported theft. Having been in that same area of Iraq at
the time on a humanitarian story, she and Bill were
each making discreet inquiries about the men impli-
cated and she had tech support looking for a lead on
the sender. Although she didn't care for anonymous
tips, no matter how often they panned out, she knew
people enjoyed the drama and adventure of being
a faceless, nameless source blowing the whistle on
some unpleasant situation.

What she'd die for about now was a tip for a juicy

exposé on local spas. Surely she could find a way to pitch that idea. She'd happily volunteer as the guinea pig for any "undercover" research too. She could already hear the laughter from her team if she made such a suggestion. Her entire MO was leaving the fluff pieces and the half-baked ratings bait to the other guys. The guys who weren't winning awards the way her team did year after year.

She reminded herself that she had left Hollywood for many reasons, not the least of which was to find a place where substance mattered more than the smoke and innuendo of the next dramatic scandal.

By the time she slid into the backseat of the commuter car waiting for her at the curb, her phone had vibrated with another three alerts. Her determination to remain accessible to her team often conflicted with her goal of developing a worthwhile personal life. With a sigh, she retrieved her phone from her purse and checked the various alerts of email and two voice mail messages forwarded from the office.

In the first voice mail, she was pleasantly surprised to hear her father's voice. She'd called him days ago hoping he had a name or some insight on getting around the army bureaucracy she'd slammed up against as she tried to find confirmation on the names listed. Her dad, a legend in Hollywood, had produced and directed movies ranging from highbrow documentaries to summer blockbusters and seemed to have friends and contacts around the world in all branches of business. According to his brief message, he wasn't ready to call in a favor for her. His best advice was to work the story from the ground up.

As if she hadn't been doing that. Well, calling him had been a long shot.

The next voice message was from Parker Lawton, making yet another terse request to meet. She deleted it and shoved the phone back in her purse. Lawton was the last name on the list, and she wanted some solid facts and a better overall picture of the situation and the men involved before they had a conversation. She didn't want a possible thief skewing the perspective on the story.

It infuriated her when the subjects of budding stories learned her team was poking around. Most likely the anonymous tipster had let something slip, unable to keep from making a not-so-veiled threat or suggestion. As a producer, she had to assess the value and impact of a story before they had the facts. After several years on the job, her instincts were spot-on, and the repeated messages from Lawton confirmed her hunch that he had either something to confess or something to hide.

She and Bill had divided the list of names and created a cover story about soldiers returning to civilian life to explain their interest in the six men named by the source. Cautiously checking into Lawton's current situation had been Bill's job. So why was Lawton fixating on her? Her mind stirred it around and around, refusing to let go of work, even as she paid the car service and entered her apartment building in the heart of Russian Hill.

Inside, she locked the door behind her. She kicked off her work heels and dropped her purse on the nearest chair, fishing out her phone and taking it with her to the bedroom. Using the voice commands, she called Bill while she changed clothes for the evening. Her date was taking her to some elite awards gala. He'd been dropping the names of San Francisco's wealthiest and brightest innovators all week, to make sure she didn't back out. She didn't have the heart to tell him she'd already met the business rock stars on his list at one event or another.

"What are you doing calling me? You're supposed to be off the clock," Bill said in lieu of anything as mundane as *hello*. "You told me you were going on the date."

Reporters, she'd learned from day one, were a habitually nosy lot. "I'm dressing while we speak."

A low wolf whistle carried through the room. "Now, *that's* an image."

She laughed. He'd seen her at her best, her average and even her worst more than once when they traveled to remote locations in search of the story. Through it all, Bill had become a hybrid of friend and mentor with a side of big brother tossed in for good measure.

"You don't scare me." She laughed, knowing Bill was far more likely to be picturing her date. "What kind of dirt are you finding on Parker Lawton?"

"Why?" Bill asked, in a whisper. "What did he say?"

Interesting. Bill was a legend in the industry for maintaining his cool in every circumstance. Why was he nervous? "Nothing. The man has left messages for me all day that don't say anything other than he wants to meet in person. His emails are the same. Shouldn't he be calling you instead of me?"

Bill's sigh filtered through the speaker.

"His assistant was a brick wall when I reached out as myself," he said. "So I tried Lawton's personal number. I left him a message as your assistant, saying we wanted to interview him for his perspective on the sudden rise of homegrown terrorism."

Her hand stilled on the hanger supporting the little black dress she'd been pulling out of her closet. "That wasn't the story we agreed to."

"I know." He sounded miserable. "Since he's in the security business, it seemed more likely to get a response."

Though she might not care for the changeup, she couldn't fault his logic. "What else is going wrong with this story, Bill?" Warning bells were ringing in her mind, and that twitch between her shoulder blades was back. "I'm thinking we need to back off and reassess."

"Not yet. I know we're onto something important."

"Where are you right now?" She swiveled around and checked the clock by her bed. Maybe they could meet and tweak the plan before her date arrived.

"Some hole-in-the-wall diner off Pier 80 waiting on Theo Manning."

Pier 80 meant there was no chance she could get there and back, or convince her date to go by the area before the gala. "We confirmed he was the command-ing officer of the team at the time, right?"

"Yes," Bill answered.

"And he's late?" Her intuition was humming. "That doesn't fit my image of a CO."

"He's a civilian now," Bill pointed out. "A crane operator. Late doesn't mean he's changed his mind about talking with me. A thousand things could have happened on the job."

"True." Propping her phone on the bathroom coun-ter, she wriggled into the dress. "Tell me what you've found on Lawton while we wait." Bill might be a ca-pable grown man, but she wasn't going to leave him sitting alone in a diner in a rough part of town until she absolutely had to end the call.

"Lawton's finances and net worth were a big sur-prise."

She unzipped her makeup bag and started adding shadow and eyeliner to go from office to gala-ready. "Is he destitute or filthy rich?"

"The latter," Bill said. "If your definition includes newly minted billionaires," he added in a low mur-mur.

Becca bobbled her mascara tube and it fell to the floor. "What?" Scrambling, she fished it out from under the counter with her toe as she kept talking. "Why did you hold on to that detail? Is private secu-rity that lucrative? Are the others rich too?"

"I didn't lead with that tidbit because I hadn't fin-ished my due diligence. Security might be that lucra-tive. His client list is privileged."

She snorted. "Not legally."

"Possibly legally. At any rate, I'm still trying to find out where and when he made his fortune."

Selling or hoarding Iraqi gold would certainly boost anyone's bottom line, though a net worth of billions seemed unlikely when the gold had been split between six thieves. Or so the source said. Huh. Maybe the source wasn't the victim as they'd inferred from the tip. Maybe their source was bitter about being cut out or shorted of his part of the fortune. "Send me what you have on Lawton right now and I'll help you sort it out."

"Your date won't appreciate you canceling at the last minute," he said.

"I'm not canceling," she promised.

"Oh?" Bill chuckled. "Even better. He'll love watching you google another man between bites of hors d'oeuvres."

She laughed with him. Better that than letting him know how close to the mark his teasing struck. "A personal life is essential to true happiness," she said. She'd written the reminder on a sticky note and kept it on her mirror where she could see it every morning. "Send it. I'll sort it out *after* my date. We can go over everything in the morning."

"Fine. I'll give Mr. Former CO another fifteen minutes and then I'm bailing. I'd rather give the Lawton tree another shake anyway. Maybe money will fall on my head."

"If he tries to bribe you, you'd better share."

Bill laughed again. "Not a chance," he said, and ended the call.

Bill was as effective and persistent as a blood-hound when he caught the scent of a story. Producing for him had taught her a great deal about how to piece together clues, unravel a background and identify the essential nature of what wasn't said in an interview. She liked to believe he'd benefitted from working with her as well. She enjoyed making sure her reporters came across with compassion as well as reliable authority for the audience. Unlike many of their competitors, they never broadcast a story until they knew they had the facts, and she used her specific skills to create a show that kept viewers coming back week after week.

They were definitely onto something with this gold theft story. She added highlighter strategically around her eyes and swept a shimmery powder just above her neckline while her mind sifted through the public records and recent articles on Lawton and his business.

They'd started the research file with the obvious and easily accessible details on each of the names listed by the source. Last known addresses, employers, positive or negative publicity, etc. Returning to civilian life as a security expert wasn't a big stretch for Lawton, who'd served in the army for twelve years. A stash of stolen gold in his pocket would have made it easier to set up shop in the Bay Area, to be sure.

She poked through her makeup bag, seeking the perfect lipstick for the evening. Finding a tube of her favorite soft peach color, she slowly dragged it over her lips. Her mind drifted to Parker Lawton's publicity shot. His thick brown hair had plenty of waves, despite the short cut. The photographer had captured a savvy glint in those serious dark brown eyes. Considering his chiseled jawline, she figured if the man hadn't stolen any gold, he'd definitely stolen more than one heart along the way in his thirty-two years.

Her front door buzzer sounded and she capped the tube of lipstick, dropping it into her evening clutch. Time to make another attempt at refining the rather abstract concept of her personal life. Whether or not the evening went well, it was a plus to have a hot date to an A-list party. She'd even convinced herself she wasn't offended that her date had probably only asked her out in hopes that he'd get an inside track to her well-known father.

She opened the door without looking through the peephole and found herself face-to-face with the man she'd been daydreaming about—Parker Lawton, accused thief. For a moment she gawked at him. She decided the photographer had been a hack to only catch the glint in his eyes. The man's allure drew her in despite his casual khaki work pants, faded blue zippered sweatshirt and black ivy cap. In her heels, she was nearly eye level with him, and the intensity in his dark chocolate gaze muddled her thoughts.

"Pardon me—"

She pushed the door closed on his greeting and he stopped her, wedging his booted foot into the space. "You're *not* welcome here." She gritted her teeth and put all her weight into the effort of squishing his foot.

"Steel-toed," he said calmly. "Can't even feel it. I just want to talk."

"Not tonight. I'll call you tomorrow."

"Pardon my skepticism. You haven't returned any of my calls or emails. Can I have five minutes?"

"No." She shoved at the door again. "I'm on my way out."

"With this guy?"

He stuck a cell phone through the space and showed her a picture of her date at the elevator downstairs.

"What did you do?"

"Bought myself five minutes."

The stunt only confirmed that he was willing to fight dirty. "You have no right to be here." She leaned into the door again, despite the lack of progress. "How did you find me?" She had an unlisted number and the apartment was rented under the network's corporate account.

"It's what I do," he replied. "Look, I've heard someone is trying to cause trouble for me and some friends. Can you just confirm if you're working up a story on me and the men I served with in Iraq?"

Working up a story? Her temper caught like a match to paper. They dealt with facts, not fiction. "I'm a producer, not a reporter," she replied with the last thread of professionalism.

"Not buying the obtuse routine, red."

Red, ha. As if he was the first to try and get away with that nickname. She was far more than the hair and freckles, and many a man had learned that the hard way. "I'll be smarter tomorrow. At the office," she added, clipping each syllable.

He leaned into the door, making it clear he could force his way in at any moment. "Tell me who told you to look into my team."

"Never," she vowed. "That's Journalism 101, Mr. Lawton. I will not reveal a source."

"You're a producer, not a reporter."

"Still applies."

The elevator at the end of the hall chimed an arrival on her floor. "Guess your time's up, Mr. Lawton."

His boot was gone and without it the door snapped shut before she finished the sentence. She opened it again to find the hallway empty except for her date, striding forward with an eager smile.

Clutching her evening bag, Becca did her best to match his pleasant expression while she willed the heat of temper to fade from her cheeks. Her date chattered aimlessly as she locked her door and they walked down the hall. She slid her hand into his at the elevator, knowing Lawton had to be close. Telling herself it wasn't misplaced paranoia didn't change the sensation that the man was watching her. He knew where she lived and she didn't trust him not to try something else.

She clung to the fact that soon she'd be out of his view and his reach. No sane man would dare make a move while she was with her date and surrounded by people at the awards gala. And afterward? The idea of coming home alone sent a little shiver of trepidation down her spine.

Well, she'd cross that bridge when she reached it. For now, she would focus on her personal life. Beaming a high-wattage smile at her date, she set out to enjoy the evening.

Oh, THAT SMILE on her face irked Parker. He hadn't found anything during his recon of Rebecca Wallace, award-winning producer, that indicated a romantic attachment worthy of that heart-stopping dress and killer heels.

He waited until they were gone to move out of the alcove near the stairwell. He was an idiot for confronting her at her door. But he was getting desperate. The bizarre blackmail note had arrived yesterday, claiming media outlets had been notified last week, and granting him five days to make restitution for the gold he and his team stole from an Iraqi family or the men listed at the bottom of the single page would be killed one by one.

Theo Manning, Jeff Bruce, Franklin Toomey, Matt Donaldson and Ray Peters were more than soldiers. They were friends. The six of them shared a bond forged on several challenging assignments during Parker's last deployment. Together they'd handled a sensitive intel-gathering mission near the Iranian border. While it might have been easy to learn they'd all served in Iraq, it shouldn't have been as easy to connect them as part of the same team on that operation.

While they'd been deployed nearby and, through

the course of the mission, had contact with the family listed as the victim, Parker and his team were innocent. None of them were thieves and he in particular had no cause to steal anything, not even back then.

He'd been ready to write off the note as a sick joke until a reporter called the office, asking for his opinion on soldiers successfully returning to civilian life. His assistant handled those comments on his behalf, as she usually did. While he was debating how to investigate the origin of the blackmail note, he'd received a call on his personal line about his opinion on locally grown terrorists. The timing was too close to be a coincidence. Someone had started snooping, and Parker needed to know who'd set them on this wild-goose chase.

Working the situation as he might do for a client, Parker scrambled to carefully reconnect with the men named in the blackmail note. He'd debated the wisdom of warning them about the note and the possibility of reporters and instead had suggested a guys' weekend. He hadn't seen the point in dredging up uncomfortable memories or causing worry over something that probably wouldn't amount to anything.

Then Theo had called back, saying he'd agreed to meet with Bill Gatlin, anchor reporter for one of the top special report shows. It was the red flag Parker couldn't ignore. He'd spent the day hustling up information on Gatlin, Wallace and the network. If other shows had the blackmailer's tip, it seemed Wallace's team had been the first to bite. And Theo's name had been the first on the list.

Parker had been given five days—four now—to return gold valued at over a million dollars. No exchange details or contact information had been provided, only an assurance that Parker would know where to bring either the gold or the equivalent in US currency when it was time. Logic and history said making the payoff was a tactical error, yet Parker planned to do whatever was necessary to keep those men alive.

Having been stonewalled by Wallace's gatekeepers at the network, he'd given up trying the polite approach. While he appreciated that they hadn't run the story on speculation and zero evidence, he didn't have time to play ethics games. He needed the name of the source or some clue he could follow so he could peel back the layers of anonymity and handle the jerk tossing around these outrageous, damaging allegations.

Parker lingered in the hallway, recalling his cursory searches of Rebecca Wallace and her reporter Bill Gatlin. At first glance, they were both workaholics and married to their jobs. He didn't know where the reporter was tonight, but he knew where Wallace was not.

He'd had his boot in her doorway long enough to learn her apartment security amounted to two dead bolts and a chain. Far easier for him to bypass the locks here than get past the systems protecting her office at the network building. He strolled up to her door, pulled his lock-picking kit from the thigh pocket of his work pants and was inside in less than a minute.

A quick survey of the space told him she was tidy,

she spent little time here or she had an excellent cleaning service. He roamed around, appreciating the decor and furnishings. She went for classy and practical, not overdone or overpriced. As a business owner and a building owner, he knew the going rate for a two-bedroom apartment in this area and decided producing for a popular network show must pay well.

The master bedroom felt more lived-in. Though the bed was neatly made and the closet well organized, the various notes she'd left for herself here and there, along with the overflowing laundry hamper, gave him a sense of her as a more accessible person. He couldn't blame her for coming off as a prim snob during their tussle at the door.

The second bedroom she clearly used as a home office and guest room. He searched the desk, found an invitation to a gala that explained the little black dress, but no sign of the lead he needed. If she'd ever brought information on the bogus theft home, it wasn't here now. Leaving the room as he'd found it, he checked the more common and uncommon places people stashed important information. Nothing. She didn't even have a briefcase or a laptop here tonight.

On a sigh, he mentally adjusted his evening plans, knowing the next stop would need to be her office at the network. With his hands fisted in his jacket pockets, he was aimed for the front door when another idea struck. Returning to her bedroom, he found a tablet as well as an e-reader. "Yes!" he cheered softly when he opened the tablet and found her email applications were still open.

He searched through her inbox and the main folders, grumbling when he found all of his email messages moved to the trash folder. Were the days of professional courtesy gone? At least his assistant had handled the initial inquiry professionally while he was still waiting for Wallace to return his calls.

Continuing his search, he learned how she organized her files. He couldn't find a way to access any progress they were making on the story about him and his team, but he could tell it had nothing to do with soldiers returning to civilian life.

Sitting on the blue suede bench at the end of her bed, he searched through her email folders until he found an email from the previous week with Soldiers Steal Gold in the subject line. *Bingo.* The email was written in a similar tone to the blackmail note Parker received. While the author of the email didn't threaten anyone on the show, the names of those involved were the same, and listed in the same order as the note he had tucked into his wallet.

The allegations in the email were ghastly, making Parker's skin crawl. His team had worked their mission and followed orders. The implications—with no evidence to back them up—that he and the others were corrupt, brutal thieves infuriated him. The last few lines and the unique closing really caught his attention. The writer, pleading to maintain anonymity, thanked Rebecca and Bill for their kindness and integrity during their visit to the Iraqi village where the theft allegedly occurred. He—Parker was certain the writer was a man—gave the producer's ego another stroke by claiming Rebecca was the only person who could be trusted to handle this the right way.

The original email was bad enough, but the instructions she added when she forwarded the email to her reporter hit him like a sucker punch.

Bill, reach out to the family. Verify their safety and if/when the gold was stolen. If this is from Fadi, why would he insist on anonymity?

Parker swore. Fadi was a common name. In context with the other details laid out in the email, he couldn't dismiss the possibility that she was referring to the same young man they'd employed as a translator when they were in that area.

Did Rebecca know who'd sent the tip raising questions and spreading rumors about his team? The way he read and reread the email, she sure suspected the tip on the theft had come from the oldest son of the victimized family. No wonder she'd avoided Parker and refused to give up her source. Hell. He wouldn't get anywhere with her if she felt some misplaced obligation to cooperate with the person trying to discredit his team.

Well, he wasn't leaving empty-handed. He had a better idea of where the tip originated from, which gave him a better starting point than he'd had an hour ago. After his service in Iraq, he had people he could reach out to as well. He set her tablet back to the home screen and wiped off his fingerprints before slipping it back into the bedside drawer.

After locking her front door, he let himself out of her apartment through the fire escape and headed home to work the new lead. He needed to find the show with their report from that trip to Iraq and start fitting the pieces together. When he went to her office in the morning, he would insist on hearing everything about her trip to Iraq and why she was so eager to believe the worst of him and his team.

He stalked down the street, needing to walk off the anger simmering in his system. It wouldn't be smart to call for a car or catch a bus so close to her apartment. From his pocket, his phone rang. Seeing Theo's name and face on the screen, he picked up immediately.

"How did things go?" he asked. There was a long pause on the other end of the line and he heard several voices in the background. "Theo?"

"Mr. Lawton?"

Parker froze. This wasn't Theo. "Yes?"

"My apologies, sir. This is Detective Calvin Baird of the SFPD. I'm calling from Theo Manning's phone, as we've just opened an investigation."

A detective's involvement could mean any number of new problems and most likely the work of a busy blackmailer. "What kind of investigation?" He put his back to the wall of the nearest building and studied the action around him on the street.

The detective ignored the question. "According to his phone log, you spoke with him recently."

"That's true." Parker's stomach clutched and his

pulse kicked into fight mode. "Where is Theo? Can I talk to him?"

"I'm sorry to say it, but he's dead," Baird replied.

No. Parker couldn't catch his breath. His hand gripped the phone hard and he slid down to land on his backside as the grief stunned him. He was on the phone with a homicide detective. What had happened to the five days the blackmailer had given him?

"Mr. Lawton?"

"Yeah." He swallowed the emotion choking him. "I'm here. What do you know? Where is he?" *Was.* Theo was gone. Parker cleared his throat. "How did it happen?"

"Nine-one-one received a call about shots fired about forty minutes ago. By the time the responding officers and paramedics arrived, it was too late. I am sorry for your loss."

"Was I the last to call him?"

"According to his phone log, you were one of two people trying to reach him."

"Who was the other?"

"I'm not ready to comment on that yet," Baird said. "I just arrived on the scene and we have very little to go on right now. Do you have time to come by the Bayview Police Station tomorrow morning? I should have more details for you by then."

Bayview? That hardly narrowed it down. The large district covered the port where Theo worked along with the southeastern part of the city. "Yes, of course." Parker knew the drill. If he wasn't a suspect, he was a person of interest. Unfortunately, his alibi was best not confirmed, since it involved his harassing a woman followed by breaking and entering.

"Thank you—"

"Hang on a second," Parker interrupted. "You mentioned gunshots. How did Theo die?"

"It's too soon for the coroner's report," the detective hedged.

Parker stood up, pulled himself together and applied the tone he'd once used to lead others in and out of harrowing conflicts. "He was my CO and a friend. What appears to be the cause of death, in your *opinion*?"

"Unofficially, sir, I'd blame the two bullets in the back of his head."

Parker's vision hazed red. Assassination less than twenty-four hours after he'd reached out to Theo. If the blackmailer thought *this* would motivate him to cooperate, to pay a debt he didn't owe, he was mistaken.

"Officers are canvassing the area for witnesses," Baird continued. "I'm hoping for a better picture of what happened by morning."

"No signs of a struggle?"

"Not at first glance, but we are in an alley."

Parker cringed at the image. "Thank you, Detective. I'll come by your office first thing in the morning." Tonight he had more work to do. He took another minute after the call ended to say a prayer for Theo. Real grieving required time he didn't have right now.

The blackmail note taunted him. Why ransom his

team for gold they'd never stolen and then ignore the timeline? Something was off, and he intended to figure it out before anyone else on that list got hurt.

Chapter Two

The gala wasn't living up to Becca's hopes for the evening. Oh, the glitz and glamour made a visual impact, although her date clearly had an agenda. His conversation revolved around her father's work, and he hoped one day to work with him on a project. The scenario was familiar territory for Becca, who listened with only half an ear as he droned on. If he could pitch his big idea to her father and add a side trip under her skirt, his life would be complete. He didn't say that last part in so many words, of course. He let his wandering hands make his point clear.

She admired the timing and efficiency of the dinner and award presentations, but now, with only dancing, celebrating and mingling on the schedule, her mind kept circling back to Parker Lawton's shocking appearance at her door.

Did he often slum around dressed like a normal person rather than a new-money billionaire? She glanced across the room, trying to picture Rush Grayson, local billionaire and one of tonight's award winners, dressed as a typical workingman. Could happen,

she supposed, squinting a little. She shook off the distraction. How Lawton dressed wasn't the point. He'd
bullied his way into her personal space. She should
report him, except the police would laugh her out of
the station. Everyone presumed reporters resorted
to similar tactics and worse when pursuing a story.

"I'm not sure I like the way you're staring at my
husband."

With a start, Becca turned to see Rush's wife at her
side, smiling and holding out a glass of champagne.
"Oh! Hi, Lucy." Thank goodness it was a friend
who understood Becca could appear more than a little fierce when she was concentrating. "Congratulations to Rush."

"I'll pass it along." Lucy was radiant in a strap-
less ice-blue gown, pride in her husband sparkling in
her dark eyes. "Dare I ask who has your attention?"

"Don't worry. It's not a story. Well, it is, sort of."
Becca clamped her lips together to cease the babbling. "I'm rattled."

"Never thought I'd see it," Lucy said, linking her
arm with Becca's. "Do you need to walk it off?"

"Sure." The warm offer drained a bit of the tension dogging her since Lawton's appearance. "Some
distance from Mr. Grab Hands wouldn't hurt."

Lucy's expression sobered. "Do you need an assist?"

"No. I have plenty of practice brushing off people
who only want to meet Dad." She glanced over her
shoulder to see her date occupied with the men they'd
been seated with at dinner. Eventually, he'd notice

she'd left and come racing after her with an inane compliment on his lips before he suggested a weekend in LA. "You'd think the red hair would make guys like that more wary of the reputed temper."

"The freckles undermine the effect," Lucy said, echoing Becca's theory. "Want me to get him tossed out? Rush and I can take you home."

"Not yet." Becca's gaze meandered as they walked from the ballroom to the mezzanine, where guests milled around between the open bar stations. She searched for a safer topic. "It seems married life agrees with both of you."

"It does," Lucy said. "I know people think I married him for the money, but the opposite is true. He married me for my common sense."

Becca chuckled. Although Lucy and Rush might not have had smooth sailing on their journey to wedded bliss, it was absolutely clear it was a love story.

"You know, most of the serious money in San Francisco is represented right here and some of it is single," Lucy teased.

Most. By reputation or introduction, she knew many of the people in the room. She was well aware of who was loaded, who liked to flaunt it and who preferred flying under the radar. Until tonight, she'd had no idea Parker Lawton had a place among the financial elite. "Do you know Parker Lawton?"

"We've met a few times." Lucy's lips pursed. "Why do you ask?"

"Put away the matchmaker ideas," she said quickly. Some days Becca cursed her rampant curiosity, fostered by her father's habit of giving everything and everyone a fascinating backstory. Unwilling to explain how she'd first heard Lawton's name, she gave Lucy the cover story. "He's local and he's had such success after his military service," she said breezily. "Bill's been trying to get him to sit down for an interview."

"I expected Parker to be here tonight," Lucy said, her eyes traveling over the guests. "I would've been happy to introduce you."

That derailed Becca's wandering thoughts. "You did? Why?"

Lucy tipped her head toward her husband, pure happiness shining in her eyes. "Because Rush invited him."

For a moment Becca's mind reset the evening, inserting Lawton as her date, replacing tepid compliments with witty banter and a discovery of mutual interests. The man probably had a tuxedo tailored to his impressive physique. *Stop it.* His wardrobe wouldn't make any difference, she decided. If he'd been here, as her date or as a guest, he would have harangued her for the name of her source. *Still better than dodging Mr. Grab Hands all night*, a small voice in her head pointed out.

"How do they know each other?" Becca asked.

"Goes back to high school, I think," Lucy replied. "Although I didn't get the impression they were particularly close then. If you need a character endorsement, I'll go on the record that Parker's a stand-up guy."

"Huh." It seemed the safest response Becca could offer. Sticking a boot in her door wasn't a stand-up kind of move in her book, but Lucy didn't toss out character references willy-nilly.

"What's next for you at the network? I know you were eyeing a move up the ladder."

Becca mimed locking her lips and tossing away the key. "I'm happy where I am. Tell me what's next for you. Off the record."

Lucy's lips curved into a smile packed with barely leashed secrets. She drew Becca a few steps away from the nearest guests. "We're expecting," she said, eyes twinkling. She smoothed a palm over her trim waistline as her eyes darted around to make sure no one was watching them. "I'll be showing soon."

"That's wonderful," Becca said. "You must be thrilled."

"We're well beyond thrilled and floating some-where in the galaxy of obnoxiously happy parents-to-be. I feel a little sorry for everyone who knows us."

Becca gave Lucy a heartfelt hug. "You'll be amazing parents. The rest of us will have to get used to a new, impossibly high standard." When she saw Lucy tearing up, she added, "I may just have to tip off one of the gossip sites."

As she'd hoped, her friend laughed out loud and the sheen of tears vanished. "You don't have such low friends."

"Of course I do," she protested. "I just keep them stashed in LA."

Lucy laughed again and, as Rush walked toward them, Becca promised to take her for a spa day soon.

Sipping the rest of her champagne, she made a game of staying out of her date's sight, making new friends as she worked her way around the room. She should just go home, though she wasn't ready to be alone and she didn't feel right about intruding on Lucy and Rush. Desperate for a distraction, she found a quieter spot and sent a text message to Bill, asking about the interview with Theo Manning.

Bill replied immediately, explaining Manning had been a no-show.

She should tell him about Lawton's visit and had her fingers poised to do just that when she changed her mind. He'd only insist she move in with him for a couple of days. Not happening. She'd be better off getting a room here at the hotel for the evening.

When Bill asked, she shared how well the evening was *not* going with Mr. Grab Hands. Welcoming the snarky replies, she was soon chuckling at herself for this latest failure at establishing a personal life. Her eyes landed on Rush and Lucy on the other side of the mezzanine and she sighed.

Love was lovely for them. Becca just wasn't cut out for the interpersonal stuff. She had her career to love. She had a stable of reporters who gave her plenty of ups and downs to juggle. She'd pit a moody reporter against the grumpiest toddler any day of the week. It might not look like a standard life, but it was hers.

Wishing Bill a good night, Becca went to find one more glass of champagne before going to the front desk to book a room. Better alone in a posh suite than home wondering when Lawton would come back and knock down her door.

AT HIS PLACE, Parker finished shaving and dressed for the gala. It seemed every breath was a new battle to keep his grief at bay. With a last check of his appearance, he decided it wouldn't get any better tonight. He grabbed the go-bag he kept ready in the coat closet, added another change of clothes and a rain jacket considering the season. Parker planned to be a much harder target for the assassin who had double-tapped Theo. Packing up his computer, he left his apartment, one eye searching for anyone too interested in the building or himself. He thought longingly of the SUV he'd had armored and knew it was too soon to reveal that asset.

Tossing the gear into the small space behind the driver's seat of his black-and-silver Audi R8 Spyder, he headed out, arriving at the awards gala well past the point of fashionably late. One perk was the lack of a wait at the valet stand. Easing out of the low-slung sports car, he tossed the keys to the valet. He flashed a fifty-dollar bill and pressed it into the young man's hand. "Keep it close. I may need a quick getaway," he said with a wink.

The kid grinned conspiratorially and promised Parker a zero wait time. Didn't matter. With the upgraded locking system, Parker could get into his car without the key he'd handed to the valet.

As he walked through the extravagant lobby, he

scanned the attendees milling about on the mezzanine level. Resisting the urge to tug at his bow tie, he did his best to believe he looked like all the rest of the men in tuxedos. Although he preferred his military mess kit on formal occasions, tonight he needed to blend in with the upper echelons of San Francisco society.

He knew it wasn't wise to pester her again after she'd made it clear she'd speak with him tomorrow at her office. He just couldn't wait. A man was dead, cut down in his prime by a coward who'd ambushed him. Eyeing the free-flowing champagne, Parker hoped to have more luck this time. He deserved a chance to share his side of the bogus story, to counter every unsubstantiated claim in that email.

More important, he intended to make her understand that Theo should be allowed to rest in peace, free of any scandal casting shadows over his honorable service.

She would give him the name of her source by morning, and he would take that information to Detective Baird.

At the top of the wide staircase, he wandered left, bypassing the first two bars and the long lines of men and women in glittering formal wear. Reconnaissance was the first step in getting a handle on the situation and the woman. After two circuits of the areas designated for the event and the acquisition of a champagne flute he was using as a prop, he still hadn't found her.

She was here. He kept his gaze roving, eager for a flash of her auburn hair or those long, creamy legs.

Striving for the patience he used to demonstrate in the field, he planted himself where he could watch the majority of the guests come and go.

At last he spotted her, walking up the stairs from the lobby alone. Where was her date? Her red hair gleamed, swept up off her neck in a sleek twist. The short black dress and sky-high heels with the sparkling straps winding around her ankles showed off her toned legs. At her door, in those heels, she'd been almost eye level with him. Her bright blue eyes, full of defiance and intelligence and amped up for the evening, had captivated him, putting an unexpected sizzle of attraction in his blood.

Forget that. He didn't need her to like him, and he'd blown any possible personal advantage by being a jerk earlier. Now he'd have to adjust his approach. He moved cautiously, using the crowd as cover to follow her when she reached the top of the stairs, so she wouldn't bolt. He wasn't in the mood to chase her around a hotel or out into the chilly October night.

He didn't want to tell her about Theo, didn't want to use his friend's death that way, but he was prepared to fight dirty and play the sympathy card if necessary. He couldn't afford to give the blackmailer any more of a head start.

How to get a stubborn woman to talk? He drifted after her as she aimed toward the ballroom where the dinner and presentations had been held. To save the rest of the men named as targets, he needed to succeed on his first attempt, not flounder around hoping for her cooperation.

His skills didn't run to charm, and with his heart in a vise over Theo, his patience was waning. The best option was to draw her away from the party, isolate her and make her see the wisdom of cooperating with him.

She tossed back her head, laughing at some flirty greeting from a man who appeared at her elbow offering champagne. Then she suddenly turned toward Parker, as if she'd sensed him staring.

Parker smiled, holding his ground while he waited for her to react. Her eyes went wide with recognition. From one second to the next, her initial shock shifted into a glare that would have split him in two if her eyes had been weapons. He merely raised his glass in a silent salute.

She turned away, returning her full attention to the people surrounding her.

He started toward her, taking his time, assessing the people around her as he practiced polite phrasing over and over in his head. She continued to check on his progress, something he found inappropriately satisfying under the circumstances. With growing confidence, he anticipated having her full attention, and the name of her source, before the night was over.

Fluttering her eyelashes at her entourage, she excused herself and moved toward the restrooms. Did she really think that would stop him?

Another man halted her, blocking her path just as she turned the corner. She stepped to the side and the stranger did the same, in that awkward dance of two people who were striving to be courteous.

Parker saw the danger a moment too late. The stranger's startled expression clouded over and he yanked Rebecca around the corner and out of sight. Hurrying through the crowded space, Parker wondered why she wasn't screaming. The woman had put up more resistance against him.

He turned into the corridor only to be blocked by a second man. Younger, trimmer than the first, he was moving into position to make sure no one interfered. *Not your day*, Parker thought. With two quick strikes, he disabled the sentry and pulled him out of sight of the partygoers.

He raced down the hall toward the stairwell, where Rebecca was struggling against the stranger's hold, fighting to stay on this side of the door.

Parker charged forward.

"Halt," the man ordered. "This is not your concern."

Parker skidded to a stop, trying to place the clipped accent. Still fighting, Rebecca glowered, pointing an accusing finger at him, her mouth opening and closing on words she couldn't get past her captor's throat-crushing arm.

"Let her go," Parker said, taking another step. The man pressed a syringe to her neck. Rebecca's body arched violently and then went limp. "No! Stop!" Parker shouted, advancing once more.

The man's mouth twisted into a nasty gap-toothed smile and as he wrestled Rebecca's body into the stairwell, Parker saw a pale scar bisecting his cheek from lip to temple.

Parker leaped into action again. The stranger couldn't have her, not when she was Parker's best chance to identify the person trying to blackmail him and discredit his team. He plowed through the door and straight at them.

Startled, the man shoved Rebecca's limp body at him and raced up the stairs. Parker eased her to the floor and pressed his fingers to her neck. Finding a pulse, he started after her assailant, only to hear the fire alarms go off. He didn't believe for a second that there was a fire, but he was the only person who had good cause to doubt the alarm.

If he left her there, the accomplice could grab her or she might be injured by people fleeing the building with the false alarm. Scooping her up and over his shoulder, he hurried down the stairs, as voices of frightened people heeding the alarms and emergency lights filled the stairwell.

Knowing he couldn't wait at the valet stand with an unconscious woman over his shoulder, he headed for the parking area. "Come on, kid, where'd you put my baby?" Pressing the panic button on the extra fob in his pocket, he waited for the response. When the lights flashed and the horn sounded, he hurried over to the Spyder and punched his code into the panel on the door.

Settling her into the seat and fastening the safety belt, he checked her pulse again before closing the passenger door and sliding into the driver's seat. The engine rumbled at the press of the start button and he maneuvered out of the parking area before it clogged with staff and guests escaping the hotel.

"Just a producer, huh?" Parker snorted as he followed the path of least traffic resistance away from the hotel. "Someone wants you as badly as I do."

This latest unexpected development bothered him. Was the goal chaos or was there a logical end game? All of his training warned him he was dealing with two opponents with different agendas, yet it seemed quite a coincidence that they would attack at the same time.

What he needed was more information from her and about her. He wouldn't get the first until she woke up. There was no telling how long that would take, or if she'd be cooperative when she did. If he could find a safe place for her to sleep off the drug, he could use the time to dig deeper into her past for a possible kidnapping motive.

At the next opportunity, Parker shifted his route to head west. There was a property with an ocean view that he kept as a rental under the company name, complete with a safe room. Initially he'd planned to live there and he'd handled every detail of the security measures as an exercise to see what could be done more than because he feared a home invasion or an attack.

The rental, currently empty, would be their safest bet. He drove around for half an hour until he was sure he wasn't being followed. When he carried Rebecca inside, he took her straight to the safe room and tucked her in on the love seat, covering her with a cashmere throw.

He removed her high heels and cleared the safe room of items she might use against him. He removed any tech that could be used to communicate with the outside world. He didn't want her giving away their position to his—or her—enemies.

With a little luck, in a few hours she'd wake up and they could have a calm conversation without any extra ears or distractions. Armed with information, they could go their separate ways and never have to speak to each other again.

Chapter Three

Becca came awake slowly, her eyes gritty and her throat dry as she tried to get her bearings. The lights were dim and she had the immediate impression of being in a pleasant small sitting room. Someone had removed her shoes, tucked her in and covered her with an incredibly soft throw. The gesture left her wary rather than comforted. What happened?

Easing herself upright, she found herself on a love seat upholstered in deep burgundy leather so smooth it felt like silk to the touch. Not Bill's house. She didn't recognize the space, couldn't name a single friend who had a room like this. Where were her shoes?

"Hello?" Her throat was dry enough that she sounded like a frog. How long had she been here? She called out a couple more times, receiving no answer.

Fear trickled down her spine, a chill under her skin that burned as questions burst through her clouded mind. Where was she? Who brought her here? *Why?*

She stood up and the room turned in a sick, lop-sided circle. Falling back, she let the love seat catch her as she tried to force herself to remember something. Anything. A bottle of water had been placed on the end table between the love seat and chair. Terribly thirsty, she reached for it and then snatched her hand back. The bottle looked new, but that was no guarantee it was safe to drink.

"Think," she whispered to herself. Someone had put her here, and she had no intention of making it easy for them to keep her. She fingered the hem of her dress, vaguely recalling her boredom with her date. They'd been at a hotel. A party. Snippets of the evening floated in a disjointed parade through her brain. A grand staircase, free-flowing champagne and beautiful people twisted in a kaleidoscope that made her eyes ache and her head pound.

When she felt steadier she stood up again. Doing a slow three-sixty, she took in the rest of the room. The space was cleverly designed in a narrow rectangle with a refrigerator, microwave, small oven and sink making up a kitchenette at one end. On the opposite end of the long room was a single door and next to that a set of floor-to-ceiling doors. She walked closer and found a Murphy bed.

"I've been kidnapped by a tiny house architect," she said aloud, imagining Bill's laughter and snarky retort.

This was more luxurious than some of the movie trailers she'd seen while working on sets with her dad. She bounced a little, discovering the floor didn't have any give the way a trailer floor often did. Another tremor slipped over her skin. A trailer could be moved anywhere, at any time. Who would do this?

There were no windows, only a lovely painting of the Golden Gate Bridge spearing out of a thick fog bank. All of the lighting came from LED fixtures in the ceiling. What she assumed was the entrance door was painted the same warm ivory as the rest of the walls, but with the oversize hinges and crossbars, it looked more like a bank vault. She walked over, pushing and tugging at the spoked handle. Her grip was weak; her entire body felt used up and she couldn't make the wheel budge in any direction.

A flat panel on the side of the door lit up and a feminine computerized voice announced, "The status of the safe room is secure."

"Good to know." Becca tapped the panel, and a command screen appeared. Not seeing an icon or a button to unlock the door, she spoke clearly in the direction of the speaker above the panel. "Unlock safe room."

After a moment, the computer denied her request.

"Thanks for nothing," Becca muttered. She walked the length of the room, looking for a switch to make the lights brighter. Apparently that too was controlled by a system outside her reach. Not even the reading lamp on the end table tucked between the love seat and the oversize tufted leather armchair responded when she flipped the switch. "Where am I?"

More silence. Apparently not even the computer had an answer.

She went to the kitchen sink and tested the water

faucet. The water smelled fine and looked clear. The cool water on her hands refreshed her and she blotted her face as well before finding a cup and drinking her fill.

Her memories returned in fractured images. She remembered walking with Lucy, but not what they talked about. There had been a strong man holding her tightly. He'd smelled funny. Odd. Too sweet and strong for a cologne, the odor had made her head swim. Chloroform? Was she recalling fact or was her mind weaving in some fiction?

Uncertain, she crossed to the other end of the room, opening the bathroom door, finding no windows and no obvious escape route. A glance in the mirror had her scrubbing away the mascara smudged and streaked under her eyes and down her cheeks. Noticing a red mark at her neck, she rubbed at the spot, remembering the pinch and sting of a needle before her world went black. Someone had shouted. Who had it been?

"Where am I?" she asked, returning to the center of the room.

"You're in a safe room."

She jumped. This reply was not automated. The voice, as rough as sandpaper thanks to one of those altering devices, filled the room. "Cooperate, Ms. Wallace, and you will be released unharmed."

She heard the unspoken flip side of the statement. If she didn't cooperate she wouldn't be released. "Come in here and say that," she said with all the bravado she could muster. "Show yourself!" Her temper mounted as she waited for a reply. "You coward! It will take more than voice alteration and an automatic door to avoid the penalty for kidnapping me." She needed to keep him talking, needed information about her captor.

"We'll see."

Male, she was sure of that much. Ninety percent sure, anyway. Those voice gadgets could do bizarre things. "Let me out!

"People will be looking for me." She hoped they already were.

There was another long delay before the reply. "Rest. Drink plenty of fluids. We'll talk again soon."

"What do you want from me?"

"For now, I want you to rest."

"Where are my shoes?" She shouted the question at the door and pulled on the handle again. Her frustration soaring to new highs, she smacked the control panel, hoping for a short circuit if nothing else.

"Escape is impossible without the code and my palm print."

She swore at the door and the electronic panel that was currently dark. "Unlock this door."

"As soon as it's safe, I will."

"When this door opens I'll—"

"I understand your distress. You will not be harmed in my care."

Becca shivered. Something about the voice, the cadence of it, felt both familiar and frightening. "I won't make the same promise to you."

"The basics are stocked for you," the gravelly, distorted voice said. "Meals will be provided three times each day."

When left to her own devices, she didn't eat three regular meals each day. "What makes you think I'll eat?" A hunger strike might be her fastest way out of this room.

"Eating is your choice," the voice replied. "But I will not allow you to harm yourself."

"Oh, that's your job, huh?" She crossed her arms to hide her trembling hands. "What do you want? Money?" Had one of her notoriously bad dates gone off the rails in an effort to get her father's attention? "Name your price." She'd gladly give up the password to her untouched trust fund account in exchange for the code to leave this well-appointed prison.

"No," the voice said. "Cooperate and this will be over soon."

Cooperate with a faceless kidnapper? No way. "Buddy, this won't be over until I'm free and you're locked up in a prison cell," she shouted at the ceiling.

The speaker crackled once and went silent. The vault-like door remained closed. Knowing the effort was futile, she walked to the panel and poked at it again anyway.

One dead end did not a hopeless situation make, she told herself, not quite believing it. She couldn't bring to mind any situation quite as bad as this one.

Her father's film company had been detained once in Turkey. It had been a miserable and uncertain forty-eight hours under house arrest, before all the paperwork was considered acceptable to the authorities and they were allowed to leave.

As stressful as that had been, this was worse. Here, she was alone, trapped by someone who had yet to make any real demands. She felt her molars grinding on the tension and forced herself to take a few calming breaths.

She'd survived worse things than this. Turkey had been dangerous. Working the story with Bill in Iraq, right on the Iranian border, had been a huge risk. Anymore, dating was akin to Russian roulette. No way was she going out of this life in the role of a helpless captive.

"What do you want from me?" she shouted at the door.

The silence built and built until she ended it with a loud, long scream worthy of the worst horror flick. Cutting loose, she released all her bottled-up fury into the sound, imagining her captor's ears bleeding from the assault.

He might be in control for now, but there had to be something here she could use against him. Her dad had gone through a horror flick phase and she'd learned a great deal about improvised weapons on those sets. Not to mention all the time she'd spent with prop masters, learning how to fashion amazingly realistic things with little more than duct tape and a good idea.

Her captor had been smart enough to confiscate her high heels. No matter. That was only the first, and most obvious, option. She reviewed the small room through a new lens, with the primary goal of escape.

The love seat wouldn't be much help, unless it had a pullout option. It didn't. She examined every inch of the shelves and the items they held. The CD cases could be sharpened with a little effort.

For at least the tenth time since she'd woken up, she reached for her cell phone and felt that swell of panic when she didn't find it. How pathetic to be so dependent on a device no bigger than an index card. She'd noticed that her captor had also stripped the space of any technology that could be used to communicate with the outside world. Not even a remote for the television remained.

That meant careful planning and forethought. Was all this for her specifically, or just because she was unlucky girl number whatever? She battled back another surge of fear and blinked away the tears threatening to turn into a pitiful sob. She would not let this bastard watch her cry.

Having noticed two surveillance cameras, she retreated to the bathroom, which was the only place he couldn't keep an eye on her. Maybe no cameras in the bathroom qualified him as a decent sort among the kidnapper set, but it did little to improve her opinion of him.

PARKER WATCHED THE woman carefully through the two cameras he'd installed in the room, feeling better now that she was moving around so well. Fighting back was another good sign.

The drug hadn't kept her down long, thankfully. In the two hours he'd watched her sleeping off the effects, he hadn't come up with an acceptable explanation to offer if he had to take her to an emergency room. The only friend with medical training he trusted in a situation as sticky as this one lived in Nevada, and also happened to be the third man on the blackmailer's list.

Her blatant search for something to use as a weapon left him smiling. She didn't give a damn that her captor knew what she was up to. Grit and courage were traits he admired. He shook off the sensation. He didn't want to admire anything about Rebecca Wallace. She was a means to an end and he should stop wasting time coddling her.

If she was strong enough to argue with him and fight with the locked door, she was strong enough to tell him her source. His finger hovered over the communication link before he pulled it back. As soon as he demanded answers, she'd know it was him keeping her locked away. What would he do with the information at half past one in the morning anyway? Better to wait, to learn more about her. He'd prefer to find a way to handle this without exposing himself to a lawsuit or criminal charges.

It was a relief when she ducked into the bathroom and out of his sight, ending his one-sided debate.

There was no way for her to escape. She'd accept that soon enough. Fortunately for him, there wasn't anyone else to hear her screaming, though he hoped she didn't do that again any time soon. The woman had excellent projection and stamina. Rubbing his aching ears, he returned to his search into her background, looking for anything that made her a target.

He glanced up at the monitor when she emerged from the bathroom. She'd let her hair down and he'd bet the clip was tucked in her bra or somewhere she thought to use it as a weapon. Fair enough. When she brushed a finger under her nose, he zoomed in on her face and cursed himself. She'd been crying. In the one place where she knew he couldn't watch.

What had he done here? After a few hours, he was already dangerously close to feeling guilty about locking her in the safe room, even if it was for her protection. Guilt didn't suit him. He assessed and took action according to mission parameters. That philosophy had served him well in the field and equally well in his civilian endeavors. It would serve him well as he tracked down the blackmailer.

Parker pulled the tie from his tuxedo collar, wrapping and unwrapping the length of fabric around his knuckles. He'd mined her school records from high school through college. She'd made straight A's through a tough course load peppered with every form of drama club and literature classes. According to her first résumé out of college, she'd held lead roles in some of the stage productions. He supposed that went along with being the daughter of a powerful force in Hollywood. Those details trickled down and eventually disappeared as she applied for jobs that took her away from Southern California. She'd had an interesting journey to her current post as a producer.

Nothing in the first layers of her background pointed to motive for kidnapping. His mind followed the logic back to his first theory that the scarred man's attempt to take her was connected to the blackmailer and the source feeding the media lies about Parker's team. It wasn't the least bit uplifting.

Satisfied she was alert and out of immediate danger, he felt better about leaving her unattended while he made the quick trip over to her place. She wouldn't be comfortable in that dress indefinitely. Hopefully a gesture of goodwill in the form of clean clothes would be a step in overcoming her justified anger.

With a sigh, he synced the app that would let him keep an eye on her and this condo through his phone. As he changed clothes, he decided the only silver lining was that she didn't seem to remember he'd been around when the scarred man grabbed her. He didn't expect that to last much longer.

BECCA PACED THE length of the room, considering her options. In the bathroom, she'd taken the clip from her hair and broken it in two pieces. One was inside her bra, the other tucked into her garter. She wanted to be prepared if her captor came in and tried something. As weapons, the pieces wouldn't cause much damage, but they might buy her a few precious seconds to get away.

She loosened the zipper on her dress, wishing she could take it off. Although the little black dress was considered a wardrobe staple, perfect for every occasion, she was ready to be done with it. What she wouldn't give for yoga pants and her threadbare college sweatshirt. And some thick socks. Her sheer stockings did nothing to protect her feet from the cold tiled floor.

It was a peculiar experience for her to not know the time. Her entire life revolved around her daily routine. Good grief, she wanted to know the *day*. Was anyone looking for her yet? Had a ransom been issued? Would her captor be demanding payment from the network or her family? She supposed that depended on the reason for taking her captive. If the goal was money, he'd be better off dealing with her directly. She could just imagine her dad ignoring a critical voice mail or email because he had a movie to finish or business to handle.

Tears threatened once more. He'd always been tough, though she knew he loved her. They loved each other. The gap had just become too wide after her mother died. Flattened by his grief, he'd never quite made it back to really connect with her. They hadn't had a real conversation in months, and that last one hadn't been uplifting for either of them. She hoped that terse exchange wouldn't be their last.

Her stomach rumbled and she decided to make use of the basics her captor had stocked. Finding peanut butter in the cabinet and bread in the refrigerator, she used a spoon and made a sandwich. "Good thing I don't have a peanut allergy," she said, raising the sandwich to the camera. "Did you check my medical records?" She poured another glass of water from the tap, not ready to trust the chilled bottles.

She ate standing up, refusing to be caught at a disadvantage. "It really is a good use of space," she said, in case her captor was listening. "Efficient too. Must have cost you a fortune with the design, the build and all the security measures."

Security. The word ricocheted through her brain. Parker Lawton handled security for high-end clients like the Gray Box data storage solution company co-founded by Rush Grayson. Could he be foolish enough to hold her hostage? It wasn't outside the realm of possibility. He had been dumb enough to stick a boot in her door and demand information.

Much as she tried, she couldn't recall seeing him at the party. Of course that didn't mean he hadn't been there, only that her memory was still recovering from whatever drug had knocked her out. If—*when*—she got out of here, if Lawton was the captor behind the speakers and cameras, she would make sure gold theft was the least of the charges against him.

With renewed resolve, she returned to the bathroom and closed the door. This was a safe room per the computer and her captor, making it a safe bet that the room was inside a building. If she could loosen a pipe or somehow cause a leak, that would draw someone's attention. At the very least, her captor would need to come in and repair it, giving her an opening to escape.

She knelt down to peer under the sink, and the lights went out. Biting back a startled scream, she scrambled to her feet and reached for the door handle. It locked under her hand. She was trapped in the dark, half expecting some monster to lunge out of the shower stall, when the deep, altered voice carried through the closed door.

"Time to talk, Ms. Wallace." He was in the safe room, having made his move when he knew she couldn't attack.

She pounded on the door. "Lawton, is that you?"

"No."

It had to be. "Prove it." She hammered another fist on the door. "Let me out."

"In good time. I need some information."

She clapped a hand over her mouth to smother the weak plea that nearly promised him anything in exchange for her freedom. Becca Wallace did not beg.

"If you cooperate—"

"Oh, stop with the threats and get to the point," she snapped, somehow keeping her voice steady.

"Your show has a good reputation."

What? She bit back a sharp retort. Maybe it was her awful date. Surely Lawton was smart enough to know he couldn't win her over with ridiculous, mild compliments. "Good? We win awards, thank you very much."

"How do you decide on ideas for the show?"

The question threw her off. Lawton or the dumb date? "I can assure you we don't let kidnappers dictate our topics."

"Walk me through it," he insisted.

She decided to play along. It was the only way to get clues about her captor. Turning slightly into the door, she tried to imagine the person on the other side. "My reporters usually pitch the ideas. We discuss them in meetings, looking for a fresh angle on newsworthy events."

"How much time to get from idea to broadcast?"

"It varies." Although the device altered his voice, she could tell the sound was originating from a point a few inches above her. More potential proof she was dealing with a man, since she was only a couple inches under six feet tall herself.

Her mind reviewed the men she could remember from the gala, starting with her date and Lawton when he'd been at her apartment door. Her date had been a smidge shorter than Lawton.

"Ms. Wallace?"

"What?" Lost in thought, she hadn't heard the question.

"I asked you how the show handles anonymous tips."

Her opinion swung back to pinning this on Lawton, though if she called him out, he'd only deny it. She had to give him enough rope to hang himself. "Depends on whether the tip is legitimate."

Practicing the same diligence they used on a story, she mentally flipped through the topics and features of their recent broadcasts. One of those had started anonymously, over six months ago. The research and legwork on that one had been grueling, but she'd refused to take the easy and obvious route simply for the sensation factor and ratings. The segment had aired last week with a fresh, objective perspective on a hot-button issue regarding energy costs.

"Is this some convoluted attempt to pitch me a show?" she asked.

"No."

The single word held a sharp edge that had her easing back from the door. Although he'd been polite so far, she had the sense that pushing him too hard and too soon would be a big mistake.

"How do you determine the validity of an anonymous tip?" he said in that same edgy tone.

"I'm not going to reveal my sources," she stated. "You can accept that right now." What if something for an upcoming show had leaked or one of her reporters had rattled the wrong cage? She had to confirm who she was dealing with, and fast.

"Isn't that a protection limited to reporters?" he asked.

"You know we could swing by a court and ask a judge," she suggested. Through the door she heard him sigh. She gave herself a point on her imaginary scoreboard. "What? Aren't you ready to accept the consequences of kidnapping me?"

"Tell me what happens when you get an anonymous tip for a story," he demanded.

"If the story is interesting, we spend long days tracking down confirmations of the allegations. We have plenty of days banging our heads against walls, stalled out when people won't talk to us. Invariably we spend a ridiculous amount of time speculating and hoping for a break. Anonymous sources can be big time and energy drains while we search. Most of the time we ignore them," she finished, hoping he'd believe it.

"If you don't get the break?"

"Without confirmation, my show doesn't tell the story. It sits in a potential idea file until additional and indisputable information comes through."

"Sounds like a strange way to run a news program."

She bristled. "You're a producer now as well as a kidnapping scumbag? Haven't you seen the show? For your information, we deliver content designed to engage and enlighten our audience. My team doesn't chase the daily or weekly news cycle. We choose to delve deep into the issues that matter, the situations—good and bad—that have a lasting impact on our community as a whole."

Silence was the only answer to her outburst. She was getting tired of him going mute. Long minutes of silence combined with the dark surrounding her made her sympathize with claustrophobics. Was he still out there? She pressed her ear to the seam of the door. Only more of that empty silence, not even the sound of his breathing. Maybe he'd left and was just being a jerk about the lights. She twisted the door handle, swearing to find it remained locked. As she'd given him a piece of her mind, he made his complete control of the situation, and of her, crystal clear.

"Let me out of here!" She pounded her fists against the door. "I will flood this room," she threatened.

"You can't," he replied. "I control the water supply."

Of course he did. The idea made her mad and she clung to the anger rather than admit to even a shred of relief that he was still in the safe room with her. "Let me go. You're making a huge mistake. People will be looking for me. Let me go and I won't press charges."

"Have you ever been wrong, Ms. Wallace?"

The question, asked so calmly, interrupted the chaotic cycle of despair and fear. "Yes." She'd been wrong to go to the gala, for starters.

"Have you ever been wrong about a story?" he pressed.

There were too many ways to answer that question, and she refused to have him twist her words around. For all she knew, he was recording this conversation to use against her and the network. "I stand by the finished product of every broadcast," she replied.

"Do you ever identify the anonymous sources?"

Almost always, usually by the process of elimination or when the person had a change of heart. "Sometimes."

"Before or after you run the story?"

This was Lawton. Had to be. She tried to take comfort in the fact that with Lawton as her captor she wasn't at the mercy of a psychopath or pervert or a flat-out madman. Only a thief bent on hiding the truth. Money and power did strange things to people. Even respected, stand-up-guy kinds of people.

"Ms. Wallace?"

"Rebecca," she said. According to the psych classes she took in college, a first name established a more personal bond. Anything for him to see her as a person rather than a useful tool.

"Rebecca." Her name, altered by the device and muffled by the door, sounded so strange. Goose bumps raced along her skin and she was grateful he couldn't see her hands shaking.

"Before or after the story?" he asked again.

"Rarely before the story airs," she admitted. "Some sources are better at disguising themselves." It was so obvious he wanted to know who'd sent the tip about the gold theft. She had her suspicions, but no proof. Just as she suspected it was Lawton on the other side of this door and couldn't yet prove it.

"In what way?"

Would he never give up? "Very few people can resist their fifteen minutes of fame. Aside from that, the bigger the story is, the more options there are for the source. Usually, though, with sensitive information, only a few people have access and we can figure it out, if only by process of elimination. I prefer..." She didn't finish the sentence as her temper flared to life again. She preferred a normal interview style. She preferred having civilized conversations.

"You prefer what?"

"My preference is to have all of our sources sign a statement with the network, under the agreement that we will never expose them. In my opinion, that choice gives them more credibility."

"Thank you."

"Does that mean I'm free to go?"

"In due time," he said. "I've done all I can to make

your stay pleasant. You'll find a meal in the kitchen. Feel free to make use of the Murphy bed."

"Wait. I don't want to stay." She gripped the door handle in both hands and tugged mightily, willing it to move. "Wait!" she cried again. "I won't tell anyone about this," she pleaded. "Please, let me go."

He didn't answer. A moment later the computerized voice announced the safe room was secure.

"Yippee." The bathroom door was still locked. She dropped her forehead to the door and debated the pros and cons of crying again. Would he see that as a ploy or a weakness?

Before she could decide if she had any tears left to cry, the lock clicked and the door opened when she turned the handle. She stepped out into the room and found herself alone. The homey aroma of pancakes and bacon wafted through the space. Was it really morning, or was he messing with her idea of time? She forgot the food when she saw the small black suitcase in front of the love seat. She reminded herself that although it looked familiar, most black suitcases did.

Becca walked over and flipped the tag and felt another spike of fear. The luggage tag sporting the network logo was hers. And on the other side of the handle she found the white daisy sticker she applied to make her black suitcase stand out from all the others.

Her brain slid into a panicked loop that she was in more trouble than she realized. It didn't matter if it was Lawton or someone else. Her captor had too much access. He'd not only been to her apartment, he'd been *through* it. He'd gone into her closet and found her suitcase and presumably packed it with her belongings. As if being held against her will wasn't enough of a violation.

Becca backed up and sat down in the chair, as far from the suitcase as she could get without returning to the bathroom. She didn't want anything he'd touched. The little black dress would do just fine for now. Forever, she added, glaring at the suitcase. And that was a dumb idea. If she cooperated, maybe he would relax his protocols. She had to make him think he was winning.

Resisting the sensation of complete helplessness, she finally unzipped her suitcase. He'd been careful here too, as if he knew how a woman's mind worked when she was cornered. He wanted to make her stay pleasant? Well, she didn't have any intention of *staying* a moment longer than necessary.

There were jeans, T-shirts, pajamas, bras and panties, socks, tennis shoes and a zip-up sweatshirt. Her travel bag of toiletries and makeup was tucked in place as well. He'd touched it all. While she was grateful to have her own things, she couldn't shake the feeling it was all tainted by the man who'd rooted through her home, her most private and personal spaces. She rubbed the chill from her arms. This situation was unpleasant, not impossible. He'd promised not to hurt her. She hadn't made the same pledge.

Shifting to block the view of the camera perched in the corner near the door, she quickly opened the pocket of her suitcase where she kept a multitool stashed. Since she always had to leave the one in her purse at home when traveling, she'd purchased an extra and kept it in her suitcase. The pocket where she stowed it was empty. He'd thought of everything.

She sat back on her heels, reluctant to admit defeat. "I'll find a way out," she whispered to herself. "I am strong and smart." Her voice cracked on the affirmation, so she repeated it until she believed it.

Chapter Four

At precisely eight o'clock Friday morning, Parker turned in his room key at the front desk and walked out of the midpriced motel in the Mission District. He hadn't slept more than an hour in the last twenty-four, and he was running on adrenaline and strong coffee.

Couldn't be helped.

Until he had a handle on this situation, he wouldn't go home again or stay more than one night in the same place. Likewise he didn't want to bring attention to Rebecca's location by staying too long at that property. Before he'd left the motel room, he'd checked the app to confirm she was still well at the safe room. He'd spent the last hour answering emails for her so no one at her office would ask questions too soon.

With the strap of his duffel slung across his chest and a worn briefcase in the old army digital camouflage pattern packed with Rebecca's cell phone and tablet as well as his devices, he stood at the valet stand and waited for his ride.

He owned three cars and stored them in various locations around town. Hours ago, he'd called in a favor and moved the Spyder away from prying eyes to the safety of Sam Bellemere's garage. The cofounder of Gray Box owned an entire building and had devoted one parking level to his car collection. Though driving on his own would be more convenient, Parker didn't want to make things too easy for whoever had set this mess into motion.

When the driver arrived, Parker climbed in and gave the address for the Gray Box offices. He figured it was the safest place in town to stow the personal belongings without undue questions. Then it would be time to meet Detective Baird at the Bayview station to discuss any progress on Theo's murder.

"I'll only be a minute or two," he said when the driver pulled to a stop in front of the building. He handed over the fare and a hefty tip. "Wait for me?"

"Yes, sir."

True to his word, Parker returned to the car without the bags within five minutes. His friend Rush Grayson, founder and namesake of Gray Box, had no problem stowing the gear for any length of time. Aside from the men Parker had served with, Rush and Sam were the only people Parker counted as friends and trusted implicitly. The pair had been instrumental in helping Parker manage a surprise windfall inheritance while Parker had been serving overseas and they'd worked on several projects together since Parker opened his security firm.

Armed only with his phone, Parker used the security app to check on Rebecca again. Switching up the camera access, he checked the street outside the building as well for any signs of trouble. Thankfully, everything remained clear for now.

For a man known for making reliable, intelligent choices even in the heat of a gunfight, he kept doing everything wrong this time. Rebecca wasn't afraid of him. She hadn't called him by name yet, though he had to be at the top of her suspect list. If he'd been thinking clearly, he would have walked into the safe room and asked her outright about her source and her plans for the gold theft story. Then, assuming she hadn't attacked him, he could have persuaded her to stay in the safe room and out of danger while he went after the culprit.

Sorrow and lack of sleep weren't good enough reasons for his flawed decisions. Saving her from the real kidnapper last night was fine, but until he identified the man and the threat, he could hardly use that moment as evidence of cause and sound reasoning for keeping her locked up.

At the Bayview Police Station, he thanked the driver and tipped generously again. Logically, he knew life's scorecard rarely balanced, and even if it did, Parker knew it would take far more than a couple big tips to offset holding Rebecca Wallace against her will.

He pushed back against a fresh wave of guilt as he walked into the station to speak with the homicide detective who'd caught Theo's case.

Detective Calvin Baird was tall and lean, with

ebony skin and close-cropped hair going gray at the temples. He shook hands with a firm economy of motion and encouraged Parker to have a seat in the chair by his desk.

"How are you holding up?" Baird asked.

"Theo was a good friend of mine," Parker began. "We served together in Iraq," he added. "Both of us grew up in and around San Francisco, but we didn't meet until the army introduced us."

"Small world," Baird said, nodding. "We have a fairly clear picture of what happened last night. No suspects so far. I assure you we will be digging deeper, interviewing witnesses and such. I'm sorry you lost a friend."

"Me too." Parker sat forward. "What do you know?"

"According to his coworkers, he planned to meet someone at a diner a few blocks from Pier 80. His shift ran late and he decided to walk it. After that, it appears someone came up behind him, shot him twice in the back of the head and pushed or dragged his body into the alley."

"Theo never had a chance?" That didn't make any sense.

"That's how it looks right now. We're still processing evidence and creating a timeline."

Parker could see the question in his eyes. "I wasn't anywhere close to that neighborhood yesterday." He pulled out his phone and sent a text to the office. "I'll have the office send over my itinerary so you can corroborate."

"I didn't ask," Baird pointed out.

Parker shrugged. "Gotta cross the *t*'s and dot the *i*'s, right?"

"Right." Baird leaned back. "Were you aware he was on his way to meet with a reporter at that diner?"

"No," Parker replied. "Was the reporter the other phone number on Theo's call history?"

Baird nodded slowly, his dark gaze inscrutable.

"No idea who called nine-one-one?" Parker asked.

"None," Baird replied. "When SFPD arrived, your friend was alone and deceased."

Parker struggled to stay seated and calm. He felt as if he could punch through cinder block about now. "He deserved a better exit from this world."

"Most of us do," Baird said. "The reporter came in when I called him earlier this morning. He didn't volunteer much about the interview topic, but he did help us with the timeline."

Parker hid his surprise over the reporter's cooperation. "Are you thinking the interview made Theo a target?"

"Anything is possible." Baird tapped his fingertips on the file. "The deviation in his routine might simply have put Mr. Manning in the wrong place at the wrong time. It's a rough neighborhood. I'm afraid it's too early to tell, unless you care to shed some light on why they were talking."

"Could be anything, I suppose." Parker propped his ankle on his opposite knee, deciding on the best way through this prickly situation. "I'm ashamed to say Theo and I hadn't seen each other recently. Didn't stay in touch as much as we should have. Overseas, we were tight. Had to be. Once we were home, we drifted apart."

"It's natural," the detective interjected, the weight of experience in his voice.

"It is." Parker met Baird's steady gaze and realized the detective really did understand. "How long did you serve?"

"Ten years in the navy," Baird said, sitting up straighter. "Another ten in navy reserves."

Parker relaxed a bit. "Doesn't make me feel any better for only reaching out to Theo a few times a year. I don't really know enough about his day-to-day life to give you a good picture of him. He didn't have any enemies during our service. Everyone liked him. Can't imagine that changed in the civilian sector. He was a good man."

Killing Theo made no sense. Why strike down anyone on the list before the ransom deadline? Whoever was pulling the strings had to know that wouldn't make Parker eager to cooperate. He had three days left to figure it out.

"I'm hearing the same. We will work this step-by-step," Baird promised. "I'm good at my job, Mr. Lawton, and I close cases. Someone has the information we need. If you think of anything else, give me a call." He handed Parker a business card.

"You got it."

Parker didn't bother pointing out Theo had been trained in enough forms of combat from hand-to-hand to rocket-propelled grenades that he might as well have been labeled a walking weapon. Baird would know that with one look at Theo's service record. The killer who'd managed to shoot him in the back of the head must have known that as well. A swift, silent surprise attack had been the best chance for success.

"Has next of kin been notified?" Parker asked.

Again, Baird consulted his notes. "His brother is on the way from Arizona. I expect the body will be released soon."

"Will you pass on my number?"

"Of course," Baird assured him.

With a handshake, Parker left the police station, the muscles in his jaw tight with frustration. Outside, he checked the app, confirmed Rebecca's status and put his mind back on his own investigation. There had to be a point where the bogus gold theft story, the blackmail note, Theo's killer and Rebecca's kidnapper intersected.

Using public transit this time, he crossed town to the network building and asked to speak with Rebecca. When they gave him the out-of-office message and expected return date he'd sent on her behalf through her email, he left his name and number and went on to Gray Box to pick up the gear he'd dropped off.

Rush, noticing his return, invited him upstairs for a quick word.

"Everything okay?" Rush asked when they walked into his office. "I noticed you were late to the gala and left without saying hello last night. Coffee?"

"Please." Parker stifled an oath. Hopefully Rush

was the only one who noticed. "Congratulations," he said. "Sorry I missed your speech."

Rush laughed. "You've heard one acceptance, you've heard 'em all." He handed Parker a mug of black coffee and sat down on the long, modern couch in front of the windows that offered a stunning view of the city. "What kept you?"

Knowing that the closer the lie was to the truth, the easier it was for the liar, Parker sat down and told him about Theo. "They called me from the scene, since my number showed up in his recent call history. It shook me up."

"Sorry, man. Are you all right?"

"Not really." Parker shook his head and dropped his gaze to his boots, startled by the sudden wave of emotion threatening to pull him under. He had to keep his cool or be faced with increasingly uncomfortable questions. "Theo was one of the good guys, you know? I'm sad I won't talk to him again and I'm pissed off that he survived a few war zones only to get shot in a stateside alley."

Wisely, Rush only nodded his agreement. It hadn't been that long ago that Rush was up to his eyeballs in unfair and dangerous circumstances. He'd called Parker to dig up dirt on his wife's former employer, who turned out to be wanted for war crimes. The man had given Lucy a terrible ultimatum: steal information from a secure cloud account at Gray Box or her sister and nephew would die. Although Parker trusted Rush and his partner, Sam, he couldn't drag them into the mess he'd made.

"You know Sam and I would do anything for you, Parker?" Rush waited until he had his full attention. "Without you, we might not even be here."

Parker wasn't here for praise. Yes, he'd lent his expertise to both Rush and Sam recently. He'd handled the building security and assisted in a couple of sticky situations. Without the sage financial advice of Rush and Sam, Parker wouldn't be independently wealthy today. Unbidden, a small voice in his head wondered if being an average guy might have prevented this situation.

No sense leaping down that rabbit hole. Better to play the cards he'd been dealt than waste time and energy on the what-ifs. The money had been a blessing, empowering him to change his life as well as the lives of those he employed. He couldn't allow one coward wanting a chunk out of his bottom line to spoil his outlook. He had to stay locked on to who he was, not how he was viewed—a lesson he'd learned on his military operations.

Deciding to make use of the time Rush had given him, Parker changed the subject. "What do you know about Rebecca Wallace?"

Rush's eyebrows arched in surprise. "Looking for an introduction?"

What was it about marriage that turned perfectly sane men turn into matchmakers? He dismissed the notion of playing along. "That's not what this is." She wouldn't have him anyway once she figured out he was the man holding her hostage. Why did that awareness annoy him? "The detective on Theo's case told me he was killed on the way to his meeting with one of the top reporters on the show she produces."

"All right." Rush frowned as if choosing his words carefully. "She's smart as a whip. Born and raised in the movie business in LA. Seemed to cause a stir when she moved up here, out of her father's shadow."

"You like her?"

"And I respect her," Rush said. "She knows the value of ratings, but she and her reporters get the facts straight. You were overseas when her show first featured Gray Box. She did another segment when we moved to this building. In both interviews her reporters asked tough questions and the end result was candid and overall positive publicity."

Parker didn't take the endorsement lightly. Rush and Sam, with their checkered pasts, hadn't always been treated fairly by the press. Now Rush and the company were big enough to effectively control any issues that might become problematic. It helped that his friends ran a clean business and maintained a product that remained impervious to computer hackers.

"Did you go to her?"

"No." Rush sipped his coffee. "Her reporters came to me."

"Why?"

"Why?" Rush echoed the question, clearly startled. "Sam and I were news. Our start-up made a splash, had huge success, and now we're investing in the community."

Parker hated lying to Rush after everything they'd

been through. "I can't think of anything newsworthy going on in Theo's life."

"You could ask her," Rush pointed out. "I can make a call and get you into the office."

Parker shook his head. "Thanks anyway. I've called. She's out of the office. Her reporter hedged with the cops. He won't be any more open with me."

"No ideas why your friend was meeting with her reporter?"

Parker shook his head again, staring into the dark coffee in his mug.

"But you're going to look," Rush said.

"Wouldn't you?"

"I have. You remember what happened when the gossip columns declared Sam married to a woman I didn't know. Lucy and I went over immediately armed with champagne and doughnuts."

"And you called me." Parker had been armed with deadly weapons when Rush asked him to help keep an eye on the newlyweds.

"Turns out it was the right call." Rush leaned forward. "We weren't soldiers, but we have skills and resources. Connections, too. If you need us, Parker, *ask*."

He knew Rush, in business mode, was renowned for his savvy, his sound strategy and his ability to apply the right amount of pressure to a decision moment. It had been a long time since Parker felt someone could see through his defenses. "It's personal," he admitted.

Rush waited him out.

"Or it's a random crime and nothing at all," he added after another minute of internal warfare.

Rush leaned back and stretched his arms across the back of the couch as if he had all day for Parker to choose between opening up and walking out.

"I have it under control," he said, standing up. "Thanks for the coffee, the ear and the insight on Wallace. If there's a point when I'm in over my head, I'll let you know." He hoped it wasn't obvious how close he was to sinking right now.

"You're the most capable man I know." Rush stood up and extended his hand. "But seriously, anything you need, just name it."

"There is one thing." Parker weighed the pros and cons of doing some of his work here. He didn't want his problems to blow back on Gray Box. It was no secret they contracted with his firm, so spending time here shouldn't raise any eyebrows. "Do you have a computer I could use to do some investigating—off the grid?"

Rush grinned with pride. "You know you're in the right place."

Parker followed Rush downstairs to an available cube on the cyber security level, just around the corner from Sam's high-tech and intimidating work space. He started his search by scouring Rebecca's cloud storage files for notes from the trip to Iraq. No anonymous sources on that story. She and Bill had gone looking for success stories between the US military and Iraqi communities and found several to use in their feature.

Her notes were peppered with locations, names, anecdotes and pictures, and once more he felt admiration and respect for her. Not for her, for her approach, he reminded himself. She and Bill had gone out of their way, two people and their crew on a morale-building tour that seemed to have positive effects. Knowing he had to get a hot meal over to her in the safe room, he transferred the rest of the Iraq files to a thumb drive for later review. If there was an overlap, it would surely be there.

When he skimmed through the broadcast history of the show, he noticed the way she balanced hard-hitting pieces with more upbeat, feel-good stories. He discovered Rebecca was just as Rush had described her. Tough, fair and thorough on the job, she let her reporters go for the jugular, but only after they'd done the research to prove the legitimacy of their approach.

He skimmed background notes on stories that were initiated with vague anonymous claims and confirmed she'd answered him honestly about how they proceeded and verified the facts in those situations.

Although he was glad to learn she hadn't lied, he wasn't happy that Theo died, likely caught in the cross fire of the typical verification process. Reading through her emails with Bill about the gold theft tip, he saw that between the two of them, they had tracked down current addresses and phone numbers on all the men listed.

Parker thought about asking Sam to look for any evidence of a hacker monitoring her email and decided against it. He couldn't abuse the friendship by asking Sam or Rush to get actively involved, just in case she did manage to drag him into court over kidnapping her.

Someone wanted the gold theft story out there, and someone, other than him, was willing to kill to be sure it wasn't told. He forced himself to look at the situation strategically, turning it over to view it from all sides as he'd done during his military days. It was possible the source had used Rebecca to flush out Parker and his team and take them out. The theory left a bad taste in his mouth and left him wondering if the blackmail note was designed to accomplish the same thing. Neither theory explained going after Rebecca.

Taking advantage of working in an area where the signal couldn't be picked up by any outside surveillance, Parker picked his way through her cell phone apps and records for a look at her life and habits. Her life seemed to revolve entirely around her work. Aside from her trips to the grocery store and gym, there were only a few calendar entries that might qualify as dates. Even her social occasions were driven by network or community events like the awards gala last night.

This wasn't his first time evaluating a target. Gathering and assessing intel and habits, despite the obvious privacy violations, created a better picture and revealed potential weak spots. Still, when he sat back and rolled the tension out of his shoulders, he wanted a shower to scour away the sensation that he'd been digging too deeply into her personal space.

"First time for everything," he said under his breath.

He blamed the bulk of his discomfort on the guilt of yanking her out of her life. Who was he kidding? The guilt was bubbling up because every time he peeled back a layer, he actually *liked* the woman more and, as Rush had said, he respected her work. She didn't allow her personal bias or that of her reporters into any of the finished broadcasts, though it cropped up in the planning stages.

Shutting down her tablet and phone, he packed up and forced himself to consider how to release her. He didn't want to let her go immediately. The risks were still too high. Yet he couldn't keep her locked in the safe room indefinitely, ignorant of why she was there, even if *he* thought it was the best place for her. Without undeniable proof that keeping her out of sight was best, he didn't stand a chance.

Outside, waiting on another rideshare driver, Parker checked on Rebecca once more. She wore faded jeans and a pale T-shirt and her feet were bare. Tucked into the armchair, she was munching on a meal bar. She had a pad of paper balanced on her up-drawn knees, and the pencil in her hand flew across the page, her head tilted to the side. For a moment, he did a double take, then recalled it had been in one of the pockets of her suitcase. He supposed a television producer raised in the movie business would have learned how to draw if only for storyboards or blocking sets, or to fulfill any number of new terms he'd learned since poking through her life. Curious, he made a mental note to check camera angles, in case she left the pad open.

When the driver arrived, he gave the address for another generic midpriced motel near the airport. Once there, he booked a room for the night under a fake name and credit card and stowed his belongings. Armed only with his cell phone and a 9mm pistol at his back, he called a cab for the ride to the west side of town, grabbed a burger and milk shake and walked to the condo where Rebecca was hidden.

He used the cameras to verify her position in the safe room and then shut off the lights, plunging the room into darkness. A moment later, he hit the microphone and used the voice alteration effect to order her into the bathroom.

"No."

He took his finger off the mic and sighed. He was too tired to fight with her. "Cooperate, Rebecca," he said, trying again.

She held her ground, standing in the middle of the room, hands on her hips, a defiant glint in her eye. Since he'd last checked on her, she'd pulled up her hair in a messy ponytail. "This has gone on long enough," she said. "People are looking for me, Lawton. Let me out."

So she knew. Or was willing to try and convince her captor that she knew his name. What was he thinking? He *was* her captor. He thought of the man with the scar who'd tried to take her. The memory put a bite into his voice when he said, "No one is looking for you." No one she wanted to find her, at any rate. "Into the bathroom."

"On one condition," she said.

"You're not in a position to negotiate."

"Don't lock me in this time. Please," she said, staring up at the camera near the door.

"Fine." He caught the flash of a triumphant smile before she turned and hurried to the bathroom. Her mind was working overtime on some angle.

When she reached the bathroom, he opened the safe room door only enough to slide the food through. Then he closed it and locked it, even as she ran across the room. He brought the lights up and turned off his mic.

"Yes!" She did a fist pump and picked up the burger and milk shake. "Thanks," she said, tossing another look at the camera before returning to the armchair with her food. "Is it lunchtime?"

He didn't reconnect the mic, just watched her happily devour her burger.

"No Q&A today, Lawton? What day is it?"

He stayed at the condo longer than he'd meant to, listening to the questions she hurled toward the ceiling while he studied her carefully. The woman was definitely up to something. He smiled, surprised how much he anticipated their next meeting.

BECCA SENSED HE was done talking to her. She suspected he might even be gone already, but she kept up a one-sided conversation just in case. He hadn't denied it when she called him Lawton. Of course, he hadn't confirmed it either. *That* would have been too much to ask.

What he had confirmed, bringing her a burger topped with sautéed mushrooms, Swiss cheese and mayo with a side of fried pickles and a chocolate-cherry milk shake was that he'd been poking through her life. Once a week, she splurged and ordered this lunch through an online app from her favorite family-owned burger joint near the office.

She wanted that to mean she was being kept near the office, and knew better than to jump to that conclusion. It was safe to assume from the hot burger and thick, cold shake that she was still in San Francisco.

"Consider this another offer to buy my way out of here. You have learned by now that I'm loaded, right?" As a new billionaire, Lawton wouldn't care about money. "I hope you didn't call Daddy. He's far too busy to bail out his daughter, even from a kidnapper."

She ate for a few minutes in silence, wondering what kind of conversational bait to dangle next. She wanted to keep him talking. Not because she was bored or lonely. That would be the definition of pathetic. No, she wanted him to talk so she could worm under his defenses and get out of here.

"Hey, Lawton, did I mention that I called him when I got stonewalled by the army?" She twirled her straw through the milk shake, grinning at the silly noise. "He has all kinds of friends in strange places. I thought he could help me get a more comprehensive look at your service record." She popped a pickle into her mouth, enjoying the tangy flavor. "Don't worry, your secrets are safe. He didn't help. Dad doesn't believe in favors or handouts."

Not for daughters who flew the nest anyway.

"Are you even there?" she asked, peering at the camera again. At the continued silence, she polished off the burger, cleaned up her trash and returned to the chair.

Picking up the notepad again, she flipped over a new page and started drawing, letting her thoughts wander aimlessly. When she paused to stretch her hand, she realized she'd filled the page with sketches of Lawton.

The first was a detailed picture of his face when he'd been at her door, the ivy cap pushed back from it. Another one was a recreation of his head shot from his security firm's website. She'd drawn how she imagined he would look in a tuxedo. No, wait. That wasn't a guess; that was how she'd seen him at the gala. She picked up the pencil again, scrambling to get the images on the page as they flooded back into her mind.

As she sat back again, several faces stared back at her from the notepad. The happy expressions of Rush and Lucy, a man she didn't know with hard eyes and sharp features, and another man with a scarred cheek. But the face she couldn't look away from was Lawton's. She'd sketched him with eyes wide, lips parted and worry stamped on his forehead. He seemed to be pleading with someone. Could he have been begging her to drop the story?

She knew it was a memory. Now she just had to figure out what it meant and where it fit in with her previous recollections of the gala.

Chapter Five

Leaving the condo, Parker walked for several blocks, stopping here and there along the way and doubling back at one point to confirm he wasn't followed. Satisfied, he moved forward with his plan to pick up the SUV registered in his name. With luck, Theo's killer had eyes on the car and picking it up would draw out Parker's enemy. He couldn't develop an effective strategy or counterattack until he knew if he was up against one man, two or a team.

There had been two men at the hotel. He just didn't know if the sentry was a local hire or into this as deeply as the man with the scar. In Parker's experience, that snarl and the delight in his mean eyes when he'd put that syringe to Rebecca's neck added up to a man who enjoyed his work.

Feeling comfortable and confident behind the wheel of his own car, Parker had watched his mirrors for any sign of a tail as he cruised through the city, eventually reaching the pier where Theo had been a crane operator. He had two and a half days left to unravel this mess, and he didn't want to lose any other friends along the way.

He'd come down to ask questions about Theo's last days, hoping one of his coworkers would give him a new lead to work with. No one had seen Theo chatting with strangers. None of his friends on the job thought he'd been behaving strangely or showing signs of stress. Everything had been situation normal for Theo until he'd been shot.

Parker walked from the pier toward the diner, daring either fate or the killer to take a shot at him. It was an idiot move, especially if Theo had been in the wrong place at the wrong time and a victim of local crime rather than the blackmailer. Passing by the alley again on his way back to the pier, he paused and stared at the fresh bloodstain about ten feet from the sidewalk.

It was too easy to picture Theo dead before he hit the pavement. The man had crossed the world going from one mission to the next, always willing to get in the trenches and get dirty and always eager to contribute to get the job done.

No one took a shot at Parker. No one spoke to him, though there were people milling about across the street and on the corner. He decided to leave the witnesses to the professionals and stalked back toward the pier.

Returning to his SUV, he watched the cargo ships and port crews work while he gave the recent events consideration. He rolled his windows down, hoping the breeze off the bay would blow out the clouds of guilt and doubt muddling his thoughts. His instincts screamed *Danger*, yet he couldn't pinpoint the source. America had enemies and the army had enemies. Good grief, Parker had enemies. Not Theo. He'd been little more than a pawn on a global chessboard.

Whether or not Rebecca's reporter admitted it, he'd contacted Theo because of that anonymous tip. This couldn't have been a coincidence of local crime. Parker wasn't confined by the laws and was therefore free to make the logical leap. Bill had wanted information on the gold theft, or more likely the details of the mission around the time the gold was allegedly stolen. If the police got those pieces out of Bill, what would happen next?

Danger. Parker could practically smell it on the air.

At least Rebecca was safely out of the office and out of the scarred man's reach. Parker should probably encourage Bill to get out of town, but with the police active on the case, the reporter had a thin layer of protection in place. Parker had the sense that if the person pulling the strings on this wanted Bill dead, he'd be dead already.

He tapped his fingers absently on the door panel as he watched a crane operator load containers to the deck of a cargo ship, maneuvering each piece like another layer in a slow-moving, complex block-stacking game.

Yesterday, it had been Theo sitting in that crane. He'd told Parker how much he enjoyed working a job challenging enough and noisy enough to mute the ghosts from their combat years.

Parker swore. They lived in the same city and saw each other only a few times a year. Benign neglect was a lousy definition of friendship. They'd been through hell together and Theo had died worried that those nightmares had come calling for them.

He curled his fingers into tight fists and drummed them against the steering wheel. He wanted a target, needed a viable outlet for the rage building inside him.

His phone rang and seeing the Nevada area code and Jeff Bruce's face on the screen, he felt dread settle like a cold lump in his gut as he picked up. "Hello?"

"Parker?" The soft, feminine voice was thick with tears.

"Yes?"

"It's Naomi, Jeff's wife. He's…"

Her voice trailed off and Parker checked the phone to be sure the call hadn't dropped. "Naomi? What happened?" he asked, his pulse pounding in his ears. *Don't say dead, don't say dead.* Parker had made those calls to loved ones, and he wouldn't wish the experience on anyone. "Take a breath. Just take your time."

He heard her suck in a ragged breath and exhale slowly. "He's been in an accident," she said. "I'm at the hospital."

"I'm on my way." He started a mental list that began with unlocking the safe room door remotely and letting Rebecca know where to pick up the belongings he'd taken.

"No." Naomi sniffled. "I mean, that's not why I called. He said don't come."

What? "Okay." Why wouldn't Jeff want him out there?

"The police said his car was run off the road. Hit and run near a bridge. Between the seat belt and airbag he survived it. Another car stopped to help. They got him out before the river took his car." More sniffles. "The doctors are sure he'll recover."

"That's good news." His pulse returned to something closer to normal. "What do you need? How can I help?" Parker had to get his head out of the sand and give clear warnings to everyone on the list. Keeping the ransom note to himself hadn't helped any of them. With two men on the list attacked, in order, he couldn't pretend the incidents were unrelated. His team deserved the heads-up, and being vigilant while separating theory from fact wouldn't hurt any of them. Hell, it might save what was left of them.

"He's back in surgery right now, but he said to tell you—only you—he saw the driver of the other car. He said it was Fadi."

Parker bit back the visceral protest. Jeff had to be wrong. Parker absolutely could not reconcile the smart, helpful young man they'd known with this cowardly act of attempted murder. "He was sure?"

"He was." She sniffled. "You know who he's talking about, who he saw, don't you?"

"Yes." He struggled to believe it. It had to be true; Jeff wasn't prone to hallucinations. "I promise I'll handle it," Parker assured her, having no idea how to keep that promise.

"When he got home after that deployment, Jeff talked about Fadi and the family frequently," she said. "He said he was one of the best locals he'd met over there. I got the impression any one of you would have vouched for him or his family. If he got his visa and made it over here, wouldn't he have reached out?"

"Yeah, you'd think so." Parker closed his eyes, but it was no defense against the onslaught of memories from those months of recon and analysis and careful interpretation of words and actions. "Are you going to be okay?"

"I'm upset," Naomi said. "Don't worry. I can pull myself together before he gets out of surgery."

"Let me know when he's out. I'd like to talk to him when he's ready."

Naomi promised to keep him updated and when the call ended, Parker sat there, dumbfounded. He felt as if he was mired in quicksand and every move he made dragged him closer to drowning.

At this point, with Theo dead and Jeff in the hospital, Parker had to assume the blackmail note was as bogus as the anonymous tip sent to Rebecca. It seemed like a safe bet they'd been contacted in order to flush out the entire team.

Although the kid was the obvious common denominator, Parker wasn't ready to take that bait. The Fadi Parker remembered had a clear head. Loyal and proud of his heritage, and aware of the political and geographical economics of the area, he wouldn't have been easily swayed by propaganda that would turn him against the Americans.

What on earth was he up against?

He needed to get back to his computer and dig into the thumb drive with the rest of Rebecca's notes from her trip to Iraq. He had to find the exact points where his mission and her visit overlapped and hope the answer gave him a worthwhile clue. Otherwise he was just spitting into the wind while someone picked off his friends.

BECCA WAS GOING stir-crazy in this room. She knew exactly how many steps she needed between the wall and the door, having counted it out a dozen times. Or more. By the same method she knew the distance in steps from the counter that served as a kitchen to the Murphy bed. Sure, the safe room was all tricked out, complete with the best of everything except a window or a clock. The indulgent decor choices didn't take the sting out of being held against her will.

There was an entertainment system, but the television and radio components had been removed, probably because the devices had been able to connect to the outside world.

"This is cruel and unusual punishment," she'd hollered at the camera near the door. "I can't even stream shows or movies." No, she was left with a small library of books and music CDs for amusement. Unfortunately for Parker Lawton, her mind needed more stimulation.

She'd spent what she considered the remainder of

yesterday focused on the gala, sketching out every scene she could recall from the time she'd left the apartment with her less-than-stellar date to the moment she'd woken up in the safe room. By the time the third meal of fried chicken salad arrived, she'd been pretty confident in the order of events.

Not too hungry, after thinking it all through, she'd picked at the salad and stashed the rest in the refrigerator. Bored and frustrated, she gave up on a novel and applied her brainpower to finding a way out of this box. She hadn't come up with a good idea before she fell asleep.

Based on the eggs and toast that had been delivered while she was in the shower, she wanted to assume it was a new day. She detested this sense of helplessness, this utter lack of control as she wandered aimlessly from hour to hour without the anchor of her normal schedule.

When would Lawton let her go?

After the burger and milk shake exchange, she'd given up all pretenses that her captor could be anyone other than him. Who else lived in San Francisco, had virtually unlimited funds at his disposal and a reason to keep her out of his business? Those facts and the questions he asked were more than enough to convince her.

She debated the wisdom of causing damage to the safe room she'd likely have to live with and making him offers he couldn't refuse.

"This won't work, you know," she said, aiming her words at the entertainment system where the speakers pushed that deep, altered voice into the small space. "The network has to know by now that something's wrong. I don't take time off without significant planning. Someone will raise the alarm."

Hopefully someone already had. What was the minimum time before the police would take a missing-person report on an independent adult? "Bring a clock with the food next time," she muttered. "It's common decency."

On a wave of uncertainty, she took a long drink from her water glass. Just to change things up, she forced herself to consider the possibility that her kidnapper wasn't Parker Lawton.

There had been someone else at the gala. Sitting down, she flipped back through the pages in the notepad and studied the face with the scar that she'd sketched. What if *he* was her captor? She shivered, remembering the way his forearm had crushed her neck, nearly suffocating her.

What if that man was working for Lawton and she'd been taken as leverage to drop the story about the stolen gold? Oh, good grief, playing the what-if game was as pointless as yet another rundown of the facts. What she needed was a distraction.

No, she needed to get out of here. Not just for her safety, but for her sanity.

She sat up and reached for her water glass, and the lights went out. Startled, she bumped the plastic tumbler with her hand and she heard the water splash onto the table and tile. "Lights! Please?"

"Remain seated," he ordered in that altered voice that scraped her nerves raw.

Once more she obeyed, despite her urge to leap into action. What good would it do when he could obviously see her with the cameras and she couldn't see anything other than layers of darkness?

She heard the lock disengage and the door open on a soft whoosh. Just as quickly, the door closed and locked again. His footsteps were barely audible as he approached.

"This really isn't fair," she protested, shifting in her seat.

Strong hands gripped her shoulders from over the back of the couch, pushing her deeper into the cushions. "Do not move."

She didn't think his hands felt as rough or heavy as those of the man with the scar, but she couldn't be completely sure. "Do I get an early release if I co-operate?" She hoped keeping it light would mitigate the strange mix of excitement and fear his presence stirred up in her.

"No."

"Then why bother?" She slid down and rolled off the love seat and out of his reach. Gaining her feet, she bolted for the door. Maybe while he was inside with her, there was a way to—

He was on her in the next instant, faster than a heartbeat, one of his arms clamped against her waist and a hot palm covering her mouth.

His chest created an unyielding wall at her back. She shifted her hips, seeking an advantage, and only managed to create an intimate contact better suited for a different kind of darkness.

"Screaming does nothing, remember?" The words, spoken at her ear, reverberated through her. It wasn't solely an effect of the voice alteration. The stubble on his jaw had scrubbed lightly across her skin with each word.

Slowly, he peeled his hand from her mouth.

She didn't embarrass herself by calling for help. Nothing had come of her one and only bloodcurdling scream, and nothing had come of any of her shouting matches that followed. When she tried again to pull away and gain some breathing room, he caught her wrists and pulled them behind her back. A moment later she felt the cool pinch of plastic, heard the rasp as zip ties were pulled snug against her skin.

"Wait a second," she protested. "You don't need to do this."

"It's done." One large hand circled her upper arm and he guided her unerringly around the furniture until she was seated in the armchair. "Now we're going to talk."

The touch branded her skin under his palm, leaving her chilled everywhere else. "No, please. Not like this." This prickly sensation under her skin had to be a rant brewing inside her. It was temper and frustration, not *attraction* to the man holding her hostage. Obviously she needed fresh air to clear away the cobwebs of being locked in here. "Please. Just cut me loose and I'll tell you whatever you want to hear."

"You don't leave until I say so," he said.

The digitized voice would have terrified her if she hadn't been so sure this was Lawton. Lucy wouldn't call him a stand-up guy if he was a complete jerk all the time. "Listen, Lawton, this is a big mistake. We all make them." She flexed her wrists, trying to get the zip ties to bite into her skin for proof later. "Restraining me only makes you look worse."

"Stop fidgeting." He leaned over the back of the chair. "You'll be released when I'm satisfied."

What did that mean? Was he suggesting she trade her body for her freedom? It sounded dreadful when he suggested it. Even though she was ninety-five percent sure this was Lawton, for the first time she was truly scared. It was one thing for her to make the offer, but to have him demand sex was completely different. She didn't care that it was a double standard.

"How many times have you been to Iraq?" he asked.

The question, so far outside her line of thinking, startled her. "Iraq? Once."

"And overseas?"

She clamped her lips together, ignoring her watery knees and the fear trickling down her spine with icy fingers. He'd been through her computer. If he wanted answers, he could untie her or go back and find out the hard way. She would not cooperate with him while he had her tied up.

"Why were you in Iraq?" He tugged on her bound wrists when she didn't reply. "Answer me, Rebecca."

"You already know." She tried to turn around, and he held her in place with one hand and his superior skills. "You can't keep this up. People will be looking for me by now."

"They aren't. Answer my questions and we'll both be out of here sooner."

No one was looking for her? He sounded too sure of himself. "What did you do?" she demanded.

"Give me a few answers and you'll be free to go find out for yourself."

Only more questions danced on her tongue. Questions, demands and promises of prosecution. She bit all of it back, swallowed it down. When she was free, she would be sure he paid the price for every inconvenience and worry he caused her.

"Why don't you work in Hollywood anymore?"

She wasn't fooled by the changeup. "It's none of your business."

"You should be glad I disagree with you." His hands stroked across her shoulders, in toward her neck and back out again, miraculously smoothing the tension out of her muscles. "Why?"

What was he up to now? Did he want to be her counselor or her massage therapist? She might as well play along until she had a better opening to escape. "Nepotism is an epidemic in Hollywood. No way to make my work stand on its own merit."

"Is your work that good?"

"Yes. My reporters are the best and we deliver a quality show. We were in Iraq because our teamwork is that good," she added. According to the source, the last village on their circuit had been attacked by insurgents the week after they left and the gold stolen by the Americans sent to clear out the intruders. "Did our presence put those people in jeopardy?"

"No."

The word rasped across her senses, a harsh counterpoint to the easy movements of his hands. "Tell me what happened during your tour," he said. "Tell me who you met, what you saw."

She gave in. What would holding back accomplish at this point? He was completely in control here, and nothing she said would change the past. Everything he wanted to know was on her computer, and she suspected he'd helped himself to that already. A small cooperation *might* get her out of these zip ties and out of this room sooner rather than later.

"We were escorted the entire time by a security detail. We only visited areas that had been clear for three weeks or so," she continued as the tastes and smells and the surprising sights filled her mind. "You remember all of that too, don't you, Lawton?"

He lifted his hands away and she could still smell the fresh soap on his skin. "Go on," he said.

She did. "We had two weeks once we left Baghdad, and we made the most of it." She shared every detail from those days packed with movement, light, trepidation and joy. The highs and lows of the trip had been fresh in her mind since the anonymous email hit her inbox.

"Did you ever see a fortune in gold?" he asked.

"No," she admitted. "The families we met and villages we visited were quite modest."

"And were they happy to chat with Americans?"

She nodded. "Yes. War is ugly, but the people were grateful for the positive changes."

"I see." His fingers lightly brushed down her arms. Calloused and cool, his touch slid to a stop just above the bindings, resting lightly on the pulse points of her wrists.

"Please let me go. I've told you everything."

"Not yet." He leaned closer, his breath warm on her hair, and somehow he managed not to touch her anywhere else. "Before someone sent you that trumped-up email about stolen gold, have you ever had contact from anyone you met in Iraq?"

She tried to stand up, but he kept her in place. "You cowardly bastard! You've been through my email?"

"Among other things," he said easily. "Answer me. Have you had contact with anyone from Iraq?"

She thought of Fadi. He'd been such an asset, helping them as a translator and sharing his remarkable culture with her, Bill and their crew. She'd been hoping since the beginning that he hadn't authored that email, if only because it meant misfortune had befallen his family. "No," she snapped. "What are you doing now? Do you think you're a human lie detector?"

"Something like that."

If an altered voice could express a smug smile, his did. Her mind filled with an image of the sexy, tuxedoed Parker Lawton at her door, lips curved in an inviting smile rather than set into an irritated slash. Her hormones took a sudden side trip down kissing lane.

What was wrong with her? They weren't holding

hands, he wasn't trying to romance her, he was monitoring her responses for truthfulness.

"Do you or the network ever trace anonymous informants?"

She stifled the first instinct to cooperate. He was treading into territory that would make lawyers salivate. "I've cooperated enough. It's your turn to share."

"You don't want to hear my secrets."

"Yes, I do," she insisted, seizing a chance to go on the offensive. "Did you steal gold while you were in Iraq, Lawton?"

"What will you do if you find out I'm not who you think I am?"

Another evasion. "Turn on the lights and prove it."

"I'll give you a truth." His fingertips slid up a few inches and back down again to settle once more. Had he felt her pulse skip in response? "I have no intention of keeping you here any longer than necessary."

Why did his emphasis on *necessary* create a swirl of warm temptation low in her belly? She scolded herself for not being revolted by his audacity. She should be resisting. Fighting. Taking action to get out of here. "Shall we define necessary?"

"Not unless you're a lawyer," he deadpanned. "I'm well aware of your position with the network, your college degrees and your grades all the way back to kindergarten. Seems you were a real chatterbox as a kid."

Now, *that* upset her. He had no right to go tearing through her life. Her work, yes. Her past and her childhood? No way. "You—"

"Cowardly bastard? I've been called worse," he said. "You might be right. Tell me how the network would track down a source that doesn't want to be found."

"No." She shifted as far from him as he allowed. It wasn't nearly enough. "Let me go or leave. I'm done talking."

"I need information, Rebecca."

Her shoulders slumped, defeated. "If you don't like what I have to say, let me go. Surely you have the skills and gadgets to keep an eye on me in the real world."

"Watching you isn't my point. I need to know you're safe while I'm gathering information. The sooner you tell me everything you know about the source, the sooner I'll let you go."

"Everything?"

"Yes. What I don't know could hurt both of us."

She fidgeted under his fingertips, seeking a bit more space. A little distance would restore her sanity. He kept his fingers on the sensitive skin, his body close enough to catch her every twitch and flinch.

"In reverse order," she began, "everything I know about this situation amounts to filing charges with the police the minute you let me out of this room."

"I'm not surprised. Go on."

Not surprised and not concerned. "I also know you're a jerk."

"So noted. Get to the part that led us to this point."

"You led me here," she muttered. "Where are we anyway?"

"Rebecca."

She sighed. Fighting him was getting her nowhere, better to just tell him and let the chips fall. At some point, her captor would make a mistake. She had to believe that much.

"Anonymous tips are the worst. I told you that before." Now she was repeating herself. "Bill and I started fact-checking the tip itself. We learned the unit accused of the gold theft was in the area at the time of the alleged theft. Parker Lawton was part of that unit, just as the tipster claimed." Did his breath catch? Oh, she hoped she was making him nervous.

"The family name caught my attention. Bill and I got to know them as well as differing cultures and a few brief days allowed. They didn't project the wealth I would expect to go with the amount of gold stolen. They were kind, helpful and articulate."

She had to stop for a steadying breath, deciding how she wanted to explain it to him. "So this tip comes in and we start working it."

"Because you were angry for the family?" he asked.

"Because exposing appalling behavior is the right thing to do," she countered.

"You're eager to assume the worst of those soldiers," he said.

"Not true. The show is about giving viewers a compelling, objective story." She paused, trying to dial down the defensive tone. "We've been doing our research. Did you know *one* man on that team has a fortune? He's inexplicably wealthy," she added, wishing she could see his face. "As in one day he was an average guy, and almost overnight he was a billionaire. That in itself is suspicious."

He snorted. "Suspicious isn't proof. Go on."

Go on. Why did that two-word directive slip over her skin like silk, even with the creepy voice alteration device? "You saw the email from the source. There were six names on the list. Bill and I divided the research to speed things along. So far Lawton hasn't agreed to speak with Bill on the record. He will, though, won't he?"

"No idea."

"The night of the gala, the night you kidnapped me, Bill called me from a diner where he was waiting to meet the former CO of the team. The guy was late. What did you do, warn him off?"

"You're mistaken."

She laughed, the sound disappearing into the dark. "Please. I know it's you, Lawton." *Please don't let it be anyone else.* "Who else has any cause to hold me hostage?" She thought of the man with the scar and the brutal grip. "I can't imagine another thief taking this much interest in me or the show. I'm not an idiot, Lawton." She had to get him to slip up and admit it.

"I'm not Lawton."

"Maybe not," she said, pretending to consider. It was difficult to sell the nonchalant bravado effectively with only her voice while he hovered close enough to catch every reaction. "I had it on good authority *he* is a stand-up guy. You sure aren't."

"Tell me more about the family you think lost the gold. The source gave you a pretty common name."

That caught her off guard. Had he known them well too? "Why don't we work together? The show is objective, remember? Together we can probably figure out who the source is. We can even tell your side, and if the men on the list are really innocent, we'll make that clear."

He made another disbelieving sound, accompanied by one more adjustment of his fingers on her pulse points. "You'd work with me? A man you believe is connected to an army unit who stole from your friends?"

"Yes." She needed to sell the lie, had to convince him she could be an asset. Once she got out of this room, she'd turn him over to the first cop she saw. "You've done your homework. You know we work with all sorts of people to get to the heart of a story. I'd work with the devil himself if it gets me out of here."

"The devil, me, but not your dad. Interesting."

Taking a play out of his book, she left that assertion unanswered.

"I'm not the devil," he said, his voice tight. "You should know Bill didn't get his interview. Theo Manning is dead."

What? She swiveled her head around to look at him, the effort futile in the darkness. "No," she murmured. "How? When?" He was only trying to shock her. Still, she felt her heart clutch, worried he might be telling her the truth. He couldn't mean it.

"Murdered on Thursday night, thanks to *your* research," he continued. "Jeff Bruce, second on that list, is in the hospital. It wasn't an accident. You, Rebecca, are a threat to all the men on that list. You'll stay *right here*."

His fingers lifted from her wrists and he caught both her hands in one of his. She felt a flare of fear and in the next moment the bindings were gone, her hands free. Her back, the air around her, cooled as he retreated. She hadn't even heard him open a knife or tool capable of slicing though the zip ties so smoothly. Maybe it was a secret trick he'd learned in the army.

His stealth was almost worse than the absolute control he held. He'd clearly thought through each step. Maybe he'd done something like this before, yet nothing in Parker Lawton's background indicated he was a serial kidnapper or worse. Nothing they'd found so far, anyway.

Other than his instant leap from middle class to wealthy, nothing indicated he was anything other than an honorable veteran. The opposing pictures painted by the anonymous source and the first layer of facts had made her want to dig deeper into Lawton, with or without an end story in mind. Now not so much.

Once more logic fed the doubt that had taken root in her mind. What if the man in control of this room and her life wasn't Lawton, but some crazy thug he'd hired to interrogate her?

"Thanks," she said, rubbing her wrists where his hands had been. The zip ties chafed her pride more than her skin, and releasing her was a move that showed trust. *Or pure arrogance*, a little voice in her head pointed out. "If you prove the tip is bogus, I won't even press charges." She lied openly now that he wasn't close enough to catch the deception. "At the very least, let's have the rest of this conversation with the lights on."

She heard the soft whir of the lock as the door opened and closed again. The lights came up and she turned a circle, blinking as her eyes adjusted to the light, searching for him. "Oh, come on!" She did another full circle, as if by willing it she could make him reappear.

"We'll talk again," the voice carried through the speakers.

She leaped for the door and hammered it with her fists. "You jerk! You need me out there!"

"We're all safer with you in there. I'll be back in a few hours."

Hours! With no windows or clocks, she had no idea what time that would be in the real world. "Wait!" She wouldn't let him go without getting *something* in return.

"What is it?" he queried.

"When you come back, be polite." Considering the vast imbalance of power here, she probably should have phrased that as a question rather than a demand.

"How so?"

Oh, good, he was still out there, listening. "Give the lights a flicker or say hello before tumbling me into the dark. Please," she added belatedly. She pointed at the upended water glass she'd hit when he turned out lights. "The floor you save might be your own."

In the corner, the tiny red light on the camera flashed. "Okay." The speaker clicked and the camera light winked out.

He was gone. She knew it even without making a request or comment that would go unanswered. The red light was out on the camera too. She assumed that meant he wasn't watching all the time, only when the light was on. She could find a way to use that.

She'd thought she had him on the hook while they were talking, and he'd wriggled off again. He was out there chasing something and she was stuck. Was Theo Manning really dead? She rubbed the heel of her hand over the ache in her chest. Whatever was going on out there, Lawton couldn't keep her here indefinitely. He had to know that as well as she did.

While she still believed it was most likely the man holding her was Lawton, she didn't *know*. Didn't have any proof.

She had to admit to herself that the search to corroborate the anonymous email combined with a friend's death—if that was true—might have pushed a man like Lawton over the edge. She could have a better idea of who she was dealing with if her dad had helped her get a look at the service records.

That didn't answer why he'd locked her up in here. If Lawton wasn't the man holding her, she might be in dire trouble. This guy could be as much of a nutcase as her captivity suggested. Dwelling on that scenario only fed the smoldering panic inside her that was all too ready to leap into a consuming inferno of debilitating fear.

Becca combed her hands through her hair and took slow, deep breaths until the sensation passed. Then she stalked up and down the room with a renewed determination to save herself and break out of here.

Chapter Six

"Another dead end," Parker told the empty room. On a weary oath, he pushed back from the wobbly table and stood up from the lousy excuse for a chair. Crossing the small room in two strides, he carefully peered through the crack in the window curtains. No one visible on the nearby rooftops, and down on the street the cars seemed to be a fresh crop than those he'd passed when he walked into the shabby motel a few hours ago.

He longed for the assistance and conveniences of his office, his condo or even the rental outside the safe room, but he needed to be as unpredictable as the enemy. Staying in one place too long or going back too frequently only made it easier for whoever was picking off his team.

Exhausted, frustrated, he wanted to get out in the city to walk and think. And yes, to tempt anyone who might be on his tail. The remainder of the night invited him to search for his opponent's weak point and go on the attack. Except he didn't know where to start looking. San Francisco, Nevada or somewhere in between?

After he'd studied the rest of her raw notes, it was clear Rebecca had told him everything about Iraq and it still wasn't enough to connect any of the dots. Although it would be easy to believe she'd held some essential detail back for the sake of insurance, he knew better.

It had taken him hours to recover from that conversation. Not only because she called him by name and she'd been so open and candid about her experiences overseas. No. It had been the citrus scent of her hair, the fragile skin covering her pounding pulse points. Her defiance and courage despite the odds blew him away and drew him closer simultaneously.

Her pulse had remained steady under his fingertips. Fast with nerves, but steady. Her voice, that cool, cultured sound rippling over him through the darkness, had held the unyielding tone of a woman who knew she was right. Until she'd heard Theo died. Her pulse had gone haywire, stuttering under his fingertips as she processed the news.

He should let her go. Beg her forgiveness. And he would. As soon as he could figure out if he would be doing it for her or to invite the scarred man back for another attempt to nab her. Until he could trust himself with that decision, until he could own it, she'd stay safely tucked away. "Locked away," he amended aloud.

What a fool! How had he let a rescue turn into this

nightmare? He could just hear the men he'd worked so closely with on that last mission cackling over his idiocy. Theo's life motto had been Think First. He'd drilled it into everyone he served with as if it was his personal mission to teach others that no matter how bad things got, there was always time to think before taking an irreversible action.

Parker hadn't taken any time to think. He'd been reactionary from the moment he heard about Theo's murder. Before that, if he was honest. The blackmail note had set his mind spinning out of control. He hooked his thumbs into his back pockets and dropped his head in shame. Reactionary was a pretty word for glossing over an outright kidnapping.

The pure shock of seeing all their names in one place had unnerved him. Still did. The six of them had been deployed to the same base, working with their individual units, until Theo had gathered them for one particular covert operation.

They'd gone out in teams of three, and after more than a month battling rough conditions and unforgiving terrain, they found and dispatched a terrorist cell moving explosives from Iran to Iraq. No one should ever have put all six names together. It should have been impossible. Except someone had proved it was possible, compounding that problem by creating a compelling story designed to discredit all of them unless Parker paid the blackmail.

He glanced back to the table where her devices and his laptop sat open. None of his extensive searches were getting him closer to identifying the source be-

hind this mess. The only thing he labeled progress
was discovering that the driver who'd run Jeff off the
road couldn't be Fadi, the young man from the village
near the Iranian border. No matter what Jeff thought
he saw, Parker's expert at the office had used amateur
radio operators to confirm that the kid was still in
Iraq with his family. Too bad he hadn't found a way
to ask if the family still had their gold.

Parker rubbed at his temples, astonished at how
small the world had become. It was nearly incompre-
hensible that he and Rebecca had met the same lanky
eighteen-year-old within a few weeks of each other.
Fadi had served as a translator first for Parker's team
and then Rebecca's crew. Logic said someone from
that village was behind this, and yet the setup was
too sophisticated, the knowledge too complete and
the reach too long.

That left him wondering if someone on the base
had learned about their operation. If so, what was
the end game here? It couldn't be about the money or
Theo would still be alive and Jeff would be home with
his wife. And how did kidnapping Rebecca fit in?

He prowled around the shabby motel room and
checked in on Rebecca. He'd expected her to be sleeping and found she was marking time in a similar
pattern of pent-up frustration in the safe room. He
turned up the audio and heard her cursing him in increasingly innovative combinations. As he watched,
he wondered if it would take all of his fortune to buy
her forgiveness. Rush, reportedly the wealthiest man

in the city, might not have enough money to buy that woman's forgiveness.

No, money wasn't the right key to her anyway. She'd offered to pay off her captor, and a quick search of her financials proved she had a hefty nest egg at her disposal. Rebecca's world revolved around the story. Would admitting he was better at being a security expert and a soldier than a wealthy civilian win her forgiveness?

The story. Parker kept circling back to that. The blackmailer claimed the media had been informed of the story. Yet no one had run it. None of his remaining friends on the list had received calls from other reporters. Only Rebecca's group had started investigating, and they'd interpreted the sudden leap in his net worth as a smoking gun.

The tip in itself could have been a story worthy of a network mention. If her reporter had run with the first suggestion of the story, tossing out inflammatory accusations of corruption, as many might have done in their places, the men on that list would be facing tough questions right now. All of them embarrassed, scrutinized and investigated, blindsided by a media feeding frenzy. Who would gain from that? And why now?

With Theo dead and Jeff still in the hospital, restitution for the stolen gold didn't seem to be the primary objective at all.

His phone chirped and hummed on the table and Parker hesitated, not sure he could handle more bad news. In his experience no one called with good news at nearly one o'clock in the morning. The screen showed the call was from Tony, one of the men he'd assigned to keep an eye on Rebecca's apartment in Russian Hill.

"What is it?" Parker asked.

"Flashlight moving around," Tony replied, his voice low. "Someone is searching the place."

"You didn't see anyone go in?"

"Whoever is in there didn't use the door."

Parker stifled the first knee-jerk response. He wanted to send Tony in and have him haul the burglar to the office so Parker could conduct an interrogation. *Think first.* "Call the police," he said to Tony. "Do what you can to get a picture and tail whoever leaves the apartment."

"On it," Tony said, ending the call.

Parker pocketed his phone and worked through the next steps. Russian Hill wasn't in Detective Baird's district, but Parker could make sure he caught wind of the break-in once they had more information. Tony knew how to call in a crime without sharing contact information and he was as good as a ghost at following people. With the apartment empty, they didn't need to worry about endangering anyone.

Glaring at Rebecca's tablet, Parker returned to the table and closed it. The missing pieces of this puzzle weren't there. Nor were they in the human-interest story she and Bill had brought back from Iraq. He couldn't write off the places where her journey and his had almost collided as coincidence.

Someone was pulling on strings Parker couldn't

see, jerking them around like puppets. Her show. His mission. Where did they overlap? He was sure her show was being used as a pawn in the effort to disgrace him and his team, but she'd also been targeted personally.

There was a way to get in front of this. With only two days left, he needed a comprehensive plan to protect her as well as the three other men on the list. He couldn't dump them all into safe rooms.

He sank into the chair and leaned forward into the table, propping his head on his fists. He'd been through everything, too many times to count. If she talked with army units during her trip to Iraq, those notes weren't on this device. It was a question to ask when he went back to the safe room.

He used the app to check on her again. She was sprawled across the Murphy bed. He watched for a minute, trying to decide if she was really asleep or faking it for the cameras. Observing her while she was vulnerable made him feel like the worst creep. He switched the view, found the camera fritzed out and took it as a sign to stop being an idiot with her. He used the app to check the cameras outside the building, relieved when he didn't see anything remarkable.

He should sleep as well. Instead, he started a new search on his laptop, looking at the world headlines during the days and weeks when Rebecca's crew and his unit were in the same vicinity. Then he saw it: 12 Dead—Village Caught in Cross Fire.

The date of the article matched up, and his blood turned cold, slogging through his veins. Not the village where Rebecca and Bill had been, farther north on the border. The article claimed Iranian smugglers had been outed to US forces and had retaliated against the community to make a point.

Oh, he should have suspected this involved the off-the-books skirmish at the border. He would have thought of this tragedy first, if there had been any survivors. He swore. At the time Jeff, Matt and he had been certain they'd cut off the head of that snake. Someone had clearly survived.

Parker stared up at the water-stained ceiling and replayed the entire week in his mind. It wasn't the first time and it definitely wouldn't be the last time those harrowing moments consumed him. Knowing he couldn't sleep, he reached for his phone and dialed Franklin Toomey, the third name on the list. He stared at the contact listing for a long time but never hit the Call icon.

He'd warned Frank and the others yesterday. The man was on guard. These new details could wait until a reasonable hour.

The blackmail note sent to him made sense now. Raw fear iced Parker's skin. The restitution demand had little to do with money or family and everything to do with honor. It was about vengeance, and more innocent lives would get caught in the cross fire. Who had the intel, the reach and the nerve to start picking off soldiers on American soil?

Of the six of them, only Theo would have had the names of likely suspects. Killing him immediately made sense now. Kidnapping Rebecca might have been a ham-fisted attempt to force her network to run the story. Instead, the scarred man had pulled Parker right into the heart of his deadly game.

Up against one or more highly-skilled assassins on American soil, Parker needed to dig deep. Gathering intel was step one. Security was step two. Too bad for his Iranian enemy, Parker happened to be an expert in both areas.

He focused his efforts on drawing out and identifying the scarred man, mining every source and latent surveillance camera for more information on Theo's death and Jeff's accident. Skilled or not, everyone left a trail of some sort. Parker drafted an email asking a favor of another friend who'd transitioned from the army and landed with Homeland Security. Maybe they had some intelligence on the man with the scar. He paused, thinking through all the pros and cons before he hit Send.

After catching a much-needed nap and making more phone calls, Parker was convinced he'd found the first bread crumbs on that trail. His friend at Homeland agreed to help, and the hotel where the awards gala had been held invited him down to look through the surveillance footage from that night.

Though the Iranians had a head start, he would catch up. He sent a few replies in Rebecca's name to the emails that seemed most urgent and then closed down her computer. Checking the window once more, he had to give the Iranians points for subtlety. If they were tracking the activity on her accounts or the devices, they were being exceptionally discreet.

He packed the gear he'd brought to the motel room, leaving only a few bread crumbs behind. If the roles were reversed, he would search the vacated room of his enemy. With luck, they'd believe he was off his game and follow his bogus clue, giving him a couple of hours to launch an offensive plan.

Luck failed him. A tail caught up with his SUV within blocks of the hotel. At least it looked that way. He checked his mirrors and swore with mild frustration.

Driving through the city congestion on the weekend had pros and cons. It was easier to lose a tail, but more difficult to confirm one. He just couldn't be sure the midsize white sedan one car back from him now was following him with a purpose. It was possible he was simply overtired and paranoid. Despite the low odds of figuring this out on his own, he had to try. He couldn't lead the killers behind the blackmail note and false story to where he was keeping Rebecca safe.

What he wouldn't give to be back overseas where support and reliable intel were a secure radio call away. He turned onto a famous street no local in his right mind would travel willingly and gently slalomed right and left to navigate the one-way intersections. The white car followed.

At the last possible moment, he swerved into the turn lane for the next block, and the white car followed again. To his right another driver blew through the now-red traffic light to a chorus of angry car horns and squealing brakes.

He glanced up at the traffic camera installed on the light pole to help the city catch drivers misbehaving. Belatedly, he remembered he wasn't nearly as alone as he felt.

Upon his latest inspection this morning, his SUV hadn't been tagged with GPS or any other surveillance devices. Pressing the button on his steering wheel, he called Sam at the Gray Box office. Sam could hack into any system, including the city's traffic cameras. Back when Sam and Rush were setting up protective measures against corporate espionage attempts to steal their tech and worse, Sam had created a specific route through the city so they could both pinpoint pesky surveillance tails and lose them as needed.

"Bellemere," Sam answered on the third ring.

"It's Parker," he said. "I may or may not have a shadow out here in the city today. Can you help me out?"

"Of course. What's your location?"

Parker heard the eagerness in Sam's voice and replied quickly, even as he kept one eye on the white sedan in his wake. "I'm in my SUV," he added.

"All right," Sam said. "Give me a minute." It only took a few seconds. "Okay, I can see you. Hmm. Take your next right."

"Got it." Parker could practically hear Sam cracking his knuckles. "I think it's the white sedan two car lengths back."

Sam hummed thoughtfully again. "Why don't you

cruise out toward the Presidio? Do you remember the route we set up on that side of town?"

"Well enough," Parker said, picturing the convoluted path in his head.

"Great. Drive happy, my friend. I've got your back. In a minute I should have his registration."

Parker kept the line open, though neither he nor Sam spoke while Parker drove the route. The white sedan, or one like it, stayed close the entire time. No way this was a coincidence. In the quiet car, he second-guessed himself. Any smart team would be subtle about tailing him. They'd trade off every few blocks, or hang back. Whoever drove the sedan didn't seem to care whether or not Parker knew he was back there.

"According to the plate, the car has a California registration and is insured with a rider for one of those rideshare things."

"Do you think the person on my tail is a fare?" If so, he could try and request any records from the driver.

"Not exactly. There's no one other than the driver in the car. The view from the last traffic cam is pixelated, but I doubt the car's owner, one Jenny Swanson, has a thick dark beard."

Neither did the scarred man or the man running interference for the attempted kidnapping at the gala. Did they steal Jenny's car or was she a connection to the team giving his team fits? "So I'm being followed."

"That may or may not be the good news," Sam agreed. "You want me to keep running this down?"

"Please," Parker answered. His mind was moving on to the next part of his problem. He wanted to get Rebecca out of the city before the assassin tracked her down again.

"And?"

Parker hesitated, unsure what he was supposed to say. "Thank you?"

"Very mannerly, although not what I was fishing for." Sam chuckled. "It was a prompt for you to ask for more help. I can send an alert to the police. You'd have some breathing space."

"No, thanks. I'd rather know exactly where this guy is."

"You got it."

When the call ended, he aimed for the condo again, careful to keep the white sedan in sight as he worked through his dwindling options.

If he didn't get Rebecca to a new hiding place soon, he had no doubt she'd get caught in the cross fire. Rescuing her had been tricky enough. Talking with her had created an entirely different and unexpected set of problems, none of which he could resolve while she viewed him as the enemy.

What he'd learned during his background search on her left him reluctant to just walk in, introduce himself and beg for her understanding. Although she had a mile-wide streak of compassion, she also held grudges. In his case, she should. He deserved each and every terrible thought and word she aimed at him.

He liked her too much. The courage and creativity she showed trying to outwit him and escape made him want to stand back and let her win. Should he do that? he wondered. Should he let her escape without any confirmation of her captor's identity? A safe option, but for some twisted reason, he didn't want to confirm he was the coward she'd labeled him.

While he debated his best approach, formulating a story Rebecca might embrace, he circled the block twice. Someone had been brave enough to take his designated parking space on the side street.

Making sure the driver on his tail was following closely, Parker aimed for the dry cleaner to pick up the dress he'd dropped off yesterday. With any luck the gesture would give Rebecca pause before she filed a report with the police. He didn't bother with a meal, since he was about to insist she hide elsewhere. He didn't expect her to let him off the hook for kidnapping. His behavior had been atrocious, his knee-jerk decisions lousy.

No, she had every right to file charges against him. The catch would be convincing her to grant him a few days to get this team of assassins out of the US before they killed anyone else. Although the police department was capable, they were no match for the coming battle, and Parker sure couldn't stop anyone if he was buried under a mountain of paperwork and complaints in a county lockup.

Chapter Seven

When the lights flickered, twice, and then went out as her captor heeded her request, Becca readied herself to fight. Today was the day she'd break free of this room. He'd been in this room with her. She had a sense of his size and power. She would have one chance, one moment when surprise was on her side. She had to make this work or he might never let her go no matter what he'd said that first night. Reminding herself she'd be fighting Lawton, she bounced a little on her bare feet. Whether or not it was true, she had to believe she was going up against someone who'd once had morals and might pull a punch rather than hurt an innocent woman.

Overnight, she'd done what she could to interfere with the camera feeds, without making it obvious she was the root of the trouble. When the red lights were out, she'd balanced on her suitcase, scraping and prying at the lenses, half-afraid he'd burst through the door and tie her up. That approach hadn't worked, so she'd resorted to using the tweezers from her toiletry case to work on the screws in the brackets. Once the brackets were loose, she jammed her metal nail file into the nest of wires behind the camera by the door and hoped for the best.

"Step back from the door," the menacing, altered voice rumbled through the speaker.

She obeyed, silently lamenting whatever sensor or gadget kept him informed of her actions in here. Did he have it wired for infrared too?

The door opened with the familiar near-silent whoosh and she heard the rustle of plastic. Her heart stuttered in her chest. Though he'd never really laid a hand on her, she feared that was about to change. Permanently. She'd seen enough true-crime documentaries and read enough fiction thrillers to know the preferred material for containing evidence of a murder was plastic.

She tried to rein in her racing imagination. While it was hard to accept that a veteran with Lawton's record would kill her in cold blood, it wasn't an unprecedented situation. People went off the rails every day, and she suspected very few of them had his motivation of keeping millions of dollars in gold.

Her skin went hot and then cold and she trembled, faced with the daunting task of survival. She would not become a victim without a fight that left her mark on *him*. She refused to die alone and unheard in this horrible room with all its comfortable amenities.

Holding her breath, she heard only his footfalls, the plastic and the whisper of the door moving on those unbeatable, industrial hinges. Timing her attack based on the way he'd entered on previous visits, she waited until he was through the door to strike.

She didn't do the obvious lunge for the open door. He had to be prepared for that option. No, she kicked the small ottoman behind him into the gap, praying it would be enough to prevent the door from closing.

Only a faint sliver of light from whatever was beyond the door illuminated the space. It was more than she'd seen during his past visits, and she used the variations in the shadows to sort out her captor's shape within the dark room. Riding a tide of desperate determination, she threw herself at him, aiming her shoulder at his midsection. He angled away, but she got enough of him to shove him back against the love seat.

As much as she wanted to pummel him or turn on the lights and demand answers, she scrambled for the door. Escape was her top priority. Five steps was all she needed to reach the door from the love seat. Five steps and she'd be on the other side looking for a cop. Let the police sort out who her captor was, how he'd brought her here and why. The state prosecutors could have a field day with him in court.

"Stop!"

No way. The heavy vaultlike door was fighting the ottoman, and winning, based on the scrape and snap of the wooden legs. She had mere seconds to make her escape. Two more strides and her ordeal was over.

He caught her ankle and dragged her back. She screamed in despair, kicking him hard enough in the shoulder to make him grunt with pain. Up again, she'd taken only one stride before he had one arm locked around her midriff. He turned her to face him and part of his arm slid over her breast. On reflex, she slapped him.

The loud crack of her hand against his face startled them both. The pure-luck shot gave her another opening. She used it, but he caught her again. She screamed for help, using her best horror flick scream. Someone must be within earshot outside this room. Though she fought him with everything, hands, hair clip, fingernails, knees, elbows and feet, he kept gaining the advantage. Her arms flailed as she reached for any object to fend him off. Nothing worked.

Even with the adrenaline shooting through her system, she was outmatched. He had every advantage from size and reach to home court. She found herself caught between the wall and his body.

"Settle down!" he snapped. "I won't hurt you."

"Yet." She tried again to knee him in the groin and missed. Again.

He swore as she launched into one more round of shrieking hostility. His expertise versus her will to survive. It shouldn't have been a shock that expertise won. He won.

She found herself pinned to the cold tile floor by his hot, hard body. His hands manacled her wrists and his legs pressed the full length of hers. In the almost near dark, her mind started cataloging the details of his build. Clearly her captor kept himself in excellent shape and she wondered if the calluses she felt on his hands were from the gym or some kind of honorable work.

And why did it matter? Her escape attempt had failed miserably, and whether or not this was Parker Lawton she knew she wouldn't have another chance. Thinking of the plastic, she felt the first tears leak from her eyes. It was over. She coughed out a sob of despair, despite her best efforts to go out strong.

"Lights to dim." The voice alteration was gone and the clear, deep voice giving the order swirled around her like a sensual fog. That he didn't sound the least bit winded while her breath sawed in and out of her lungs made her want to start fighting all over again.

The small pinpoints of light in the ceiling came up in clusters and illuminated the room, confirming her suspicions. Parker Lawton was her captor. He stared down at her, apparently in no hurry to move from his position on top of her. Relief and temper warred for dominance while her traitorous body enjoyed every sensation. Her gaze drifted from his dark eyes to his full lips, and for a long moment she wondered how those lips would feel on hers.

"Rebecca?" Her name in his normal voice sounded strange, broke the spell she'd fallen under.

"Get off me!" She swallowed a fresh burst of frustrated tears and bucked and twisted under him, to no avail. "You did this!" Furious, she flung a string of obscenities at him until her breath was gone. With him on top of her, she couldn't quite get her lungs refilled. "Why?" she gasped.

"Take it easy." He levered himself up just enough for her to breathe. "I'm not here to hurt you."

He already had, in more ways than she cared to admit. She had always believed she was strong and smart. Then he'd come along and kidnapped her from a public building and held her against her will. She hated the things she'd considered doing to gain her freedom.

"I'm going to press charges," she said with as much dignity as she could muster. She glared up at him as he hopped to his feet. She was already feeling the effects of their fight. "By this time next year, I'll own your security company and anything else with your name on it."

"Probably." He held out a hand to help her up and she batted it away.

His easy acceptance of her claim was the equivalent of pouring gasoline on a fire. "How long have you kept me here?" she demanded, standing up without any help from him.

"Too long. You're free to go."

Her knees nearly buckled with relief. She leaned into the love seat for support. "Do you mean it?"

He nodded, tucking his hands into his pockets. "I want to explain a few things before you go."

The red imprint of her hand on his cheek gave her a little satisfaction. She was still outraged that anyone thought they could smother a story by holding her here in a safe room. That he was a veteran honorably discharged with combat hero medals made it worse.

"Start talking while I pack." The statement was ludicrous, but she owned it, turning around to gather up the belongings she hadn't expected to take with her.

"I have your phone, uh, in my car."

"How convenient for *you*." She didn't want to know what he thought he'd found in her call history and the other apps. He'd picked through her life, she knew that from his questions. She slid a look over her shoulder at his continued silence and caught him looking through the sketches she'd made. "Stop that. Hand it over."

He shook his head, flipping the pages back and forth, engrossed in her drawings.

"It's private," she said, resisting the urge to stomp her foot like a three-year-old. "Like a journal." She made a grab for it and he swiveled out of her reach.

"You're good," he said absently.

"Gee, thanks." *Ignore it, ignore him*, she coached herself, zipping her suitcase. "Open the door."

He held up the notepad and used his phone to take pictures of the pages. "Stop that," she said.

To her surprise he did stop. He held out the notepad, open to the page she'd devoted entirely to sketches of the man with the scar. "Do you know this man?" His eyes held the same worry she recalled from the night of the awards gala.

She took a half step back, unnerved by his intensity and the mean eyes leering at her from the page. "No. Do you?"

"But you've seen this man," he pressed.

"Obviously we both have," she replied.

"Where did you see him?"

"At the awards gala. He reeked of onions." She gripped the handle of her suitcase. "Open the door, Lawton."

"Call me Parker."

She wouldn't. "Open the door."

"Have you seen him anywhere else in town? Do you remember what he did to you?"

Becca squared her shoulders and set her teeth against the tremor that threatened at his questions. She remembered feeling caught and the scent of onions overpowered by something sweeter, stronger. "No," she lied. She didn't owe Lawton anything. "Open. The. Door."

He handed her the notepad. "I am sorry, Rebecca, for everything." Stepping to the panel, he pressed his hand to the screen. There was a soft beep, and then he did something else and the door swung open.

She hurried by him, stopping short when she found herself in someone's magnificent home. "Have you been right out here the whole time?" She gazed around the gorgeous, modern decor of the condo, drank in the wide view of the ocean. Freedom had never looked so wonderful.

His eyebrows flexed and, smart man, he didn't take his gaze off her. "Here in the condo? No."

She pushed away the flood of questions about his whereabouts, focusing on the most important issue. "I'm leaving. You can keep the phone. I plan to burn everything you've touched once I'm home." She started for the door.

"I'll let you leave once we come to terms."

She plowed forward, determined to get as far from him as possible, until she saw the security panel at the front door as well. Naturally, when she tried the doorknob, it was useless.

"Terms?" She folded her arms over her chest. "I will only agree that I won't kill you for this. Everything else is fair game." She held up a hand when he shifted his feet. "Hold still," she ordered. "I mean it. I can get this story out and moving with a single email. I can ruin you, your company—"

"You can," he said as if it wouldn't bother him in the least. "Or you could listen."

Listen? She'd been listening since he locked her in here. He'd terrified her, shocked her and annoyed her. She was done playing this game his way.

He moved again and she braced to fend off an attack. Her gaze locked on the dry cleaning bag on the floor behind him, just inside the safe room. *That* was the plastic she'd heard in the darkness. He turned slightly, following her gaze. He plucked it from the floor and smoothed the plastic and the fabric, then draped it neatly over the back of one of the dining room chairs.

"That's my dress."

"Yes."

"You had my dress dry-cleaned?" Her gaze darted from the bag to him and back again. "When?" Why couldn't she figure out if he was a good guy or a bad guy? What kind of kidnapper would be so thoughtful?

The sick kind, she told herself. He'd held her against her will for two days? Three? She had no real way of knowing aside from the meals. Her thoughts were pinballing through her mind. "How long has it been?"

"Almost two days," he said, his gaze steady. "It's Saturday morning."

She wanted to hate him for his steely composure as her self-control frayed. "It's already Saturday?" She thought of Bill's failed interview with Manning and her Thursday date. "Has anyone reported me missing?"

"No." He shifted. It was barely perceptible, but she was an expert at the subtleties of body language.

"Because you did what exactly?" She gestured for him to fill in the sentence.

"I've been managing your emails. The office thinks you're out of town dealing with a family emergency."

Only the calming methods she'd learned in yoga class kept her from launching herself at him. Well, that and the physical scuffle that proved she was grossly outmatched. The element of surprise had been her only advantage, and she sensed she would never have it again. Not with this man.

Figuring out who he was before she made her move didn't change what he was. He was a soldier, an expert in covert operations and financially blessed by fair means or foul along the way. She took a step toward him. "Did you steal the gold?"

"No." His gaze was steady and the sorrow in his dark brown eyes was obvious. "No one on that list has ever stolen anything." He gestured for her to sit down.

She remained where she was.

"I know this isn't ideal," he began.

"Which part?" By sheer willpower, she kept her hands loose when she wanted to ball them into fists. "Being held against my will or being able to identify you as my captor?"

"None of it is ideal," he snapped. "Please sit down."

She shook her head. "Not here. Not until I'm far away from that obnoxiously tiny room. Just say what you need to say so I can leave." She was coming dangerously close to begging again.

A crack of laughter startled her and she aimed her notorious glare at him. At the network, it was the expression known to silence argumentative reporters and send interns scurrying for the nearest shelter. He only laughed again. "What's so funny?"

"This. Us." He tipped his head toward her. "I imagine that scowl works on most people."

"It does, yes."

He bobbed his chin as if seeing the merits. "If our lives weren't on the line, it might have worked on me."

"Don't patronize me."

His slashing dark eyebrows lifted a fraction. "You make patronizing sound worse than kidnapping." He sat down and leaned back into the cushions of the plush sofa. "Yes, the doors are locked right now. You will be allowed to leave once you understand the stakes."

"I can take care of myself."

"I believe you. In most circumstances, you

wouldn't need me at all." He shook his head. "This is different."

She suppressed a shiver at the hard edge in his voice. She took a seat on the edge of the black sofa facing him. Her body thrummed with tension from head to toe. "Get to the point. I have a couple days' worth of work to catch up on before Monday."

"First, please accept my apology. Kidnapping you was a knee-jerk reaction. It started as a rescue and just spiraled out of control. I regret how you've been inconvenienced by my fear-based decisions."

She couldn't imagine him afraid of much of anything. "Are you afraid of me?"

He nodded, a rueful smile on his lips. "On a few levels."

A rescue—her mind latched on to that detail, refusing to let go. She crossed her legs at the knee and let her foot swing a little as she studied him. He meant it and his sincerity knocked her further off balance. "Then why did you do it?"

"Because I thought you could help me save my men," he explained. "Your reporter called my office. It raised red flags on my end." He sighed. "I wanted the name of the source who accused us of stealing. At the gala, the man with the scar grabbed you. He drugged you and was headed for the stairwell when I intervened."

"You didn't steal anything."

"No." Restless, he leaned forward and propped his elbows on his knees. "Unless we count stealing you from the scarred man."

"It counts." She just wasn't sure where to put the tally.

"Tell me what you remember about him," he said.

She bristled. "I'm not under your control or command anymore. In case you didn't notice, I've always been bad at taking orders."

His brown eyes flashed with something. Lust or temper? Either way, she was chagrined that the look sent a ripple of anticipation through her body. "I'm listening," she continued through the awkward silence. "You still haven't explained why you kept me here so long."

He reached behind him, and her breath caught, afraid he was pulling a weapon on her. Instead he held out an envelope that had been folded until the paper was nearly worn through at the creases.

"What's that?"

"Just read it." He inched closer, holding it out to her.

She took it but didn't open it right away. "Mr. Lawton—"

"The sooner you open the envelope the sooner you can get back to your life."

Parker Lawton had proven himself adept at several skills during her stay in his safe room. Deception topped the list, though his gift for igniting her temper was a close second. She stopped listing off his skills right there, before she could add his seductive voice and his ability to kindle her darkest sensual fantasies in absurd situations.

More annoyed with herself now than she was with

him, she opened the envelope and removed a half sheet of standard white copy paper. She read the brief message twice over, trying to make sense of it.

"Oh. We've been played," she began, her voice colliding with his. "Pardon me?"

His brow furrowed. "I said it's bogus," he replied. "Why are you on my side?"

"I'm not exactly on your side." *Yet.* The note, the *blackmail*, nudged her closer toward his corner. She dropped the note on the sofa and stood up, crossing the room to watch the ocean, needing some movement to think through the details. "You read the anonymous email I received, right?" she asked, without looking at him, still angry about the violation of her privacy.

"Yes," he admitted. "You believed it was from the family. Possibly from Fadi."

She nodded, her eyes on the waves moving with such constancy toward the shore. Watching the ocean soothed her. Always had. "The email was written to push my buttons, and the note was written to push yours." She turned to face him again. "It worked. Bill and I led the killer right to the targets they wanted."

"Once I read the email I was sure it was written by the same person who wrote the blackmail note," Parker said.

"I agree," she said, rubbing her hands over her arms. "Fadi would never threaten to kill, especially not our soldiers. He was proud of how he helped the US."

"I thought the same," he said. "Come sit down

a minute. We need to figure out why you were targeted."

She stayed put, keeping her back to the window and maintaining some much-needed distance. "Probably to mess with you," she suggested.

"I was thinking it was an attempt to force the story out."

She tipped her head to the side, considering. "Taking me removed your best access to the anonymous source. You'd come by the apartment earlier to hassle me. It might even have been an attempt to frame you."

"Hassle you? I only wanted to talk."

"And here we are." She spread her arms wide, let them fall to her sides. "Good job." He'd been cornered, his CO murdered and his best lead nearly captured. Sympathizing with him didn't excuse his actions, yet she understood why he'd done it. She fought that kernel of compassion. He didn't deserve it, not after scaring her and cuffing her and…her pulse was fluttering at the memory of his hands on her yesterday. She turned back to the ocean, willing herself to regain her common sense.

"I want to go home," she said. A hot shower, clean clothes and some tea would ease her sore muscles and pave the way for a good night's sleep in her own bed. In the safe room she'd been too nervous to really sleep.

"You shouldn't do that." Color flooded his face.

"Why not?"

"Someone was in your apartment last night. We don't know why yet."

With a groan, she held out her hand to make him stop. "Enough with the cloak-and-dagger routine. Just tell me, yes or no, is it safe for me to go home?"

"No." Worry flashed in his eyes again as he checked his phone. "The police are probably trying to reach you. We'll go see them first."

That explained his change of heart. "You're letting me go so the whole kidnapping thing won't come out."

"Not exactly." He stood up and retrieved the blackmail note, returning it to his wallet. Picking up her dress, he walked to the door, opening it wide. "You can tell the cops whatever you want, but we need to leave. Now."

"Why?"

He arched an eyebrow. "Didn't you just jump me to get out of here? You're free. Let's go."

His sudden urgency raised her suspicions. "I didn't jump you," she protested hotly. "If I'm really free to go, I'm going home."

"You can't."

"Why not?" She wanted the pieces to fit together and give her a complete picture. She understood the investigative process, but she also understood the value of a narrative. "Tell me."

He pulled the door shut and programmed an electronic lock. "Because my best guess is the guy with the scar is an assassin working on behalf of someone powerful in Iran who blackmailed me and involved you."

For a moment, she just stood in the hallway, gawking at his back, then rushed forward to catch up before he reached the stairwell. "If you don't have the gold, why would the blackmailer think you could pay the ransom?" she asked in a low whisper.

"It's an excuse. He found out I have deep pockets, I guess." He shrugged and took her suitcase in his free hand as he marched down the stairs. "Think what a coup it would have been if I paid him off."

"How did your pockets get so deep?" She was close enough she could see that his jaw set and his breath caught. The question bothered him, though he hid it quickly. "I can research too."

"I know." He sighed. "I inherited a chunk of money just after I joined the army. Two friends gave me some excellent investment advice." The stairs let out into a small alcove and mail room for each of the three units. "Factor in that I was deployed with almost zero expenses, and it snowballed quickly, even while I set up my businesses."

No wonder he didn't flaunt his money; he'd never learned how. "Care to share your investment strategy?"

"No."

His deep voice rolled over her, pulling at her senses like an ocean wave. "Fine." Two could play the monosyllable game.

His eyes heated and his lips slanted into an expression caught between regret and frustration. Good grief, the expression left her wondering what she might have missed if they'd met under better circumstances. He said he'd rescued her and she believed him. He'd apologized as well, but still, actions had consequences.

Donning his ivy cap, he drew her aside. "My car's this way. I'll take you to the police station and then preferably to a friend's place to lie low. Have you decided if you'll wait or are you set on filing kidnapping charges against me today?"

"Why should I wait?" she asked, incredulous. "You removed me from my life for no valid reason."

"I had reason," he countered, his voice low and rough. "You were in danger."

"You could have taken me to a hospital," she said.

He didn't reply, his expression an inscrutable mask.

"You could have just talked to me."

He closed his eyes and murmured what might have been a quick prayer. "Just give me forty-eight hours. Please," he begged. "I can't stop the men hunting my team if I'm in jail."

The *please* landed on her heart with the weight of an anvil. "All right," she said. "I won't go to the police. Not about the kidnapping or the break-in."

His eyebrows dipped low over his eyes. "I didn't break in."

She gave her suitcase a spin. "You did at some point," she said with a syrupy smile.

The tops of his ears turned red. "Thank you, Rebecca."

"Call me Becca," she corrected. "And not so fast. You're not going hunting alone."

"You?" He started to laugh, but then the sound

dried up. He leaned in, his voice intimidating without the device. "You'd drag those men through the mud for *ratings*?"

She swallowed back the instant lecture. He was stressed out and had just lost a good friend with another in the hospital. He deserved compassion and patience. If only there was someone else nearby who could offer him both. Someone he hadn't *kidnapped*. "The idea of an assassin with orders from Iran to attack soldiers on American soil is a major story. Yes, it would be nice to get the scoop, but more important than that," she pressed on when he tried to interrupt her, "is the safety of your team. You kidnapped me because you thought I could help. So why not let me help?"

"Because you're not qualified," he said. "We both know that." He started for the exit to the side street.

His flat dismissal jacked up her temper again. "We know nothing of the sort." She paused for a deep breath. "I was qualified enough to be kidnapped." She snapped her mouth shut and looked around for anyone listening. "You're innocent," she added. "Bill can tell your story better than anyone else."

"I don't need my story told." He shut his mouth and swiveled away. "I need to save the rest of my team. You can't help me with that."

There was more to this situation, details he was keeping locked up tight. For national security or personal reasons? Who was Parker Lawton under the impenetrable military past and the current security expertise? Why couldn't she shake this deep-seated need to find out?

She folded her arms, refusing to budge from her spot in the narrow hallway. "If you're shutting me out, I want your word you'll let me know what happens."

He rolled his eyes, swearing under his breath. "You'll know it turned out okay if you don't see my name or any of the others in the obituaries."

That wasn't the reassurance she was looking for. She was tired, sore and hungry. Rather than keep arguing, she figured the best way forward was for him to think he'd won this round. She probably shouldn't feel protective of the man who kidnapped her, even if it had started with a rescue.

However, she was perfectly content to feel protective of her nation, state and city. Parker might think he could do this alone, but someone needed to watch his back. She and Bill knew how to unravel rumors to find facts and locate people who didn't want to be found. By the time Parker realized she was still in the thick of it, it would be too late for him to shut her out.

Chapter Eight

The moment he turned up the lights in the safe room and revealed his face, Parker knew the charade was over. He understood her fury, gave her points for her cleverness as well as her elbow strike. The woman put up a good fight and he wanted to know what she'd done to his cameras. Beyond all that, he appreciated her resiliency and her willingness to write off his behavior as mindless stupidity rather than criminal intent. At least for the next two days.

Right now he just wanted to get out of the building before anyone saw them together. That would undermine every effort he'd made to create a plausible reason for her absence and break from the well-oiled routine. She could hardly be tending to a family crisis in a pricey condo with an ocean view.

Every time he looked at her, one of two things happened. Either he wanted to plunder her lush mouth or he wanted to apologize again for being an idiot. Since groveling only put him in a more precarious position and he was skating on thin enough ice at the moment, his brain kept returning to the kissing option.

Twice now he'd come close to giving in to that urge. Yesterday when he'd had her cuffed with zip ties and his hands on her silky skin had been a test of his willpower. Today was worse, after he'd finally subdued her attack. He wouldn't forget the feel of her sumptuous curves under his body any time soon. It was a wonder she hadn't snarled at him about his inappropriate desire or erection.

As she stood there stubbornly in the hallway, he thought she looked as delectable now in the snug jeans, college sweatshirt and worn high-top sneakers as she had in the dress he carried for her. She pursed her lips, rolling her daisy-tagged suitcase back and forth, and it was all he could do not to gather her into his arms, march back upstairs and lock them both in the safe room until they were too sated to move.

From a security standpoint, it wasn't a bad plan, actually. Even if the assassin found the condo, there would be no way through unless Parker willingly opened the door.

"What's that look about?" The natural wariness in her blue eyes brightened. "Did you change your mind?"

"No." He reached for the door. "You must be hungry. Come on."

He realized there were parts of his story she wasn't sure she could believe, and knowing who she was and what she did, he also knew she would do her best to figure them out. He had to convince her to drop it.

One crisis at a time, he thought, and at the moment the Iranians took precedence. Assuming he survived this insanity, he could find a way to distract her from digging too deeply into his real mission with Fadi and his family in Iraq. He was all for transparency, but not when it was sure to be misunderstood and freak out the general population. Sometimes good people had to do difficult things for the betterment of the world.

The door opened and the building maintenance man walked in. Parker forced a smile across his face and prayed for a distraction. "Good morning, Alan."

"Morning, Mr. Lawton. What a surprise."

"How's the wife?"

"Doing fine. You know, I—" Alan stopped and stared. At Becca. His genial expression transformed into a starstruck glow. "My goodness. Is it really you, Miss Wallace? The wife and I have watched every episode of your show," he gushed.

"Thank you, that's very kind." She extended her hand and let Alan give it a vigorous shake.

"My Sylvie will never believe it. Never." He patted his pockets and came up with his cell phone. "Would you mind terribly if I took a picture?"

"We really should be going," Parker said. Since when did television producers get celebrity status? "Maybe another time, Alan."

"Oh, don't listen to him. We have a few minutes." The gleam in Becca's eyes said it all. She wanted proof she'd been here as much as he didn't want to leave any evidence.

"How do you know each other?" Alan asked.

"I'll just take your suitcase out to the car," Parker said, resigned to his fate. He walked out while Alan asked her about a show last season, making Parker wonder how he kept each reporter and segment straight.

Returning to the building, he admired Becca's boundless patience even more when his snapped. Men he'd served with were in jeopardy. And with a soulless assassin on their trail, standing here in plain view, chatting up a storm, put all three of them in danger.

"Rebecca." He tipped his head toward the door.

She shifted in that direction, and Alan moved with her. Stifling a curse, Parker took her hand and guided her closer to the door. Alan didn't let up.

Though the white sedan was gone and he couldn't spot anyone on the street, Parker's instincts were snapping. Someone was watching them. Desperate to get out of here, to take whatever fight was coming away from Alan and the other innocent civilians in the neighborhood, he raised the key fob and pressed the button to start the SUV.

The big vehicle seemed to bounce on the tires and then the front end was immediately engulfed by a ball of flame. "Get down!" he shouted, knowing it was too late.

His vision registered the fiery explosion in slow motion long before the sound or the concussion wave from the blast blew out the glass door and window. The three of them were tossed around the hallway like leaves in a gale, and he did his best to shield Becca. The flash knocked the air from his lungs, and it felt as if someone had stuffed cotton in his ears. For long seconds all he could hear was the sound of his heart pounding.

Heat from the explosion pressed in on them, making it hard to breathe. Becca was under him again, her hands patting his face and arms. He asked if she was okay, but he couldn't hear her answer, only saw her nodding. She seemed generally unharmed, although her eyes were wide and swimming with tears, her face, hair and clothing covered with dust and debris.

Parker peered through the smoke and rubble, searching for Alan. The man's face was a study of contrasts, his skin pale and bloodied from the flying glass. More blood flowed from his lower leg, pooling on the slate floor. Parker called his name, having no idea if his voice worked or if the man could hear him.

Keeping Becca between him and the burning car, Parker moved toward Alan and tried to rouse him. He didn't respond and Parker couldn't find a pulse. The man was dead. Because of him. Alan had paid the ultimate price for Parker's screwups. The truth leveled him as effectively as the bomb flattened his SUV.

Becca's lips were moving, although he couldn't make out the words through his battered ears and torrent of guilt. Dumbfounded, he watched her reach out and close Alan's eyes.

"Parker!" she cried. Her smaller hands shoved at his shoulder. "What do we do?"

He heard her, barely. It didn't matter really. He didn't have an answer. Might as well let fate come to him.

She caught his face and forced him to meet

her gaze, held him so close his nose brushed hers. "Parker. Help *me*. I don't know what to do."

It might have been the tremor in her hands, or the way she said his name, but something finally cut through the shock. He leaned forward and kissed her, fast and hard, startling them both.

"No sense dying with regrets." As a romantic gesture, it didn't qualify, though her lips tilted into a bewildered smile. It gave him the hope he needed.

Lurching to his feet, he said a quick prayer for Alan while his mind leaped into tactical mode. Everything had been in that vehicle. His go-bag, her suitcase, her electronics and his were ash. They were down to the cell phone in his pocket, the pistol in his ankle holster and the torn-up clothing they were wearing.

Outside, the SUV continued to burn. People were inching closer, cell phones held high as they took pictures and video of the flames dancing and smoke billowing up into the blue sky above. Still a bit dazed and half deaf, the coppery sting of blood in his mouth, he understood the fob must have triggered the explosion. He tossed it into the debris scattered across the floor. Maybe it would help the police.

The safe room upstairs beckoned, but he'd stripped it of anything that would help them now. Hiding up there while they waited for help meant putting more lives in the line of fire. And for what? This was his fight. "We have to get out of here." Any one of those bystander phones might already have caught a glimpse of them.

He drew her down the hallway, back toward the front door of the building, and checked for anyone keeping watch outside. He caught sight of a slender man with dark hair leaning against a parked car, smoking a cigarette. He bore a close resemblance to the sentry at the awards gala. While Parker watched, the man's gaze drifted lazily from the scene of the explosion, up to the roof and then down the block.

"Who is that?" Becca's breath whispered over his cheek.

"No idea," he replied. "I'm guessing he's not on our side." He ushered her away from the slash of light from the front lobby door, into the shadows of the stairwell.

Every second counted and each minute felt separated, standing apart from the minute before it, the minute that would follow. They had to move, to hide or they'd both be dead by the end of the day. Noticing the scratches on the backs of her hands and the small burns on her clothing, he was furious for his errors that had painted a target on her head. It had been a narrow miss.

"Do you trust me?"

"Yes." She put her hand in his and kept pace with him as they ran back upstairs.

At the top floor, he turned toward the service hallway and entered the code for the roof access. He paused long enough to send a text message to the office. The short sentence was a code for his assistant. Though it was possible the assassin had managed to track him through his phone, it was a risk they had to take if they were going to get away.

He slid his phone into a pocket and zipped it shut. He eased open the door to the roof, relieved they weren't greeted by a shower of bullets, and closed it again quickly. Reaching for her, he tipped up her face to the faint light coming through the screen at the top of the door. He stroked his thumbs over her cheeks, wiping away the smudges and turning her face side to side. Other than the shallow scrapes along her jaw-line and under her ear, she looked all right.

"You can see okay, right?"

"Yes," she said, her auburn eyebrows knitting together over the wary gaze that seemed to be her default way of viewing the world. "Can you?"

He grinned. "I'm good. We're going straight out this door and over the edge. Fast as you can move. Stay low, don't stop and know I'll catch you."

"You can fly now?"

"I wish. There's a balcony. From there, we work our way out of the neighborhood." And eventually he'd get her out of the city and out of harm's way. It was an argument they could have later, assuming they survived the next few minutes. "Ready?"

"One second." She fisted her hands in the panels of his jacket and pulled him close. Her lips met his with an urgency that shot through his veins like a bolt of lightning.

He wrapped his arms around her, bringing her flush against his body. At last, he indulged the fantasy of claiming her mouth. Her lips parted and his tongue stroked across hers. The pleasure and heat wove a spell around him. He ran his hands up over her ribs, his thumbs following the soft curve of her breasts.

He was seeing fireworks behind his closed eyelids, but the sound track of heavy boots thundering on the stairs brought him slamming back to reality. Breaking the kiss, her taste lingering on his tongue, he pushed open the door and they ran.

He kept his body between her and the door, sheltering her until the last possible second. Surging around her, he went over the roof first. He heard her swear when he dropped out of sight and suppressed a chuckle. He liked her creative vocabulary.

Landing, he turned and looked up in time to watch her make the leap. Grit, determination and blind faith were a heady combination, he thought, catching her, letting her slide down his body until they were both safe on the balcony of the second-floor condo. "Nice job."

"Thanks. I dated a stuntman for a while," she said.

Part of his brain mulled that over with a foreign twitch of jealousy as he guided her to the balcony on the next building. From there he followed her down a large cypress tree as easily as descending a ladder. Hearing a loud crack, he looked up as a bullet tore through the branch he'd just left.

Glancing back to the rooftop of his building, he saw the man with the scar raise a rifle. Parker ducked around the trunk of the tree, covering Becca. Two more gunshots ripped through the air, biting into the tree trunk, followed by the welcome sound of emergency sirens.

BECCA, WRAPPED IN Parker's protective embrace, felt his body jerk and heard him groan while they waited out the shooter. "Are you hit?"

"He missed me."

She suspected a lie, but this wasn't the time to debate it. "Where to?" The tidy courtyard garden between the buildings seemed as big and open as a football field now that someone was shooting at them.

His embrace eased, his hands light on her shoulders as he squared her in the direction he wanted her to go. "Through the gate, over the fence and across the next street. I can borrow a van from the inn on the next block."

Borrow. She wondered about his definition. "All right."

"Run and don't look back."

She wasn't about to make that promise. "Then you'd better keep up, because I'm not leaving you behind."

Before he could argue, she grabbed his hand and used every ounce of the adrenaline coursing through her body—from that searing kiss and the outrageous danger—to get through the gate. Remembering her days on various movie sets, she released him just long enough to get over the fence. Hand in hand, they raced across the street and moved from one bit of cover to the next as they headed for the low-rise inn right on the ocean.

Although the bullets had stopped, Parker wasn't behaving as if the immediate threat was over. "What are you thinking?" she asked.

"Keep moving," he said, his voice tight. "We're almost safe."

She glanced up at his smudged face, relieved his eyes were alert when he met her gaze. She squeezed his hand, grateful he'd pulled himself away from the abyss that had nearly dragged him under when he saw Alan's body.

Becca promised herself she could vomit later. Not now when it could slow them down. "Your phone is ringing," she said when she heard the classic rock riff emanating from his pocket.

He waited to check it until they were safely inside the rear lobby of the inn. He swore as a faint smile ghosted across his lips. "Change of plans."

She tried to get a peek at the screen, and got distracted by the blood on his hand. "You're hurt. How bad is it?"

"It'll wait," he said. "One more sprint and we're out of here. Can you do that?"

"No borrowed van?"

"We've been upgraded," he said with a bewildered expression.

She suspected running from an assassin didn't often go as planned, and this twist appeared to be in their favor. "I'm game if you are," she replied. "Lead the way."

She tucked herself under his injured arm as they walked out of the inn, marveling at how quickly opinions could change. This morning, she'd been willing to cause him any harm to get away. Now a part of her ached knowing he'd been hurt protecting her. When he'd asked her about trust, her affirmative answer was pure instinct. She'd made a gut call in the heat of the moment, but she knew when the dust settled the answer would be the same. Despite all the things she should still be furious about, she did trust him.

A nice bonus, considering she was already addicted to his hot, possessive kisses.

She noticed the wince of pain when he broke into a jog as they reached Golden Gate Park. "Are we still being followed?"

"Not for much longer." He pointed to the sky. "Hear that?"

It took her a second to realize it was a helicopter rotor. "That's our upgrade?"

He nodded, taking her hand again as they ran toward the sound. They reached the soccer fields, and a moment later the small helicopter with the Gray Box logo set down long enough for them to climb on board. When they were buckled in, the pilot lifted off and circled, getting to altitude.

Becca watched, more than a little awed at the views of the city flowing by below. "Where are we going?" she asked.

"I'm not sure," he replied. "Sam Bellemere seems to have hijacked my escape plan."

"That's what happens when you hang with billionaires," she said.

"Rush and Sam were outcasts when we were in high school." He brought her hand to his lips for a moment. "Thanks for sticking with me." He loosened his grip on her hand, making it clear that any continued contact was her choice.

Lacing her fingers with his, she connected the dots between what he'd said and left unsaid. She knew a bit about Rush from her interviews. Although some of his competitors had labeled him and his partner as cocky, she'd always found he could back up even the biggest claims. "Those two were your investment strategy?"

Parker gave a nod, his gaze locked on the view through the windscreen. "I didn't have anything better to do with the money when it landed in my lap." He shrugged a shoulder. "They needed investors. It worked out for everyone."

"You don't need to be ashamed of being wealthy," she said, earning his full attention.

"I'm not." His brown eyes were filled with emotion, his lips pressed into a flat line. "I should've paid the ransom."

"No." The man was hurting, not just from the wound in his arm, and she wanted to make it better. "You said it yourself. If the blackmailer wanted money, we wouldn't be here."

"At least not until next week." His laughter was bitter and weak.

"Don't start second-guessing now, Parker," she said in the tone she used with unruly reporters. "Your car didn't explode from a random malfunction. It certainly wasn't a typical act of terrorism." They both knew terrorists wouldn't risk exposure and criminal charges over such a low potential casualty count. "This was personal."

"That's what scares me," Parker admitted.

She could already see where this conversation was headed. He wanted to send her away. Fortunately for him, the argument would have to wait as the helicopter began its descent over a building in the heart of the city.

Chapter Nine

Parker's gaze drifted around the sparsely furnished condo and he thought billionaire lessons might be a good idea. Sam and Rush had conspired to keep an eye on him after his visit to Gray Box yesterday. Parker hadn't considered the idea that doing research from a location protected from prying eyes might have prying eyes on the inside.

Not that he wasn't grateful for the assist.

Sam had tapped into his cell phone GPS and kept a police band open. Parker had only made it easier when he called for help identifying the driver tailing him. When the emergency crews were dispatched to a fire near Parker's location, Sam had leaped into action, reorganizing Parker's most trusted team and sending the helicopter to bring them to the building Sam had purchased, stripped down and rebuilt per his exacting specifications.

While Parker was relieved to know he and Becca were completely off the radar, guilt gnawed at him. There were three men on a list with targets on their backs. Tony hadn't checked in since following the burglar from Becca's apartment, and Alan was dead. For a security expert with a military background, Parker was doing a lousy job of keeping people safe.

He replayed the explosion over and over, looking for the next step forward, while he showered off the smoke and debris and let the doctor Rush had sent over treat the wounds in his shoulder and leg. The assassin's bullets had missed him, but not the splinters from the tree. Parker turned down the offer of painkillers, wanting to keep his head clear.

Recognizing his primary mistake, he wished he could go back for a do-over. It was as if his military background had fallen out of his head. He'd slipped into the civilian tendency to underestimate an opponent. Cocky and overconfident, he'd relied too much on his home field advantage. The world was a smaller place in recent years and it was too easy for people to travel and train with experts anywhere around the globe.

The man—or men—hunting him and his team were definitely in the top of their class.

He'd seen it in those eyes when the man had the syringe to Becca's neck. Recalling those first images of her coughing and sputtering from the smoke, tears rolling down her soot-smudged cheeks from red-rimmed eyes, he swore. He'd nearly gotten her killed too.

"Are you hurting?"

He turned at the sound of Becca's voice and tried to dredge up a smile despite the guilt weighing him down. "I'm fine."

Her blue eyes searched his face and he knew she saw the lie. He waited for her to call him on it. She didn't. She crossed the room and wrapped her arms around him in a gentle hug that felt like a cool balm, soothing him from head to toe.

She'd been seen by the doctor and given a chance to shower and change as well. He breathed in the fresh clean scent of her hair, appreciated every healthy inch of her in his arms. "You smell fantastic."

"Thanks. You too." She stepped back and grinned at him, turning in a circle. "What do you think?"

Sam had checked their sizes and had clothing delivered for both of them. Parker had pulled on jeans and a blue button-down shirt, while Becca had chosen black slacks that hugged her hips and an ivory cable-knit sweater. "You're gorgeous, Becca."

And he needed to get her far away from him to make sure she stayed that way.

"We should—"

"Go upstairs and thank Sam and Rush," she finished for him. "Lucy and Madison are bringing lunch." Catching his hand with hers, she tugged gently on his good arm, leading him closer to the elevator. "I'm not letting you overanalyze this alone."

"It's better to pick apart my mistakes as a group?" He knew he sounded like an ass and couldn't get a grip on the emotions slamming through him. The loss was bad enough, and the fear layered over all of it was paralyzing him. If another wrong move resulted in losing another friend, it would break him.

There had only been one other time in his life

when he felt this overwhelmed, this uncertain of his ability to create a positive outcome.

She stopped at the doorway and laid her hand on his cheek. "Parker. Everyone upstairs is here to help."

"It's not their fight."

"It is now. This isn't the time to fall on your sword in a solo act of honor. You need your friends. *We* need them."

He arched an eyebrow. "We?" She couldn't mean it the way some part of him wanted her to mean it.

"If you didn't want me involved, you shouldn't have kept me locked up like a pet hamster in a cage."

"That's not what happened," he shot back.

"Facts are so often a matter of perspective," she said with a shrug. "Now you're stuck with me. Come on, they're waiting for us."

"Won't you please go visit family or friends? Preferably in Europe." His throat felt raw as he posed the question and he knew better than to blame it on the earlier explosion.

"No." She pursed her lips, linking her hand with his again. "Not without you." She walked out into the hallway, dragging him along, and pressed the button for the elevator.

"I've got a car downstairs," he said. Any woman who jumped off rooftops and dated stuntmen had to know how to handle a car like his Spyder. "Sam is storing it for me. You can take it anywhere you want." He told himself the offer didn't mean anything. He could buy another one any time he wanted.

"Not without you," she said again. She crooked her finger as she stepped into the elevator.

"Becca, be reasonable."

"That, I can do." She gave him a soft kiss, eased back as if gauging his reaction. "I can't seem to stop doing that," she mused. "Let's share a meal with friends and we'll both be reasonable."

Parker knew he'd been manipulated. He just couldn't work up much irritation over it. She was right. They needed the meal, the sense of normal conversation to push aside the last of the morning tension.

He'd never been up to Sam's home after it was complete, only to the garage and the computer lab, and on one emergency response to the lobby downstairs a few months ago. Until he met and married Madison, Sam had spent most of his time at the Gray Box offices.

It was a temporary reprieve and all six of them knew it. An outsider would probably think they were three happy couples gathered for a relaxing weekend. While happy might apply to Rush and Lucy and Sam and Madison, he and Becca needed a different descriptor.

By some tacit agreement, they kept the conversation on lighter topics while they made the most of the big sandwich platters and sides of potato salad, fruit and coleslaw Lucy and Madison had brought over.

As Lucy passed a plate of chocolate chunk cookies around, Sam broached the topic with an apology.

"Being such an introvert myself and so protective of our work, I thought it was hypocritical for me to poke into your searches, knowing you expected privacy," Sam said to Parker. Turning to Becca, he added, "I'm sorry."

"I'm grateful," she replied with a warm smile. "You were a huge help today. All of you."

"What are you going to do about it?" Rush asked Parker.

"Does everyone know the basics?" There was concern on each face around the table.

"I filled in a few missing pieces while the doctor was working on you," Becca said. "Resistance is futile," she added with a quick flash of that smile.

He kept expecting her to come to her senses and withdraw from him. She didn't, staying close, showering him with inexplicable affection. Yes, they'd come through a harrowing morning, but he'd treated her poorly since rescuing her from the gala.

Parker pulled out his phone and shared his latest efforts. "No word yet on the favor I called in at Homeland on the man with the scar. I thought it would help to know how he got into the country."

"I can follow up," Madison offered. "Maybe a call from the State Department will light a few more fires. Do you think he is Iranian?"

"I'm ninety-nine percent sure the person paying his way is." He pulled up the pictures and handed her the cell phone. "Becca did sketches. I haven't had a chance to send them out for facial recognition."

"I can help with that too," Sam said. "We might find a trail of where he's been around the city."

While Parker's phone made the circuit around the

table, he explained how he'd also sent reinforcements to help watch the backs of the other men on the list.

Becca swiveled in her seat to face him, her knee bumping his. "You have offices in other cities?"

"No. I made calls," he said. "Traded a few favors among colleagues."

Her auburn eyebrows gathered in a thoughtful pucker over her freckled nose, but she didn't say any more. He knew that look meant her mind was working overtime. Maybe she'd finally come to her senses.

"I appreciate what you've all done." This had been one of the toughest briefings of his life. Admitting his faults to clients who trusted him with their security wasn't the way to keep them on board. "Staying here puts you in jeopardy." He caught a speaking glance between Sam and Madison. "If you can help Becca get somewhere safe, I'll send a protective detail with her."

"No," Becca said flatly. "We still need to speak with the police."

His first instinct was to forbid her to leave Sam's building until he took care of the assassin. As the words danced on the tip of his tongue, he realized how ridiculous such an order would sound. That didn't even factor the uselessness of it. He could practically hear her laughing in his face. When she made a decision, she stuck with it. He just couldn't figure out why she was sticking by him after what he'd done.

"We can invite Detective Baird here," Lucy suggested.

"Or send you to his station by helicopter," Rush added.

Parker gave a snort. "By now, the team after us has probably acquired surface-to-air missiles."

"If you want to give a police statement, I can arrange that from the lab downstairs," Sam said. "You can do phone, video or secure instant messaging. Whatever you prefer."

"Baird would prefer face-to-face," Parker murmured.

He would prefer to get Becca out of the way and set a trap for the man hunting his team. He'd assisted in the security design here. Sam's building might as well be a fortress between the physical and technological barriers. They could hide in this building indefinitely, or until Sam's generous hospitality wore out. Parker's skin crawled at the thought of being trapped, being dependent on others to bring in supplies.

The irony of it, considering he'd done the same thing with less explanation to Becca, put a knot in his stomach. He stood up, distancing himself from the group to stare through the floor-to-ceiling windows. He couldn't enjoy Sam's superb panoramic view.

Someone was down there wreaking havoc on his team, on the city, on innocent bystanders.

"I still haven't heard from Tony," he said abruptly. "Set it up so both Becca and I can check in with the police and we'll go from there."

"On it," Sam said.

A few minutes later, while the others were chatting, Becca joined him at the window. "You have good friends," she said softly.

"They are." In a terrifying flash he saw them all dead, the scarred man standing over the bodies, sneering at him. Similar artificial scenarios had bothered him in the past, usually before a mission. It wasn't foresight, just the brutal awareness of how quickly a plan could go awry.

He turned to look at her. "I considered asking you to stay put until the threat is contained."

Her lips twitched. "And you've reconsidered, I hope?"

"Would you leave town?" he asked hopefully. "Think of it as a vacation."

She reached out and smoothed the shirtsleeve at his shoulder. "You're kind of cute when you're trying *not* to be a dictator."

"Could I convince you to cooperate with a twenty-four seven protective detail?"

"Only if you're on it," she replied breezily.

He'd never met a woman who could flirt over life and death. If this was flirting. Maybe she had a thing for the bad-boy types. He had a laundry list of credentials to back up that label. "Why are you here?"

She lifted those big blue eyes, holding his gaze, but before she could answer, Sam called up from the lab, "We're ready to roll."

Why are you still here? His question and how she could best answer it swirled in the back of Becca's mind as they went down to Sam's isolated computer lab. The obvious reply was that she could see Parker faltering under the weight of his burdens and she wanted to help. He was compounding his grief by stifling it. She knew because she'd seen a similar expression in the mirror after her mother died and her father pushed her away a little more each year.

Alone wasn't an ideal way to get through life. Sinking into work and calling it thriving in order to avoid personal attachments wasn't the answer either.

Lucy and Madison had cornered her as soon as the doctor had examined her, vowing to have their husbands help them have Parker drawn and quartered if he'd done something out of character and hurt her. He hadn't, she assured them. He'd confused her, infuriated her and saved her life more than once. Through it all, he hadn't hurt her.

Yet. She kept that to herself.

Deep down, she knew he could. Not physically, never that, but emotionally. Although that should scare her, she couldn't seem to stop moving toward him. She recognized attraction and lust well enough. She knew she had adrenaline-junkie tendencies, and the last few days had tested that facet of her personality. This was different. Parker signified something far more dangerous than all that.

Why are you still here? It was only a matter of time before she had to answer that—for both of them. She hoped courage wouldn't fail her.

They were seated together at one of Sam's workstations, and after the brief introductions, Detective Baird aimed most of his questions at Parker, starting with his statement on the explosion. He wasn't happy they'd fled the scene, but he was very interested in Parker's take on the details.

"I left the key fob behind," Parker was saying.

She hadn't seen him do that.

"The thing went up like a Roman candle when I hit the remote starter."

Baird scowled as he made notes. "This guy wasn't expecting that."

"No. Early detonation saved us."

While he explained Alan's injuries, she shifted, rubbing his knee with hers so her support wasn't too obvious.

She appreciated that Parker kept up the reassuring knee-to-knee contact as she gave her account of the morning's events.

"Anything else you'd care to add, Mr. Lawton?"

"I was aware they were tracking the car," Parker said. "I'd planned to go straight from the condo to the police station."

She bit back the interruption. The tracking detail was news to her.

"They must have set the bomb while I was inside with Ms. Wallace. Since Theo's murder I regularly scan my car for threats. It was clean a few hours prior."

Detective Baird turned his focus on her. "Can you explain why you were staying there rather than your home?"

She felt Parker tense up. Years of living and working with her father had honed her ability to deliver a role convincingly. Clearly he expected her to tell the detective she'd been kidnapped and locked in the safe room. "Mr. Lawton was concerned for me after I was attacked at the awards gala on Thursday night. He suggested I might want to take a break from my routine and generously offered me the space. Since he's the expert, I took his advice."

He arched an eyebrow, clearly skeptical. "You didn't report the attack." Baird shifted his attention to Parker. "Neither did you, Mr. Lawton, when we spoke on Friday."

"There was no evidence linking her attack and Theo's murder," Parker replied flatly. "I was just in the right place at the right time."

"Uh-huh. And now?"

"It would seem the two events may be connected after all," he admitted. "There was a second man serving as a lookout when Miss Wallace was attacked at the hotel. I believe he was also observing the scene at the explosion."

"I tend to draw the way other people journal," Becca volunteered, as Parker's jaw tensed. "I have sketches of the man with the scar and a profile of the other man."

They gave Baird a description of both men and Parker sent him an email with the picture of her sketches as well.

Parker leaned closer, draping his arm across the back of her chair, his fingers stroking her shoulder in a soothing motion. The detective narrowed his gaze at the protective gesture. "Have you made any progress on Theo's case?" Parker asked.

"No. We'll canvass the area again with this picture," Baird promised. "Has the brother called you?"

Parker shook his head.

"We expect to release the body later today. I got the feeling he wanted to discuss final arrangements with you."

"I'll keep my phone on," he promised.

"The Northern Police Station has been trying to reach you, Miss Wallace."

"My phone was in the SUV," she said, well aware that didn't account for the hours before the explosion. "I haven't had time to replace it. What was the trouble?"

The detective made a note and continued. "A bystander reported a burglary in progress at your address last night. Someone broke your window and searched your apartment."

She trembled at the idea, imagining what might have happened if she hadn't been in Parker's safe room. "Did they take anything?"

"Best we can tell, the obvious targets of electronics and personal valuables were ignored, but only you will know for sure. It's possible the bystander's call interrupted the burglar's plan. You'll need to schedule a walk-through with the officer on that case."

"Of course," she replied with a tight smile. "It will be my next call." She didn't want to go anywhere near her apartment without Parker. The police were more than capable in most circumstances, though she didn't know how they'd hold up if the assassination team from Iran showed.

"Is there any way to speak with the bystander who called it in? I'm sure Becca would like to thank him."

She smiled on cue, struggled to hold the expression as the detective scrubbed at his jaw. The man was stalling, debating what to share with them.

"We don't know for sure who called it in," Baird said, toying with the pen in his hands. His gaze shifted from her face to Parker's. "There's another matter I'm not sure is related. The unit that responded to the burglary call stumbled across a body a block from the scene during their search. No ID on him."

Parker's arm stiffened behind her shoulders. "You think the dead body is related to the burglary simply because of proximity?"

"We have to keep that in mind as we investigate."

Becca waited, her heart thudding against her rib cage.

"And?" Parker prompted.

"It caught my attention that the man they found in Russian Hill last night was killed in the same manner as Theo Manning. Two small-caliber bullets in the back of his head."

Becca pressed her fingers to her lips.

"Description?" Parker asked through clenched teeth.

Baird held up a picture of the man's face to the camera.

Parker swore under his breath. "That's Tony. He was in the area because I asked him to keep an eye on her apartment after the attack. I'll have my office send over his information."

Baird added more notes, then lifted his head and glared at them. "Come clean with me, Lawton. You know something. How are these crimes connected?"

Becca turned as Parker did and they stared at each other a moment. Silently, she asked the obvious question with a slight tilt of her head. He gave her a reluctant nod. "Detective Baird, I may know a possible common denominator."

Surprise flowed over Baird's career-worn face and he leaned back a bit in his chair. "I'm all ears."

"Parker told me yesterday when and where Theo Manning died," she began. While she explained the email from the anonymous source and how she and Bill had proceeded, Parker grew more and more edgy. She made every effort to make it clear she didn't credit the claims against Parker or the other men, but he didn't relax. Not that she blamed him after the losses he'd suffered personally and professionally over recent days.

She didn't bring up the blackmail note—that was his decision. She also neatly avoided any mention of his visits to her apartment before and after the gala. Still, Parker was wound so tight she wondered when he'd snap.

"I'll need to see that email, Miss Wallace."

"Of course. We'll send it over right away."

When the call ended, Parker moved with silent, slow deliberation as he closed the camera and conference call applications. His lips were pressed into a thin line, and the dark circles under his eyes were more pronounced in his pale face. He'd lost another friend, and she ached for him.

"We'll send the email and Tony's details from another computer," he said. Taking no chances, he shut down the computer.

"Already done," Sam replied. "Seemed more expedient."

Parker gave him a short nod and stalked out of the lab.

"Thanks for all your help." Becca's relief that the conversation with the police was over was short-lived. She didn't know how to reach Parker, or if she should try. "I guess I'll go upstairs."

"Would you like to stay with us?" Sam asked. "Or I can open up another apartment. Just because you showed up together doesn't mean you have to stay there."

"Did you furnish all of them?"

"Four," he said sheepishly. "A friend needed the design practice."

"Lucy called him a stand-up guy," Becca said absently.

"He is," Sam agreed.

"That wasn't my first impression, in person," she admitted.

"And your second impression?"

"Different." Becca rubbed her arms, remembering those moments with Parker in the dark, as a delighted shiver skated over her skin. She'd been angry as his captive, but only her doubts about his identity had given her a reason to be afraid. "I'll go talk with him, if he'll let me."

"Make him listen," Sam suggested quietly as she reached the door.

Regardless of Parker's interpretation of the circumstances, he needed her. She couldn't leave him to brood about it too long, or they'd be back to square one with him pushing her away. The man had generously shared his resources and friends and even called in favors to protect her.

It was time he accepted what an asset she could be in the task of protecting him and the men on that list.

Chapter Ten

Becca walked into the apartment and found him in the kitchen slamming down a beer. Someone had stocked the refrigerator and brought in a basket of snacks while they were hashing things out with the detective. Parker wanted his own place, his own *space*. He just didn't trust himself to get there quite yet. He was too angry. He'd rather head down to his cabin in Big Sur. No one would pester him there.

Except a nasty, scar-faced assassin.

That was what he wanted, what they all needed. He should lead the bastard away, finish it one-on-one where he couldn't murder any more innocent people.

Might not win that fight, said a pesky little voice in his head. If he lost, would Jeff and Franklin and Matt and Ray really be safe? He slid a glance at the woman sitting at the counter, contemplating the snacks. Would she be safe?

"You know Sam has stronger stuff upstairs," she said, catching him watching her.

"I need to be alone," he snapped. He needed to

think about how to reel this guy in close enough to finish him off.

"All right." She gave him plenty of room as she went to the couch and sat down.

He set his beer aside and went after her, perching on the coffee table in front of the couch. "Why didn't you tell Baird I kidnapped you?" He wanted an answer. Nothing about her made any sense to him. He wanted to drink her in, from the rich red silk of her hair to the creamy tips of her toes. He jerked his gaze away. It was official. He'd finally lost his mind.

"Because it was a rescue."

"I should have let you go right away." He paced away from her. "I wasn't thinking."

"Grief makes us do strange things. I'm over the awkward start, Parker. Are you?"

He stared at her. Was she that generous or that foolish? "You need to get away from me." Begging went against his nature, but he'd do it to spare her from the looming battle. This was too serious. A team of assassins had targeted him for things he'd done in a remote area on the other side of the world. Twelve people had died over there. Three people were dead here—so far. She'd nearly joined that inexcusable statistic.

Even if they got around the man with the scar and his pal, that didn't mean it was over. There might be someone else later who would be even more ruthless. He had to make her see reason.

Think first. He raked his hand through his hair. If only he had taken time to think first, she might be on a second date with the weasel-faced man who'd taken her to the awards gala. *Or at the mercy of the man with the scar*, a cruel voice in his head added.

"Parker."

When she squeezed his hands he dragged his attention away from the charred wreckage of his thoughts to study her face. "You have to get out of here, Becca. Out of the state, if possible. You have to see how dangerous it is to be around me."

"On the contrary," she said, massaging his hands. "You keep proving how adept you are at keeping me safe." She lifted those clear blue eyes to his. "Even when I didn't know I needed it."

He tried again. "This is my fight. My problem." If they'd done the job right the first time, there wouldn't have been anyone left to come after them.

Her jaw set into a stubborn line and her eyes sparked. "It may have started that way, but—"

"No buts." *You're too important to me.* He managed to keep those words tucked away where they couldn't create more trouble. "You need to get out of the cross fire." How could she overlook the obvious fact that sooner or later people got hurt around him?

If she got hurt, or worse, he'd never forgive himself. She wasn't an innocent bystander, some faceless collateral damage in a godforsaken war zone. He'd come to care about her, though none of his actions could remotely be interpreted in such a positive or benevolent way.

"It's too late for that. You can't finish this alone, Parker."

He wrenched his hands from her grasp and stalked back to the kitchen.

"How about this?" she said, following him. "I'll leave town when you do. After."

"After what?" he asked.

She drilled a finger into his chest. "After you."

"Of all the stupid criteria..." He stopped when temper flashed over her face. He rolled his shoulders back. She needed to accept the facts. "It may surprise you to hear you're not in charge, Rebecca."

Her eyes went wide. Her lips twitched and suddenly that remarkable laughter tumbled out of her, spilling over him. "It might not have shown up in a background check," she said, mimicking his dry tone, "but that's never stopped me before."

He sidled away as she leaned close. Touching her would be a mistake to pile on to all the others he'd made with her. He crossed the room, putting the couch between them and praying for the ache in his gut to go away. It *was* too late. He was addicted to her already. The best solution was to cut himself off cold turkey.

He stuffed his hands into his pockets. "I'll take you to LA," he said.

"That's not a bad idea," she said thoughtfully. "My dad is away and we can stay at his place in Malibu."

"Stop being difficult." He clenched his jaw, searching for the patience he'd been praised for during the most grueling covert operations. "*You* can stay in Malibu while I finish business with the guy hunting my team."

Her gaze narrowed on him. "You're thinking of paying him off?"

"It's not so absurd." He had more than enough money.

"You said it yourself! It's not about the money," she shouted. She picked up a pillow and threw it at him. "What if—and I'm just brainstorming here—what if we worked on ending this *together*? There's Sam and Rush, Detective Baird, Madison and her contacts in the State Department. You might have noticed, I'm not without skills."

His shoulders locked as he turned away. Why wouldn't she leave him? "This is a mess from *my* past. You're only peripherally involved."

"Ohh."

He spun around, glaring at the way she dragged out that single syllable. "What does that mean?"

She hitched a shoulder. "It means this makes sense. You're wanting to do the whole martyr thing."

He stared at her.

"Is *penance* a better word for you?" she asked sweetly.

"Becca." Her name was little more than a growl. Too bad she wasn't easily cowed. "I'm done arguing." He caught her elbow and steered her toward the door. "Be smart and go up there and tell them you want to leave." Her escape window was quickly closing. As soon as the assassin learned where they were hiding, it would be a tougher task to get her out safely.

"I'm not leaving," she snapped. "And I have some ideas."

"Fine. Let's hear them." He let her have her say uninterrupted, listening with half an ear as he worked out the next steps. She could argue while he focused on getting both of them out of this alive. A plan was taking shape in his head while she tried to convince him she could be helpful.

He had the money and connections to buy a new identification and background for her, but that took time. Although he barely knew her, he figured once her father learned of her disappearance, the man would move heaven and earth to find her.

She was equally valued at her network. They too would search for her if she just went off the radar. Plus, she loved her job and was good at it. A new identity meant no-turning-back changes he didn't want her to suffer. He had to solve this in a way that didn't leave her career in shambles.

"You're not listening," she said abruptly.

"I am," he protested.

She folded her arms and dared him with a raised eyebrow to tell her what she'd just said.

"A memorial service," he said. He'd heard that much. Studying her face, he tried to sort out how that would work.

"Oh, give up." She put her hands on his shoulders. "I suggested we stage a memorial service for Theo and invite the other men on your team."

"Are you crazy? It would be shooting fish in a barrel for the assassin if we were all in one place."

"I said *stage*," she said patiently. "I know plenty of

actors in the area. You might have heard I have some experience with putting on a good show."

He caught himself before voicing his doubt about her idea.

"I don't mind that you don't believe me yet," she said with a serenity that put him on edge.

"You don't?"

Her lips curved into a sassy grin that lit a fire in his system and left him wondering why he'd limited their previous interactions to darkness. "Your disbelief doesn't make it less true."

He pondered that statement as he paced in front of the windows. "I considered a trap," he said.

"Great minds think alike," she said confidently. "Setting a trap with backup in place is a better idea."

"How would we be sure the assassin takes the bait?"

"Why don't we go ask Sam for advice on that?"

The smile that curved her lips had a sharp edge that made him thankful she was on his side. He just wasn't sure he could hang on to that hope when he didn't understand why she didn't leave him to deal with the mess on his own. Admittedly, his brain was muddled from grief and guilt. Maybe he was missing an important detail. Was she really willing to help? "One second," he said, catching her hand, needing the contact. "Becca, why are you still here?"

"You don't think I should be?" Her gaze dropped to their joined hands.

He reached out and tipped up her chin until he could see the flicker of nerves and excitement in her eyes. Her teeth bit into her lower lip as she stared at his mouth.

His body reacted predictably, going hard in an instant. "I want you, Becca."

She slid her tongue across her lips. "It's mutual, Parker."

The husky confession threw his lust into overdrive. He was no saint, just a man who knew how fleeting life could be. He crushed her mouth under his. Tasting and taking, letting her do the same. Her lips were soft and her response firm and willing as she met him move for move. Slipping his hands over the glorious curve of her hips, he pulled her close. Leaving no doubt about his need or intentions.

She rocked against him and moaned, winding her arms around his neck to press closer. Her fingernails grazed the edge of his ear, up into his hair, and he nearly lost it.

He pushed a hand up under her sweater. Her warm and supple skin rippled under his fingers. "Ticklish?" he asked, peppering kisses along her cheek and jaw.

"Maybe."

He tested the theory, drawing a helpless giggle out of her as she squirmed away and then closer. Something they could explore later. Right now he wanted her, wanted to bury himself deep inside her and forget everything but her.

He slid her sweater up and over her head, tossing it aside and guiding her back toward the couch. She stretched out and pulled him close. Her bra was black satin, cool and dark against her lovely, ivory skin. She worked open the buttons of his shirt and he'd never felt anything as wonderful as her palms running up and down his chest.

She pulled his mouth back to hers, her tongue tangling with his, and her hands seemed to be everywhere. His body reveled in her affection, even as he struggled to slow things down for their mutual pleasure.

Life offered no guarantees, and if this was the only chance he had with her, he wanted to make it unforgettable. She had his jeans open and her hand glided over him. He bucked at the touch, craving more.

He blazed a trail with his mouth down the column of her throat, dipping his tongue under the edge of her bra, then suckling her through the fabric. She cried out his name, arching into him and holding his head close.

He heard chimes and counted it a new high until Becca pushed at his shoulders. "Your phone," she said, pointing to where it had fallen on the floor.

"It's Sam." He sat up to answer the call, his eyes cruising over Becca's luscious body. Unless the building was under attack, this wasn't over.

"Parker, we've got company. You guys need to come upstairs."

He immediately snapped back to business mode. "We're on our way." He ended the call and leaned over her, giving her a scorching kiss. "To be continued," he said, meaning it. He stood and helped her up.

"What's wrong?" The question was muffled as she pulled the sweater over her head.

"We've been found sooner than expected."

"Iran has a new enemy," she grumbled as they walked out.

"Then my money is on us." He laughed, reveling in the wonderful, normal feeling of holding her sweet, shapely body close to his on the brief elevator ride down to Sam's lab.

He hoped what they'd been doing wasn't too obvious to Sam and Rush when they walked into the lab. He shouldn't have worried. His friends were studying a monitor array with four views outside the building. Two more monitors showed Sam's open searches and a list of names.

Parker instantly locked on to the white sedan. "He's still using Jenny Swanson's car?"

"Looks like," Sam replied. "The beard is gone, but he hasn't changed the license plate."

Parker puffed out his cheeks and rocked back on his heels. "Send the cops out to her residence."

Becca gave his hand a gentle squeeze and he saw the comprehension in her gaze.

Sam opened an email window and sent the message along with still-capture pictures from the current surveillance feed, as well as the earlier shots from traffic cameras around the city.

"Should we invite Detective Baird over for dinner?" Rush asked.

"Becca came up with a different idea." He explained the concept of a fake memorial service for Theo, staged for the sole purpose of capturing the assassin and his partner staking out the building.

He let her explain how she planned to get actors to play the role of the other men on the list. "We would need to fake the travel records and credit cards," she added, layering in more details.

Uneasy, Parker amended her plan. "I'm not comfortable putting innocent people in this guy's sights. Let's assemble the team from my own crew and local experts."

Sam nodded. "We can do that."

Becca gave him a warm smile. "Parker said the two of you would have come up with some idea to be sure the assassin takes the bait."

"He's sitting right there," Rush said, scowling at the monitor. "We could just go down and tell him."

"Whatever we do, I want Baird in on it," Parker said. "I want this guy to go down the right way." Theo, Jeff, Alan and Tony deserved justice more than revenge.

"Since your SUV blew up, I've been working to get an ID," Sam said. "Anything the police can use to haul this guy in."

Parker sensed a plan brewing. "What's on your mind?"

Sam was locked in to something. "There are two of them out there in one car." He zoomed in so they could all see. "How do you feel about a wild-goose chase?"

"I like it," Becca answered, her eyes bright.

"They're parked where they can see the garage entrance. Rush and I have a fleet and drivers who can meet us around front. All of us leave at the same time, head different directions."

Parker shook his head. "I won't take a chance on them hurting any of you or your employees."

"So we modify it," Becca said, touching his arm. "You and I leave, from the garage. Let them tail us."

"He must be monitoring you through the cell phone GPS now. I can add text messages that allude to a small private service tomorrow evening. Gives the others time to travel."

"Choose a location that gives him an easy point of attack and escape," Parker said. "We want him to be comfortable enough to take us all on."

"Right." Sam brought up overhead views of various funeral homes around the city. After a few minutes, he used a stylus to circle the area. "We can put the service right here. It gives the appearance of being convenient for his coworkers, and it's close to the airport too."

Parker stepped up, analyzed it. "Looks good." He picked up a notepad and pencil and wrote down a series of instructions, waited for Sam and Rush to read them through. Both men nodded in agreement.

"We'll go pack a bag," he said. Then they'd be as ready as they could be. "Let's get this goose chase started."

Becca grinned and slipped her hand into his.

Chapter Eleven

Becca watched the world fly by as Parker worked his way south along the Pacific Coast Highway. The scenery was gorgeous with the sun falling toward the ocean, and once they'd left the city behind, there were stretches of the road when it felt as if they were the last two people on the planet. "Have you decided how far we're running?" she asked when they stopped for gas.

"Maybe once I decide where to stash you next." At least the suggestion was delivered with a wink this time.

"That's rich," she said, laughing a little. "Please be over the loner thing. We need to be a team."

"We certainly have some unfinished business." The heated look he aimed at her did crazy things to her belly. She checked the phone Sam had given her, just to keep her hands off Parker.

"Any word?" he asked, his gaze on the road.

"Sam says he's still in the city."

"Good."

She didn't understand all the technical details as

Sam developed an electronic net to track the men hunting them while Parker arranged a bait and switch with his company trucks. He'd had a driver pick them up at Sam's building, and another crew took his cell phone and became the target of the sedan's interest when they circled the funeral home that would host the fake memorial tomorrow night. Sam was keeping tabs on all the players so they would know if and when they had to move.

Parker had headed out of town, just in case the ploy hadn't worked, while the team pretending to be them had retreated to the hotel where the other members of the team were expected to stay after the memorial. Assuming the plan succeeded, Parker and Becca had the rest of the night to themselves.

It was exciting and terrifying all at once. She felt safe with Parker, even safer now that they had backup, yet the high stakes made her cautious. "Do you ever wonder why they grabbed me?"

Parker's expression sobered and she wished she could erase the question, except now that it was out there she wanted to hear his answer.

He finished with the gas pump and gave her a hard look through the open car window. "It has to be my fault," he said. "Somehow the scarred man was on my tail when I went by your apartment. I was an idiot and I'm—"

"Don't apologize again." Without Parker's intervention, she might be dead by now. "And he tossed my apartment for a lead?"

"Probably." Parker shrugged and hopped back into

the truck. "A lead on either one of us, I'm betting. He didn't find me until I used my SUV. It's the only car registered in my name."

She looked around. "So, where to next?"

His expression was unreadable. "There's a great little place down the coast, if you're up for another hour on the road."

She was up for just about anything with him, and an hour later he pulled the truck off the road and parked in front of a wind-battered restaurant perched on the edge of the cliff. Below she could hear the surf crashing into the coast. The sound put a smile on her face, and when Parker took her hand, her heart melted.

Inside, the ambience was a throwback to a classic diner, including padded chairs and stools upholstered in cherry-red vinyl. Tables were arranged to make the most of the view, including a long L-shaped counter. "Can't you just see this place fifty years ago with a full soda fountain?"

Parker took the counter stool next to her, chuckling as she swiveled back and forth. "You having fun?"

"Yes, actually." Her stomach rumbled and they ordered burgers, milk shakes and a double order of loaded French fries as soon as the waitress came by.

He dragged his hand down her arm when they were alone. "If you could live anywhere, where would it be?"

"Where's that coming from?" She leaned back, startled by the curiosity in his gaze.

"I snooped through your life, remember? Your

work has taken you all over the world. What have you enjoyed most?"

While they watched the ocean, she relayed some stories of working on her father's sets in the United States and abroad, traipsing merrily through the good memories, the awkward and absurd moments in other cultures and her time with the various people who made productions possible. "It's the same kind of fun with my reporters, just on a smaller scale."

"Your dad doesn't get that."

She understood it wasn't a question and still she felt the need to defend him. "My dad is busy."

"I've only traveled with the military. They give us culture training, and it helps, though not nearly as much as meeting people one-on-one," he said. "And traveling with pals isn't the same as traveling with someone important."

Was he implying she was important to him? It gave her a little shiver of happiness. She bounced a little on the seat, her stomach growling in anticipation as her strawberry milk shake arrived. "I want you to know I was suspicious of that email from the start," she said after she managed to get her first taste of the treat.

"Why?" He stirred his milk shake with his straw, eyeing her closely.

"Gut instinct. The family that was supposedly robbed of their fortune would never have reached out to *me* for help. A news story would have been too shameful." She handed him a napkin from the dispenser on the counter when their food arrived. "I still had to verify it."

"I understand," he said. "In your shoes, I would've taken a deeper look too. Sometimes my clients give me the problem in a way that paints them in a better light than it should."

His words lifted a weight off her shoulders she hadn't realized she'd been carrying. "Thank you," she murmured.

He spread mayonnaise and mustard on the bun and stacked up his burger. "Want my tomato?"

"You're kidding." She gawked at him. "That's a heritage beefsteak tomato."

"Is that important?"

"Have you ever had one?" He shook his head and she bit back the lecture. "Taste it. If you still want to give it up, I'll gladly take it off your hands."

He pulled the tomato aside and cut off a small bite. She watched the reactions play over his face as he went from skeptic to believer with just one taste.

"Remarkable."

"I know, right? Of course, you've just been spoiled for all tomatoes in your future."

"I think it's worth it," he said, stacking up his burger.

They ate for several minutes in a satisfied silence.

"While we were working in that area of Iraq, we worked with two of the sons of the family named in your email and the blackmail note," Parker said quietly. "They're good people. According to Jeff, the oldest son, Fadi, is the driver who ran him off that bridge."

"Not a chance," she said. "I know we weren't there

long, but I'm pretty good at reading people. Everyone in that village was relieved, delighted and hopeful about the efforts of our armed forces."

"You thought I kidnapped you," he pointed out.

"Well, I was on drugs." She grabbed another French fry from the platter between them. Anything to chase away the grim fog of those minutes. "Bill and I spoke with the oldest boys about coming to America, and they only wanted a better life where they were. I don't believe anyone in that family would sink to the lows we've experienced."

"I double-checked anyway and called in a favor to confirm that Fadi is still at home," Parker said. "We know the blackmail letter was a ruse." He pushed a hand through this hair, ruffling the thick waves. "I played right into their hands."

They both had. There was something he wasn't saying, and she wasn't sure how to ask in a way that he would answer. Parker Lawton was an enigma wrapped in secrets and sealed with tape stamped Privacy Line. Do Not Cross. To respect and honor that line meant walking away, leaving the mystery of him unsolved.

He kept asking why she was here and she had to admit wanting to know his story was part of the answer. Not for the show, but for her heart.

"You've done the right thing every step of the way."

He shook his head and hunched over the rest of his meal. She didn't push the issue further, letting them both eat and rest and fuel up for the events ahead.

She suspected even a fake funeral would take its toll on him.

"You know what bugs me most about all this?" she asked when she finished her burger.

"I wouldn't hazard a guess," he said, his gaze on the ocean.

She nudged his knee with hers. "Why? Why now, why this method and why the six of you by name?"

"Important questions," he said. "There's only one reason I can think of, and even after everything that's happened it still seems implausible."

"Spit it out."

Parker pushed his empty glass and cleaned plate toward the back of the counter. "Not here." He balled up his paper napkin and dropped it on the plate. "Is there any hope of having you sit somewhere safe until we spring the trap tomorrow?"

"No." She mimicked his move with her napkin. "We're in this together, Parker. Surely you've noticed I'm not a fragile, porcelain doll. You're stuck with me."

"Becca." He dropped cash on the counter to cover the meal and tip. "A ruthless, creative killer believes his targets will all be in one room tomorrow evening. There's dedication to a cause and loyalty to friends, and then there's insanity."

She studied his face, and although he didn't move, she sensed he wanted to fidget. She covered his hand with hers. "I was willing to call in my actor contacts for this." Although she felt confident her contacts could have managed the ruse with his team working behind the scenes, she was grateful he'd assembled the stand-ins. It was progress for him. "I wouldn't have offered if I didn't believe the good guys will prevail."

"I appreciate all the positive thinking."

"You do not." She stood up. "I grew up in Hollywood. I know how to set a stage, create illusion and see through a smoke screen." Parker was blowing all kinds of smoke. She just didn't know why.

"And I know how to set security."

She bit back her assessment that his constant worry for her safety was stemming from misplaced guilt as much as good reason. If he heard her at all, he'd hear pity, which wasn't the point she was trying to make. "Do you want to take a walk on the beach before we head back?" she asked when they reached the truck.

"Sure." He guided her out of the restaurant with the whisper of a touch on her back.

She wanted to lean in or touch him in return. As he'd said, they had unfinished business. She couldn't forget the feel of his mouth and hands on her skin. Her body hadn't really stopped humming since Sam interrupted them.

Well, we have the evening to ourselves, barring a surprise attack, she thought as they took the stairs carved into the cliff down to the crescent of a beach. She intended to put it to good use.

They sat on a rock and he drew her close, keeping her warm as they watched the ocean swallow the last rays of the sun. In that lovely, quiet twilight, as the first stars winked on in the velvety sky, she brought his hand to her lips and kissed his palm, then curled his fingers around it.

Back in the truck, she wondered if he'd ever opened up to anyone. He dealt in secrets for a living. Who was his confidant, his release valve? She shouldn't press him for how those six men from different units came to be on one list assembled by an assassin. If asked, he would surely prefer that she leave it alone, but she would regret it for him.

That was the crux of it, she realized. Parker might have everything in place on the surface, yet underneath, a part of him was lost. She recognized it because it had happened to her. The solution required someone to point it out and then a conscious choice to change.

She was more than a little surprised that the place he had in mind for the night was a courtyard of individual log cabins a couple miles inland from the diner. Although it didn't look like much on the outside, it was off the beaten path and they had an opening for the night. Inside the room, she was startled to see all the amenities of a five-star hotel, complete with a stocked mini fridge, a microwave and a king-size bed topped with pillows and fluffy white linens. "How did you discover this place?"

"A client," he said. "Referral from Rush, actually. We worked out a new surveillance system that doesn't go off every time a raccoon wanders across a porch. I come out once or twice a year just to clear my head."

"It's so unexpected," she said, trailing her fingertips over the smooth linen.

He sat down and started unlacing his boots. "I can order wine if you want. They have a good cellar."

"Really?"

He slid a look at her and she felt a blush stain her cheeks. They had the whole night ahead of them, and suddenly she was shy. "I'm good." Ignoring her surging hormones, she grabbed her overnight bag and headed for the bathroom to freshen up after the beach. At the last second, she decided to change clothes too.

In a T-shirt and comfy leggings, her hair brushed smooth, she stared into the mirror. Until Parker wanted to open up about his enemies, maybe they shouldn't take this further. Her body protested the idea and she sighed. Together they were combustible, that much was clear. She should just enjoy whatever they could share in the moment.

Her concerted efforts at personal life planning had fallen flat. She could hardly expect him to open up while she stayed safely in her shell. She walked out of the bathroom, determined to clear up a few misconceptions. "Parker—"

Her mouth went dry. He'd moved the chair around and his feet were bare, propped up on the edge of the bed, his laptop balanced on his thighs. Inwardly, she groaned. She couldn't have designed a more drool-inducing scene for herself.

She knew how strong he was, knew what those muscles felt like in fighting mode, and she wanted to discover what he would feel like in more intimate, uninterrupted pursuits. This afternoon hadn't been nearly enough to satisfy her curiosity and desire for him.

"Where'd you get the laptop?" She perched on the far side of the bed, tucking one leg underneath her. "Stupid question. Sam gave it to you."

"No such thing as a stupid question." He looked up from the screen, and the scowl on his face vanished, giving way to an intense, hungry smile.

Her skin warmed under his gaze. "You found something?"

"I wasn't in a patient mood. This can wait."

"Tell me." She joined him when he waved her over. "My friend at Homeland hasn't found anything helpful about how the men entered the country. Madison, however, has made progress. And I called in another favor, so the hotel emailed me the security footage from Thursday night. They'd invited me to their office, but I convinced them to send it out."

"How many people owe you favors?"

He looked up at her, considering. "Several."

"It must be interesting work you do." The weak response annoyed her. She should tell him what it meant to her to see him go to such lengths for her as well as for his well-being. She'd forever be frustrated that her own father had never shown such willingness to help her with far more typical concerns.

He set the computer aside, giving her his full attention. "It's what I do. It's all I know."

Though she didn't believe that for a minute, she changed the subject quickly. "What did Madison come up with?"

"This." Parker adjusted the screen so she could view it easily. "Look familiar?"

"Maybe?" The man in the picture was much bigger and a bit older than the slim man they'd seen watching the fallout from the car bomb.

"I'm not surprised," Parker said. "He grabbed you so fast."

"There's no scar." She laid a hand on his solid shoulder and leaned a bit closer to the screen. "Makeup?"

"No." He went still beneath her touch. "This is Samir Abdullah before..." In a flurry of action, he closed the laptop and stood up.

Before what? She didn't ask, refused to push him. He had to choose to open up.

He didn't. He retreated to the small refrigerator and pulled out a bottle of water.

She scrolled through the pictures Madison had sent. In one, the man, before he was scarred, stood with his hand on the shoulder of a lanky boy, beaming as if he'd caught a prize fish. There was something familiar about the boy's face as well, though she couldn't put her finger on it.

"He was basically a tyrant king running the insurgents in the area where you met Fadi and his family," Parker said beside her. "With his identity confirmed, Sam notified the authorities. If we're lucky, they'll drop a net over him tonight."

"I'm sorry I mistook you for the bad guy," she said.

"I wasn't exactly the good guy, keeping you locked up."

"Keeping me safe." She turned to him and smoothed a hand up the placket of his shirt, resting it lightly on his shoulder. "And *you* never smelled like onions."

Parker's lips twitched, but he didn't laugh. He cleared his throat and hooked his hands in his back pockets. "I should apologize."

"I believe you've done that already," she said, holding her ground, holding his gaze.

"Not for that, for not being truthful about the whys."

"It can wait." She hooked her finger in his shirt collar and tugged a little, until his lips were within reach. The kiss she gave him was light, a flirty invitation if he wanted to play.

He didn't even blink.

Releasing his shirt, she stepped back, racking her brain for the right words to sweep this awkward moment under the nearest carpet.

"Becca. I want you." His voice cracked on the words. "You shouldn't want me."

The pain in his voice sliced through her, and anger followed. "I can *want* whomever I like," she replied. "We might want each other, but I believe you need me as well. I'm not perfect and I don't expect you to be."

"Perfect?" He groaned. "I'm a killer," he said suddenly. "We were in the area, a task force sent to stop Samir." He turned his back on her, and the story poured out of him in a rush that had his shoulders quaking. "The man had stolen children, among other heinous crimes. We shouldn't have been surprised he used the villagers as an escape strategy."

She wanted to comfort him, to erase the pain, and knew letting him share was the only way.

"Fighting amid the villagers, we couldn't call in a drone strike. It was all hand to hand, up close, personal and bloody as we cut down his group one by one. We cornered him and eventually chased him out of that village. Blew up his car as he made a run for the border. I don't know how he survived, or who helped him identify the six of us. God. There was so much blood and chaos."

"It sounds like hell."

"It was." He choked on the admission.

"And you survived." She moved to him, rubbing his back and then hugging him from behind, laying her cheek against the solid strength of his back. "You all came home and thrived."

"Hardly. He used me to find them, and is mowing us down in retaliation."

"Hush." She slipped around in front of him and cradled his face. "You did what had to be done, Parker, that's all. I'm so sorry for the price you've paid in the process."

She pressed up on her toes and kissed his lips. "We have a plan." She kissed his cheek. "We'll take care of him once and for all." Kissed the other cheek. "Together." She smiled, wondering if anything she said was sinking in. "Trust your friends and favors and resources."

He blinked away the sheen glistening in his dark eyes. "You're still here," he murmured, trapping her hands against his cheeks.

She nodded, not trusting her voice.

He reached over and turned off the floor lamp, throwing the room into darkness. A moment later, a thrill danced up her spine when his strong hands gripped her hips, pulled her flush against his muscled body. "Becca," he whispered against her lips.

She nipped his lower lip, clinging to his shoulders for balance as his kiss set her head spinning. She reveled in the heat, the velvet stroke of his tongue against hers. Under her hands she felt his breath stutter in and out. Good. She ran her hands over the hard planes of his chest and fumbled with the buttons of his shirt. Nothing would stop them this time.

As if he could see in the dark, his gripped her hips and boosted her up. She locked her legs around his trim waist as he carried her unerringly to the bed.

This. Yes. More. The world dwindled down to the two of them. Nothing else existed, nothing was needed, beyond the delight and indulgence right here.

His fingers sank deep into her hair and he pulled just enough to bring her head back so he could feast on her throat. She shoved at his shirt and hers until at last they were skin to skin. His mouth traced her collarbone, then drifted lower, pressing kisses over her heart while he thumbed her nipples.

She cried out when his mouth closed over one taut peak and suckled hard. He broke contact and she whimpered until she heard the sound of his zipper lowering. She scrambled to get out of her leggings and panties and heard a thud as something hit the floor.

"What was that?" she said.

"Not important."

He was right. She reached for him, explored him in the darkness as he worshipped her with his mouth and hands, every wicked touch bringing her closer to the peak. She tasted the salt on his skin, inhaled the scent that was him alone, found the places that made him shudder.

She was begging, her body eager, when he spread her thighs and filled her. She nearly came at that first touch. He changed the angle, and pure pleasure flamed through her. Gripping his hips, she matched the rhythm as relentless and timeless as the ocean until she had to let go and surrender to the shattering climax.

Her body shivering around his, she could only hang on as he brought her to another peak before giving in to his own release.

They drifted there, in that starry bliss, with soft kisses and softer words.

When he drew her to his side and pulled up the comforter over their cooling bodies, she remembered the thud and the laptop he'd put on the bed. "I hope the computer's okay," she said with a giggle.

"Sam has more." His hand danced down her rib cage, tickling her.

On a glorious burst of laughter, she let him roll her over and start thrilling her again.

Chapter Twelve

Parker woke to a spill of sunlight through the curtains, surprised to find he'd slept soundly for the first time in recent memory. As he felt the warm, seductive curves of Becca snug beside him, the reason for this bone-deep happiness filtered through him and left him smiling.

Everything about her tempted him, enticed him. She was brave, bright and sexy as hell. And for some reason he wasn't ready to label, he got a hollow feeling in his gut when he imagined going back to his life without her in his face, challenging him on every detail.

Before reality could intrude, they made good use of the oversize shower and the breakfast he'd ordered last night while she dozed.

As they drove back to San Francisco, they talked more about Theo and the others, as well as her career path at the network. Not knowing what the evening would hold, or if she'd even want to stick around once the rush of their ordeal was over, he didn't want to jinx these priceless moments.

Sam had called before they set out, to let them know Samir was still locked on to the hotel where he thought Parker and Becca had spent the night, so they drove straight to Sam's building and a meeting with Detective Baird and Special Agent Spalding, an FBI connection of Madison's.

They reviewed every detail. "The only person who isn't a stand-in is Theo's brother David," Special Agent Spalding reported. "We couldn't convince him to stay out of it."

Parker glanced at Becca and caught her smirk. "I can sympathize," he said. "As long as he knows how to get out of the room, that's all we can do."

Just as Becca had assured him, the plan was in place and working. It was simply a matter of waiting for the right time to move in.

The countdown was running in the back of his mind as they gave their statements to the police and FBI and connected the dots on Samir, his revenge mission and the other man whom they believed to be a cousin of Fadi.

Finally, it was go-time and he could stop thinking about the what-if and what-next questions. He had a target and he meant to hit it.

When they walked into the small chapel at the funeral home, Parker's brain kept flip-flopping about Becca at his side. He wanted her safely away from this potential nightmare, and yet if she were out of his sight, he knew he'd be distracted with worry. Samir had gone after her before. There was nothing to say he wouldn't try again.

She looked stunning in a quiet black dress with pearl earrings and a long strand of pearls that draped to her waist. He wanted to run his hands through her gorgeous auburn hair, remembering the feel of the silky waves against his skin.

"All clear, survey one." The voice in his ear brought him back to reality with a jolt. Surveillance one was stationed on the street out front. He and Becca, David and the crew posing as Theo's mourners were all in place. In the still, somber mood in the room, aware he'd have to do this for real if he survived, Parker found it hard to breathe. Without the distraction of the trap, he'd bolt for his cabin in Big Sur and work through this as God intended: alone with his thoughts and a bottle of whiskey.

Make a move, Samir, he thought. *Let's end this.*

"Relax," Becca said, slipping her hand over his arm. "It will be over soon."

"I want my target," he murmured for her ears alone.

"I understand." She leaned in just a bit. "The service will begin shortly."

He hadn't wanted to take the charade that far, but David insisted he could handle it, especially if it meant catching Theo's killer.

"You've set a good stage here," Parker said, trying to steel himself against the emotion threatening to swamp him.

"Thank you." She rubbed her hand up and down his arm.

He relaxed a fraction under the soothing touch. "The flowers are a nice touch."

Plants and floral arrangements had been placed about the room, all of them props that hid weapons. "Why doesn't the bastard make his move?" he asked after another round of check-ins sounded in his ear.

"You're antsy. It's understandable. Let's get started. Just to keep up appearances."

Parker nodded at David, who stepped to the podium near the closed casket. As David played his part, Parker calculated angles and choke points. They were dealing with two men, a leader and an accomplice or more likely an apprentice. Unless Samir hired more to tip the odds in his favor. Though it was possible, Parker believed the home field advantage, and a room filled with experts would be an effective balance. *Make your move.*

He had to give the entire setup praise for authenticity. The three men playing the parts of Franklin, Matt and Ray looked remarkably similar to his friends and comrades in Iraq. It was the equivalent of a dress rehearsal, and the finality of it all seeped into Parker, turning him numb from the inside out. Without Becca, warm and real beside him, he might have disappeared.

As those present shared memories of Theo in his various roles, Parker's mind carried him far from the quiet room and back into the heated combat zones they'd survived. He felt a nudge and glanced over to find Becca eyeing him with expectation as she tilted her head toward the podium. There too he was met with the expectant expression of Theo's older brother, his eyes puffy and red. The man was the bravest of them all today.

Parker walked to the front and turned to the small gathering. He had to play the part as well as the rest of them. He thought of the people he'd served with through the best and worst of military conditions. They all knew death was part of living and risk part of military service, but he found himself speaking to Becca.

He shared what Theo had meant to him. Not in recent years or as part of Samir's revenge, but as a unique and strong-minded personality, as a competent and willing leader. He wasn't sure how long he spoke, only that he continued when his voice wanted to crack because Becca's gaze held his, giving him courage.

He returned to his seat and let her warm his chilled hand with hers until the service ended.

"No attack." He didn't bother to hide his disappointment from Becca. "So much for being an irresistible target."

She slipped her arm around his waist as the others moved out to secure the room until they could clear the weapons. "I find you irresistible," she said.

Her quirky humor made the failed plan easier to bear. Becca's resiliency had captivated him from the moment she tried to shove his boot out of her door. Had it only been a few days? Another round of checks in his ear claimed no sign or sighting of Samir or his accomplice.

"I was sure this would draw them out." He loosened his tie and unbuttoned his collar as they walked toward the hotel where David and the others were staying, according to Sam's maneuvers. He wasn't afraid of being on the street with her, knowing the SFPD and the FBI had spotters all over.

"Did we scare him off?"

"Possibly. None of this is making sense." Parker sighed. "I shouldn't be surprised. He's made a study of being unpredictable since he put this in motion."

Suddenly there was shouting and chatter on the comms from the surveillance teams. A fire alarm went off at the hotel. Parker and Becca exchanged a glance and broke into a run up the block.

Keeping her safe was essential, and he looked around for someone he trusted to hand her off to while he went after Samir. Everyone was converging on the hotel, and when they joined the fray, they found the lobby teeming with every brand of law enforcement, including Detective Baird, who walked over immediately.

"Did you see him?"

"No." Parker's stomach clutched. "What happened?"

"We've got the accomplice upstairs," Baird said. "Attacked the agent playing Franklin."

"And Samir?" Parker demanded.

The detective swiveled toward the front doors. "He should have passed right by you."

"I'll find him." He'd studied the area, chosen this place because of the escape options for Samir. He gripped Becca's shoulders, firmly. "Stay with the detective." Kissing her forehead, he bolted for the door before she could argue.

BECCA WATCHED HIM GO, wishing she'd found a way to keep him out of town and away from trouble. Last night had been the best of her life. She didn't want to contemplate that it would be the only night with the man she loved.

Loved.

She turned the word around in her mind, still not sure how or when she'd started to fall for him. During her initial background search? Looking into his eyes for the first time at her door? Maybe in the dark of the safe room, when she'd all but known Parker was holding her. Any and all of those moments had solidified into an emotional certainty. She'd fallen with no chance of recovery when they were in the darkness of his grief, and he'd finally been brave enough to open up. To her.

She ran her fingers up and down the strand of pearls. She loved the man and he'd gone charging out after a vengeful assassin. "Who has his back?" she asked the detective.

"I'm not sure. We have spotters and cameras all over the area."

"Right. And who has eyes on Parker?"

She'd told him that he didn't have to finish this alone, that he had backup. She would damn well be sure it was true. She followed the detective to what appeared to be a staging area of sorts in the hotel security office. Sam was there, furiously working on camera angles.

She wedged her way closer to Parker's friend. "Do you see him?"

He shook his head.

She stifled the frustrated scream, watching the various images for any glimpse of Samir or Parker.

"There." She pointed and Sam did something to magnify the view. She'd seen little more than a shadow moving through the construction zone across the street, but she knew Parker's build and the way he moved.

"Are you sure?" Sam asked.

She was. As far more qualified people around her debated and assessed, Becca slipped out to do whatever she could to save the man she loved.

Rushing across the street, she ducked through the fence surrounding the scaffolding. Hearing the sounds of a fight several stories up, she cringed and started up the stairs. She didn't focus on her lack of weapons or skills. She trusted her ability to create a distraction that would give Parker an opening.

When she reached the floor, she hit the lights and tucked herself low, hoping she wouldn't be seen yet as she peered through an opening. The men broke apart for a moment, both of them raising an arm to shield their eyes. Parker was on one knee, breathing heavily. Samir breathed hard as well as he rolled to his feet.

"Who's there?"

Now that she saw the scarred face, she recoiled. If not for Parker, she might still be Samir's captive. Or worse. Though fear left her trembling, she would not back down or leave Parker to handle this alone.

"Your accomplice is in custody," she shouted. "Give up now."

"Get out of here, Becca!"

"Help is coming," she called out. They had to be closing in.

Samir turned to run, but Parker lunged after him and tackled him, driving him farther from her. They were exchanging punches and kicks and getting dangerously close to the edge of the construction where only plastic sheeting guarded the long drop-off.

He couldn't believe jumping was an option, could he?

"I brought your money," she shouted at Samir's back. "Take it and escape. Go home while you can still leave the country."

Samir pulled a knife on Parker and drove for his midsection. Parker feinted, his jacket getting sliced in the process. As he dropped and rolled away from another swing of that wicked knife, the loose fabric caught on a piece of equipment.

Samir went for a killing strike and missed. He cursed at Parker and raced for the stairs. "We are not finished."

"That's what you think." Parker leaped up and attacked again, heedless of the knife.

Becca covered her mouth as she watched the fight.

The heavy blows and near misses were more than she could bear. Where was their backup?

"Let him go!" she cried, giving the performance of her life. Hearing a helicopter rotor overhead, Becca shouted at him again, "Take the money and go!"

When Samir hurried toward the stairs, she moved to block his escape. The man skidded to a stop, glancing over his shoulder as Parker closed in from behind.

"It *is* over," she said. If she could keep his attention, Parker would have room to seize the advantage. "You can't escape."

The assassin faced her, his mouth twisting into an ugly sneer. "I came to kill my enemies, not die on foreign soil."

"Plans change," she said, holding his attention.

"There is no honor among thieves, only power and respect," Samir said in his heavy accent. "To bring the head of the enemy to my people will restore my rightful place as leader."

She wanted to vehemently deny the idea of Parker fatally wounded here, in this skeletal construction zone. "There is no honor in murder, you freak."

Samir advanced. "I am justified. He is the killer!"

"You're a tyrant." She scooted back another few steps, buying more space for Parker.

"My *cause* is justified," he roared, pumping the knife into the air.

Under his raised arms, she saw Parker pick up a length of scrap metal. She held her ground. "Petty vengeance is not a cause."

He reached out, grabbing her by the strand of

pearls. She leaned back, putting all her weight away from him. The necklace broke and she tumbled backward into the stairwell, hearing Parker's voice as the world faded to darkness.

Chapter Thirteen

One week later

Parker kept peeking at Becca, watching her carefully for any lingering sign of pain or distress during the drive to his cabin in Big Sur. He wanted to impress her, and despite the doctor's assurances, he wanted to be sure she was healthy enough to be impressed. Now that the danger was over, what he had to say could wait a little longer, if necessary.

Of course it had been too much to expect her to stay with the detective when he'd chased down Samir. He'd been by her side from the moment the ambulance had transported her from the construction site, only leaving her long enough to shower and change into clean clothes once a day. She'd been unconscious for thirty-six hours, the worst hours of his life. It had taken several attempts before his friends convinced him it wasn't all his fault she'd ended up in the hospital.

When she'd finally woken, sore and disoriented, her first word had been his name. It had done more to heal him than all the legal fallout and justice combined. As she recovered, Lucy and Rush and Sam and Madison had all stopped by to keep them company and commend her for her bravery.

Eventually he'd explained Samir had committed suicide by law enforcement, refusing to surrender when he was surrounded, and by charging the officers he'd sealed his fate. With the cooperation of the accomplice, the FBI and other authorities were piecing together all the clues to the Iranian's crimes—from the original email and blackmail note to the assaults and murders.

He parked in front of the cabin and hurried around to open her door and help her out.

"I'm not fragile," she promised, but she didn't shrug off his assistance.

"I've never brought anyone else here," he said, throwing open the door to his private retreat.

"Oh, Parker." Becca immediately moved through the space, complimenting various things along the way until she reached a wall of glass with a western view of cliffs and ocean.

"You like it?"

She shot him a look over her shoulder. "You knew I would." She stood at the window, her hands rubbing some heat into her arms. The sunset on the other side of the wide bank of glass caught the fiery highlights in her hair. "The view is gorgeous. I don't know how you drag yourself away."

"I've been tempted to hole up here and live like

a hermit." Thank God he hadn't done so or he never would have found her.

The temperature had dropped on the drive, and the forecast called for a cool night. To Parker it made the perfect excuse for cozying up to the fire. He knelt by the fireplace, and once the kindling caught, he joined her at the window, wrapping his arms around her waist. Giving her his warmth until the fire chased the chill from the air.

"I first saw this place in late afternoon," he said. "The Realtor and I walked the property first and then the sun was just starting to set when we stepped inside. I think he did it on purpose to get the sale."

"Smart Realtor," Becca said.

"Definitely." Parker chuckled, remembering it fondly. "I should've known I didn't stand a chance. He was referred by Rush and Sam. They don't tolerate slow or second-rate in any area."

Through the years, the number of people Parker trusted with his life could be tallied on one short list. He'd never expected to share his deepest thoughts or secrets with a woman. Of course he hadn't believed a woman like Becca—smart, funny and safe enough to trust—existed.

He'd treated her badly, yet every chance she had to turn on him, she'd turned toward him instead. He wasn't sure he would ever really be worthy of her, but he wanted to spend a lifetime trying.

"Becca." He turned her away from the view, and when he looked into her big blue eyes, all the things he wanted to tell her jammed up inside his head. He dropped his forehead to hers and just breathed her in. She was alive. They were alive.

It was time to take the next step. Well, it was time to *ask* her if she was interested in taking the next step with him. No more issuing orders or fighting for control. He wanted her in his life, as his equal partner in all the days to come.

He nearly swore when the sapphire-and-diamond ring in his pocket seemed too heavy. How was it he could blow a hole in an enemy stronghold with confidence and the idea of popping the question had his knees knocking? He knew it wasn't second thoughts or cold feet. He was entering uncharted territory.

"Becca, thank you for coming up here with me."

Her generous mouth spread into a wide, happy smile that made her eyes sparkle. "We deserve some time to recoup and recover, just the two of us."

Her words warmed his heart, steadied him. "We do," he agreed. "This place means something to me and I wanted to share it with you."

Her auburn eyebrows arched toward her hairline at his admission. "Thank you."

"You know, after handling the earlier, um, situation so badly."

Her blue eyes twinkled with amusement. "We're both past that now, right?"

"Right. I just—I mean." He clamped his mouth shut. He would not stammer and bumble his way through a marriage proposal. He leaned in and kissed her. Her lips, soft and yielding beneath his, settled his racing thoughts. When he lifted his mouth from hers, the words tumbled out exactly as they were meant to. "Becca Wallace, would you please be my wife?"

"Oh, Parker." Her eyes glistened with emotion and then her gaze dropped to the ring he held up for her.

Although the blue sapphire reminded him of her eyes when she laughed, he suddenly worried that he should have chosen a traditional diamond ring. "If you don't like it, we can—"

She pressed a finger to his mouth to silence him. "It's a beautiful ring. Perfect." Still, she didn't take it.

Was that a no or a yes? Would it be pushy to ask for clarification? If other men had this much trouble, they sure didn't tell anyone about it. "Is it too soon?" He pulled the ring back. "Can you forget I asked? We'll just take it a day at a time." He should've known it would take more time to win her over. They'd been through too much.

"Hang on." She caught his hand, her eyes on the ring for a long moment before she raised that gaze to his. "Parker, I knew you, I fell in love with you in the dark." She lifted his free hand and pressed a kiss to the center of his palm.

The move sent a tremor through him, stole his breath, just as it had done the first time when they were on the beach, watching a different sunset.

"I love you, Parker. You can count on me to always stand by you forever. Yes! My answer is yes." She bounced a little on her toes. "I can't wait to be your wife."

Her words, the sincerity in her vivid blue eyes smoothed away the last of the rough edges, even before she kissed him tenderly. At the sweet, familiar contact, he felt everything inside him click into place like the proverbial key in the lock.

"I love you, Becca. No matter what has been or what will be, you'll always be my light." He guided the ring onto her finger, where it sat, a perfect fit, just like the two of them.

* * * * *

Can't get enough of bestselling duo
Debra Webb & Regan Black?
Check out MARRIAGE CONFIDENTIAL
and INVESTIGATING CHRISTMAS,
available now from Mills & Boon Intrigue!

MILLS & BOON®

INTRIGUE
Romantic Suspense

A SEDUCTIVE COMBINATION OF DANGER AND DESIRE

A sneak peek at next month's titles...

In stores from 16th November 2017:

Just can't wait?
Buy our books online before they hit the shops!
www.millsandboon.co.uk

Also available as eBooks.